Lines That Drew Us

Palisade Trilogy 3

Amber L. Werner

Contents

NORTHERN DEPTHS
DOLN
NORWICH
MIDSPORT
GRANSEA
KINGDOM OF
DRACWOOD
MAGE KEEP
ABANDONED LANDS
EPRORA OCEAN
ORDDON OCEAN
GREENVALE
FLAMESMOAT
BOGSMOUTH
THE BOGLANDS
STONESHORE
MIDO ISLANDS
RAIMIRE
SLINAS
SALT CLIFF
SULAND WASTE
JORIA
SOUTHERN SEA

Prologue

Ereni doubled over and retched, praying her breakfast wouldn't make a reappearance splattered across the fine silk carpet. The moment passed. The nausea retreated.

She lifted a steaming cup of ginger tea and took a tentative sip. The hot fluid slid down her throat, banishing the sting of bile. Every day had become a ghost of the same in Flamesmoat. All spent waiting.

She leaned back on the plush feather bed, lifting her brown cotton tunic for a peek at the vibrant purple glow emanating from her belly.

At least some things were worth waiting for.

A knock at her door chased away her smile. She slipped her tunic down and cleared her throat. "Come in."

"Sade Pr—"

The icy glare she sent across the room stilled the young mage's lips.

"Sorry, Ereni. Old habits die hard." Baris sheepishly raked a hand through his curly brown locks. The blue aura around him blazed bright against the floral wallpaper.

"It's all right. Have a seat." Ereni's gaze softened, her blue eyes meeting Baris' directly. She stood, leaving the bed and taking a seat at the tea table.

"Thanks." He pulled out a chair, the wooden feet sliding soundlessly, courtesy of felt pads wrapped around the bottoms.

Nothing but the best furnishings adorned the home she found herself in. The family who'd once lived here no doubt spent many lifetimes and a massive fortune to surround themselves with all the trappings of wealth. All abandoned now. They were likely among the first to hightail it out of the city when the scourge came knocking.

"What brings you by?" Ereni quirked a brow and lifted the teapot in invitation.

Baris shook his head, sliding forward the delicate, intricately painted teacup and saucer in front of him. "It's the tunnels. We're doing all we can, but they won't hold much longer."

"Show me." Ereni tied her long brown hair up in a quick ponytail and pulled her thick fur cloak from the closet. In a matter of moments, they found themselves on the streets of Northgate, surrounded by a wall of flame.

She hadn't chosen her opulent house for comfort but for proximity to the flame moat that kept the scourge at bay. Here, the mages worked around the clock, shoring up the magic that stood between them all and certain death. But that was not where she was needed today.

Ereni followed Baris through the empty streets, the echo of their boots clattering loudly on the cobblestones.

In the time they'd spent here, the crowded city had dwindled to a meager population of mages, castle guards, and a handful of stubborn fools too stupid or set in their ways to flee. The empty houses and shops were left to greet them, their bright painted facades garish and laughable in light of the demise they faced.

Baris stopped in front of an abandoned bakery. He threw open the front door. Ereni breathed deeply as they entered, greeted not with the aroma of fresh baked bread but the dank scent of the deep earth. They hurried past an array of tables and chairs, which once held patrons gathered around a pot of tea and delectable scones, all empty now, covered in dust and pushed to the sides of the cheery yellow room.

Behind the counter, a hole in the ground beckoned, lit with a warm glow.

Baris grabbed an oil lamp from the counter and held out a hand. "Watch your step."

Ereni followed him down a set of steep steps to a narrow underground passage. Her skin came alive with the hum of vibration that signaled the use of earth talent.

The tunnel was lit with a series of torches, the flickering flames sending shadows dancing across the dirt walls. She passed by a handful of harried faces, all covered in a fine layer of grime that did nothing to dampen the blue glow surrounding them. A few spared her a smile, but most just kept at their task, tirelessly bracing the tunnels with layer upon layer of dirt and mud.

Baris led her further east until the tunnel dead-ended. Three mages furiously flung mud and chunks of rock at the end of the tunnel.

Baris cleared his throat loudly. "Any change?"

The weary mages lifted their heads in unison, their hands still moving as they worked.

"No. Still the same," the closest woman replied, her blond hair pulled back in a tight bun, the yellow strands doused in a liberal dusting of brown.

"Why don't you three take a quick break?" Baris asked.

"Are you sure?" The woman eyed the tunnel wall dubiously.

Baris patted her shoulder. "Just for a moment. Grab a drink. Ereni needs to hear it."

All three nodded, their hands falling slack at their sides. The heavy vibration in the tunnel faded, but it didn't evaporate entirely with the rest of the earth mages still working nearby. The trio retreated a few steps, talking in hushed tones and sipping from a pile of waterskins stacked on the ground.

Ereni strode to the end of the tunnel. She bent sideways and set her ear directly against the freshly packed earth. Her eyes widened. The scratching was the loudest it had ever been. Baris was right. There wasn't much time.

She turned to the mages, smiling at each of them. "Thank you all for your hard work. Do you think you can handle a few more hours?"

They all nodded quickly, moving back into position. Vibrations hummed to life in the air. Ereni's skin tingled with the force of it as she grabbed Baris's arm and tugged him back toward the entrance. "Have everyone stop just before dusk. Don't waste any time crossing the bridge."

Baris left with a parting wave and circled back, no doubt on his way to spread the news throughout the entire network of tunnels beneath Northmoat.

Ereni made her way to the surface. She walked a circuit of the empty city, calling out to everyone she saw. Her breath clouded in the chill air as the day rolled on, yet still she searched, tugging her cloak tighter and ignoring her sore feet. No one could be missed. She had to be certain.

Before she knew it, she stood on the wide wooden bridge spanning the Riddle River that cut the city of Flamesmoat in two. The river churned beneath her as she waited. As the final stragglers arrived, the sun sank down, leaving the gathered mages awaiting her on the Southmoat streets swathed in the light of dozens of torches.

"Is that everyone?" Ereni peered behind Baris as he approached, bringing up the rear of a small group of mages she recognized from earlier in the tunnels.

His brown curls bobbed inside the hood of his dark cloak. "Yes. I'm the last."

They hurried together across the icy bridge, careful not to slip. Within moments, they arrived safely on the other side. They joined the group of huddled mages standing on the dirt road in Southmoat.

Ereni smiled at them. All of them glowed blue so strongly. "Is everyone in position?"

A chorus of nods answered her.

"Let's begin."

Two fire mages approached the edge of the Riddle Bridge, each holding a torch. The air, already cold enough to force Ereni to stuff her hands into her pockets, grew even colder as the pair called forth the flames. Fire lit the night, flowing from the mage's hands. The scent of charred wood filled her nose.

"Wait!" a familiar voice called out. One she was not expecting to hear tonight.

"Izora?" Ereni whirled on her heel just as the elderly mage burst through the crowd of young mages, her cloak buttons done up askew, leaving it halfway open, showcasing her gray castle servant's uniform beneath.

"The king. The king is missing!" Izora sucked in a gasp, her breathing harsh and labored. "We have to find him!" Her gaze finally fell on the burning bridge, and her brows shot up, disappearing beneath the white curls that covered her forehead. "Are you mad? What are you fools up to?"

A white-haired mage plowed through the crowd, one Ereni didn't recognize, wearing the signature white robes of the Palisade Mages.

"Izora." He grabbed the blustering woman's elbow. "What's happened? You tore by like you saw a ghost."

Izora turned to the mage, her face lighting with what looked to Ereni like recognition, even as she continued to shake her head, inching closer to the bridge. "The king. I have to find him."

Ereni frowned, stepping into her path. "Wait, you can't charge over there now. It would be suicide. Surely the king is somewhere in Southmoat. I watched him cross the bridge earlier this afternoon."

"No. No, I heard it from his own lips. He's headed to the stables."

Ereni pressed a hand to her chest. "The king is speaking?"

Izora sucked in another gasp, trying to push past her again. "That's what I said, isn't it?"

"Look." The white-robed mage's arm shot out, pointing across the river.

There, on Northmoat's cobblestone streets—where no one was supposed to be—strolled King Quinton in a bright red bathrobe and a pair of red silk pajamas. His gray-streaked blond head was unmistakable as he passed beneath a torch someone left behind.

"Blazes!" Ereni exclaimed.

Izora was back in motion, heading for the burning bridge.

Ereni caught her cloak sleeve, her stomach sinking. "You can't."

But the old mage shook free, her mouth set in a grim line. "I told Kayda I would keep him safe. I've never broken a promise to her before, and I don't plan to start today just because you fools feel like burning the place down."

Izora swept past, setting her hand down as she reached the bridge, banishing the flames in a line down the center. She turned back. For a moment, Ereni was sure she'd changed her mind. But a smile crossed her dark face, and she lifted a brow at the white cloaked mage. "You mind?"

The man strode forward and leaned down to lift a handful of soil from the dirt road. He closed his eyes briefly, and when he opened them, a tremor whispered over Ereni's skin. The dirt flew from his hand, forming a flat disk before his feet, the size and shape of a stepping stone. He grabbed Izora around the waist with a wink. "Hop on."

All the young mages crowded behind Ereni, and everyone watched the pair hover across the burning bridge, the flames reforming in their wake to swallow the wooden boards behind them.

"That was either incredibly brave, or incredibly stupid," Baris said as the old mages reached Northmoat and hopped down onto the cobblestone road.

Ereni sighed, meeting Izora's gaze just before she disappeared behind a building, following the king. "A bit of both, I'd say."

"Should we follow them?" Baris asked.

As if to punctuate his question, Riddle Bridge chose that moment to crumble, breaking in two with a deafening *crack*, followed by a massive splash as it slammed into the icy water below.

"No." Ereni raised her voice to be heard over the din. "We go ahead with the plan. Maybe it will buy them time to find the king and get to shelter."

They all stood in silence, watching, waiting for the signal. Waiting. Always waiting.

Finally, it came. A whistle split the night. The earth and water mages strode forward to the river's edge, twisted the lids of their vial necklaces open, and linked hands.

A vibration thrummed through the earth, shaking Ereni's feet. A massive chunk of the riverbed on the riverbank's northern side broke off and splashed into the churning water.

Moisture flooded the air, making Ereni shiver. But her gaze locked on the dark river below. Slowly, the roiling waters stilled. Then the flow reversed, forced by the water mages to flood into the gaping hole revealed by the fallen earth.

The mages stood in deep concentration beside the riverside for so long the cold numbed Ereni's toes. Then they stepped back, weary and spent, clutching at each other and falling to their knees.

Ereni didn't move from her spot. Not even to shake the feeling back into her feet. She stared down as the water reversed course, rushing back to the river. Rushing back filled with countless drowned scourge corpses floating in its wake.

Baris whooped beside her, pumping his fist in the air. "It worked! Ha, drowned like rats, the ugly bastards."

Ereni smiled sadly. The victory didn't feel so great now that they had a stranded king and rogue mages to rescue.

Even as the river below bobbed with the dark corpses of an uncountable number of scourge, she knew there would be more. She didn't delude herself into thinking they'd slayed even a tenth of their ranks.

As she stood there staring, the light of the flame moat surrounding Northmoat flickered and faded. The last of the laumarle oil they'd used to light the moat in place of the fire mages had finally died out. Almost instantly, the snarling and screeching across the river intensified as hundreds upon hundreds of vermin flooded the streets of Northmoat.

"Hang on, Izora." Ereni whispered. She turned toward the docks and closed her eyes. "Help will come."

Tarquin pulled himself free of the earth, breathing deep the chill afternoon air.

"Bloody blazes those vermin are rank," he murmured. He shook himself and stood to his full height for the first time in ages, the bones in his neck and back cracking.

"How you can stand it down there in that hovel, I'll never understand."

A chuckle sounded in his mind, reverberating darkly. *"I'm where I need to be."*

The stench of the scourge clung to his nostrils, covering him like when he'd awoken underground. Tarquin shuddered, shoving aside the memory of the darkened tunnels where he'd found his savior. He buried the memory of the unspeakable things he'd suffered in the red gloom. He needn't go back there again. It had been a necessary evil. A means to an end. And now, it was time to take back what was his.

"Soon, my son," the voice whispered.

His gaze flicked over the desolate landscape. He recognized it instantly. The Eastern coast of Dracwood, in the Abandoned Lands.

He bit back a chuckle. It almost felt like yesterday when he'd stood with that traitorous bitch mage surveying the lush fields and rolling hills that dominated the coastal plain. Now the place was completely unrecognizable. Charred plants, torn up earth, and the bones of thousands littered the ground, crunching beneath his boots as he strode forward.

He headed for the river, passing the bare skeletons of metal and charred wood that were all that remained of Mage Keep's ugly buildings. The mages were all gone, scattered in the wind like so many flakes of ash.

Soon he approached the slow-moving Palisade River's banks. He shucked off his soiled clothing, all of it covered in layers of dirt and shit. Then he plunged himself into the icy water, frantically scrubbing his skin. The water clouded, hazy with all the grime of his weeks underground.

After scrubbing his skin till it was practically raw, and washing the filth from his clothes, he emerged from the river, shivering, flushed pink and totally spent. He collapsed on the riverbank, the hard ground ice cold against his naked flesh.

"My boy, you do too much. What good will it do you to freeze to death?"

"I'd rather be dead than forced to smell that filth," he retorted, his chattering teeth not affecting the conversation in his mind.

"No matter. Take what you need. You must keep up your strength."

Tarquin raised his head from the ground as the skittering of claws approached. Another of those damned scourge came, bringing with it its foul, musky stench, its beady eyes staring blankly ahead.

"Take it," the voice demanded.

Tarquin grasped the quivering beast. His hands closed around its throat. He watched the life fade from those beady black orbs and felt a change come over him. His skin warmed, all of his muscles infused with new strength. And beneath it all, he sensed the whisper of something *more*. Something he'd been chasing all his life. The power he'd been promised.

Tarquin smiled, sitting up on the cold ground. *"Send me another."*

Chapter 1

Lark reached into the bucket at her feet and lifted another handful of soil into her hand. She gazed off *Nova's Champion's* port side as they sailed up the western coast toward Flamesmoat.

She closed her eyes, visualizing the shape of a dart in her mind. A tremor whooshed over her skin. Then she lifted her eyelids and let loose. A clump of soil flew from her hands and splashed into the sea below.

"Ha, keep it up. Maybe you can nab us a fish for dinner."

Lark shot her bondmate Muse a glare where she sat preening on the midship deck but didn't bother with a response. Silly falcon. One would think she was training to be a jester with all her jokes.

"That's it. You're getting the hang of it," Kayda said, at her side. The sea breeze tousled her flowing white silk shirt and brown trousers, whipping at her braids and tangling her long red hair.

Lark frowned and dumped the dirt back into the bucket and leaned over to stare at the dark sea. "I was picturing a dart. That looked more like a marble."

Kayda patted her shoulder. "Don't be so hard on yourself. I'd say that's pretty impressive for your first training session."

Mika dumped out another handful of soil. "You'd think after a lifetime spent healing, this would be child's play, but I don't seem to have the knack for it." He brushed his hands over the bucket, then curled his dark brown locks out of his eyes.

Kayda turned to him, the freckles on her light brown skin illuminated by the afternoon sun. "Don't give up. It gets easier with practice."

Lark sent Mika a smile and squeezed his arm. "We can practice together."

Conall strolled to the side rail, leaving his bonded wolf, Shadow, curled with his mutt Sunny on the midship deck. "Need any help training?" he asked with a grin, the sun's rays glinting off the silver streaks in his curly brown hair.

"No, I've got it," Kayda said, her tone a touch more abrupt than it needed to be.

Lark sighed as her brother's shoulders sank. It wasn't entirely his fault. His actions may have chased Kayda's dragon away back on that lonely island in the sea, but he'd only been doing what he thought was right, at the time. Yet it seemed that Kayda still hadn't forgiven him for that mistake.

She opened her mouth to say something, to break the tension, but snapped it closed at the tapping of booted feet approaching. The tension thickened so much it was almost tangible, hanging in the air like a cloud of smoke, dense and choking.

"Jett," Conall said through clenched teeth.

The older man strode forward, his hazel eyes and gray-streaked brown hair a perfect match for his son's. Now that all the folk from Raimire donned cotton and wool in preparation for the colder climes they sailed toward, the familial resemblance was even more striking, leaving little doubt in Lark's mind that what Conall had said about the stranger was true.

Lark still couldn't wrap her head around it. How had their father returned from the dead?

"Conall, Lark. I'd like to talk to you now, if you have a moment." Jett cautiously stopped beside them at the side rail.

Mika took that as his cue to leave. He disappeared into the depths of the ship without a word. The squeak of a wooden door swinging on its hinge sounded over the breaking waves and wind.

Kayda's brow furrowed, her brown gaze flicking between the three of them before she let go of the rail. "I'll leave you to it then."

"Wait, Princess." Jett held up a hand, tilting his head back to the rail. "I have a feeling you'll want to hear my tale, too."

Lark frowned. What did the princess have to do with their father faking his death and disappearing to Raimire for the entirety of her life? Was that a crime in Dracwood? Maybe he was planning to ask her to put in a good word for him with the magistrate...

Jett sighed deeply, angling his face into the wind. "I'm sure you're all wondering how I ended up in Raimire." His gaze darted between her and Conall. "Does Kayda know who I am?"

Lark crossed her arms and shook her head.

Conall's stare dropped to the wooden boards. "He's our father."

Kayda's lips pursed, her brow wrinkling. "Are you sure I should be here for this?"

"Yes," Jett blurted as Kayda moved to leave. "Stay. This concerns you, too."

Kayda stopped and turned. "All right."

Jett stared at the sea, his knuckles turning white as he gripped the rail. "Before I moved to Raimire, I lived in Southmoat. I was born and raised in the slums." He swallowed, his Adam's apple bobbing up and down. "You weren't yet born, Lark." His gaze flicked to Conall. "But I'm sure you remember those years back in Southmoat. There was never quite enough to eat. And no matter how hard I tried, my hunting and trapping was never enough to get ahead like I would've liked. Your mother even needed to keep her job in that shit tavern just to make ends meet."

Conall's face screwed up. "It wasn't that bad... was it?"

Jett smiled sadly. "I'm glad you remember it that way, son. Your mother and I did our best to make your childhood normal. To shelter you from the hardships we faced. It was the least I could do, after the way I was raised."

"Is that why you left? You couldn't stand a life lived in the slums?" Conall asked.

"Wait, that doesn't make sense." Lark clasped her brother's forearm. "What about the farm?" She pivoted to Jett. "You inherited the plot in Greenvale just before I was born, didn't you? You already had your ticket out of Southmoat."

"I'm getting to that." Jett rolled his neck, his gaze shifting nervously between the three of them. "I don't want you to feel sorry for me, or to forgive me even. I just wish I could make you understand... leaving you and your mother was the hardest decision I ever made."

Lark leaned forward, angling her head so he'd meet her gaze. "Then why did you?"

His hazel eyes met hers, glossy with unshed tears. "It all started when a mage came to see me."

Conall stiffened. He gripped the back of his head, his hand clenching in his unruly locks. "Always the damn mages," he muttered.

But though the announcement seemed to unsettle her brother to no end, Kayda drew closer, quirking a brow. "What happened?"

"It was strange. Some old man in white robes found me one day. Offered me a sack of coins to answer some questions." Jett tugged his collar. "Well, times were tight. Of course, I accepted. I would've been an idiot not to."

Lark crossed her arms. "What did he ask you?"

"At first, he asked me a million and one questions about my mother." Jett rubbed the back of his neck, eyeing the deck again before his gaze lifted. "I never got around to telling you, Conall, what with you being so young. My mother wasn't your typical moral citizen. There's no easy way to say this..." He grimaced. "She was a whore."

Her grandmother—Lark shook her head, fighting to reconcile the facts with the picture she'd created in her mind. She'd never met the woman, never even known her name, but it hadn't stopped her from imagining what her father's mother might've been like. Never in a million years would she have pictured this.

Conall appeared to struggle with the news as well. His tanned skin took on a white pallor, and he leaned back against the rail and gripped the wood tightly with both hands.

"She wasn't a bad sort, your grandma," Jett hurried to say. "Just a bit absent. She never confided in me the reasons why she did what she did." He shrugged. "Southmoat... it's a rough life. Hunger and poverty will drive folk to do desperate things."

Kayda splayed a hand on her chest. "I had no idea."

Lark lifted a brow, glancing at the princess dubiously. Had they kept her so sheltered she had no clue what happened in the city she ruled?

"In any case," Jett rambled on, "that was just the start of the questions. After he finished asking about my ma, they tried to locate my whole family tree. I told him the truth—I never met my father, and as far as I know, I don't have any siblings. If my mother even knew who sired me, she took the secret to her grave."

He turned again to stare at the sea. "Then he started asking about my wife and children. That's when I stopped answering. I was so angry, so disappointed in myself that I might've gotten us all tangled in some mage's scheme. I ran out of there. I left that old geezer without even bothering to ask for the coin he promised me."

Jett laughed, a single bitter scoff. "I didn't hear from them again for some time. Not until Rhea had a run in with a group of local thugs on her way home from the pub one night. If that was even what they were, and not puppets of the damned mages."

Lark's stomach dropped. "What happened?"

"They beat her bloody. Stole her wages for the week." His jaw tightened, and his eyes narrowed. "Happens in the slums every day."

"Then why do you think the mages were behind it?" Kayda asked.

"I didn't at the time. It's only looking back that I start to wonder, because of what happened next." Jett's gaze flicked to Conall. "Your mother was in bad shape. We didn't have the coin for a healer. Rhea did what she could with her herbs and tinctures, but she was in so much pain. We'd only just learned we were expecting a new baby." He sent Lark a sad smile before returning his gaze to Conall. "I brought you with me the next morning to search for work so your mother could rest. That's when the mage came back."

Jett wrinkled his nose. "He wasn't alone this time. He brought a woman with him. She did all the talking."

"Did you learn their names?" Kayda asked.

Jett shook his head. "I likely did, but it's been so long now. Can't say I remember."

Kayda frowned. Nodded.

"They found me at a local pub, begging for work in the kitchen. The woman invited me to sit down with her to chat."

"And I was there?" Conall asked. "I don't remember any of this."

"They brought a hound in for you to play with, Conall. You know how you always used to light up around dogs. It was like the whole world stopped every time you met a mangy old mutt in the street."

Conall gaze darted to where his bondmate and mutt lounged on the deck before he waved a hand and nodded.

"The woman offered me a job. They needed me to complete one week of work, and after that, I would be free to go on my way. In exchange, they offered me the plot in Greenvale. Said they'd set it up to look like I just inherited it from some distant relation."

Lark gasped. "You're kidding!"

"'Fraid not. Of course, I was suspicious. Especially when she wouldn't explain what I'd be doing." Jett grimaced. "And even more so when they named their conditions."

"What conditions?" Lark asked.

"After the job, I had to leave Dracwood for good. She didn't seem to care where I went, only that I never returned."

Conall scoffed. "And you agreed? Just like that?"

Jett sighed heavily. "It took some convincing. She said they would make it look like I'd died at sea. Rhea would receive a widow's stipend to help the three of you get on your feet at the farm. And they offered to send your mother a healer, too."

Lark's heart twisted. Who would turn down a deal like that? Certainly not a man on the brink of poverty, whose only desire was to protect his family. To gift them the kind of life he'd tried, and failed, to give them.

"I took the deal. I left you all behind. I'm sorry."

Conall bowed his head beside her, his hands clenched into fists.

"What was the job?" Kayda shifted, leaning closer to Jett. "What did the mages have you do?"

Jett, his hand outstretched toward Conall, stilled. He turned to Kayda with a pained grimace. "We sailed down the coast. We met a Jorian shipping vessel on its way north. They introduced me to a girl on board. Her name was Chanti."

Kayda's face paled. "What did she look like?"

"She looked an awful lot like you, Princess," Jett replied somberly.

Kayda blinked repeatedly. "Another mystery solved." She muttered something under her breath so quietly it was unintelligible.

Lark's brows furrowed. "You mind filling me in?"

"I only had one task on board that ship. They wanted me to lie with her. An easy enough task for the son of a whore. At first, I refused. But the mages can be persuasive when they need to be. And Chanti convinced me she was willing." Jett shrugged. "We did what they asked."

Lark's stomach churned. It was so strange. Why would the mages go to such desperate lengths to make their father sleep with some woman from Joria?

Her mind racing, her gaze flitted between everyone. Jett was looking sheepish. Conall murderous. And Kayda, like she'd just been told someone drowned her kitten.

"How could you do that to our mother?" Conall asked through clenched teeth. "She was back in Dracwood, pregnant with your child!"

Lark swallowed hard and stared at her father. "The better question is why? Why would the mages ask that of you?"

"Because of me. Chanti was my mother." Kayda twisted to face Jett. "And you're my father. The timing fits. She must've already been with child when she married the prince."

Lark rocked back on her heels and steadied herself against the railing. "You're our sister, Kayda?" They certainly didn't share much of a resemblance. In fact... "Wait, that would make you slightly younger than me." She set a hand on her hip, eyeing the princess up and down. "You're only sixteen?"

"Yes, I am." Kayda reddened slightly, rubbing her arm. "I summoned without a source once."

"Oh." Lark cringed, her gaze darting to her brother, who'd also suffered the effects of premature aging, although on a much greater scale. "Sorry."

"No, I'm the only one who should be apologizing," Jett jumped in. "I should've told those mages they could take their deal and shove it. But I didn't. I'm sorry for all the pain I've caused you. All of you."

"Did Mother know?" Conall asked. "Or did you let her believe all the lies?"

Jett shook his head. "I never told her. After that week, I left the boat and never looked back. I figured that was the least I could do for Rhea, after what I'd done."

Conall sighed. "I guess that was for the best. She went to her grave thinking her husband loved her, instead of knowing you'd betrayed her." He pushed off the railing and charged away.

Jett moved to follow, but Lark grabbed his arm. "Give him some space. Conall's always been one to work through things on his own time."

"I need some time to think, too. Thank you for telling me the truth." Kayda flashed them both a half-smile then strolled away in the opposite direction Conall went.

Lark's stomach rolled and swayed, and for once, she was sure it wasn't the ship's motion upsetting it. It was all so much to take in.

"I'll give you some time, too, I guess." Jett started to leave.

"Thanks, Father," Lark blurted out on a whim.

The smile he sent her looked so much like her brother's it made her heart ache. "You're welcome, Daughter."

He left her standing there, staring at the sea, wondering if her life would ever be the same.

Chapter 2

Conall stomped past Shadow and Sunny, heading for the bow of the ship.

"You all right, little brother?" Shadow lifted his head from the deck and gazed at him curiously as he strode by.

Conall paused. *"Not really, but not much I can do about it,"* he grumbled in his mind.

"What's wrong?" Shadow rose on his front paws and shook out his gray fur. Sunny perked up, her yellow tail wagging.

"Don't get up." He waved them off. *"I'll explain everything later. I just need some time to think."*

Shadow lay back down. *"I'm here when you need me."*

Conall reached down to pat Sunny between the ears and resumed his walk.

Nova's Champion was a fine boat. A welcome change from the rickety mess that was *The Lady Luck*. Instead of warped, dented boards and tattered sails patched in a hundred places, this ship was practically new.

The fresh scent of spruce and oak lingered beneath the tang of salt air. The deck gleamed in the midday sun, shaded by huge yellow sails. Deckhands scampered about, handling their tasks with smiling faces and ribald jokes on their tongues.

Conall wasn't in the mood to appreciate any jokes today. He stormed off, passing the wild Sul captain Jayan at the helm, and he didn't stop until he'd reached the bow's rail.

His thoughts swirled as he tried to piece together the crazy tale his father spun and the fragmented memories from his childhood. Had it really been that bad?

It was true a home in Southmoat wasn't something anyone yearned for. The lower section of Flamesmoat was cramped and dirty, inhabited by all kinds of riffraff. Not just regular, honest, poor folk, but thugs and thieves—whores. He grimaced.

His grandmother... that'd been an unpleasant surprise. A part of him wished he'd been told of his family's humble origins, but he couldn't say it surprised him that they'd sheltered him from the truth. It's not exactly the type of profession people bragged about.

But a rotten childhood didn't give his father the right to abandon them for a new life. Even if he secured them a ticket out of Southmoat in the deal. They were family. They were supposed to stick together.

"Conall?"

He turned and found one of the mages his sister had rescued on the Mido Islands approaching. Her clothing was no longer tattered and torn, but he still recognized her, though at the moment her name escaped him. What could she want?

He didn't know if he could handle any idle chit-chat. "Yes? Can I help you?" he asked, trying to tamp down the hint of annoyance in his tone. He must not have managed it well enough.

The girl flinched and backed up a step. "I can come back later."

He shook his head, forcing his voice to soften further. "No, don't. I'm sorry. I didn't mean to snap at you." He raised an arm toward the empty rail beside him in invitation. "Would you care to join me?"

She nodded once and slid up to the rail. They stood in silence for a time. Long enough that he began to think she'd simply come to the bow for the view.

His mind wandered back to his childhood, before his father left. All those days spent together in the woods. He'd only been a boy, but his father had been so patient attempting to teach him all he knew about trapping and hunting, while all Conall had been interested in was goofing off. He'd probably scared away all the game with his antics, but he couldn't recall a single time his father raised his voice to scold him.

His father was always smiling, his hazel eyes filled with laughter. When Conall looked back on those days, that one image always stood out in his mind, crystal clear.

"I heard you traveled through Doln with the mages after the Palisade fell."

"Hm?" The girl's statement drew him out of his reverie. He cleared his throat. "Yes, I did."

She picked at a spot on the bow rail, rubbing at a tiny imperfection in the wood. "Did you happen to run into a boy named Quent while you were there?"

Conall spun to face the girl and surveyed her more closely. Those bright green eyes, that pale freckled skin. How had he missed it? "Oriana?"

Her gaze lifted from the rail and connected with his. "Yeah, that's me."

"I met your brother. He's alive and well—or at least he was when I left Gransea—if that's what you're wondering." Once again, he fought to keep the annoyance out of his tone.

That poor boy was so worried about his sister. Another family split up when they should've stuck together. His stomach clenched as he remembered how torn up Quent had been, thinking he'd failed his mother.

"Good," Oriana said quietly. A small smile flitted across her lips. "That's good."

"Did you know your mother asked him to look out for you before she left?"

Oriana's face fell, and her smile vanished. "She did?"

"Quent befriended me while we trekked through the mountains." The side of Conall's mouth lifted in a crooked grin. "More than that. He saved my life once. Used his air talent to build a cave in the snow during an avalanche. Your brother is a hero."

"He can summon? At his age? That's... it's incredible."

He crossed his arms. "How could you leave him? He's just a kid, all alone. You're his family."

"I know it was selfish." She sighed. "I believed in Ereni. I still do. I wanted to be part of it all. Saving the world."

"Is that what Ereni sold you?" Conall wanted to scream. "Mages and their damn fate. And we're all just puppets in their show."

Oriana seemed to sense his mood shifting. She backed away, rubbing her chest. "Thank you for telling me about Quent." Then the tapping of her boots faded as she disappeared.

Barely a moment passed before boots pounded again, headed toward him. What now?

The frown plastered to his face faded as he spotted the footfall's source. A white and gold-feathered falcon landed on the railing beside him, just before his sister marched into view.

"Lark."

"Were you just talking to Oriana?"

"Yeah. Why do you ask?"

Lark scowled. "Oh, no reason. She definitely wasn't just racing away from here in tears." She cocked a brow at him, hand on her hip.

"Maybe I was a little hard on her." Conall grimaced. "I met her little brother on the trek to Doln. I had a few choice words to say about how she shouldn't have abandoned him at Mage Keep."

Lark joined him at the rail. She tugged her long brown curls over her shoulder and stared down into the dark sea. "You expect so much from everyone. Sometimes people make mistakes."

He tilted his head to glare down at his sister. With her bent beside the railing, she barely made it up to his shoulder. "This isn't just about Oriana, is it?"

"Do you ever think you can forgive Jett?" Lark's hazel eyes shone up at him, the color a perfect match for his own. For their father's as well.

Conall shook his head. "I don't know. I'm just so angry with him."

"Yeah, I get that." She slid her hand over his where it rested on the rail. "There's nothing wrong with being angry about the whole situation. I am, too. But when I look at it from his point of view, I can see why he did what he did."

"That doesn't make it right."

"I know." She squeezed his hand. "I believe him, though. When he said he was sorry, I think he really meant it. And I don't want to waste this second chance. We already lost our mother."

Conall pulled his hand free. "He's nothing like Mother."

"He made a mistake."

"Why are you sticking up for him?"

"Maybe because I know what it's like to do something you regret." She wrapped her arms around her chest. "I never told you what happened at the farm."

Conall's heart twisted as he recalled standing outside the burned-out shell that had once been their home. "What do you mean? It burned down." But even as the words left his lips, the image of the half-sunken foundation returned to his mind, and a sick feeling settled in his gut.

"I returned there after I escaped from the slavers." Lark turned to him, her shoulders trembling. "I set the fire. Gael... I killed him."

Conall gulped. "You didn't."

"I did. I set the fire. I stood there and watched it burn. And when I heard that bastard drunkenly stumbling around, trying to escape, I sunk my fingers into the earth and used my talent to trap him there."

He closed his eyes, just for an instant. Then he opened them and pulled his sister into his arms. "It's all right. He deserved it."

Lark shuddered, and he wished he could take away all her pain. He should've been there for her in that moment. Instead, he'd been recovering in the woods from the arrow wound Gael inflicted on him. If anyone deserved a violent death, a man who would leave his own stepson for dead in the woods certainly qualified.

"If I could go back, I would've done things differently." She sighed. "I know he deserved it, but I still wish I wasn't the one to kill him. To have his death weighing on me." Her voice wobbled. "I'm supposed to be a healer, not a killer."

He rubbed her back, not saying anything. Just holding her close while she dried her tears.

Eventually, she eased out of his arms and looked up with a wobbly smile. "Thanks. I just hope you can forgive our father for his mistakes one day, like you have mine."

Conall barely resisted the urge to roll his eyes. "It's not the same."

"I know. Except, it kind of is." She shrugged. "Either way, Jett gave us one thing we can be thankful for."

Conall cocked a brow. "What's that?"

"More family. Kayda. Nox. We've got two new siblings now." Lark grinned. "That's pretty exciting, don't you think?"

He flashed her a half-smile. "I guess you're right. I forgot about that."

Lark beamed up at him, her eyes shining. Then she tilted her head sideways, her gaze landing on her bonded falcon, Muse. She gasped.

"What is it?" Conall asked.

"Flamesmoat." She squinted at the horizon beyond the bow. "We're here."

Chapter 3

Kayda paused on the midship deck of *Nova's Champion*, her gaze drawn to the spot where Druturion used to laze in the sun, as content as a cat with a bowl of cream. A bittersweet smile crossed her face.

Then the smile vanished just as quickly as her bondmate had when he chased after Belstasia into the unknown. No matter how many times she reached out to him through their bond, he never replied.

Where was he?

Kayda pushed her worry for her bondmate aside and resumed pacing. They'd be approaching Flamesmoat soon. She'd not forgotten the promise she'd made to herself. She wouldn't just stand by and allow the city she'd grown up in to be destroyed without doing something to help. Even though parts of it seemed to be less than worthy of salvation.

Her stomach churned, her mind still reeling from all she'd learned from Jett. Had she been so blind she'd not noticed the common people suffering? Looking back, she realized that even though she'd lived in

Flamesmoat all her life, there were vast swaths of the city she'd never stepped foot in. Why hadn't she ever thought to ask for a tour of the rest of the city?

She was too comfortable in the keep. Too complacent. Too trusting that the loving faces she interacted with in church and at public feasts were all that the city had to offer.

She should've done more. Her heart had broken as she listened to Jett's tale. All of that suffering going on right under her nose. As princess, she could've helped them.

Not that she even deserved to be princess. That fact was blatantly obvious now. She didn't share any blood with the king. All her life, she'd been an unwitting imposter. A product of the mages' schemes.

Her chest burned. Just one more thing for Izora to explain, once she found her.

Kayda's pacing brought her within shouting distance of the helm. Jayan waved her over.

She sighed and headed over to chat. "Captain. How's the sailing?"

"Smooth as silk." He sent her one of his signature toothy grins, his teeth gleaming against his dark skin and his chest on display beneath his wide open cloak. Even the steadily decreasing temperatures as they made their way north couldn't convince him to button his shirt. Although, he appeared to have taken a shine to his new, expensive boots. "How's your day treating you, Princess?"

She bristled and wrinkled her nose. "Kayda," she blurted, holding back a wince at her own clipped tone. "After all we've been through together, you can call me Kayda, Jayan."

"Aye, Kayda." He peered at her more closely. His smile slipped. "Everything all right with you?"

She waved him off. "Yeah, it's nothing." She patted his arm. "Just nervous about what we'll find when we arrive at Flamesmoat."

"Well, you won't have to wonder much longer." He nodded in the bow's direction. "Flamesmoat, ahoy," he said with a playful smirk.

"Already?" Kayda left Jayan at the helm and strode forward toward the bow. Conall and Lark were already there, staring up in the air and shading their eyes.

"What are we watching?" Kayda asked as she reached the rail.

Lark spared her a glance, then went right back to craning her neck up at the sky. "Muse. I sent her ahead to scout."

"Good plan," Kayda admitted. She joined the pair in their staring, finally glimpsing a bird high in the air and closing in on the far-off city.

It would likely still take the boat the better part of an hour to arrive at the docks in Southmoat. Her heart fluttered, and she tapped her foot on the wooden deck. If only Druturion were here, she might be the one flying ahead. More likely, she'd have arrived days ago.

Lark gasped.

"What is it?" Conall asked.

Kayda's heart dropped to her feet as Lark's normally tan face lightened to a ghostly white.

"We're too late," Lark whispered.

Kayda gripped the railing with both hands, her knees wobbling.

"Wait." Lark splayed a hand on her chest and bowed her head. "It's only half." She laughed. "Damn bird had me scared out of my wits."

Kayda frowned. "What's only half?"

Lark twisted sideways to face her, looking sheepish. "Sorry. Muse overshot the city, then swung down on it from the north. She thought the whole place was overrun with the scourge. But it's only Northmoat. Southmoat still stands."

Lark was smiling, obviously elated with the fact that half of the city still stood, but Kayda's blood turned to ice. Kings Keep was in

Northmoat. Her home was lost. What of her family? The king and prince? Izora?

"Northmoat is gone?" Kayda gulped and stared down at her boots. "How could that happen?"

Lark's hand landed on her shoulder. "I'm sorry, Kayda. It looks like the fire moat was breached. The scourge are running rampant on the streets."

Conall loosed a loud sigh. "How does Southmoat fare? Can Muse see any people there, still?"

Lark was silent for a moment, then she nodded. "Yeah, there are people there, scattered all over. There're a few ships at the docks, taking on passengers. The fire moat is still lit. But Muse says the streets are practically deserted." She grinned. "Sounds like the mages have been busy."

Kayda's heart lifted, if only for an instant. She sucked in a breath and said a silent prayer that all of those she loved were on one of those boats already.

The mages had accomplished at least one task they could be thankful for. Emptying a city of tens of thousands was no small feat. But had they evacuated everyone out of Northmoat before it fell?

They spent the next hour rousing everyone from below deck and preparing to dock. The Raimish warriors they'd brought with them readied their bows and knives. Everyone watched as Flamesmoat loomed larger on the horizon.

From their southern approach, the devastation Muse reported in Northmoat remained largely hidden. Only the smoke of some smoldering blaze, left to burn unchecked in the distance, rose as evidence that anything was happening in the city's northern section.

The docks were alive with activity as they pulled into port. Jayan parked them on one of the innermost docks in the bay. All the while,

Kayda felt that same crawling itch creeping up her back, the sensation becoming nearly overwhelming when she spotted the scourge prowling the Riddle River's banks on the city's Northmoat side.

Kayda was one of the first to hop off the gangplank. She strode down the dock, heading for a group of young people who appeared to be directing foot traffic onto a rickety old wooden ship. Dozens of people rushed about, young and old, loaded down with bags and whatever valuables they could carry.

A man who looked to be in charge whirled around to greet them. But instead of addressing her, he brushed his curly brown locks aside and his brown eyes lit on the young mages behind her. "Oriana, Edrik. You're back!"

"Baris!" Oriana rushed forward and clasped the man in a hug. "We've brought help from Raimire."

"Good, this boat is almost full. We still have some stragglers we need to evacuate." He turned and shaded his eyes, scanning *Nova's Champion* up and down. He whistled. "That's some ship. We'll be able to fit a lot of refugees on that."

Conall strolled up beside her with a smile. "Well, I'll be damned."

Kayda raised a brow. "What is it?"

He pointed at the old, beat-up ship being loaded. "*The Lady Luck.* I hired them to sail me from Doln to the Mido Islands." He chuckled. "I guess the captain couldn't turn down a second payday ferrying refugees."

Kayda spared the ship another glance. It didn't look like much, but—she gasped. "Father?"

She raced forward, her boots slapping loudly against the wooden docks. Prince Gideon wheeled around at the sound of her voice, his brow furrowing until he spotted her racing toward him. Then his face lit with joy.

"Kayda!" He stumbled down the gangplank, reversing course so quickly his round belly nearly knocked the man beside him into the bay.

She hadn't given it much thought at first. Her reaction had been purely instinctual, calling out for the man she'd always considered her father and running to greet him. But as he met her gaze and pulled her into a hug, all the knowledge she'd learned over the last few weeks rushed to the forefront of her mind.

This man was *not* her father. He'd never been her father. She was a sham princess.

As he squeezed her, embracing her so tightly she struggled to breathe, she had to tamp down the desire to scream out the truth. But if she knew anything, she knew now was not the time. She couldn't have that conversation on a crowded dock with the city crumbling beneath them.

"I'm so glad you're back." Gideon held her at arm's length and smiled down at her, his blue eyes misty.

She sent him a tremulous smile, then shifted up on her toes to peek behind him. "Are you the last to leave? Where are Grandfather and Izora?"

The prince sucked in a shaky breath. "I—about that..." He dropped her arms and frowned down at the docks.

"What?" Kayda couldn't keep the hint of anger from her voice.

"I know I promised you I'd look after him. And I did. I swear I did." Gideon curved a hand through his blond hair. "But just before the bridge burned down, Father took off into Northmoat."

Kayda's heart dropped. "He's out there, all alone?"

"Not exactly. Izora followed him."

She turned from her father, doubling over and gripping her knees.

"Kayda, what's wrong?" Lark rushed up the dock toward her, followed by a gaggle of her friends from the boat. She reached Kayda and rubbed her back. "Hey, it's all right."

Kayda allowed Lark to soothe her for a moment, her mind racing. Then she straightened, spinning to face her father.

"How long have they been stranded in there?"

He shook his head. "Not long. Northmoat only fell last night."

Kayda nodded. "Then there's still a chance they're alive." She scanned the city. "I have to find them." She started walking.

"Wait, where are you going?" Lark called out. "Slow down."

Conall jogged up to their group and grabbed her arm before she got far. "Hey, what's wrong?"

Kayda shrugged off his hand. "The king is in Northmoat. I'm going to find him," she announced again.

"You can't," Prince Gideon said. "They burned the bridge down."

"I don't care. I'll find a way."

"Wait, Princess," Conall said.

She glared at him but halted.

"We just got here. Let's get some more information and piece together a plan before we do anything."

Kayda inhaled through her nose, forcing her body to stay still when all she wanted was to move. How long could they last there, surrounded by the scourge?

Conall turned to the prince. "What exactly happened? How did the king end up stuck there?"

Prince Gideon's brow furrowed. "I wasn't there at the time. I can't tell you exactly."

By now, a small group had gathered around them, including several young mages. The brown-haired man who'd greeted them, Baris, stepped forward. "I was there. We gathered everyone in Southmoat before we set fire to the bridge. Somehow, the king snuck back into Northmoat. A couple of mages followed him before the bridge collapsed. After that, we just moved ahead with the plan, hoping they managed to make it to shelter. With how many scourge we killed, they might've had time to hole up somewhere before the fire moat ran out of fuel."

Kayda clenched her fists. It didn't make any sense. "The king just wandered off with no one noticing? The last time I saw him, he would only move if you led him somewhere."

Baris shook his head. "Izora said he'd spoken to her before he left. Told her he was going to the stables."

Lark perked up. "Where are they? Tell me how to get there from here, and I'll send Muse to scout from above."

Baris started detailing directions but Kayda wasn't listening. She stared up at the sky, her mind reeling.

The king had broken free of his stupor! After those days they'd spent together, locked up in the tower room, she'd believed he'd never be the same again. But now he was back! She *had* to save him.

As Muse rose into the sky and disappeared across the river, Mika approached Kayda. "The king, his condition, was he that way from having too many bonds?"

Kayda met his gaze. "He was attacked at the Harvest Festival, but ever since his second bondmate passed, he'd been acting differently. Do you think bonding magic had something to do with why he wouldn't recover?"

"I believe so," Mika said. "I've had some experience with healing his condition. I'd like to come with you. I think I can help."

Baris jumped in. "That's all well and good. I mean, someone ought to save the king, but we've got a host of problems to solve on this side of the city."

"What problems?" Conall asked.

"The fire moat and the tunnels are close to failing. We just don't have enough mages to keep up with the scourge. Now that they've realized there isn't anyone left in Northmoat, they've redoubled their efforts to tunnel in over here."

Kayda stared across the river. He was right. The crowd of scourge snarling at them from the riverbank had already thinned in the time they'd been standing here.

Baris continued, "It's insane, the way they act. I've never seen another animal so coordinated, except maybe a hive of bees when they've been attacked. Like they're all connected, or under orders or something."

"What do you mean?" Kayda asked, a sick sense of dread settling in her stomach.

"They all swarmed Northmoat last night. But after only a few hours, they started retreating. We didn't know where they were going, but this morning a huge crowd of them arrived on this side of the river. They must've doubled back, found a bridge outside of the city to cross. What kind of animal does that?"

Kayda's stomach churned. More evidence of the Unseen at work. But maybe the scourges' cohesion could work to their advantage. It certainly helped that there were a lot less of them in their way of finding the king.

"How close are they to breaking through Southmoat's defenses?" Conall asked.

Baris rubbed his chin. "I'm not sure. I know they can use all the help they can get in the tunnels and moat. I'd be there myself if I hadn't used all the magic I could handle already today."

"I'll go," Edrik offered.

"Me, too," Oriana said.

Conall turned to Lark. "We should head there, too. You can help in the tunnels, and I'll lend a hand at the moat."

Lark nodded. "Agreed, just as soon as I hear back from—wait, Muse reached the stables." A wide grin split her face. "Sounds like they made it. She says all the doors are barred and there's a white flag hanging from a window."

Kayda's heart lifted, and she sighed. There was still a chance.

"How can the rest of us help?" asked Dausius, the leader of Lark's gang of traveling entertainers.

"There are still pockets of citizens refusing to leave. We could use help finding them and convincing them to evacuate," Baris said. "I'm afraid we don't have much time."

All around Kayda, the others discussed plans to split up—who would head where and when to return—but the conversation slid around her, unheard. She was busy trying to think of a way to cross the river. The churning waters were full of rapids and scattered rocks, making boat travel unlikely. But there must be another way. How else had the king crossed with no one seeing?

But though she racked her brain, she just couldn't—unless...

Kayda smiled, a snippet of a conversation from long ago in the king's chambers flashing in her mind. She'd thought it was just more of his mad rambling, but maybe it wasn't. Maybe it was the answer she was searching for.

Mika turned to her. He pointed across the river. "Looks like the path is clear, for now. How are we getting across?"

"I know how to get us there; it's getting back that will be a problem," she admitted.

Prince Gideon leaned forward. "I might have the solution for that."

Kayda turned to her father and lifted a brow. Her entire life, she'd never been able to count on him. Even after he'd apologized for ignoring her, he couldn't handle watching the king like he promised. Could she really trust him to help?

Maybe she could give him another chance. Besides, it wasn't like she had many choices. "I'm listening."

Chapter 4

L ark sighed and shook her head. No wonder her father wanted out of this place. Southmoat was a dump.

Conall, Oriana, and Edrik weaved through the empty streets with her, hurrying to reach the underground tunnels and fire moat. The dilapidated houses loomed over them, just as shabby and run-down as she remembered them from her last trip through the slums.

Back then, she'd been forced to view them from the cramped confines of the back of a horse cart, smashed together with Tiora on her way to becoming a slave in Doln. She shivered, shoving aside the memory of the terror that'd overcome her that night.

Things were different now. No one would force her to do anything ever again.

Edrik stopped at a fork in the road. "Here's where we need to split up. The fire moat is this way." He pointed at the eastern road. "Ori, you should head there with Conall. Your wind talent can help fan the flames. Me and Lark need to go this way." He pointed south. "The closest tunnel entrance is over here."

Lark responded with a curt nod, but inside, her heart thudded wildly. Was she really about to split up with Conall again, after everything he'd gone through to find her?

Conall seemed to sense the uncertainty warring within her. "Hey." He grabbed her arms and stared down at her face. "Don't worry. We'll meet up back at the ship. I won't lose you again."

"All right." She offered him a wobbly smile. "Keep him safe, Shadow," she said to the gray wolf at his side. Maybe it was her imagination, but her brother's bondmate looked like he understood, even inclining his head in her direction.

"What, do you speak to wolves now?" Muse asked from her perch on a ramshackle roof of a nearby house. *"Should I be jealous?"*

Lark rolled her eyes, setting off on the road beside Edrik. *"Don't be silly. You know you're my tweetheart."*

"Ha! Was that a joke? I'm finally rubbing off on you."

Lark cringed inwardly. Yeah, maybe she was. After so long listening to awful puns from her bondmate, it was no wonder she was coming up with a few of her own.

Edrik turned a corner, revealing another street just as run-down as all the rest. But unlike the others they'd passed, this one was occupied. A woman sprawled in the middle of the road, a bevy of sacks loaded full to bursting scattered in the dirt beside her. Two filthy, raggedly clothed children glanced up as they approached, tears painting clean tracks down their dirt-encrusted cheeks.

"Help!" the larger of the two exclaimed. He hopped up and raced toward them. Lark guessed he was likely around ten-years-old, and the little girl who stayed crouched by the woman's side, probably only around five.

"Please, you've gotta help us!" he pleaded. "My momma fell down on our way to the docks. She hurt her leg."

"It's all right," Lark said with a gentle smile. "I'm a healer. I'll take a look at her leg."

"Thank you! Thank you so much," the little boy gushed, rushing back to his mother's side.

Lark knelt down beside the woman's face. "Hello, my name is Lark."

The woman's brown eyes shot open. A sheen of sweat covered her forehead, even though her threadbare cloak appeared far too thin for the chill in the air. Her teeth gritted shut, and her brows pinched tightly together. "My ankle." She moaned. "We were rushing, and I tripped over something in the road. I felt something snap. I think I broke it."

"Do you mind if I take a look? I'm a healer."

The woman nodded, wincing.

Lark moved beside the woman's leg, gently lifting her wool pants. She scowled at the swollen flesh she found underneath. "I'm afraid you're right. It's either broken or badly sprained."

"Oh, what am I going to do?"

"Hey, don't worry." Lark kept her voice as soothing as possible. "Did I mention I'm a mage?" She quirked a brow, aiming a smile at the boy and little girl—who hadn't yet said a word, only sat clutching her mother's hand with trembling fingers. "I'll get you all fixed up in just a moment."

She shucked her bag off her back and dug inside. To heal bones, she needed greens or beans, and for the swelling she'd need—

An explosion of sound blasted through the air, followed by a vibration in the ground so strong it shook the earth where they sat.

"What was that?" the little boy asked, his voice thready and quavering.

Edrik, the only one still standing, wobbled beside her. He stared at a brick building at the end of the road—one that had a cloud of dust escaping from the open door and windows.

"Lark, that's where we're headed," he said after he caught his balance. "I don't know what that was, but I should probably go check it out."

"Go," she waved a hand, shooing him toward the dust-clouded building. "This will only take a moment, then I'll meet you there."

"Are you sure?" he asked, but he was already in motion, turning backward for a final glance in her direction.

"Yes. Go. I'm right behind you."

Edrik took off at a jog, and within moments, he ducked inside the doorway and out of sight.

"Where were we?" Lark said, more to herself than the confused faces crowded around her. That's right—swelling. She rummaged in her pack again, found what she needed, and exhaled, then met the woman's wide eyes. "I just need to press this to your injury. It will hurt for a moment, but then you'll be good as new."

The woman set her jaw. "Yes. I'm ready. Just get it over with."

Lark pressed her hand against the wound, ignoring the woman's yelp of pain. She closed her eyes and wished. The earth trembled again, much fainter than before, but still enough to be discernible. The vibration flowed through her, coalescing on her palm and flooding into the wound beneath her. When she lifted her hand, the flesh was no longer swollen.

"Try moving your ankle, please," she instructed.

The woman complied, her eyes widening even further as her ankle twisted and turned. "It's like I never hurt it. Bless you!"

Lark's cheeks warmed as she cinched her bag closed and brushed the dirt off her knees. She stood, glancing at the overloaded bags once more. "You should be able to make it to the docks now, but you might consider leaving some of this stuff behind. I'd hate for you to fall again."

The woman flushed, nodding sheepishly. "That's good advice. I promise I'll heed it. Thank you!"

"You're welcome." Lark flashed the kids a smile and set off after Edrik.

Her heart lifted. Just a few weeks ago, she would've been helpless in that same situation. She couldn't be thankful enough for all the knowledge Mika had taught her. Not to mention the confidence he'd helped instill in her.

Of course, she had someone else to thank for that as well. After all, it's not every day her mother sent her a message from the grave.

"Muse, I'm going underground, you better stay—"

Noise from somewhere close by halted her. A pained voice, crying out.

"Did you hear that?" She swiveled her head around, looking for the source but finding nothing.

Muse darted off. *"Yeah. Let me see what I can find."*

Lark stopped just outside the doorway to the brick building. Whatever explosion happened inside hadn't repeated itself, but dust still swirled in the doorway, motes catching in the sun's rays and dancing in the air. She leaned closer, listening carefully for any sign of distress coming from within. After a moment, she heard a male voice speaking calmly and someone else chuckled gently in response, though they were too far away for her to make out their words.

"I found something," Muse said.

"What is it?"

"A tall building, just up the road from where you are. There are people on the top floor. I think they're trapped."

Lark gulped, sparing a glance at the doorway. But her feet were already moving. *"I'm coming."*

She broke into a run, her boots pounding on the dirt road, ignoring the twinge of guilt in her stomach and the tiny voice in her mind that told her to return to the tunnels.

There were people—her friends among them—out here searching for stragglers. She was supposed to be helping the mages underground. But she couldn't just leave those people there to die. What if they weren't discovered in time? Surely, she could free them quickly and return before the mages realized she was missing.

As she drew closer, the voice reached her ears, clear as day. "Help!" he cried, over and over, the voice hoarse and distinctly masculine.

She arrived in front of a circular tower built of stone and mortar and spotted Muse circling it. It had to be at least four stories tall, far larger than any of the buildings surrounding it. The scent of decay hung heavy in the air. One she recognized intimately from her time in the Boglands. The road ended beyond the stone tower, and the tops of mangrove trees rose on the horizon behind it.

"Are we back at the bog?" she asked.

"Yep, this building is built right on the border. It's all water on the other side."

"I didn't realize we'd made it that far south." She slowed down and climbed the steps to the doorway. The door was barred, a wooden bar nailed down over the entrance.

"What in the world?" she said aloud, all thought of the Boglands driven from her mind.

"The door's barred with a wooden beam," she explained to Muse. *"Why would someone lock people inside of here when everyone is supposed to be evacuating?"*

She craned her neck up and shaded her eyes. The unmistakable shape of a hand slipped out of a top floor window and waved down at her. "Help! Please, help! We're in here."

"Are you going in there? I've got a bad feeling about this," Muse said.

"I'll be all right. I can't leave those people in there to die." She scanned the doorway, searching for a way in. The door looked like it was made to swing outward, but maybe with a little magical push, she could knock it off the hinges and slip inside.

Lark hopped down the stone steps and scooped up a handful of dirt. She rose to her feet and turned, but then she swiveled back around and leaned over again, slipping a few handfuls of dirt in her cloak pockets—just in case.

Then she returned to the door, exhaling a deep breath and slipping her hand beneath the beam on the wooden door next to the lower hinges. She closed her eyes, visualizing the door breaking. A tremor filled her, rattling her jaw and thrumming through her blood.

Crack. She opened her eyes and smiled. The door still hung there, but the lower half tilted ajar, the hinge blasted to nothing. She knelt down and pushed. The heavy door protested, but with a shove of her shoulder, it opened just wide enough for her to shimmy inside.

Lark's eyes took a moment to adjust inside the dimly lit interior. The room looked curiously more like a dock than the inside of a building.

Brick shelving lined the wall next to the door, with piles of neatly stacked poles, rope, and tackle resting next to buckets full of dirt that likely held live bait. Skinny canoes hung on the rest of the walls, smaller than the ones Fillan and Dal had ferried them through the bog on. Half of the back wall was open, and a hole in the floor on the far side even allowed some of the sulfuric water to creep inside, providing a second entrance to the building. One that led directly to the bog.

A shadow darted inside the opening, setting Lark's heart racing. She shrieked.

"It's just me." Muse landed gracefully on a rafter crisscrossing the high ceiling.

"You scared me half to death," Lark admitted with a chuckle, a hand clutched to her chest as her racing heart slowed.

She spun in a slow circle, scanning the building's interior. In here, the lapping water and the distant croaks of bog life dominated her ears. The cries from upstairs were so muffled she could barely hear their echo.

At first glance, she didn't see any way to climb to the top floors. But as her eyes fully adjusted to the dim light flowing in from the hole in the wall, she spotted a rope dangling down, and the shape of a wooden rectangle set in the ceiling.

Walking beneath it, she raised up on her tip-toes, reaching for the rope. It dangled just out of her reach.

"Of all the times to be short," she grumbled under her breath.

"Ha, you need a hand there, runt?"

"Very funny." She crossed her arms. *"See if you can pull that down for me, would ya?"*

Muse flew down from her perch, clasping the rope in her beak and flapping her wings furiously. But after a few moments, she dropped the rope and returned to her perch. *"It's too heavy. Too bad. It looks like those folks upstairs are out of luck."*

Lark's heart sank. She couldn't just give up. *"Can you fly out of here and find Aren or Daus, bring them back with you?"*

"You don't quit, do you? Fine, I'll be back."

"Thanks, Muse."

Lark sighed, watching her bondmate disappear outside. So much for being back before the mages noticed she was missing. She tapped her foot, scanning the walls again. All those canoes. They must use this place for fishing.

A smile crept across Lark's face as a thought crossed her mind. She approached the closest canoe, and bending her knees, hefted the small vessel off the wall. It almost knocked her over, but she managed to slide the craft onto the stone floor, upside down. Then it was only a matter of scooting it across the floor, and she stepped atop the bottom of the boat, and grabbed the rough rope in her hands.

She pulled. The wooden hatch door swung down, and a folded wooden staircase came with it, unfolding so quickly she had to jump down off the boat to avoid being struck. It smashed into the canoe with a loud *crack*.

Lark wobbled on her feet, her heart slamming to life. She came dangerously close to falling into the bog before she righted herself. Blowing out a shaky breath, she shoved the boat sideways so that the ladder could completely unfold.

The cries returned, louder than before. She could hear not just one, but dozens of voices screaming for release.

She mounted the stairs, taking her time, the rickety stair swaying with every footfall. The second floor was even dimmer than the first, and she cursed herself for not bringing a torch. The only light filtered in through the barred windows.

As her eyes adjusted, she gasped. She stood in a hall surrounded by dozens of cells, all of them empty, the metal doors shut tightly. On the wall beside the door, dozens of weapons hung. Cudgels and staves mostly, many of them covered in dark brown stains.

A sick feeling rose in her gut. She was in a prison.

The scared little girl inside of her screamed to turn around and leave. To abandon these criminals to their fate.

But beneath the fear, a different voice was there, convincing her to stay. Telling her that these men were someone's father. Someone's brother. Did they really deserve to be left here to die? Starving to death, locked up in a cell, alone and forgotten while the rest of the city fled. Or worse yet, torn to shreds and eaten alive by the scourge.

Lark remembered the woman on the docks in Bogsmouth. She'd watched helplessly as a horde of the vicious beasts ravaged her.

She shook her head. No one deserved that death. No one.

Lark found a stairwell leading up. She passed another floor, opened the door from the stair, and peered within. All the cells were just as quiet and empty as on the last. In a matter of moments, she found herself on the top floor. Here the voices of men greeted her as she pushed open the stairwell door.

"Help, please help us!" called out the voice she recognized hearing outside.

She strode over to the nearest cell. Inside, there was a man, bearded and clothed in tattered rags, his right arm torn to shreds. Dried blood encrusted the sleeve of his gray prison coveralls. The cold wind whistled through his window. He clearly used his bare hands to smash a hole in the glass between the metal bars.

A chorus of pleas surrounded her, all the men shouting and screaming at her.

"Help!"

"Free us!"

"I don't want to die," one cried out, voice thick with fear and desperation.

Lark shuddered, her heart breaking for these poor, abandoned men. Who could leave someone here, alone, to die?

She grabbed the metal bars of the man's cell by the broken window, tugging with all her might. It was no use. The door was locked. She reached into her cloak pocket, the cool soil sliding in her fingers.

The man within raced over and shoved his face against the bars just beside her. His eyes were wide, cheeks streaked with tears.

Lark gasped, backing up a pace.

"Hey, you're here. Thank the Lord Dragon!" His chin wobbled, and his hands trembled. His voice choked with emotion. "The keys!" He pointed behind her to a set of keys dangling from a hook on the wall beside the doorway. "There, grab the keys!"

Lark nodded, strode back to the doorway, and removed the key ring. Then she slid the key into the man's cell door.

The door swung open, and the man stepped out. His face, which only moments ago had been the picture of suffering, morphed before her eyes. His gaze landed on her, and he licked his lips, smirking. "Well, well, well. Looks like my prayers have been answered. What do you say, boys?" Hand moving lightning quick, he snatched the keys from her grasp. "It's time to have some fun."

As the pleas for help died down, replaced with raucous laughter, Lark gulped.

Blazes. She just made a terrible mistake.

Chapter 5

Conall followed Oriana through the ramshackle streets of Southmoat. Silence surrounded them. And not just from the empty buildings and deserted streets.

Shadow strolled beside him, just as quiet as Oriana. He'd left Sunny back on *Nova's Champion*, sleeping peacefully on the deck. But even the presence of his bondmate and the thought of his beloved mutt couldn't calm the discomfort roiling in his belly every time he glanced over at the silent girl beside him.

He cleared his throat, slowing as the first flicker of flame rose in the air beyond their path. "I'm sorry for the things I said earlier."

Oriana's step faltered, and she nearly fell face-first on the dirt road before she righted herself. "What?"

Conall winced, watching her wobble. Even apologizing, he still managed to frighten the girl. "You just wanted to know about your brother. I shouldn't have chewed your head off."

Oriana's chin quivered, and she sniffed.

Blazes. What did he do now? He didn't want to make her cry—again.

But then she flashed him a smile and shook her head. "No, I'm glad you didn't hold back." And the next words she uttered made him certain the moisture in her eyes were tears of pride, not sadness. "Our Quent—a hero. I'm glad he had you for a friend, Conall."

He rubbed the back of his neck, his own eyes feeling a tad teary. Surely it was just from the fire moat they were fast approaching. "He's a good lad. I'm glad to know him, too."

Oriana sent him one last bright grin, then faced forward, her step quickening. "C'mon, we're almost there."

As they passed the last buildings, the road ended. Instead of more city spread out before them, a chest-high wall of flame burned, forming half of a semicircle and shielding the city's lower section.

The flame's warmth kissed his cheeks. Conall turned his head slowly, gazing in awe at the incredible display of magic.

He'd been to Flamesmoat countless times in his life. Before now, the ancient moat had been barely discernible; a shallow depression ringing the city, overgrown with grass and weeds. Now, the moat stood out starkly against the surrounding ground, the dirt freshly dug, so deep that even without the flames, the average man would likely struggle to climb out.

The mages had been busy. The lengths they took to protect the common folk of Dracwood were impressive, to say the least. If only they hadn't been the ones responsible for the Palisade's fall, he might think them all heroes.

A petite young woman noticed them approaching and cut off the stream of fire flowing from her hands to turn and greet them. She rubbed the sweat-slicked brown hair off her brow. Even in the chilly air this far north in the late fall, she sweated, clothed only in a short-sleeved tunic and what appeared to be light cotton trousers.

"Oriana, is that you?" she asked.

"Karina, I'm back from Raimire. We've come to help man the moat."

Karina drew closer and shivered. She chuckled, rubbing her bare arms. "You tend to forget it's almost winter when you spend half the day roasting next to the moat." She smiled crookedly. "Forgive my rambling. You've come to help, you said?" Karina flicked a glance at Conall and Shadow, her brows lifting, face lighting with what might be curiosity. "Both of you?"

Oriana nodded. "This is Conall. He can summon fire."

"Conall. I remember you from Mage Keep." She stuck out a pale hand expectantly.

Conall grasped her hand and shook firmly. "Can't say I can admit the same."

Karina released his hand. "You wouldn't. We weren't properly introduced." Her gaze flicked down, and she crossed her arms. "I was there, watching, when the Palisade fell. I'm sorry for what happened to you."

Conall tilted his head, examining Karina. This was the first time anyone who'd sided with Ereni had apologized for the trial they forced him to undertake.

Karina stared at the ground for a long moment before lifting her gaze to meet his. He could sense her apology was sincere. This girl, who didn't know him beyond watching him age before her eyes, seemed to be the picture of remorse. Could it be that the mages who had followed Ereni had as little say in what had happened to him as he had?

Conall flashed her a tiny smile. "It's ancient history. How can I help?"

Karina pointed south. "The two mages stationed next to the Bog-lands are due for a break. If you follow the moat until you hit the bog, you'll find them."

He and Oriana headed south. They passed several pairs of mages stationed alongside the moat, directing streams of fire and air. Most paid them no mind, their stares locked on the moat, intent on their task, keeping the city safe.

It wasn't long before twisted mangroves appeared on the horizon, and the distinctive stench of decay filled his nostrils. The walkway ended at the edge of a small cliff, and beyond that, the bog stretched out far as the eye could see. Murky water was dotted with so many mangroves it looked more like a maze than a proper waterway.

They stopped. Oriana spoke briefly with the two mages they'd been sent to replace. The hum of their pleasantries buzzed around him, but he was too distracted to focus on the words spoken.

They were so close to the fire moat now that the flames, which only provided a pleasant warmth on their walk, blazed with enough heat that he had the urge to remove his thick wool cloak.

But more than that, the scourge were finally visible, sending a chill through his veins that lessened the effect of the heat before him. Their musky scent competed with the stench of the bog for dominance, and their snarls roared in his ears. And underneath it all, the faint scratch of digging reverberated, causing the pit in his stomach to grow.

Worry swamped him for his sister, sudden and sharp. Would she be all right in the tunnels?

Shadow stopped beside him. His lips curled back in a snarl as he spotted the vermin crawling all over the ground beyond the moat. *"Ugly little beasts, aren't they?"*

"Yeah." Conall bit back a grimace.

The creatures they'd feared for so long were small—barely bigger than squirrels—but much more vicious. Covered in black and silver striped fur, their teeth snapped as they crawled atop each other, each of them vying to reach the moat. Their beady black eyes roved all around, and their wicked claws dug at the dirt or slashed through the air in a constant show of aggression.

He squinted, trying to see as far beyond the moat as he could. The entirety of Flamesmoat was bordered by large swaths of farm and pasture land, which would normally be used to feed the city, either with crops or livestock.

Now, as far as he could see, stretching back to the beginnings of the thick forests that rose beyond the fields, the scourge swarmed. They covered the ground like a living blanket, squirming and snarling, altering the landscape from the unrelieved browns and greens of fallow fall fields to a scene from a nightmare.

"Be careful, and good luck," one of the retreating mages called over his shoulder with a wave as he hustled off.

"What was that about?" Conall glanced briefly at Oriana.

"Weren't you listening to anything they said?"

Conall grimaced, sending her a half-hearted shrug. "I got a little distracted," he admitted, his gaze returning to the scourge beyond the flames.

"They said the scourge have been acting strangely today. Even more so than usual."

"Oh?" He turned to look at her, his curiosity piqued. "How so?"

It was her turn to shrug. "They couldn't put their finger on it exactly. But they both agreed they seem less combative today. Almost like they're working in unison."

Conall's skin prickled with gooseflesh. The Unseen. Was that phantom here, now? Pulling the strings on the scourge like so many puppets, there to do its bidding?

The fire before them wobbled, the chest-high flame guttering and fading to merely waist-high. Oriana lifted her hands. A tingle of static flashed across Conall's skin before the wind whipped to life, fanning the flames before them.

"C'mon." She stopped beside a lit torch the retreating mages left half-planted into the ground. "We've got a job to do."

Conall stepped beside her. His lashes fluttered closed for an instant as he visualized the flames he wanted. Then he brought forth the image of Lark's face. He needed to do his part to keep the city safe. To keep her safe. A chill settled over his skin and sank into his chest. Then twin flames shot from his palms, flowing freely, joining with the massive fire wall before him. Within moments, the two of them returned the wall to its former height.

Conall grinned. This wasn't so hard.

But then the moment stretched out, time passing slowly. Fatigue set in. The cost of summoning so much magic weighed on him. His back and legs ached. Not for the first time, he cursed the changes that had aged his body far more than his mind. If he didn't have these old bones, he might not be so wiped already.

Finally, Oriana dropped her hands and stepped back. "Time for a quick break. You, too." She set a hand on his shoulder. "We have to pace ourselves. If we don't rest every now and then, we'll be worn out too quickly."

The flames shooting from Conall's hands disappeared. His arms fell slack at his side, and he slumped to the ground, resting on his knees.

"Are you all right, little brother?" Shadow asked, sidling up beside him.

"Yeah. Just a need a moment to rest." He pulled out his waterskin and gulped down a long swig. *"You thirsty?"*

Shadow's tail wagged. *"Yes."*

"Here." Conall cupped his hand and filled it with the cool water, which Shadow lapped up quickly.

As he refilled his palm, Oriana chuckled. "Sometimes I forget Shadow isn't a dog, with how he acts. I can't believe you trained a *wolf* to eat out of your hand."

Conall smiled. "I didn't train him at all. Shadow's my bondmate."

Oriana settled down next to him cross-legged, quirking a brow. "What's the difference?"

"It's hard to describe. He's more like a brother to me than an animal. We share our thoughts. Our hopes and fears. He's always there for me, and me for him."

"That sounds incredible."

"It is. I wish more people could know what it's like. But from what I've seen, the talent is extremely rare. Much rarer than summoning the elements." It was strange to think that all the people he'd met so far with bonding magic were actually his siblings. But he'd met mages who hailed from all over the world.

"You're lucky to have both talents, then."

"Yeah, really lucky."

He sighed. Sometimes it didn't feel that way. Especially when the only people he knew who possessed both talents were the same people who'd been embroiled in the mage's schemes: Kayda, Lark, and himself.

"We better get back to it." Oriana rose to her feet and stretched.

Conall shoved his waterskin back into his pack and set it on the ground beside Shadow. He rose to return, then turned back. He shucked off his thick cloak, folded it, and rested it atop his bag. The fire moat would keep him warm enough.

Then he was back beside Oriana, fire once again flowing from his hands. The work was tiring physically, but he found once he started summoning, continuing didn't require much mental concentration. It wasn't long before his mind began to wander.

He couldn't help but see the irony in his situation. Here he was, with the same mages that'd brought down the Palisade, working to keep a different wall standing. It was funny how things happened like that; everything repeating, coming around full circle. He hated to say it, but it felt—fated.

He kept telling himself it was ridiculous to believe his future was preordained. But he'd drunk the dream elixir. He saw the battle in his vision. His stomach clenched. Was his future really set in stone, or could things change?

His gaze was drawn to the scourge, the lot of them, blanketing the earth with fur and claws and teeth. Their numbers were daunting. How could they hope to defeat them? Especially now that they knew the beast's vicious nature was not controlled by instinct alone. They would never give up. Never surrender. Not with the Unseen driving them.

What did the Unseen want? Why did he seek to destroy them? It was all so strange and confusing, trying to predict the motivations of something so unknown.

From across the fire, one of the scourge opposite him stilled, its beady eyes locking onto his. He gazed into the black depths of its stare and thought he spied something there. A hint of intelligence the rest of its brethren lacked.

He tried to shake the thought from his mind but couldn't. It stuck there like a thorn caught on his trousers. He went to move his gaze instead, to break the stare he held with the beast, but found his gaze just as fixed. Panic gripped him, and his muscles tensed, his heart pounding out of control.

"You've returned," boomed a harsh, gravelly voice in his mind. And though he'd never heard the voice before, instinctively he knew who it was. The Unseen.

Fear joined the panic slithering up his spine. That sick feeling he remembered so well crawled up with it, making his stomach spin.

"What do you want?" he spat.

"Conall?" Shadow paced to his side, backing away from the heat still streaming from his hands. *"What's wrong?"*

But he couldn't answer. Not while that vile voice infected his mind. He wouldn't let the Unseen hear him speak to his bondmate.

"Who is that?" The Unseen asked, curiosity clear in his tone. *"Who's speaking to you?"*

"That's none of your concern."

"Ah. I see." Laughter filled his mind. A gurgling chortle that made his skin crawl. *"We have more in common than you'd like to admit."*

"I have nothing in common with you."

"That's not true. We're cut from the same cloth. One day soon, you shall see."

Conall shuddered, trying with all his might to break free from the hypnotic stare he was locked in. To break the hold that allowed this thing to pollute his mind. Shadow circled him, ducking beneath the flames flowing from his hands, whining and shoving at his legs.

"You will come to me," the Unseen said, voice thick with glee.

Oriana's head spun to him, no doubt alerted by Shadow's strange behavior. She frowned. "Conall?"

Shadow rammed into him again, harder than ever. But though the blow would've been enough to topple him at any other time, he stood fast, his stance just as locked as the rest of his body and mind.

"You'll join me," the Unseen said.

"Never!" Conall shouted.

That laughter reverberated in his mind. Madness echoed inside his head. He wanted to claw his eyes out to break the stare. To silence that sickening voice.

Oriana's brows furrowed. Her gaze locked on Shadow as he reared back for another shove. Just as he connected, she turned her hands on Conall, blasting him with a wall of wind.

Slam. He landed in the dirt, hard on his back. The fire flowing from his hands halted, his chest heaved. Without the scourge's stare, he broke free from the Unseen's hold. The laughter cut off in his mind, and the sick crawling itch dissipated from his skin, vanishing as quickly as it had come over him.

Oriana and Shadow appeared at his side and tugged on his legs. He peeked behind him, and his heart skipped a beat. He'd fallen a mere handbreadth away from the cliff leading to the bog. Scrambling away from the edge, he rolled onto his knees and met Oriana's and Shadow's gazes.

"Thank you," he said.

"Thanks, brother," he thought.

"What was that?" Oriana asked.

"Was that the Unseen?" Shadow asked in unison.

Conall held up a hand, still reeling from the unexpected invasion. After a few deep breaths, he answered his bondmate first. *"Yes, I don't know how, but he used one of the scourge to connect with me."*

"Are you all right, little brother?"

"Yes. I am. Thanks to you." He reached over and pet Shadow behind the ears, the simple action bringing him a measure of comfort.

He turned to Oriana and scrubbed his face. "I don't even know where to begin. It's a long story, one I don't have the energy to dredge up at the moment. Just... thank you for what you did. It was the right call."

He spotted the mages they'd replaced earlier returning. They were chatting among themselves, smiling and laughing. But then one mage—the same man who'd warned them to be careful—flicked his gaze away from his companion and at the wall of flame. His eyes widened, his tanned face blanching. He raised a hand, finger pointed at the wall, a wordless scream forming on his lips.

Conall's gaze shot from the mages to the moat. At first, he noted nothing out of sorts. The fire still burned, just as strongly as before. But then he looked beyond the fire, and his stomach sank.

The scourge piled atop each other, forming a massive mound of creatures that reached high in the air. High enough he could see a tiny sliver of shining silver fur peek out above the chest-high wall of flame. Before he could do anything other than gasp, the top creature leaped straight for the fire.

It slammed into the fire moat, lighting up instantly, its dying screech pained and shrill.

"What are they doing?" Oriana yelled, bouncing to her feet.

Conall scrambled up as well, his stare locked on the climbing vermin as the scent of burning hair and roasting flesh clogged the air.

The pile beyond the flames steadily grew. More *ichneumon* ran to join their brethren, stacking atop each other higher and higher. In the space of a few heartbeats, the pile grew so tall he could clearly see the top few rows of beasts above the flames.

When the next beast jumped, it cleared the flames and landed on the ground at their feet. Shadow jumped for it in a flash, and the beast zeroed in on him, the two animals quickly turning into a snarling blur of ferocity.

"Breach!" one of the approaching mages screamed. "Quick, make the wall higher!"

All four of them summoned. The flames appeared in Conall's hands, quicker than ever before, with his fear for his bondmate at the forefront of his mind. He had to protect him.

The moat roared to life, the flames rising to reach the height of the pile. But not before a half dozen beasts cleared the wall and landed on the ground beside them. Three of them tore off straight for Shadow, but the other three bolted toward Conall and the mages.

Conall turned from the wall, still summoning fire. He aimed his hands at the scourge. A smile lit his lips as they burst into flames and shrieked, screaming in pain.

That still left the rest of them on his bondmate. While they'd been focused on the wall, he'd managed to latch his teeth around the first of the vermin. He clamped the beast in his powerful jaws, blood gushing out from his mouth as he shook his head wildly.

But with three more after him, Shadow struggled. He ducked and weaved, inching ever closer to the cliffside that bordered the bog. He dodged two of the beasts, but the third vaulted atop his back, digging its wicked claws in an instant before it bit the nape of Shadow's neck.

He dropped the carcass in his jaw, letting out an ear-splitting howl.

"Shadow!" Conall raced closer, shooting a ball of flame at one beast as it reared back for a second leap at his bondmate. The satisfying sound of its shriek filled the air as the flames roasted its face, and the beast dropped to the ground. He sent a second blast engulfing the vermin's body.

Another growl tore from his bondmate. The second scourge leaped on Shadow, its claws dug into his flank, teeth latched onto his hind leg.

He couldn't strike them with fire now. Not with them on Shadow. He'd hit him, too. He could run back and grab a waterskin, but that would waste too much time. Even the air, always present, might end in a disaster with Shadow so close to the cliff. If he pushed him off with a blast of air, Shadow would tumble down to the bog.

The mages furiously flung magic at the fire moat, fanning the flames ever higher. He'd have no help there. What could he do?

Desperate, he lunged, intending to rip the bastards off with his bare hands if he had to. No one messed with his bondmate.

He saw what was happening an instant too late. The beast on Shadow's leg bit down harder, just as he attempted to shake it off. His leg buckled. Shadow dropped sideways and fell off the cliff, splashing into the bog below with the beasts still latched onto him.

Conall screamed, "Shadow, no!" He landed on his stomach on the cliff's edge, right where Shadow had just been. He stared down with wide eyes, watching the current tug him away.

He didn't give his decision a second thought. He scrambled up on his feet and jumped. *"Brother, I'm coming!"*

Chapter 6

L ark shuddered as the man's smirk spread. His chapped lips cracked and bled, but he didn't even wince, only grinned ever wider, giving her a glimpse of his rotten teeth.

Immediately, her mind flashed back to the last man who'd looked at her like that. To that tiny warehouse room in Southmoat, where two vile men kept her against her will. She stood frozen, staring, her heart beating like a caged bird desperate to escape.

Then the man turned from her, his head and shoulders thrust back, reveling in the laughter and hoots of his cellmates.

Her gaze locked on that sickening grin, she started to back away.

"Hey," he crowed, his head swinging around to watch her, "don't leave so soon. The fun's just getting started."

He grabbed her cloak—just as fast as he'd snatched the keys from her hands—and shoved her into the cell she'd freed him from. He seized her pack while she staggered on her feet and ripped it off her back. Before she could right her balance, the door slammed closed behind her. The man sent her an evil smirk as she spun around, and he dropped her bag on the wall hook where the keyring had once hung.

"Hey, what'd you do that for?" called out a dark-skinned man a few cells down. "I want a taste of that little morsel."

The freed man laughed. "Can't have the first few ruining the meal while I free the rest of you blokes, now, can we?" He twirled the key ring on his fingers. "This way, we all get a taste."

More laughter and cheers met that statement as the man moved to the first cell door, and then went about methodically opening them, one by one.

Terror threatened to immobilize Lark. Her breath came hard and fast, her gaze darting across the men's faces. They stared back at her with violence and something more sinister in their eyes.

No. No! She stared down at the hard stone floor, forcing herself to take a calming breath.

She was not the same powerless girl who'd been tricked into bondage all those months ago. These men would not get what they wanted from her. She'd rather die fighting.

"Muse? I'm in a bit of a tough spot here... Please tell me you've found someone."

"I've got Daus. We're headed back. What's the trouble?"

"Remember that bad feeling you had?"

"Yeah..."

"You were right. I get the feeling these people were left here for a good reason."

"Bird brains! You went up alone?"

"Yes, just hurry back with Daus. I'm seriously outnumbered here, and I'm gonna need your help."

Lark slipped her hands into her cloak pockets, sinking her fingers into the smooth soil she'd picked up outside. The echoes of laughter and the squeals of the rusty metal doors swinging open reverberated in the air.

Let them come. They were in for a big surprise.

Moments ticked by. Her stomach roiled, but she set her stance, boots firm and hands clenched around the cool dirt. Except for a pair of men who only spared her a quick glance before they hustled to the stairwell door then quickly disappeared, all the freed men gathered around her cell. They yelled out taunts, licking their lips and tugging at their groins.

Lark waited.

Finally, the first man returned, the key ring swinging. Flecks of dried blood flicked off his sleeve, and his smirk spread wide. "Fellas. I'm sure you'll all agree, seeing as it was my plan that saw us free, first turn goes to me."

"Aww, there's plenty to go around, Ulric. You really gonna make us all wait?" yelled out a man in the back of the crowd. There had to be at least twenty, probably closer to thirty men in front of her cell. The sight of so many sent a spike of fear up Lark's spine.

Ulric's grin turned feral. He shouldered through the crowd to the front of the cell. "You blokes can divvy up the spoils how you like once I'm done. I won't be long."

Lark's stomach turned at the undisguised glee on their faces. And the way they spoke about her—like she was a thing and not a person—was sickening.

Ulric slid the key inside the door. The dark-skinned man grabbed his elbow before he could swing the door open, and Ulric turned a menacing stare his way. The man dropped his arm immediately and retreated a step. "You sure you don't want a few of us in there? Lass looks like a fighter."

The smirk was back, and a cruel glint lit Ulric's eyes. "Perfect. Just the way I like it."

Then the door swung open, and Ulric slid in, then pulled the door firmly closed behind him. He stalked closer, the key ring enclosed within his fist with the sharp ends sticking out menacingly.

"What's your name, Pretty?" he asked.

Lark panicked. Her mind raced as she tried to plan something to say that would make this vile man think twice about laying a finger on her. An image of Meital flashed in her mind. The way she'd dealt with those creeps back in that little inn. Fierce and fearless.

Lark stared Ulric in the eyes and channeled Meital, her voice just as sharp and sweet as hers had been. A dagger drenched in honey. "Call me Death."

The fiend laughed in her face and circled around her, the keys pointed at her neck. "Lady Death. Do you hear that, fellas?" He rounded her back, his gaze roaming over her body with overt lust. "Won't be the first time I screwed death."

Lark swallowed a grimace as laughter exploded from the men. Not quite the effect she was going for there. Maybe she could try another tactic.

"Is that right?" Lark purred. "Or has Death been waiting to screw you?" She forced a coy smile across her lips as Ulric turned to face her. She ignored the cold metal key poking into her neck and spread her hand over his chest, caressing him softly.

"Ha, she ain't a fighter, boys. She's a whore," yelled one of the men.

"We're almost there, Lark. Hold on!" Muse called out through their bond.

"We'll see about that," Ulric smirked again, his lips aimed at her own.

She closed her eyes and wished. A vibration thrummed through her body, racing into Ulric's chest through her palm before his vile lips descended on her. She threw everything she had into it, and her eyes flew open as Ulric slammed into the metal bars, grasping his chest, a look of horror on his face.

"Mage! The bitch is mage!" someone screamed. A few men scattered, but the dark-skinned man reached his hand into the bars, swiping the key ring from Ulric's dying grasp. Before they could get far, the stairwell door swung open.

Dausius and Muse! They'd come to—

A stranger leaped through the doorway. It was a young woman, her long brown hair pulled back in a ponytail. Her blue eyes were cold as steel, and in her hands, she wielded a swirling ball of vapor.

She took one glance inside and sent air blasting into the crowd. Chaos ensued. Lark used it to her advantage, flinging darts of dirt at the men still crowded around the bars of her cell. Cries of pain rang out, and bodies fell, smashing into the cold stone floor.

The dark-skinned man still grasped the key, clamping it tight to his chest. But with the bodies tumbling around him, he tripped, and the ring went flying. It skittered across the stone toward the brunette. Lark's heart skipped a beat. She needed those keys!

The brunette spotted the ring hurtling toward her and caught it with a blast of air, sending it flying back into the cell. "Get out of there, quick!" she ordered.

Lark scrambled to grab the key ring. By now, all the prisoners either sprawled on the ground or had been blasted deeper into the hall, held immobile by the mage's constant stream of wind. Lark's shaking hands slipped the key in the lock. It turned. She stepped over Ulric's dead body and out of the cell. She was free!

Then the same heavy wind keeping the prisoners back caught her. If she hadn't still clutched the cell door, she would've surely lost her footing and slammed back into the crowd of prisoners.

But then the mage cut off the wind. "Let's go!" she screamed, frantically waving her arms.

Lark didn't need to be told twice. She raced to the stairwell, only pausing to swipe her bag off the wall.

The mage slammed the door closed behind them. She sent another blast of air at the door. "Do you have more earth? Jam the door, quick!"

Lark dug in her pocket and flung earth at the door's seams, picturing it caked fast with mud.

A moment later, the brunette tugged her elbow. She pulled her away from the door and down the stairs. "That won't hold them forever. Hurry."

They raced down the stairs, taking them two at a time. Lark bit back a gasp as they passed the two men who'd fled on the stairwell, lying in matching pools of blood, their throats slit.

The brunette stepped over their slack bodies without a word. Had she killed them?

Soon they descended down the rickety wooden staircase to the bottom floor. As they hopped off and the girl turned around to send the folding stair back up into the ceiling, Lark spotted a problem.

The racks of shelves she'd noticed when she'd entered had been smashed to pieces. The supplies that had once been neatly stacked, lay scattered and broken. Piles of brick littered the floor in front of the door, blocking the bottom section she'd knocked askew. She reached into her pocket again, preparing to call on her talent to move the bricks.

"No." The brunette grabbed her arm. "We can't let those men into Southmoat. There's not enough time for us to climb out and barricade the door again."

The pounding of footsteps echoed above them. She was right. The men had already broken the door holding them upstairs. It wouldn't be long before they made it downstairs.

"What are we going to do?" Lark eyed the canoes on the wall, seeing only one other viable exit. "The Boglands are a maze. We'll be lost if we try to escape that way. Do you mean to stay and fight?"

Her stomach churned. They'd barely fought them off upstairs, and that was before the men spotted the weapons hanging on the first-floor walls. Thirty armed men against two tired mages were not great odds.

The girl lifted her hand, using the wind to send the canoe she'd used as a footstool earlier into the murky water. Then she shucked off her cloak, nodding for Lark to do the same. "We'll hide underneath that canoe. Let's hope the prisoners leave out the docks. Let them be the ones to get lost. If we hear them moving the stones to escape into the city, we'll need to take our chances fighting them off."

The brunette grabbed Lark's cloak and pack and marched to the chamber's wall. She pressed on a stone, one that looked just the same as all the rest.

Lark gasped. A hidden chamber popped open. Lark peered inside, hopeful they could hide inside it instead of jumping in what would no doubt be freezing water, but the stone drawer was far too small, barely large enough to fit their cloaks and her bag inside. The girl shoved them inside, then shucked off her boots, too. Lark's boots joined hers atop the piled clothes a moment later.

"C'mon." The girl shoved the drawer closed. She hopped into the water with a splash, winced, then quickly smiled. "It's not even cold. Jump in."

Lark sensed she was lying about the cold. But the footsteps above were only getting louder. She took a deep breath and jumped.

The breath gushed out of her lungs as the freezing water surrounded her. Definitely lying.

"C'mon," the brunette demanded, then she ducked beneath the overturned canoe.

Lark wondered—not for the first time—who *was* this girl? Obviously, she was a mage. That much she could be certain of. One with an intimate knowledge of the city and this building. Whoever she was, Lark owed her life to her. That fact made it easy to duck her head beneath the water and follow her beneath the canoe, even when she didn't yet know her name.

The cold was like a slap to the face, sapping her energy. When she resurfaced under the overturned canoe, her teeth-chattered, and she gripped her chest tightly beneath the water. Luckily, the depth was shallow, and she could hold herself up on her tiptoes so that her mouth and nose cleared the murky water's surface.

The brunette, being taller, was steadier on her feet. She held the canoe in place around them as the water swayed.

"Who are you? How did you know I was in trouble?" Lark wasted no time asking, her voice a harried whisper.

"My name is Ereni. I'll explain later. They won't be long now." She cocked her head sideways, listening intently to the footfalls above as they grew louder.

A prickle of recognition came over Lark at the name. She could swear she'd heard it before, but where and when she couldn't put her finger on.

Lark couldn't waste time racking her brain for where she'd learned the girl's name. Instead, she took the opportunity to update her bond-mate. *"Muse? I'm safe for now. I'm hidden beneath an overturned canoe in the bog. You better stay hidden, too. The prisoners are on their way to the bottom level.*"

"*Hidden? Prisoners? Oh no.*"

"*What's wrong?*"

"*Daus, he's at the entrance trying to move the rocks and make his way inside.*"

Lark's stomach sank. "*Get him to stop! He has to hide!*"

"*I'm trying!*"

She started to explain, "My bondmate—"

But Ereni slapped a hand over her mouth, her gaze darting sideways.

An instant later, the folding stairs crashed down.

Blazes! Dausius came running to help, and she was about to get him killed.

"*Is Daus still out there?*" she asked, her own voice in her mind panicked.

"*I can't get him to stop digging! Damn humans, the whole lot of you don't know when to quit!*"

Lark clutched her chest beneath the icy water. She prayed for the men to leave through the bog. Ereni said they needed to fight if they made for the city... The odds were certainly stacked against them, but she wouldn't leave Daus to die. Never.

Time to change strategy. "*Can you find somewhere to watch the men in here without being seen? I need you to be my eyes. If Daus is in trouble, I have to know right away.*"

"*On it,*" Muse replied.

In the room beyond their little hidden shelter, the lumbering thuds of the prisoner's footfalls reverberated on the creaking wooden ladder, making it impossible to hear any of their conversation. Were they already attempting to dig their way out into the city streets?

"*I can see them. Looks like they're all just standing around, arguing.*"

Lark blew out a heavy sigh. Just then, the ladder's creaking stopped, and the door slammed heavily. They must've sent the trapdoor back up into the ceiling. The men's conversation finally became intelligible. Muse was right. They were definitely arguing.

"We should escape to the bog. There are plenty of canoes," one man said, his voice firm.

"The bog is a deathtrap. We'll be lost or eaten alive. I'm taking my chances in the city," another insisted, his voice deeper than the first.

Ereni tensed beside her at that.

"Are they digging at the door?" she asked Muse.

"No... wait. The man who just spoke is headed there. A few of the men are following him."

Lark shuddered. She stared at Ereni, tilting her head sideways. The mage's stare bored into hers and spoke volumes without having to say a word. She gripped the canoe's edge, ready to flip it aside and fight.

"Wait!" A third voice yelled from further away. "I can hear something on the other side. Shut up and listen!"

Lark stilled and forced her teeth to stop chattering, listening just as intently.

"Someone is digging out there." A pause. "Shit! It's the guard!"

Deep voice spoke up again, "How do you know that? It could be anyone!"

"Listen, you ass! I can hear the man bellowing out there. It's the Guard Captain! He says there's an entire contingent surrounding us."

A chorus of shouts and chatter exploded at that announcement, with everyone talking over each other. Lark couldn't make heads or tails of it until she heard the far away voice frantically shushing the lot, and they quieted down again.

"How do we know it's not a trick?" a new voice asked.

"Shh, you idiots," the far voice demanded. "I hear horses nickering. And a horn blow. It's them. It's the guard!"

"Is the guard out there with Dausius?" she asked Muse.

"No, I would've heard or seen them. It's just Daus out there."

Lark almost laughed. That old showman. He was out there putting on the performance of a lifetime.

"That settles it. Out through the bog if you want to stay free," someone yelled.

"Pull down the canoes. Quick!"

Grunting and noise resounded as the men got to work. Lark's heartbeat slowed a tiny fraction. Daus was going to be all right.

"Lark, one of the men is heading for your canoe!"

Shit! Her eyes widened as booted footsteps came closer and the canoe rocked around them. What were they going to do?

Ereni caught her attention. She sucked in a deep breath and pointed a finger down an instant before her head disappeared beneath the water.

Lark gulped down a breath and followed. Not a moment too soon. The water above her head splashed and heaved as the canoe they'd hidden under flipped over.

"Lark, where are you?" Muse asked frantically. *"Are you all right?"*

"Yes. I'm underwater. I'm fine," she insisted. But even as the thought left her mind, she couldn't escape the panic. How long could they last under here? Surely not long enough for all those men to clamber into boats and set sail.

Her bondmate wasn't buying it either. *"How long can humans hold their breath?"* Muse asked.

Lark's mind raced. She struggled to come up with a reply. Her lungs were already burning. Daus was safe, but she was about to drown. The canoe above her sank in the water, no doubt with the weight of the man jumping in, forcing her to sink down to the very bottom of the bog.

Something grabbed her beneath the water. Lark's heart skittered and her eyes popped open.

Ereni. It was hard to see in the murky water, but she could make out her outline as she lifted a hand. A sphere formed, floating in the water between them. Ereni shoved her face toward it and the bubble shrank.

That's right—Ereni could summon air. Lark pushed her face to the bubble and breathed deep, sucking air into her lungs.

"Muse, I'm all right. There's an air mage here with me." Her voice was almost giddy. *"I need you to keep watching. Tell me when the coast is clear."*

"Sure. I can do that."

Time passed by excruciatingly slow. She and Ereni drained a bubble of air with a few breaths, and then the mage formed another one. The cold seeped into Lark's skin, deep down into her bones. Her body shuddered so much she worried the men atop the water would notice the ripples she made.

As Ereni formed another bubble, Lark saw her shuddering just as strongly. How much longer could they stand the cold?

"They're almost all gone." Muse announced. *"When this pair of canoes leave, you'll be safe to resurface."*

"Thanks, Muse." Lark sighed internally. She couldn't wait to escape the bog. This day had certainly taken a turn on the strange side, but thankfully, the danger was almost over.

Finally, the water above them stopped echoing with splashes.

"They're gone," Muse confirmed.

Lark grabbed Ereni's arm and tugged. They burst out on the water's surface and took deep gulping breaths of air.

Lark turned to Ereni, a smile on her lips. "That was clos—"

The word caught in her throat as Ereni's eyelids fluttered shut and her head slipped under the water.

"No!" She dove under, frantically searching for the mage in the murky water. There! She grabbed her and hauled her to the surface.

Ereni was unconscious but breathing normally. Her dead weight was such a burden Lark struggled to hold them both above the water. How in the world would she pull them both out when she could barely keep them floating?

Then the skittering of rock sounded.

"Daus, help, we're over here."

A few moments later, Dausius peered down at them, the beads in his braids clacking together as he shook his head. "How did you end up here?" He reached out, frowning. "Here, hand her to me."

"Thanks."

He hauled up Ereni's motionless form, then reappeared a moment later, his hands slipping beneath the water and under her armpits, to help lug her out of the bog.

She slapped onto the stone floor. Her chest heaved, her entire body shuddering violently with cold.

"You've got to get out of those wet clothes," Dausius said. He swiveled his head, scanning the room. Then he made his way to a bin with crumpled cloth sticking out the top. Reaching inside, he pulled out a set of prison coveralls.

Lark wrinkled her nose. The thought of wearing the same garb as the men who'd nearly attacked her didn't sit right. But it was that, or staying in her wet dress. There wasn't much of a choice.

Dausius tossed her a coverall and grabbed another, heading for Ereni. "I'm sorry for this, whoever you are," he muttered as he peeled off her soaked trousers.

Lark finished changing quickly. The cold still clung tightly to her, but without the soaked clothing, her teeth finally stopped chattering. She let out a sigh as she buttoned the last button on her chest.

"Um, Lark. We have a problem," Daus announced.

She turned, her eyes bulging as she spotted where his gaze was locked. Ereni slumped on the ground, still unconscious. Dausius had stripped her of the wet clothing but hadn't yet reclothed her in the coveralls. Her stomach curved up into the air, the skin stretched taut around her huge belly.

How had she missed that before? Lark scrubbed at her eyelids. The mage was heavily pregnant. From the looks of it, she was due any day.

Dausius spoke up again, his voice filled with panic. "I'm no expert now, but I think her water just broke."

Chapter 7

Kayda scanned the riverbank beside the docks, her eyes peeled for any sign of the conveyance that would see them across the Riddle River. Where was it?

"What exactly are we searching for?" Beside her, Mika adjusted his brown cloak's collar.

Kayda spared the Raimish healer a glance. He and a handful of castle guard trailed after her, their faces painted with a mixture of curiosity, annoyance, and fear.

"If you're looking for a boat, we're heading in the wrong direction," the Guard Captain grumbled, scrubbing at his sweat-slicked forehead. He was one of those portly men who perpetually sweated, even with the chilled breeze blowing up from the fast-moving river to cool them.

Kayda spotted it finally. "We're not sailing across." She crept closer to the riverbank's edge and brushed aside a row of weeds overgrown around a huge stone boulder, revealing an old rope tied around it. A rope that stretched taut across the river, from one bank to the other. "We're flying."

"Blazes," exclaimed a young guard with a stubbly chin and shaved head. "You expect us to cross the river on that old thing? It'll never hold!"

Kayda smiled. "It held the king. It's the only way he could've made it across with no one noticing."

The Guard Captain scoffed. "How would he even know this rope was here?"

"Because he used to slide across the river on this supply line as a youth, for the thrill of it. He told me the story, once. Said the dockmaster ruined all his fun when he found out and told his father."

Well, those weren't the exact words he'd used, but close enough. If she explained how he blurted out the story to her in his wreck of a room—dressed in his underclothes no less—her reasoning might start to sound a little crazy.

Mika crouched beside the line and scanned the rope. "Is that what this is used for? Moving supplies?"

Kayda nodded. "It's the quickest way to move goods from the docks to the castle. They don't use it much anymore."

"Why is that?" Mika rose to his feet.

Kayda shrugged. "I'm not sure."

The Guard Captain spoke up. "I know why. Goods tend to *disappear* more often when they're sent this way. The dockworkers claim some are lost in the process, falling into the river, but more often than not they end up in the same workers' pockets." He shook his head. "The king would rather wait longer for his goods to be carted over the bridge than send a handful of workers who can't handle the temptation to prison every year."

Kayda's heart stirred at the reminder of her grandfather's inherent goodness. He was one of the kindest, most caring people she knew. Just one more reason she *had* to find him.

She exhaled, eyeing the rope. The ground on this side of the river was a great deal higher than the opposite bank on the Northmoat side. It should be a simple matter to slide across. Kayda knelt down and shucked off her bag, pulling out the supplies she'd brought with her.

"Here." She pulled free a stack of handkerchiefs she'd pilfered from an abandoned clothing shop bordering the docks. She handed one to each of the men with her, then stuffed the rest down the top of her blouse beneath her thick wool cloak. "We can wrap these around the rope and slide across."

Kneeling back down, she pulled out the second item she'd insisted on finding before heading for the riverbank. This one she'd located in a Jorian antique shop. The little can of oil she'd filled it with, she'd borrowed from the hold on board *Nova's Champion*.

Mika peered over her shoulder. "What's that?"

"We're bound to run into the scourge in Northmoat. I need my source readily available." Kayda finished pouring the oil inside and lifted the delicate glass oil lamp aloft. She'd wrapped a length of cord around it, to enable her to wear it around her neck. Standing, she walked to the closest guard holding a torch and stuck a dried twig into the fire then used it to light the lamp.

"Isn't that going to get hot?" Mika asked.

Kayda patted her chest, her palm denting the stack of handkerchiefs. "That's what the extra padding is for." Kayda pointed to the rope. "Once I make it across, I can take it off my neck if it starts to burn."

Mika grinned. "Very impressive. I see you've got this all thought out."

"Thanks." She ducked her head, hoping no one noticed the blush she felt warming her cheeks. Pacing to the edge, she started to slip a handkerchief over the rope.

"Nope. No way are you sliding over there first, Princess," the Guard Captain said. "Let me do the honors."

Kayda backed away, watching as the burly man slung his handkerchief over the rope. Then he drew a deep breath and leaped off the edge.

"Ahh!" he screamed, his voice surprisingly high pitched for a man his size.

She bit back the tiny smile that fought to appear. The guards surrounding her had no such qualms. Hearty laughter rang out, rising in volume when the Guard Captain slammed onto the ground on the Northmoat riverbank.

He walloped into the dirt, luckily landing on the side of his body that didn't have an enormous sword strapped to it. The other side of the rope was attached to a thick limb on a huge oak. He'd hopped off before crashing into the tree trunk, but his landing had certainly been less than graceful.

Kayda winced as she watched the man lumber up off the ground. She started to second guess her plan to wear the lamp around her neck. What if she landed on it? She'd end up with a chest full of glass, not to mention, covered in oil and potentially set on fire...

Kayda gulped. No. She had to be prepared. If the scourge showed up and she didn't have a flame, she'd be utterly defenseless.

Well—not quite—but if she was forced to summon without a source, she'd be trading years of her life for the magic. Lighting a torch with her tinderbox would take time. Time she might not have if the scourge arrived.

It appeared Mika held similar reservations. Frowning, he shot the lamp on her chest another glance before heading for the rope. "Let me go next. The captain and I can help steady you when you land."

She nodded her assent.

Mika slid across silently, and even landed on his feet, though he wobbled a good deal and would've likely lost his balance if not for a helping hand from the captain.

She stepped up to the rope next, her mind and heart racing. Despite seeing the two men make it over successfully, the thought of sliding across the rope still raised the hair on the back of her neck. If she lost her hold on the handkerchief, she'd tumble into the river below, swept away out to sea in the strong current, battered between boulders and drowned in the rapids.

Kayda sucked in a deep breath and shoved aside her fear. She needed to do this. For her grandfather. And her grandmother.

She clutched the handkerchief tightly and jumped.

Sliding through the air brought back a tiny sliver of the thrill that ignited within her every time she rode atop her bondmate's back. The wind surrounded her, and she raced across the river.

A smile flashed across her face. Why had she been so scared of this? It was exhilarating.

Before she knew it, she was barreling toward the riverbank. That's right. The landing.

Fear returned, slamming into her as the first sign of dirt appeared beneath her feet. She jumped, her heart hammering, and landed with a jarring thump on her feet. She tilted forward, eyes bulging.

Two pairs of strong hands caught her, steadying her before she landed face-first on the ground. "Thanks," she exclaimed as she found her balance.

Snarling cut through the air. The scourge had found them! The sound had them all tensing, their heads swinging to find the source.

Kayda was the first to spot them. The sight sent a cold chill through her veins. A half dozen at least, climbed the big oak. They were headed right for the rope.

"There!" she pointed up in the branches.

"They can't cross that? Can they?" Mika asked.

Kayda gulped, watching as the leader gripped the rope with its claws, swinging its sleek little body atop the thick rope.

"We can't let them climb across," the captain yelled. He unsheathed his sword and swung, severing the rope with a single stroke. The beast attached to the rope tumbled down with it, screeching.

A second scream came from behind them, and a splash. Kayda's stomach dropped. With the scourge ahead of them, she didn't dare turn around, but she was certain that scream belonged to one of the guards. The captain didn't just send one of the scourge tumbling down when he severed the rope, he'd sent one of his own men to his death.

The thought was sobering, but there was nothing she could do for the poor fellow. And with the rope cut, there would be no more help from the rest of the guard. The three of them had to complete their mission alone.

They'd be enough. She'd make sure of it.

With that thought echoing in her mind, Kayda inhaled, concentrating on the flame on her chest. A chill spread over her skin as a ball of fire appeared, hovering above her open palm. She sent it soaring, catching the scourge on the ground before it could leap up and attack.

The satisfying sound of its dying scream flooded her ears. In another heartbeat, she shot a ball of fire at another. Then another. Soon all the little beasts were roasting. They littered the ground, tiny scattered piles of flame and writhing, screeching bodies.

"Wow, that was fast," Mika said. He rose from a crouch, his hand full of dirt. "I didn't even have time to visualize yet."

Kayda shrugged. "I've had a lot of practice." She swung her head around, looking for more vermin. The coast appeared clear for now, but with the sound of the burning scourge's death throes inundating the air, it wouldn't be long before more came. "C'mon, let's go."

They jogged off, quickly traversing the deserted streets of North-moat. The shops and homes all stood empty, except for the occasional scourge who sprang at them from the shadows. Fortunately, they seemed to have mostly cleared out. The few that ran at them were all swiftly dispatched, either on the captain's blade or to a ball of flame.

They turned a corner and Kings Keep appeared. The sight of the stately stone castle—the home she'd lived in practically every day of her life—stirred warmth in her heart. This place held so many memories, some wonderful—others, not so much. But even though she'd never felt entirely comfortable there, it was still her home. A small part of her rejoiced over knowing it still stood, as permanent a fixture of the city as it had always been.

As they approached the entrance to the Royal Grounds, Kayda's stomach churned. It was all going so smoothly. Too smoothly. She kept waiting for them to encounter a huge crowd of scourge. One that would actually prove a problem for the three of them.

Rounding the massive square keep, the Royal Stables came into view, and her prediction proved true. Surrounding the stables, hundreds of scourge gathered. They rammed the building, scratching at the ground beneath the thick wooden doors, attempting to tunnel underneath.

Kayda's hand flew to her mouth, and she stopped in her tracks.

"Damn." The Guard Captain halted beside her, his breath coming hard and fast. "We're too late."

"Or we're just in time," Mika retorted. He alone continued jogging, calling over his shoulder, "They wouldn't be trying to dig in if there wasn't someone alive inside."

He was right. They had to be alive. Kayda dropped the oil lamp back around her neck and closed her eyes, embracing the icy chill rushing through her veins. Then her brown eyes flashed open, and twin flames hovered over her hands.

"Hurry," she yelled to the Guard Captain as she broke back into a jog. Within a few moments, she'd caught up to Mika. The slight vibration humming across her skin told her he'd summoned too, even before she spotted the chunks of dirt and rock hovering above his hands.

Dodging immaculately trimmed bushes, and hopping over flower beds bursting with zinnias and mums in the gardens, they quickly closed in on the stables.

Kings Keep featured one of the finest stables in the kingdom. Due to the king's condition—even before he'd been stabbed and nearly died—the building remained largely unused, only housing the mounts of visiting dignitaries and guests. None of the royals kept horses, not since the king lost his second bondmate a decade ago.

But clearly that had all changed now. What drove Grandfather to risk everything to hole up in the stables with the scourge on the loose? Had he truly found another bondmate?

Kayda shoved the thought aside as they drew closer, and the first of the scourge turned toward them. A scream tore out of her throat, and she flung fireballs in every direction. The sick stench of burning fur filled the air.

Beside her, Mika scattered dirt and rock into the crowd. Being practically untrained in combat, he missed as many hits as he landed. But the flying debris caught in the scourges' faces, confusing and infuriating them. The guard captain stayed close by Mika's side, his sword swiping through the throng, felling all the beasts who came close enough for his blade to reach.

Though it had seemed impossible when viewed from a distance, the three of them pushed through the crowd, unleashing death on all sides. The door was within reach.

"Grandfather! Izora!" Kayda yelled. "We've come to save you!"

A heartbeat passed. Then two. Three. No movement came from the door. No sound. Kayda's heart twisted.

Instead, something flew at her from above. A scourge descended from the roof in a desperate leap. She reacted an instant too late. The beast caught in flame, but not before its claws connected with the cord around her neck, slicing it clean in two. Her eyes widened with horror, and she jumped back just in time to avoid the splash of oil as the glass shattered on the ground in front of her.

"Blazes!" The dirt and grass lit up everywhere the oil spread, catching a few scourge who'd been unlucky enough to get in the way. But Kayda's stomach dropped. When those flames on the ground died out, her source would be gone.

She sucked in a deep breath, determined to make every moment count. She screamed again. Her battle cry rang out, echoing loudly above the screeching vermin. Fire flew from her hands furiously, a constant stream of death aimed at the crowd. But still the scourge came. More and more appeared on the horizon, no doubt attracted to the spot by the sounds of battle.

For a few moments, she held them off. But then the fire on the ground guttered out, and exhaustion slammed into her hard. Kayda staggered on her feet, letting go of the flames.

Instantly, her strength returned. The heavy weight on her limbs lifted. But terror pummeled her instead. Her source was gone. And the scourge still pressed in all around them.

The Guard Captain yelped in pain as he darted forward to block her. One of the scourge raked its claws through his leg. He sliced it clean down the middle before it could leap atop him, but more pressed forward to take its place.

Mika still flung dirt, but his face had paled, shoulders slumped.

How long could they last out here? Kayda's stomach sank. She didn't like the answer.

The stable door burst open, scattering the scourge in every direction. A wall of earth and straw appeared, encircling the three of them.

Izora's dark face popped out of the doorway, and a blast of fire flew from her hands, landing on one of the scourge who'd been close enough to the doorway to be included inside the protective barrier of earth. "Get in! Now!"

Kayda grabbed the Guard Captain's arm, helping him hobble forward. Mika raced inside before them, throwing the remaining dirt in his hands at the trio of scourge left. Izora shot fire at the group, all of them bursting into flaming piles of fur and gnashing teeth.

"Hurry!" called another voice from inside.

Kayda turned, staring behind them as she crossed the threshold. The scourge outside threw themselves at the barrier, then bounced off covered in dirt and straw. None of them made it through, but the top of the wall slowly dissipated with every strike. Soon, they would be able to leap over the crumbling barrier.

It didn't matter. The door slammed shut, shielding them within the dimly lit stable house. The slight chill and hum of vibration in the air halted as all the mages let go of the elements. She dropped the Guard Captain in a pile of hay, and Mika crouched beside him, attending to his slashed leg.

Her breath coming hard and fast, Kayda swiveled around. She spotted the king slamming a wood bar down into place on the heavy door.

"Grandfather!" Tears blurred her vision. She ran to him, clasping him in a tight embrace. He clutched her back just as tightly. As his warm arms connected around her, the tears spilled free, running down her cheeks and wetting the king's silk tunic.

He was hugging her back! All those days spent together in the tower, he'd never hugged her back. It was true. Her soul rejoiced. She didn't need to hear him speak to feel it. He was back. Her grandfather was back!

"Little Red." Hearing his special nickname for her caused her heart to practically burst. He pulled free from her arms, and his blue eyes connected with hers, the hazy clouds that'd once filled them gone. "What are you doing here?"

Kayda laughed and scrubbed her face with her sleeve. "We came to save you, Grandfather."

The king's eyes grew misty. "I've been a bit of a fool, haven't I?"

She shook her head. "No, don't say th—"

Izora scoffed. "Don't sugarcoat it for him. He's a blazing fool, if I've ever seen one."

"And you haven't let me hear the end of it since you followed me out here, you old witch," the king retorted.

Kayda's brows shot up, but despite his harsh words, Quinton's voice was filled with humor and not malice.

Kayda turned, her gaze connecting with Izora's across the dim room. So many conflicting feelings slammed into her. All the lies her nurse had been party to, all the deception—everything she'd discovered on her journey to find out her true parentage rose in her mind. But underneath the anger, the hurt, and the confusion, something stronger lived—love.

She raced across the room and collided with Izora. Their arms clasped around each other. And for the second time that day, her heart felt full enough to burst.

"My princess," Izora whispered, her voice thick with emotion. "I've missed you so much."

"I've missed you, too," Kayda choked out, her voice a strangled whisper. "Grandmother."

Izora pulled back far enough to meet her gaze. She gently grasped one of the tiny braids framing the left side of her face, her brown eyes full of love and warmth but shadowed with the ghost of all that lay unspoken between them.

"I hate to break up this touching reunion, but we don't have much longer before they break in," announced another voice. One she vaguely recognized.

Kayda eased free of Izora's arms and turned to the white-cloaked mage behind her. She found a kind face she'd never forget. One that had saved the king in his time of greatest need and led her through a rain of arrows to find her bondmate.

"Vespen?" She stepped closer to him, her eyes filling with tears again. "I thought I'd lost you!"

"Not forever, it seems. I'm glad to see you again, Princess." He reached out, clasping her shoulder gently.

Kayda smiled up at him.

The wooden door, which had been pounding constantly since it slammed shut, shuddered on its hinges. All eyes turned to it, and everyone present held a collective breath. But the door stood. For the moment.

"I'm afraid we can't stay here much longer." Vespen frowned at the door.

"Don't worry." Kayda grinned. "We have a plan."

Chapter 8

Lark knelt beside the naked, unconscious mage, examining her swollen belly. The water continued to gush out between her thighs. She sniffed. Definitely not urine. Lark gently stuck a hand on Ereni's belly. She could feel a contraction tensing her muscles.

Dausius was right. Ereni was in labor. Lark's heart hammered. She had to wake her up.

She leaned over, slapping Ereni's face gently. "Wake up. Your baby is coming."

Nothing. The mage still slept. Through the slapping and the contractions.

Lark wrung her hands, staring down at the motionless young woman. What was she going to do? She couldn't deliver this baby *here*, could she?

Mothers died in childbirth every day. Was Ereni destined to do the same, after using so much of her talent to keep them alive while the prisoners fled?

No. Ereni had saved her life. She wasn't about to quit on her now. She would save her and the baby.

She tilted her head up, catching her bondmate's eye where she perched in the ceiling rafters. *"I need your help again."*

"What can I do?" Muse sounded alarmed. *"My kind lay eggs!"*

Lark bit back a chuckle. *"Nothing like that, silly. Can you find Aren? Or Tiora, or Meital, or even Mazen? If things here go sideways, I might need another set of hands."*

"That I can handle." Muse lifted into the air. *"Be back soon."*

Lark turned to Dausius. His brown eyes were wide, his mouth hanging open. "You have to help me deliver the baby, Daus. Can you do that?"

Daus shook himself, blinking repeatedly. "What do you need?"

"Bring me more of those coveralls. And my pack! There's a hidden drawer, set into the wall. She hid our cloaks and my pack inside." She pointed in the general direction she remembered the drawer being, though she couldn't pinpoint the exact spot. With the drawer closed, it blended into the wall so perfectly she would've never known it was there if she hadn't seen it opened with her own eyes. "Just start pushing on the stones until it pops open. One of them triggers the drawer."

Dausius nodded, then he stood and got to work. Soon he dumped a huge armload of coveralls beside her and started prodding at the stone wall.

Lark shoved the coveralls around Ereni, using them like she would normally use blankets. This wasn't her first birth. Her mother had worked as a midwife and a healer. She'd witnessed and assisted with dozens of births in her lifetime. Even so, this situation made her stomach churn. Never once had she birthed a child with the mother unconscious. She needed to find some way to wake Ereni.

Lark took a peek between Ereni's legs, and her stomach clenched even tighter. The baby was crowning! It didn't seem possible. How had things progressed so fast? Had Ereni been in active labor the entire time they were escaping? No, that couldn't be. She'd shown no signs of contractions while they were underwater or running from the prisoners. And besides, her water just broke a few moments ago.

"I could really use my pack," she said, hoping Dausius didn't notice the fear tinging her words.

"I'm working on it," Daus grumbled. "You sure it was over here?"

"Yes, I'm sure."

"Well, I'm moving as fast as I—"

The drawer popped open, nearly catching Daus in the shins. He hopped back, then bent down and pulled everything out. He returned with a victorious smile painting his lips. But when he met her gaze, the smile dropped.

"What else can I do?" he asked.

"My pack." Lark thrust out a hand expectantly. "I need to wake her. Hold her shoulders so she doesn't jolt up and hurt herself." She grabbed the bag, breathing out a sigh as the reassuring weight of her supplies settled in her grasp. She dug inside and pulled out a tiny glass vial.

"What's that?" Daus asked.

"Smelling salts." Lark twisted off the stopper. "If this doesn't wake her, I'm out of ideas."

Lark slid the little jar beneath Ereni's nose. She held her breath, waiting, the sound of the water lapping against the bog and her own heartbeat pounding loudly in her ears.

No reaction. She started to despair. Would this baby lose its mother before it even drew its first breath? Would it even be born at all without Ereni pushing?

But just as she pulled her hand away, her heart full of defeat, Ereni's blue eyes snapped open, and she cried out in pain. Dausius gripped her shoulders, keeping her firmly pressed into the pile of coveralls Lark had slid beneath her head.

Gaze flitting around, Ereni's breathing quickened, a groan tearing out of her throat. "What's happening? Ah, it hurts! Am I dying?"

Lark leaned closer, staring Ereni straight in the eyes. "No, you're not dying. Your baby is coming."

She expected the statement to calm the panic flooding the mage's face, but it did the opposite. Her eyes widened as she stared down at her stomach, shaking her head. "No. It's too soon. It's months too soon." She gasped. "The air. No source..."

Lark's stomach dropped. Did she mean... Blazes! The pieces finally clicked together. That's why she didn't appear pregnant before she resurfaced from beneath the bog. Why the baby was coming so quickly.

"You've been aged." Lark held back a gasp. What did that mean for the baby? She'd never heard of a mage aging while pregnant...

Ereni screamed again. Lark grabbed her hand, wincing as Ereni's grip turned crushing. It seemed she wouldn't have long to wonder.

Soon, the contraction passed. But Lark knew from experience another would come, right on its heels. "Daus, hold her hand, please." Lark moved back down into position between Ereni's legs.

"I can't do this. I can't have a baby *now*. The fire moat, the tunnels... the blazing scourge!" Ereni moaned, her eyes wild.

"Don't worry," Lark said, adopting the most calming voice she could muster under the circumstances. "I've delivered lots of babies. The mothers always think they can't do it, but they can. You will, too. And I'll be right here with you, every step of the way."

Ereni locked gazes with her. She sucked in a deep breath through her nose. "All right. All right, let's do it."

Lark smiled, then took another peek between Ereni's thighs. It was good she was ready. The baby was coming, whether she liked it or not.

"The next time you feel a pain, I need you to push."

Ereni nodded, her jaw set. They didn't have to wait long. A few heartbeats later, Ereni screamed. Dausius looked like he wanted to scream with her, his teeth gritted and eyes pinched closed. But Lark couldn't concentrate on them. She reached down, preparing to catch the baby.

"Good. You're doing so good," she said as the screaming died down, and Ereni sucked in a series of gasps. "One more push. The baby's almost here."

Lark stared down at the baby in her hands. Its head was already out, covered in flecks of blood and wispy little blond hairs. She'd never witnessed a birth progress so fast.

Her stomach churned as she waited for another contraction to come over Ereni. Was it just luck? Or was something wrong? Was some effect of the magic that'd aged her so unnaturally fast contributing to the super speed birth?

Lark shoved her misgivings aside. As far as she could tell, the birth was going smoothly. The baby was in the proper position and just moments away from letting out its first cry. She had to concentrate.

Ereni let out another scream.

"It's time to push," Lark instructed. "That's it."

The baby's shoulders popped free, and then the whole torso. Ereni bore down, her teeth gritted. And then the baby was out. Lark pulled her free, a huge grin on her face.

"You have a daughter." Lark quickly checked her over, scanning her little body for any issues. She was tiny. Far smaller than most babies born full term. In fact, she reminded Lark of the litter of piglets she'd helped Gael birth last year on the farm in Greenvale. The infant was closer in weight to one of those tiny piglets than most of the babies she'd birthed.

But the girl's lungs certainly weren't affected. As Lark reached into her mouth to clear her airway, the babe let out a loud wail. With the supplies in her pack, she took care of the cord. Then she grabbed a coverall, wrapped the baby quickly, and handed her to her mother.

"She's small, but she looks healthy. Congratulations, you're a mother," she said.

Ereni's eyes filled with tears as she gazed down at the tiny babe, her cries still ringing out through the air. "She's so beautiful. My Violet."

"Is that her name?" Dausius asked.

Ereni flashed a grin at him. Nodded. "Yes. Violet." Her nose crinkled, her smile luminous as she cradled the infant in her arms.

"It's a wonderful name," Daus said, teary-eyed. He turned to her. "We did it, didn't we? We birthed a baby!"

"Well, Ereni did most of the work." Lark chuckled. "You were great, Daus."

But Dausius' expression of wonder shifted to one of confusion. "I've heard that name before..."

Suddenly Ereni cried out, another contraction hitting her. "What was that? Is there another?" Her brows nearly disappeared into her hairline.

Lark frowned, taking a peek. "No, It's just the babe's birth sack. You need to push that out, too. It's all very normal, don't fret." Even as she finished speaking, the sack began to slide out.

Lark's frown deepened. There shouldn't be so much blood.

"Dausius, why don't you take a turn holding little Violet?" Lark said, forcing a smile. "Ereni has a bit more work to do."

Dausius kneeled, grabbing the bundle. Violet had quieted and appeared to be content, her tiny fist shoved inside her mouth.

Ereni surrendered her reluctantly. Then she craned her head down and stared at the mess between her legs. "I think I might be sick." She shook her head. "There's so much blood. Is there supposed to be that much blood?"

"It's all right," Lark lied, her chest twinging briefly at the words. But she needed her to stay calm while she worked. "Don't worry, I have everything well in hand." Lark dug in her pack searching for what she needed to stop the bleeding.

Ereni didn't look like she was buying it. Her breathing was labored, her stare still locked on all the blood flooding between her legs. She needed a distraction.

"You still haven't explained who those men were or how you found me," Lark said. "Tell me, please."

"What?" Ereni asked. "You want to know that *now*?"

Lark nodded. "Yes. Were those men meant to stay locked up in here while everyone fled and left for the scourge? What did they do to deserve that?"

Ereni leaned back on the pile of coveralls, closing her eyes. "This is a prison. I take it you figured that much out already. When it became obvious the city would fall, we had to decide what to do with the men and women inside. With the king incapacitated, the decision fell to Prince Gideon. From what I gather, he and the Guard Captain reviewed all the prisoner's cases individually. Anyone who'd committed minor crimes was set free. That's why most of the cells were empty."

Lark finished gathering what she needed from her pack. "And the men who were left?"

"Repeat offenders and violent criminals. Those they deemed irredeemable or who'd committed the most heinous crimes."

Lark gulped. She set the handful of fresh green herbs beside her and opened a jar of her mother's ointment, and slathered some on Ereni's stomach. She'd just released murderers and worse into the world... The thought was unsettling, to say the least.

Ereni's eyes popped open as the cream touched her belly. "What's that?" Her gaze slid back down, and she caught another glimpse of the blood soaking the coveralls stuffed there, her chest heaving.

"This will heal you," Lark insisted, infusing her voice with all the confidence she wasn't feeling. She'd certainly never had to contend with a birth under such strange circumstances. She wasn't entirely sure this would work, but she wasn't about to tell Ereni that when she was already acting panicked. "What about me? How did you know I was in here?"

Ereni's brows furrowed, but she tore her gaze away from her torso and leaned back again, closing her eyes. "It was just pure chance. I was walking outside when I heard a loud bang. Then I spotted the door ajar. Once I ducked inside and saw the stair hanging down, I knew someone was upstairs."

She must've heard the stairs clattering when they'd descended from the ceiling. That'd been extremely lucky for her. Without Ereni's help, she might've met her end on the top floor at the hands of those prisoners. She owed her a great debt.

Lark drew a deep breath, smoothing the fresh green herbs against Ereni's flesh. It was time to repay the favor. She would not let her bleed out here.

She closed her eyes and wished. Her talent flowed through her, the vibration humming to life. A tremor rattled the bones in her arms, then shot through her palms into Ereni. Lark opened her eyes.

Ereni's stomach shrank beneath her fingers. Lark removed the bloody coveralls between her legs. Lark blew out a sigh. "The bleeding stopped. You're going to be all right."

"I am?" Ereni laughed. "You had me worried for a moment there."

Lark knelt beside the bog and washed the blood from her hands. Ereni grabbed a pair of clean coveralls and blushed, seeming to notice for the first time that she was lying on the ground practically naked.

Just then, a series of splashes sounded. Lark's heart skipped a beat. "What was that?" she whispered, peering into the bog but seeing nothing. "Do you think the criminals have returned?"

"Hey," Dausius said. "Could you give me a hand with little Violet?"

Ereni looked torn, her gaze flitting between the bog and the babe. But after a few heartbeats she set her stare on the bog. "Go," she said, "Take care of my girl. I'll keep watch."

Lark crossed the room to Dausius. "What's wrong?" She peered down at the tiny babe in his arms. Her eyes were closed, her hand still shoved in her mouth as she sucked on her fingers furiously.

"I'm not sure if it's wrong, exactly. But it's strange." Dausius frowned. "It's her eyes. I always thought babies were born with dark eyes. Hers..." He glanced up at her, then gently tugged Violet's fist free. Her eyelids popped open.

Lark's brows lifted. Violet's eyes were different. They were a far lighter blue than any newborn she'd ever birthed, and her irises even had a slight red tinge. She took a closer look at the babe. At the light blond tuft of hair on her head. Her pale, creamy skin. In contrast, Ereni's hair was dark brown, her skin tanned.

"She's albino. It's rare, but sometimes children and even animals are born this way." She smiled down at the tiny infant as she found her fist again with her mouth, her eyes closing as she started sucking. "It's not life threatening or something I need to heal, but thank you for telling me, Daus."

Another splash sounded, this one much louder. Lark whipped around, her mouth dropping open.

"Where are you going?" she demanded.

Ereni had pulled the last canoe from the wall and was already halfway out the opening to the bog. "No time to explain," she yelled. "Take care of Violet. Keep her safe. I'll be back. I'll find you. I trust you, Lark!"

Lark stared at the retreating canoe as it rounded a bend in the bog and out of sight. Where was Ereni headed? And what in the world was she going to do with a newborn baby?

Dausius' mouth was agape, too. "Did that just happen? Why would she leave?"

Lark shook her head. "I don't know." She glanced around, scanning the mess of bloody coveralls on the ground. "Hey, she stole my cloak," she said, incredulous.

Dausius peered around, frowning. "My pack is missing, too."

Then a thought struck her, and she rocked back on her feet, her knees feeling weak.

"What is it?" Daus asked.

"I never told her my name. How did she know my name? This day just keeps getting stranger."

"Lark, we're back. I found lover boy," Muse announced.

"Muse! Do you see a canoe nearby?"

"Hold on, let me look."

Aren's blond head poked through the opening Daus had dug at the entrance. "Lark." His voice cracked. "You're all right! When Muse showed up without you, I feared the worst."

Lark smiled gently, her heart fluttering as Aren's blue eyes met her own, filled with concern.

"Thanks for coming, Aren." Lark gestured to the baby Dausius cradled in his arms. "I thought we might need help to deliver baby Violet, but her birth went much faster than I expected."

"Good thing you're finished." Aren scanned the room as he finished crawling into the building. "We need to leave. Now. They're saying the moat is about to fall." He offered her a hand, his brow furrowing when he ran his gaze down her prison coveralls.

Lark's cheeks warmed under his scrutiny, but thankfully, Aren chose not to pepper her with questions. He grasped her hand and silently led her back to the doorway to Southmoat.

"Did you find it yet, Muse?"

"No, it must be hidden beneath the mangroves. Should I keep searching?"

"No. We have to return to the docks." Lark's stomach sank. As much as she hated to leave Ereni, it looked like she had no choice. Without a canoe, following her wasn't happening, and she couldn't stand around waiting and put Violet in danger. Ereni would have to take her chances in the bog on her own.

Chapter 9

Conall smacked into the water. Cold enveloped him. The shock would've stolen his breath, if it wasn't for what came next.

He slammed into the bog bottom and screamed, the sound muffled by the water flooding his mouth. Pain flared up his leg. He didn't have to look down to realize that something was very wrong. He didn't have to look—but he did, regretting the decision instantly.

Blood clouded the murky water. His right foot stuck out at an unnatural angle, bent at the ankle. Broken. Definitely broken.

It didn't matter. He was alive. He was alive, and he had to save Shadow.

Conall burst to the bog's surface and spit out the bitter water, searching frantically. There. He swam for the flash of gray fur disappearing in the distance.

Swam was a generous description for the flailing half-hop, half-stroke he maintained in the shallow bog. The water was low enough he could reach the bottom in most places, but being forced to keep his weight off his injured leg, he couldn't swim or walk properly.

It could've been worse. It was a miracle he hadn't broken his neck instead.

"Shadow," he called out through their bond. *"I'm just behind you. Hang on!"*

"Hurry, brother," came his reply.

A spike of fear lodged in his gut. Conall picked up his pace, rounding a bend. A thrashing, snapping scourge was there to greet him. Its beady eyes locked onto him, and it lunged through the water like a starving child grasping for food.

Conall pushed off the river bottom with his good leg, launching himself forward. He would not be that vermin's life raft. Leaving it behind to drown, he swam onward.

Shadow floated in the waterway's center, just ahead. Clearly, he'd dislodged one of the scourge, but the last held on, its foreclaws sunk into Shadow's jaw.

Shadow was not faring well. His head hovered above the surface, but most of his body remained submerged, the water surrounding him tinged red. As Conall approached, even his head began to bob.

"Hang on, brother," he ordered.

Conall lunged again, desperate to reach him. Pain was his reward. He screamed, locked in place. His injured leg exploded with agony, like a thousand daggers stabbed into his muscles. Something clutched him in its grasp, beneath the water.

Conall grabbed the top of his thigh with both hands and tugged. Another flash of pain shot up his leg. Dizziness washed over him. He gritted his teeth, shaking his head. He couldn't pass out. Not now.

Shadow had just been almost within reach. In the few heartbeats he'd been trapped, the current pulled his bondmate halfway to the next bend in the stream. He needed to free himself, fast.

Sucking in a deep breath, he dove beneath the water. The cold smacked his face, banishing the last of the dizziness. He held still, waiting for the murky water to clear enough that he could see what had him trapped. After a moment, he realized it would take too long. He contorted himself under the water instead, using his hands to feel what gripped him in its grasp.

The silky length of a plant wrapped around his injured foot like a tourniquet. His first thought was to slip the boot off. He tugged and pain shot up his leg again. When the boot refused to budge—his ankle no doubt swollen fast around it—he pulled out his crafting knife.

By now, his lungs burned, the need for air hard to ignore. But swimming back to the surface would only waste more time. He needed to pull his leg free now.

He sawed at the plant, slicing through the tendrils in a few harried strokes. This time, when he tugged his leg, it pulled free.

Conall burst out on the water's surface, sucking in a grateful breath. He thrust off of the river bottom with his good leg, only to be met with a set of angry beady eyes—again.

The beast he'd left to drown floated directly in front of him, holding fast to a piece of driftwood. When it spotted him bursting free of the water, it sprang, shrieking and aiming for his face.

Conall reacted too slowly. He barely had time to dodge, and with his feet still flying out behind him after his last push off the river bottom, he couldn't propel himself out of the beast's path like last time. Claws sank into his shoulder. He screamed.

Blazes! He slammed back under the water, taking the scourge with him.

How long would it take to drown it? Too long. And he still clutched the knife in his fist.

Conall resurfaced, stabbing, catching the beast in the side. He tugged and twisted, not stopping until the vermin's entrails spilled out into the water and its claws detached from his shoulder.

He didn't have time to celebrate. The river rushed past him, blood pouring from his body in two places now. The cold, the pain, both worked together to sap his strength, but he shoved them aside.

Shadow. He had to save Shadow.

By now he was out of sight again. He had to make it around the next bend in the river. Avoid the vines. Catch up. Kill the vermin and pull Shadow to the bank.

Slow push by slow push, he forced his body to move. With one arm and one leg screaming in agony with every flailing stroke, it was slower than he'd like. But when he made it around the next bend, he spotted Shadow, caught against a mangrove tree's twisted roots.

Finally, some luck! He closed in quickly. But he spotted a new problem that made his stomach sink. The scourge had abandoned Shadow in the water, and climbed up in the mangrove's branches. But it didn't appear content to escape to the relative safety of the treetops. It flipped around, poised to leap on Shadow from above.

Dropping his knife, Conall lifted his hand and shot a blast of water at the beast as it leaped. He caught it in midair, enclosing the vermin in a bubble of water that he suspended, immobile, floating above his bondmate's head.

The beast didn't give up easily. It squirmed in the bubble, limbs flailing, claws slicing through the water and teeth snapping. But it was no use. He held the creature aloft until it drowned, then let go. Its limp body slapped onto the bog's surface and floated off in the current.

Finally, he reached his bondmate. He slid his good arm beneath his chest, helping hold him afloat. While he could stand, Shadow had been forced to tread water, and his weariness was evident.

"Little brother, you came for me." Shadow's tail wagged weakly on the water's surface.

"Of course, I did. I'll always come for you, brother. Always." He met his golden eyes and smiled, the pain in his ankle and shoulder fading in the moment of triumph. *"Hey, at least this time it wasn't me doing the falling, huh?"*

The sound of his bondmate's laughter echoed quietly in Conall's mind. Shadow was all right. For now, at least. Blood still seeped out into the water, far too much to be coming from only his injuries.

Conall allowed himself a moment to rejoice, but then he broke eye contact with Shadow and set his gaze on his surroundings. *"We need to find dry land before we both bleed out. How badly were you injured by the scourge?"*

"I... It's hard to say. It feels like my whole body is aflame," Shadow admitted.

Conall's stomach churned. That didn't sound good. *"Don't worry. I'll get us both out of this."*

The mangrove they rested against was one of many lining one side of the river in a scraggly line. But the mangroves didn't need dirt to grow. Their twisted roots plunged into the murky water, taking root far below. They wouldn't find what they needed on this side, unless they lucked into one of the marshy islands scattered somewhere further down the river.

The far bank, the one that bordered Dracwood, sported a high cliff. It appeared just as high from down here as the spot where he'd been forced to jump in, and equally steep. There was little chance he could haul both himself and Shadow up the cliff with his injuries.

With any luck, the river they found themselves in would flow toward the ocean. At least there, he might have a chance of someone on the docks spotting him and Shadow and lending them a hand.

He could only see two choices: try their chances at finding dry land and help further down the riverside, or try to use magic to save them. Maybe he could do both? He didn't know if he had enough strength left to force the air to lift them that high up the cliffside. And if he dropped them halfway, he might actually break his neck this time. But the water might be easy enough to manipulate... the current already wanted to sweep them forward, after all.

"C'mon. We need to find a spot that's easier to scale and make our way back into the city. I'll help you float, all right?"

"I trust you, little brother," Shadow said.

Keeping his good arm slung beneath Shadow's torso, Conall pulled them away from the mangrove and out into the waterway's center.

Then he closed his eyes, picturing what he wanted, the image of Shadow at the forefront of his mind. This had better work. He could feel his strength ebbing. They didn't have much time.

Conall bent the water flowing around him to his will. He lifted his foot from the river bottom and used the current swirling around him to carry Shadow and himself through the water. They picked up speed quickly.

He grinned. It was working. The water lifted them, and the current tugged them forward. Without him constantly jerking his limbs, the pain faded to a dull ache. But even as the agony of his injuries lessened, his body grew weary. He kept a close watch on both sides of the river, searching for any people, or somewhere he might be able to pull them free.

The waterway wound and twisted, and they lost sight of the cliffside and Dracwood several times in the bog's maze. Conall began to despair. Would they ever find a way out of this blazing swamp?

The magic propelling them was a blessing and a curse. Keeping still, the constant cold wore on him. His teeth chattered, his entire body wracked with shivers. It certainly didn't help that he kept bleeding, his injuries and Shadow's painting the murky water red.

Shadow wasn't faring any better. His body soon went limp in Conall's arms. He shook him awake each time it happened, but eventually he lost the strength to do even that, barely keeping them both aloft and the magic flowing around them.

Within a few moments of Shadow passing out for the last time, even that strength faded. Conall's grip on his talent slipped. The water slowed around them. The current stopped holding them aloft. Using the last of his strength, he scrambled to keep both of their heads above water.

As he bobbed and splashed, he glimpsed a building sitting on the riverbank's far side, on the Dracwood border. Was that a dock?

Hope erupted in his chest. He turned toward it, managing a single stroke in its direction before Shadow's head dipped underneath the water.

No.

He ducked under the water, searching. He spotted Shadow and grabbed hold, hauling them both to the surface.

It was all he could do to keep them both afloat. Despite the water helping boost him, Shadow's weight was a heavy burden. Conall refused to drop him, even as the dock disappeared from sight and his last shred of hope that he'd be able to reach the shore evaporated.

The current towed them into the waterway's center, where the depth increased slightly. His good foot barely grazed the river bottom. The lack of footing and his increasing exhaustion did not bode well for them. His shoulder and ankle screamed with agony as he flailed in the water, but he welcomed it. The pain was likely the only thing keeping him awake.

Even so, he could sense the exhaustion winning. It was just too much.

Curiously, he thought he heard his sister's name. His heart clenched, his body overcome with a different kind of pain. He should've never left her. He'd promised he'd make it back to her, but now his death would just be another unanswered question. Another mistake weighing on her soul.

With that morose thought ringing in his ears, his hold on Shadow slipped. Shadow sank without warning, his gray snout the last thing to disappear.

Not again.

Conall sucked in a breath, preparing to dive and find him. But the next instant, his breath flew out in a gasp and his eyes bulged. Static crackled around him, the air above the river's surface suddenly dense, like he was floating through a cloud of mist.

Shadow reversed course all on his own, his snout emerging from the water first, then his head. But it didn't stop there. His body quickly followed until he floated above the water's surface. Conall scrubbed at his eyelids with his good hand, his body whipping around as his bondmate floated over his head.

A canoe!

Shadow drifted down inside the wooden vessel, his body landing with a gentle *thunk*. And as soon as he landed, Conall began rising from the water. The tingle of electricity intensified, thrumming all over his skin. The water pushed him up from below, the pressure on his bad ankle causing a pain so intense he closed his eyes and bit his tongue, lest he cry out and break the spell.

Then he was out of the water. A blast of air took over and lifted him, gliding him toward the canoe. The pressure on his ankle subsided, and he opened his eyes just in time to see himself hovering over the small boat. Then the air cut off. He dropped onto the canoe, much less gently than his bondmate had. His back flared with pain. He landed half off, half on a wooden bench before sliding off onto the bottom of the boat. The fall to the bottom jarred his shoulder, and the deep gash there screamed again.

He groaned, but popped up off the floor, crawling for Shadow.

Please, be all right...

Conall collapsed beside him, resting his hand on the soaked fur on his chest. The slow rise and fall of Shadow's breathing pressed against his palm. Conall's eyelids fluttered shut, the exhaustion and the pain too strong to ignore.

A tiny smile tugged at his lips. They were alive.

Something warm landed on him. From somewhere far away, he heard a woman's voice—the same voice he heard all too frequently in his dreams—whispering, "It's all right, I've got you. I'll keep you safe."

Chapter 10

"What's the plan, Princess?" Vespen asked.

"There's a cliff behind the tower that overlooks the ocean. We need to make it there."

The thudding on the stable door intensified. It wouldn't be easy, but with two more mages to help, they should be able to make a run for it.

Kayda shifted to look at Mika. He was crouched beside the Guard Captain with his hand on his calf. "How's he doing?"

Mika rose and lifted his hands from the gash, revealing smooth, unmarred flesh. "He's healed. We can leave when you're ready."

The Guard Captain hopped up. He brushed the straw from his backside and tested out his leg, stomping his foot and swiveling his knee. "Thanks." He grinned.

A screech rang out. Kayda jumped, and her hand flew to her chest. She turned in time to see Vespen slam a pile of dirt in the face of a scourge who'd dug far enough beneath the wooden doors to stick its snout in the crack.

"Better go sooner than later." Vespen sighed. "Are we ready?"

"Wait," the king shouted. "We can't leave without Valiant."

"Who's that?" Kayda asked, peering around the darkened stable. The light of a handful of torches illuminated the interior. Stalls lined the walls, most of them empty. But just to her right, a chestnut stallion stuck its head free of a stall and whinnied loudly. His muzzle sported a long scar on the right side. As she drew close enough to peer within the stall, more appeared, dotting his hide all over. It was clear Valiant was not some horse of leisure; he was a seasoned fighter.

"This is Valiant." King Quinton strolled to the beast's side, a proud smile lighting his face. "My new bondmate."

Kayda's heart lifted. She couldn't remember the last time she'd seen her grandfather so happy. "Hello, Valiant." She walked directly in front of him, meeting his dark brown eyes, grinning just as widely. She glanced at the king. "How did you find him?"

"It was only when the bridge was about to fall, and the scourge descend upon Northmoat, that his voice reached me. The bond did what no magic, no healer, could. It gave me a new reason to live. And a way to escape from the strange prison trapping me within my mind. I owe Valiant everything." His eyes shone with unshed tears, his smile turning tender but just as radiant.

"Well, then we'd better bring him along," she said, squeezing her grandfather's shoulder. But then she tilted her head, frowning.

"What is it?" Izora appeared at her side, her brow furrowed and the corners of her eyes crinkled.

"The escape route, I don't know if—"

A hole burst open in the ground in the back of the stables.

"Hurry!" Vespen yelled, throwing dirt at the breach. "I can't keep this up, forever."

The king threw open the stall door, and in a fluid leap, he bounded atop the horse's back. Kayda's eyes widened momentarily at the incredible jump from a man who, until yesterday, had been one step away from being bedbound. But then she remembered the boons. Perhaps sharing a bond with horses awarded increased jumping capabilities?

She raced toward the doors and pulled a torch from the wall. Izora grabbed another while Mika and Vespen frantically scooped dirt into their pockets and the Guard Captain drew his sword.

"Rally around the king and his steed," he ordered, holding his blade aloft like a talisman. "On to the tower!" Then he lifted the wooden beam and shoved the door open with his shoulder.

A cold chill spread through Kayda's veins, and vibration hummed to life around her. The scourge were quick to jump into the gap as soon as the door sprang open, but they were ready for them. Fire and earth flew, and steel shredded fur and flesh. They forced the horde to fall back, laying waste to any that pressed too close.

The five of them formed a loose circle around the king. He alone remained unarmed. He made a peculiar sight, riding bareback on a horse in his robe and pajamas. But though he lacked a means to fight, he helped as he could, yelling out encouragement and a word of warning when any of the crowd attempted to sneak up on one of them from behind.

The tower loomed large on the horizon. It perched on the Royal Grounds' northwest corner and would normally only take a few moments to reach from the stables. But with the scourge pressing in around them, they had to fight for every step.

They fought for what felt like hours. More and more scourge came, flooding in from every direction. It seemed like with every one they slew, two more rose to take their place. By the time they reached the tower door, all of them showed signs of exhaustion. Izora nearly stumbled as she sent a wave of fire into the crowd. Mika drew a hand across his forehead, smearing sweat and dirt across his brow. They couldn't keep this up much longer.

The Guard Captain pivoted, heading for the cliffside that stretched out behind the tower as planned. But then, the scourge surged forward.

"Izora, behind you!" King Quinton yelled.

The old mage reacted an instant too late. A scourge jumped onto her back, sinking its claws into her flesh. She screamed, her knees buckled, and she fell to the ground. Her torch spilled from her hands and rolled into the crowd, guttering out almost instantly.

"Izora." Kayda leaped into action, rushing to her side.

Vespen beat her there. He jammed a dart of dirt into the scourge on her back, flinging it aside. Kayda reached her the next instant and threw an arm under her shoulder, pulling her to her feet as Vespen threw down a barrage of dirt for cover.

"Quick, into the tower to regroup," King Quinton yelled. He'd already dismounted beside the wide wooden doors and ushered his mount inside. The Guard Captain hovered at his side, his teeth gritted and sword slashing furiously.

They all piled inside. Mika barred the door after the Guard Captain rushed in. Kayda gently set Izora down on the cold stone floor in the entranceway, then rose to her feet and hung her lit torch on the wall.

She turned back to find Vespen pulling Izora's cloak off her back and examining her wound. "I'll fix you right up," he murmured. Mika hovered beside him, but Vespen waved him off, determined to heal Izora despite his obvious exhaustion.

Kayda sighed, scanning the tower. The last time she'd entered these doors, the building had been full of activity. Now, it was cold and empty, only the brightly painted murals of battles left as a reminder of the men who once worked and lived in these halls. Even the weapons that festooned the walls had been removed, leaving brighter spots of paint below the bare hooks and nails; shadows of what once was.

The Guard Captain mounted the first flight of stairs curling around the circular tower. He stopped when he reached the height of the high glass windows and peered outside. "Where do all the bastards keep coming from? I thought they'd all headed for Southmoat?"

Kayda's stomach sank. The tower was the most secure building in the entire keep. Originally built as a prison, the stone walls stood strong and sound. But given enough time, the scourge would undoubtedly find a way in. And with more beasts arriving every moment, they would have just as hard of a time advancing through the horde to reach the cliffside.

"How much farther do we have to go?" Mika leaned against the wall, his breath heavy.

Kayda gulped. "At least triple the distance we just traveled."

Mika's face paled.

The king patted his bondmate's hide, his gaze locked on Izora's back. She hissed as Vespen pulled down her gray servant's dress low enough to attend to the wound on her back.

King Quinton frowned. "Kayda, I think I know what you're planning." He turned to her. "I'm not coming."

"What? No, you can't, Grandfather." Tears prickled the corners of her eyes.

"I can't leave Valiant behind." A sad smile painted his lips as his fingers trailed down Valiant's mane. "I've heard about your bondmate. A dragon." He shook his head. "Incredible. But I can't help noticing you're alone."

Kayda took a deep breath, the reminder of her bondmate's absence wrenching her chest. She nodded.

Her grandfather clutched her hand. "Then you understand, don't you? I can't go through it again. I won't."

Mika pushed off of the wall. "Sir? I can help. Back in Raimire, I have a patient who's lost four bondmates. There is a way to remove their voices from your mind. It's risky, but I've seen it wo—"

The king held up a hand. "No. I'm not leaving Valiant. Absolutely not."

Kayda's eyes swam with tears. The pain that welled within her from Druturion's absence—she wouldn't wish that on anyone. But she didn't want her grandfather to die. If he stayed behind, with no one to protect him, it would only be a matter of time before the scourge found him.

"Please, Grandfather. We're so close. I can't go back without you."

"You can and you will." Quinton squeezed her hand, his blue eyes soft, but his voice hard as steel. "I'm so proud of you. Everything that you've done for this country—for our family—I couldn't have asked for more." He beamed, his eyes shining. "You're going to make a marvelous queen one day."

Kayda shook her head, her gaze downcast. "I'm not who you think I am—"

He reached up, cradling her cheek. "Stop. You are everything and more, Little Red. I've watched you your whole life. I might not have been around as much as I would've liked, but I wasn't blind. You have a kind heart, you're bloody smart, and tough as nails." He laughed. "Just look at you, now. You fought your way through a mountain of monsters to save us. You are a wonder, Kayda."

Her heart warmed at his words. But they sounded too much like goodbye. The tears were spilling now, flowing down her cheeks, splashing on her grandfather's wrinkled hand. "Maybe we can slow his fall. Mika and Vespen can—"

"No. You'll never make it with the two of us slowing you down." His gaze shifted to Valiant. "We've already discussed it. We'll leave first, lead the beasts away. Give the rest of you a chance." He brushed away her tears. "Take it, Little Red."

Kayda gasped, backing away. "You're going out there all alone?" The door they'd entered slammed for the hundredth time as the vicious beasts fought to break in. How could he even consider it? The scourge would tear them to pieces.

"My king." The Guard Captain hopped off the bottom step, then bowed before them. "I would be honored to stay behind and protect you."

King Quinton waited until he stood to his full height. Then he focused on the captain, peering straight into his eyes. "Gawain, your service has been exemplary. The depth of your loyalty, sacrifice, and courage is beyond compare. I would ask you to use those qualities now to protect my granddaughter." The Guard Captain looked like he wanted to argue, but Quinton grasped his shoulder and continued, "Not as your king. I'm asking as a friend. Protect Kayda for me, Gawain. Please."

Kayda pressed her fingers to her temples, watching the Guard Captain—Gawain—nodding in agreement. She'd never even learned his name. How could her grandfather expect her to make a good queen?

Inside, she seethed, sorrow and disbelief warring in her chest. She couldn't let him go through with this. But the one thing that might make him change his mind could ruin her forever.

"I'm not your kin," she blurted out. "Don't throw your life away for me."

King Quinton turned from Gawain. Kayda steeled herself, preparing to greet his shock and anger. But when he met her gaze, a soft smile lit his face. Her brows knitted together.

"I told you, Little Red. I'm not blind. You were still in the womb when I learned the truth. Your grandmother isn't the only one in Kings Keep who can keep a secret."

Kayda bit her lip, her gaze flitting between Izora and Quinton. He already knew? He'd allowed an imposter to be princess all these years? It didn't make sense.

"I wager I even know more than you think you do. But none of that matters. This is my choice. Valiant and I, we've both had long lives already. And both of us are itching for a good gallop." He sighed. "Oh, it's been so long." A wistful smile flashed on his face. He spun back to his bondmate, caressing his mane once more. Then he leaped atop his back and set his shoulders straight and his gaze forward. Valiant trotted up to the vibrating door.

"You can't, Grandfather! Please, see reason," Kayda tried again, her heart breaking.

"This is happening, Little Red. You won't sway me."

"No, she's right," Gawain said.

Kayda's heart jerked. Was someone finally going to stop this mad plan?

But Gawain only beckoned the king away from the front door. "There's too many out there. You won't make it more than five steps before they're all on you. Leave out the back door instead."

Izora, now healed, her clothes back in place, rose from the floor and wrapped an arm around Kayda's shoulders.

The king met Izora's gaze. "Keep our girl safe."

Izora lifted her chin. "You know I will." Something unspoken passed between them. An understanding that Kayda was not privy to.

Kayda sucked in a breath, ready to demand an explanation, but then the king guided Valiant toward the back door. She raced over to his side and stared up at him. "I love you, Grandfather. Please don't do this. We'll find a way... I—"

Valiant halted, and King Quinton leaned down. "I love you, too, Little Red. I'm sorry I wasn't there for you when you needed me. I wish I could stay with you forever. But I can't." He caressed her cheek, staring down at her. All signs of that far away longing that always filled his eyes had vanished, leaving them shining—radiant. "Let me go. I need to feel the wind in my hair while I ride, one last time. You wouldn't deny an old fool one final wish, would you?"

Izora caught up to her again and pulled her into her embrace. Kayda sank into it, allowing herself a moment to weep. But when the door slammed open, she pushed free of Izora's arms and raced to the back window.

Valiant burst free from the back door and tore off like a shot. King Quinton rode atop his back, his head held high, a laugh bursting free of his chest. They bowled through the few scourge gathered around the back of the tower with ease and pulled up to a stop after galloping back toward the stables.

"Try to catch us, you bastards!" The king's shout was loud enough to reach her ears through the stone walls, though barely above a whisper. "I dare you." Then they tore off again, galloping into the distance.

Kayda pressed her hand to the glass, chin quivering, tears flooding her cheeks. She watched the scourge take off after them. Dozens of the beasts zipped through the grass, slowly gaining ground.

"It's working." Gawain peered through the glass behind her shoulder. "C'mon, Princess. Now's our chance. We need to leave."

She let herself be pulled from the window, numbly following the others to the front door.

Izora grabbed the torch from the wall and shook her hard. "Kayda, listen to me. You have to fight now. He made that sacrifice for you. For us. Don't let it be wasted."

Kayda met her gaze. Nodded. She was right. It was time to fight.

The front door slammed open. She burst out first. Cold swam through Kayda's veins. She welcomed it, lifting her hands. And for the first time, the fire didn't just flow from her hands in a stream; it burst out in a wide semi-circle, incinerating everything in front of her.

She reveled in the flames, the power. The cold grew so intense she shivered, even as the fire before her blazed so hot the scourge's carcasses melted before her eyes. It felt like she lived in that moment forever, but before she knew it, it ended, and she fell to her knees.

"Blazes." Gawain knelt beside her. "That was incredible."

Kayda smiled weakly, allowing him to slide an arm underneath her and tug her to her feet.

"C'mon." Izora turned around. "Keep close to me, Captain. The princess needs to stay close to the torch."

Slowly, Kayda's strength returned. What was that blast? She'd read about something similar in the ancient book Conall brought back with him, but she'd never experienced anything like it. Whatever it was, she didn't have the strength to repeat it.

It was good then that most of the scourge had taken off after the king. The five of them ran, making much better time with only a few beasts leaping out at them instead of a vast crowd surrounding them. Kayda allowed the others to dispatch them, focusing on moving one foot in front of the other.

Finally, they made it to the cliff. Kayda stepped up to the edge and stared down at the sea below.

"You want us to dive down there?" Mika asked. "Are you sure?"

Gawain grinned and thumped Mika on the back. "Oh, it looks scarier than it is. The guard jump in from this spot during training. A test of courage. And fortitude as well." He frowned at Izora. She was doubled over, her chest heaving after the short run. "The swim to the docks tests even the most seasoned of men. Are you sure *all* of us are up for it, Princess?"

"We won't be swimming to the docks." She hoped they wouldn't, at least. Kayda shaded her eyes, staring past the setting sun. "There." She pointed, a tiny smile creeping across her face. Her father could be counted on after all. There on the horizon sailed the rickety old ship, *The Lady Luck*, ready to scoop them up like promised.

There was nothing left to do but leap. She took one last look at Northmoat. Already the scourge were regrouping. More of them barreled up the path from the tower, chasing after them.

Tears welled in her eyes as her thoughts drifted to her grandfather. Was he still alive? But she shook her head, biting them back. He'd believed in her enough to sacrifice himself to ensure her survival. She would not let him down.

Kayda turned her back on Northmoat and jumped.

Chapter 11

Lark mounted the gangplank to *Nova's Champion* as the sun sank down over the sea. Jett and Jayan were there to greet them. Her father lent her a hand as she struggled up the swaying boards.

"Thanks," she wheezed out around a sigh, still fighting to catch her breath. They'd sped through the streets of Southmoat to make it back. From how crowded the huge boat appeared, with folk peering over the sides of every rail, they'd come none too soon.

Jayan assisted Aren, then rose on his tiptoes to peer within the makeshift carrier Lark had fashioned out of a pair of coveralls strapped to Dausius' chest. His dark brown eyes widened before a grin spread across his face. "So that's what has you folks arriving so late. I've never seen a babe so small." After a moment his gaze lifted, and his smile fell. "What of the mother?"

Dausius shook his head sadly. "Gone."

"Oh, that's a shame," Jayan said.

"It's not what you're thinking," Lark hurried to say. "She took off on a canoe into the bog."

Jett's brows shot up. "Into the bog? Whatever for?"

Lark shrugged, then grabbed hold of Jayan's cloak sleeve. "Have you watched everyone boarding?" At Jayan's nod, she continued. "Are there any mothers with infants on board?"

Jayan's gaze flicked back to the babe, and he raked a hand through his braids. "I don't think there are…"

Lark's stomach dropped. What were they going to do with a newborn on a boat at sea with no milk to speak of?

Aren rubbed her back, pointing toward the city. "Look, there are more people arriving. We might get lucky."

Lark bit her lip, standing by the rail to watch the group approaching. Jett joined her, frowning as he stared into the city.

As the people drew closer, Lark's heart sank. No one carried a babe in their arms. In fact, they all appeared worse for the wear, their hair and faces dusted with dirt and their boots caked in mud. But it wasn't until they began making their way up the gangplank that she recognized one of them.

"Edrik." She waved him over as he boarded. "I'm glad to see you."

"Lark, oh thank goodness." He pulled her into an embrace, and a cloud of dust rose from his clothing, tickling her nose. "I was so worried when you didn't show up in the tunnels."

"Sorry about that." She grimaced. "I ran into some surprises. It's a long story."

Edrik opened his mouth, but then shut it again, swiveling to view a commotion headed their way from the city. A crowd of young people raced toward them, flinging blasts of air and fire behind them.

Lark gaped, her keen eyes spotting the beasts chasing after them, teeth snapping. "Pull up the gangplank and shove off!" she yelled.

Jayan turned to her, his eyes widening. "What of the young mages? They won't be able to board."

"Yes, they will. Trust me."

Jayan stared at her. For a moment, she feared he would ignore her command, but he must've seen something in her face that convinced him. He spun on his heel after only an instant, barking out orders to his crew.

Lark whirled around and shouted across the deck, "Any mage who still has the strength to summon, gather around. Now."

Soon a crowd of harried young folk joined the dirt-dusted mages already nearby. They all aimed curious looks in her direction, their jaws dropping as they spotted the mages rushing toward them, and the gangplank disappearing.

When the ship slowly began to move, a burly mage rushed to the front of the crowd. "What are you doing? We can't just leave them there to die. Put the gangplank back!"

Lark patted the mage's shoulder reassuringly. "Don't worry. We'll make a new gangplank. Everyone, gather around. Link hands."

She blew out a steadying breath and stuck her hand in her pocket, then removed a handful of fresh soil from her coveralls. This had better work or those mages would be stranded.

She reached out, clasping hands with Edrik, squashing the handful of earth between them. "Everyone, call forth your talent, please."

Lark closed her eyes, reaching for the magic all around her. Her palm warmed as she connected to the linked mage's pooled energy. Then she snapped open her eyes and held out her free hand. The boat shook and swayed, the wooden deck vibrating. Slowly, a wide curved bridge formed between the dock and the ship.

It appeared not a moment too soon. The first of the running mages arrived, and wasted no time leaping atop the dirt bridge and up onto the ship. Lark kept a constant watch on the bridge, adding more length to the ends as the ship slowly drifted away from the dock.

Before long, a half dozen boarded, but there was still a pair lagging behind. A crowd of scourge—a few dozen, at the least—trailed at their heels, and they kept twisting back to throw blasts of air and fire behind them.

"Hurry," Jett yelled.

The folk at the rails joined in, shouting encouragement. A few of the guards on board picked up bows. Arrows sailed through the sky, skewering the vermin, their dying shrieks setting off whoops of glee from the watching townspeople.

Even with all the mages lending her their strength, Lark could sense her hold on the magic fading. The bridge stretched the length of half a city block, and with every passing moment, she was forced to add more dirt to the end. Her shoulders trembled, and her knees buckled. She would've surely smacked down atop the deck if it weren't for Edrik's tight grip on her hand and Aren throwing a hand around her waist when he spotted her staggering.

Still, she kept the bridge going, until Edrik's grip slackened. She chanced a glance behind at the mages, and spotted several of them wobbling on their feet. Mika's words echoed in her mind and she recalled the weariness washing over her after linking—the same weariness all the mages linked with her must be feeling now.

But when she flicked her glance back to the docks, her heart lifted. The pair finally made it to the bridge. As soon as they both jumped upon it, she breathed out a sigh. Carefully, she shifted the dirt from the far end to the end resting against the boat. Soon a gap appeared, so large not a single scourge took the chance of leaping after the racing mages.

As soon as the last mage's boots smacked down on the wood, Lark dropped Edrik's hand, and the last of the dirt splashed into the sea. All the linked mages sagged in relief. A few of them dropped to the deck, holding hands to their stomachs and heads.

Lark winced. Had she held on too long? But soon, they all lurched back up on their feet, and she loosed another sigh, turning to greet the newcomers.

She'd been so completely focused on holding onto the bridge she hadn't bothered to examine the mage's faces closely. As she approached, she scanned the crowd, and when she recognized one of them, her heart skipped a beat.

"Oriana?" She pushed through the throng to reach her, frantically searching the newcomers, again and again. "Where's Conall? He was supposed to be with you."

When Oriana's face fell, Lark's heart twisted. "Lark, I'm so sorry. There was a breach at the moat. Shadow fell into the bog, and Conall leaped in after him. We were so busy keeping the fire lit I didn't have a chance to search for him."

Lark's gaze connected with Jett's across the deck. She watched her father's face sag at Oriana's announcement. Then he strode away, weaving through the gathered townspeople, his shoulders slumped.

Lark pressed a hand to her chest. Not again. Blazes. They should've never split up.

She paced back to the side rail and turned to stare at the city growing small as they headed out to sea. Would Conall be all right? Would she ever see him again?

The shrill cry of a newborn broke her trance. Dausius strode up to her, gently rocking the baby against his chest. "What do I do? She won't quiet."

"Hand her to me." Lark stretched out her arms. She stared down at Violet as she wailed, then cradled her tiny body against her chest.

Violet's face immediately sought out her breast, instinct driving her movements. But she wouldn't find any succor there.

Lark crossed the deck, shouting to be heard above the infant's wails. "Are there any wet nurses on board?" She walked to the aft rail, repeating her question every time she reached another group of huddled townsfolk. Every time, she was met with shaking heads and grave stares.

After reaching the stern, she veered toward the bow. With every group she approached, and every denial, her heart sank lower, until she found herself with no one left to ask, the crying child silent again. The walk had lulled her to sleep, but it wouldn't be long before she awakened again, even hungrier than before.

She found Tiora, Mazen, and Meital standing at the bow rail with Aren. Her friends and fellow performers had been true to their word, sticking with her as she left Raimire. She exhaled a deep sigh. At least they'd all made it back on the boat in one piece after the madness in Flamesmoat.

"Lark." A soft smile lit Tiora's beautiful face as her brown cloak billowed around her curvy frame. "I hear you had quite the adventure without us."

Lark's cheeks heated. "I seem to have a knack for finding trouble."

Mazen grinned, knife in hand, hard at practice balancing the sharp blade atop his knuckles. "You don't say?" His multi-colored tunic flashed beneath his cloak in the fading afternoon sunlight.

Meital elbowed her twin, nearly making him drop his knife into the sea. "Who do we have here?" She flicked her long brown braid over her shoulder and peered at the bundle wrapped in Lark's arms.

"This is Violet. I'm stuck playing nursemaid until her mother returns." Her shoulders sank. "I'm making a real muck of it already."

"What's wrong?" Tiora asked.

"I need to find her a wet nurse. I've already asked everyone on deck with no luck."

"Have you gone down below?" Meital asked.

Lark shook her head, a seed of hope taking root within her. "Below deck—of course. Maybe I'll find someone down there."

Tiora took a turn peering at the sleeping babe, and her golden-brown eyes shone with warmth. "Let us ask around. You don't want to wake the little doll."

"You don't mind?"

Her friends all insisted they didn't, then disappeared into the bowels of the ship, leaving her alone at the bow.

She didn't stay alone for long. The light taps of paws on the deck sounded. Lark whipped around, praying for the gray fur of her brother's bondmate to appear with Conall beside him. But it was only her brother's mutt, Sunny, approaching. She wagged her tail when she spotted Lark, rushing over to greet her. A small smile graced her lips in the face of Sunny's enthusiastic welcome, but it didn't stick around for long.

The flapping of wings alerted her an instant before her bondmate touched down beside her, digging her talons into the deck railing.

"I didn't see your brother and his wolf make it back on board. Are you all right?" Muse asked.

Lark quickly relayed Oriana's story. *"He found me once before. He'll find me again."*

Muse was silent for a long moment before she finally responded. *"Hey, what if that mage went after him? She could've seen them splashing out there and left to save them."*

"Yeah, wouldn't that be crazy?" She stared down at the baby sleeping in her arms. She still couldn't wrap her head around Ereni's motivations. Why would anyone leave their newborn in the care of a stranger?

Could she be just that selfless that she saw a man drowning and rushed off to save him? Surely stranger things had happened, but it all seemed so farfetched. Then again, what other reason could she have to disappear into the bog only moments after giving birth?

But was it too much to hope that Ereni had found Conall? Something tickled her mind at the sound of both their names in the same sentence.

Of course. That was where she'd heard the name Ereni before... Conall asked if she was in Flamesmoat right before he raced out of the Mata's hut on the night they'd arrived in Stoneshore.

If they knew each other already, maybe it wasn't such a crazy idea after all...

The inner hatch swung open, and Aren climbed back above deck. Lark's heart picked up speed when his gaze zeroed in on hers, but she did her best to ignore it. Now was not the time for flirting, no matter how handsome he might be or how much she wanted to sink into his embrace.

"Any luck?" she asked.

He shook his head. "Speaking of luck..." He pointed ahead, beyond the bow's rail. *The Lady Luck* was fast approaching, readying to pull alongside their boat. "Maybe we'll have better luck among the townsfolk over there."

"Good thinking, Aren." She rushed over to the side rail where sailors flung ropes between the two vessels, latching them together in the water. Soon, long wooden boards joined the ropes, and chaos ensued as people began hopping from one ship to the other.

"Everyone headed to Doln, make your way on board *The Lady Luck*," Jayan called out. "*Nova's Champion* sails for Joria."

Lark stepped closer to the barrier, but Aren squeezed her arm before she made it to the side rail. "Why don't you stay here? Let me hop over there and ask among the folk who're on board. You can ask all the newcomers on our boat."

She watched him hurry across, then got to work, asking the handful of people who came aboard the same question. She asked so many times the words *wet nurse* felt like they lost all meaning. But it was no use. The people joining them on the journey to Joria were young and fit for the most part, or grizzled old men. All of them carted weapons and fierce expressions, ready to partake in the fight to come.

Lark sighed, taking another look at the folk gathered on deck. Most of the families and almost all the children had departed, boarding *The Lady Luck* to join the other refugees fleeing to Doln.

"Lark?" a familiar voice called out behind her.

She turned and spotted Kayda returning across the makeshift plank bridge. Mika and a handful of other people trailed in her wake.

"Kayda, you made it." She smiled, walking up to greet her.

Kayda's answering smile was not as bright as she'd expected.

"What's wrong?" Lark asked.

Kayda bit her lip. "The king... I couldn't save him."

"Oh. I'm so sorry." She reached briefly before remembering the baby cradled against her chest. "I would give you a hug, but my hands are a little full at the moment."

Kayda quirked a brow, looping her braids behind her ear and smiling down at the baby. "Who do we have here?"

"Her name is Violet. I'm in desperate need of a wet nurse for her. You didn't see any nursing mothers on *The Lady Luck* by chance?"

Kayda shook her head sadly. "Can't say that I did."

Just then, Lark spotted Aren making his way back across the planks. He met her gaze and shook his head. Her heart sank. The future appeared bleak for little Violet. What was she going to do?

"She's so tiny. How did you end up with a newborn in your care?" Kayda asked.

"I helped birth her, actually. It's a bit of a crazy story. Violet's mother saved my life. She and I hid below water in the bog to avoid a bunch of armed criminals. She summoned enough air to keep us alive while we were below water, but because she didn't have a source, little Violet made an early appearance."

"Wow. That is pretty crazy." Kayda stared at Violet again. "What happened to the mother? Did she..."

Lark frowned as Kayda trailed off. "No, that's even stranger. She took off on a boat into the bog. Left the baby behind. Told me to take care of her until she could find us again."

Baris, the mage they'd met on the docks earlier that day, approached them. "I'm sorry. I couldn't help but overhear your tale. Tell me, what was that mage's name?"

Lark glanced at him. "Oh, it's all right. Her name was Ereni. Do you know her?"

Baris' eyes widened. He nodded. "Yes. She's missing." He rubbed a hand across his face. "That explains why she was always holed up in her chambers every morning. And that awful ginger tea she'd offer me when I'd come to her with a question." He peeked at the sleeping child. "This is her daughter? You're certain?"

It was Lark's turn to nod. "Absolutely. I witnessed the birth."

"Well, I'll be." Baris smiled. "I wonder who the father is?" Then his eyes widened again, and he shot a glance at Kayda before flicking his gaze back to the baby. "Exactly how early was her appearance, do you think?"

Lark shrugged. "I'm not sure. She said something about it being months too soon, but how many, I have no idea. Why do you ask?"

Baris gulped, his Adam's apple bobbing in his throat. "It's just, I've only ever seen one man who looked like more than a friend to Ereni. When the Palisade fell, her and Prince Tarquin were acting awfully cozy."

Kayda's brows shot up at that. "Is she the brunette with the ponytail I remember from the fight back in the Abandoned Lands?" Baris nodded, and she flashed a grin at the baby. "It would be kind of nice, knowing a part of him lived on."

Lark sighed, shaking her head. "I guess I better change ships before they pull apart."

"Wait." Kayda frowned. "I thought you were coming with us?"

"I was, but Violet will never make it to Joria without a wet nurse. Even Midsport..." Her stomach twisted. "I just don't know. But I need to give her a chance."

"Lark, there you are." Tiora bustled up to her, a wide smile on her face. "We found someone."

"You did?" Her heart lit with joy. "Below deck? What took you so long?"

"That's the thing." Tiora drew closer, speaking softly. "She's not a normal wet nurse. She's just a mother who lost her baby yesterday."

Lark's brows pinched together. "Oh."

"She had some reservations at first, as you could imagine. But she finally agreed to help our little Violet out," Tiora said. "Her name is Elmena. C'mon, I'll show you where she's holed up below deck with her other kids. They have family in Joria, so they were already planning to stay on board."

Lark waved goodbye to Kayda, Aren, and the others, and followed. Tiora pulled back a curtain a few moments later, revealing a small corner of the hold where several families gathered, seated on the floor, the adults chatting quietly together while the children played. When

Lark's gaze landed on the woman seated next to Meital, a wide grin broke out across her face.

"Hello. It's nice to see you made it," she said to the woman whose ankle she'd healed on the road in Southmoat.

Elmena smiled back, hers much more tentative. "Lark, was it? It's nice to see you again as well." She rose to her feet, cooing at Violet, her expression turning bittersweet. "Look at you, what a tiny little gorgeous girl you are." Elmena met Lark's gaze, her brown eyes swimming with tears. "I'll take her, now." She held out her arms.

"Thank you, so much." Lark handed Violet to Elmena. "I can take her when she's fed, if you need to tend to your children."

Elmena shook her head, settling back down, already tugging her breast free from her tunic. Violet clasped on instantly, not even bothering to open her eyes. "Oh, she'll be no bother. What a beauty." She rocked her gently, staring at Violet, tears falling soundlessly down her cheeks.

Lark's heart squeezed. Was she doing the right thing, or was she only traumatizing this poor woman who'd just lost her own child?

But then Elmena lifted her head and smiled up at her. "When your friends first asked me to do this, I didn't want any part of it. But now..." She gazed down at Violet again. "It feels right. Even though my Landra isn't here anymore, I can still help this little one. Landra was only three months old. She was never well, her entire life. It's a miracle she lived as long as she did; all the healers thought so. They told me she'd be lucky to live a few days when she was born. But she was a fighter. I did everything I could to make her comfortable. To make her short life one filled with love. Even when having her at home, too ill to travel, meant that we had to stay in Southmoat while all our neighbors fled. Now, I have to believe she held on for this. So that her milk could save another. Isn't that beautiful, in a way?"

Tiora knelt down beside her. "It is. It's wonderful." Her voice was choked, tears in her eyes.

Lark had tears in her eyes, too. Her brother might be missing, and the whole world faced with war, but here on this boat, she was witnessing something to be grateful for. People banding together to survive against all odds. In her eyes, that was the most beautiful thing of all.

Chapter 12

Kayda pushed open the door to the former captain's study on board *Nova's Champion*. The sight of her hammock swaying invitingly with the motion of the surf sent a wave of weariness washing over her. But she couldn't sleep. Not yet.

She held the door wide open. "Come in, we can speak privately in here."

Prince—no—King Gideon strode in, his nose wrinkling at the modest room. "This is what they expect a princess to use on board?" he grumbled under his breath, scanning the chamber with undisguised disdain.

Kayda pinched the bridge of her nose, seating herself atop the large desk by the window. She hadn't come here to discuss the quality of the housing arrangements. She had much bigger problems to discuss. Like the fact that she was an imposter. She could only hope her father would be as understanding as her grandfather had been. With him gone... She couldn't have the lie weighing on her with everything else happening. She needed to come clean to her father and accept the consequences, whatever they may be.

"Take a seat," she offered, easing the single chair away from the desk with the toe of her boot.

King Gideon lifted a brow, but he sat in the chair, groaning as his large girth settled atop the cushion. "I'm pleased you asked to speak with me. We have much to discuss."

Kayda gulped. "We do?" A pit coalesced in her belly.

Had the Guard Captain spoken with him already? He'd been privy to her conversation with the king before his... sacrifice. Did he confess the truth to his commander immediately?

But the next words out of her father's mouth made her shoulders sag. "Tarquin. Tell me, how did he meet his end?"

Kayda pursed her lips. She still had conflicting feelings about that day. Her half-brother had been so confident he could destroy the scourge—the evil that an entire order of mages dedicated their lives to caging for hundreds of years—in a single afternoon, leading dozens of men to their deaths. But looking into her father's eyes, seeing the pain that lurked there at the memory of his lost son, perhaps it was best to spare the man all the gory details.

"He and his men fought valiantly until they were overwhelmed. The vast number of scourge was simply too much. I'm sorry I couldn't save him."

Gideon closed his eyes and drew a deep breath through his nose. Then his eyes snapped opened, and he nodded once. "Don't blame yourself, my dear." He patted her knee. "No one holds you responsible for your brother's foolish decisions."

Kayda flinched. She'd expected a bit more sadness, but perhaps he'd cried all his tears already in private. "I—"

"Have you heard what they're saying about that little albino brat on board?" The king rolled his eyes. "It's Tarquin's bastard, apparently."

Kayda stifled a gasp. "Yes, I've met *her*. Violet. She's a lovely child."

The king scoffed, shifting in his chair. "Lovely or not, she could become a problem for us. For you. I've half a mind to arrange a little swim for the brat before we dock in Joria."

Kayda saw red. She hopped to her feet, her nostrils flaring. "I'm going to assume you aren't thinking straight after hearing the news of Tarquin's death. That innocent little *baby* will not be touched. Is that clear?"

The king bristled, blubbering incoherently, his face flushing.

Kayda turned her back on him, fighting not to lose her cool. How could he even suggest that? It was beyond the pale. About his own grandchild, if the rumors proved true. If he was willing to murder an innocent baby just for being born a royal bastard, what would he say to her confession?

All thought of coming clean fled her mind, replaced with a rage that burned as hot as the flame in Druturion's throat. She had to send him away before she said something she would regret.

She spun to face him, forcing a smile. "I'm feeling very tired, Father. Can we continue this conversation later?"

King Gideon heaved off the desk chair and smoothed the front of his tunic. "I see my joke was in poor taste. Of course, I wouldn't dream of harming that child. I'm simply frustrated, is all. We don't need her growing up and staking claim to the crown. A child of a mage, no less." He shook his head. "I'll leave you to your rest, my dear."

"Goodnight." Kayda walked him to the door, feeling marginally better after his parting words. Still, she knew so little about her father. Was his *joke* really that, or was he just saving face after how she'd reacted?

She closed the door, paced back to the desk, and leaned against the top, staring down at the jagged holes dotting the surface. The former captain had the habit of stabbing his knife into the wood like a pincushion. Kayda rolled her neck, suddenly understanding the compulsion. If she owned a knife, she would've added a few marks of her own.

Grandfather. He would've known what to do. But he was gone, and she was even more alone than she'd ever been before.

A knock drew her from her grief. "Come in."

The door opened, and Izora slid in. "Kayda, I thought you might want to talk."

She took a deep breath and perched atop the desk again. "I do." She inclined her head to the chair her father had just vacated. "Have a seat."

Izora's boots tapped across the floor. She smoothed her skirt and settled down on the chair, cocking her head sideways, her gaze landing on the tiny braids covering the left side of Kayda's head. "You've been to Sul Hollow."

Kayda grinned. "I have. I met my uncle. Your son. You have three grandchildren out there in the desert."

A wistful smile lit Izora's face. "That's good. I'm glad to hear it."

"Don't you want to meet them?" She ran her gaze down the gray castle servant's dress Izora still wore. "How could you do it for so long? How could you spend so much of your life living a lie?" Her voice cracked. "Lying to me?"

"Oh, Kayda." Izora stretched out her arm, her brow wrinkled, but Kayda folded her legs beneath her and shifted out of reach before Izora's hand landed.

Izora curled her fingers in her lap instead and let out a weary sigh. "There were so many times over the years I wanted to tell you. Every time your father ignored you to drown himself in his cups, or that brat brother played another dirty trick on you, I wished I could scoop you up and secret you away with me back to Sul Hollow. But don't you see? You had to grow up at Kings Keep."

Kayda sent her a glare. "No, I don't see. I never belonged there at all. My mother was an imposter, and so am I."

Izora met her gaze, smiling warmly. "That's not true. Not entirely, at least. Let me explain."

"I'm listening."

"I'm sure Bazman told you the story of how I disappeared from Sul Hollow after Chanti's birth."

Kayda nodded.

"What he couldn't have told you was why. After I set that fire, I was terrified. My grandfather had been talented, too. But instead of going to the mages for training, he hid his talent, refusing to leave my grandmother and his children." She shook her head sadly. "It was a decision that eventually led to his demise and took my grandmother with him. They both died in a massive fire he set unintentionally. My mother was the only survivor out of her entire family of eight. When I discovered I'd inherited the same power, I knew I couldn't make the same mistake."

"So, you went to Mage Keep."

"Yes. Even though it broke my heart to leave my family, I left. I refused to do what my father had done. Leaving them was the hardest choice I ever made, but if I hurt them by staying there... that would've been so much worse."

Kayda chewed her lip. Another family driven apart, just like Lark and Conall with their father.

Izora continued, "At Mage Keep, I discovered so much more than just how to control my powers. I learned about the mission that drove the mages to keep watch over the Abandoned Lands. I befriended a young mage named Delyth and joined the future Sade Prim on her voyage to the Northern Depths. There I witnessed a glimpse of my own future. I learned the role I would play in the battle to come. The role you would play."

Kayda wrinkled her nose. More of that damned prophecy.

"It might sound odd to you, but there is a power in that knowledge that is hard to escape. I spent many years trying to hide from it. But when news reached Mage Keep of Tarquin's talent being skipped, Delyth pulled me aside. She knew, the same as I did, that if the Palisade fell with no one left of the first king's bloodline in power, then the whole world would be doomed."

"But I don't understand. I'm not—"

"Oh, but Kayda, you are." Izora smiled. "Let me finish, dear, you'll see."

Kayda crossed her arms, frowning.

"It was apparent something fishy was happening with the royal bloodlines. The rumors flew about Tarquin's mother. Everyone assumed the fault lay with her. But she was innocent. Tarquin was the true son of Prince Gideon. The bloodlines were broken before that."

Kayda gasped. "It wasn't Father's wife who'd been untrue. It was his mother." Her brows drew together. "I would've never suspected—the resemblance all three of them share—how can they not be kin?"

Izora shifted on the chair. "It's because they are still kin, in a way. King Quinton's wife fell in love with someone very close to him."

A portrait flashed in Kayda's mind. Her grandfather smiling with one arm wrapped around his lovely wife—and the other around his beloved brother. "My great uncle." Her eyes widened. "Tarquin wasn't King Quinton's grandson. He was his grandnephew."

"Yes. Luckily, the mages had enough eyes and ears within Kings Keep that we figured it out before it was too late to fix. You see, the king had not been entirely faithful either."

Kayda cringed inwardly. It was all so sordid—her own grandfather—learning the ins and outs of his sex life made her skin crawl.

"We knew he frequented a few working girls. Delyth sent seers through Southmoat, searching for anyone who showed signs of bonding talent."

"And you found Jett."

Everything clicked into place. He said himself he was the son of a whore. That his father could've been anyone.

"I gather you've met him as well." Izora sighed. "Tales had spread about the little boy who could charm any dog. Delyth went personally to make sure. Brought the meanest, most vicious dog she could find with her." One side of her mouth quirked up at the memory. "Apparently, the hound was snapping and barking like mad, but the instant she caught sight of Conall, she ran over, tail wagging and begging for belly rubs. She didn't even need the seers' confirmation after that."

The lengths they'd gone to... it was insane. How far had they gone to ensure those prophetic visions came to pass? "What about their mother? Did you arrange her beating as well? And Grandfather. Did you have a hand in arranging his attack?"

Izora frowned. "No. We would never harm the king. And Delyth wouldn't condone injuring an innocent woman. But she certainly took it as evidence of fate in play and used it to her advantage. Can't say that I blame her when it led to your birth."

Kayda rubbed her brow. "Why didn't you just make Conall the prince, then? If what you say is true, then he and Lark are of the king's blood, too."

Izora shook her head. "We considered it. But King Quinton wouldn't allow it."

Her jaw dropped. "He knew? The whole time, he knew?"

"Yes. Delyth approached him after the seer first spoke to Jett. The news only confirmed the suspicions he'd long harbored." Izora twisted her hands in her lap. "But he'd also raised Gideon as a son. He loved him dearly and insisted on keeping the truth from him. That's why we switched Chanti for that trader's daughter the prince had agreed to marry. We needed to ensure she was pregnant before the wedding, to set the bloodline straight."

Kayda hopped off the desk and strolled to the window. She stared down into the dark sea, glistening in the moonlight.

So, she was the king's true granddaughter, after all. She almost laughed. To think, only moments ago she'd been about to tell her father she was an imposter... All the while, he was the one who didn't belong.

"What do I do now?" she mused aloud.

The chair creaked, and boots tapped lightly behind her. Izora joined her at the window. "That, I leave entirely up to you. I've spoken to everyone who was with us when you came to save your grandfather. They've agreed to keep silent about what was discussed. Tell everyone, tell no one—the choice is yours."

Kayda closed her eyes, breathing deeply. She wasn't sure what to do. At the very least, Lark and Conall deserved the truth. But with Conall missing, now didn't seem like the right time.

And her father—now her king. Did he even deserve to rule? For that matter, did she? Should she seek to dethrone him, or should she honor her grandfather's decision to keep the secrets of Gideon's birthright hidden? The whole situation was mind-boggling.

"Why her?" Kayda shifted to meet her grandmother's gaze. "Why did you pick your own daughter when any young mage would've surely been willing to step in as the prince's wife?"

"The vision. I saw you fighting, Kayda. I never truly returned to see my family until the day I came to take Chanti, but I kept tabs on them, watching in secret whenever I could. You do look so much like your mother..." Izora smiled sadly.

A sudden thought struck her. "You told me she was a mage, but she wasn't, was she? If you inherited talent from your grandfather... she would've been skipped."

"You're right. Chanti was never a mage. I couldn't exactly tell you it was me who you'd gotten your talent from back when you were training, now could I?" Izora chuckled, then her face turned serious. "She might not have had talent, but your mother was an incredible woman. Fierce and strong, just like you."

Kayda sighed. "I wish I could've known her."

"She would've been so proud of you."

A wave of exhaustion hit her right between the eyes. She yawned.

Izora took that as a sign to depart. "Get some rest, Princess. Things will look clearer in the morning."

As Kayda closed the door to her room and climbed into her hammock, she hoped Izora's words would prove true. But for once she didn't fall asleep with a thousand questions plaguing her. Only one remained, repeating in her mind like the strangest of lullabies.

"Dru—where are you?"

Chapter 13

"Conall," a voice called to him.

He ignored it. He was having the most wonderful dream.

The summer sun's golden rays kissed his face. Warmth flooded him from above and within as he watched Sunny zip around the grazing field on his farm in Greenvale, happily nipping at the goats' heels to herd them inside the barn.

Shadow trotted out of the woods, a fresh kill dangling from his jaws. And in the distance, his home stood as it once was, whole, not the burned-out shell he'd last seen. Someone stepped out of the door, calling his name.

"Conall."

It was a woman with a babe in her arms. Blue eyes met his. She smiled.

"Conall, wake up."

He jerked awake, groaning. The blissful dream evaporated, chased away by the awakening agony in his limbs. Every muscle in his body ached. Sharp needles stabbed at his shoulder. But worse of all was the constant throbbing of his ankle.

Where was he? Why was his bed swaying?

He rubbed the sleep from his eyes as the memory of his swim through the bog surged back.

The scourge—Shadow.

He shifted so fast he jostled his broken foot and hissed in pain. But he spotted Shadow beside him, his chest rising and falling beneath the cloak draped atop them, and he heaved out a sigh.

"I've stopped the bleeding, but I'm afraid that's the extent of what I can accomplish with my earth talent. I'll need your help to heal you both fully."

Conall's heart seized. He knew that voice.

As if they had a mind of their own, the fingers of his good hand rose and tugged down the wool cloak covering his face.

"Ereni?"

She stood at the front of the canoe, securing a rope around the mangled roots of a mangrove tree in the fading light of sunset.

"What... how?" A thousand words were on the tip of his tongue, but all he could manage was the strangled questions before his throat locked up. She'd saved them? Alone?

"I happened to be on the docks when the two of you floated by. I could see you were in need of assistance." She turned and met his eyes for the first time since she'd ripped the bindings from his wrists and ordered him to place his hands on the Palisade, setting into motion the chain of events that brought him here. That unleashed the Unseen on the world.

He wasn't sure what he was expecting. Did he want her to break down in tears and beg for his forgiveness? Maybe some small part of him had. But it looked like that wouldn't be happening. Not now, at least.

Ereni's eyes were clear, direct, and so blue. Her gaze pierced him, setting off a ricochet of conflicting feelings. Anger and hurt quickly rose to the surface, but deep underneath, there was the shadow of something softer. Something he was quick to bury before it could fully surface.

There were so many things he needed to say. But seeing her there, dressed in a ridiculous, oversized set of coveralls, it was as if he'd been transported back to that moment when she crested the hillside before the wall fell and grabbed another man's arm. Struck dumb, waiting for the next words to escape her mouth.

"Do you think you're up for it?" she asked finally.

He blinked. "What?"

Her gaze flicked between him and Shadow. "Healing. I only have a small affinity for earth talent, I'm afraid. But if you lend me your strength, we should be able to take care of both of your injuries."

He had half a mind to tell her where she could shove her talent. To demand they return to Southmoat and find another healer.

Conall stole a look at his bondmate. He slept uneasily, twitching, his gray fur caked with blood in more places than he could count. If Shadow didn't make it because he'd delayed healing over a grudge…

The thought of sharing his talent with the woman who'd betrayed him had his palms sweating, even with the still damp clothing chilling his skin. But for Shadow, he would do anything. Even put his trust in the woman who'd shattered him so completely.

"What do you need me to do?" he asked.

Ereni slinked closer, her step slow and measured, like a cat stalking its prey. She settled down beside him and dug into a pack resting on the canoe bottom. Leaning over Shadow, she placed her palm over one of his wounds, a flash of bright green peeking out from the edges of her hand. Shadow twitched at the pressure but didn't awaken.

Ereni extended her empty hand to him. Conall stared at it, wanting nothing more than to slap it away like he would a snake coiling to strike.

He heaved a deep breath and grasped her hand. For an instant, he could've sworn she shivered at the simple touch, but then her gaze snapped to his. "Call on your talent," she said flatly.

He nodded and broke eye contact, staring at Shadow. This was for him. Warmth tingled across his palm, seeping up his wrist and through his arm. Then the boat shuddered, shaking in the water far more than it should have. A whisper of exhaustion slunk up his spine. But then, Ereni removed her hand from Shadow's hide, and the weariness lifted.

Conall peered down at the spot. Just moments before a jagged gash puckered the skin, now it was healed. He tugged gently on Ereni's hand, but she tightened her grasp. His gaze shot to her face. She scanned Shadow's body, her palm slipping down to another wicked gash.

"We're not done." She met his gaze. "Again. Please."

His breath caught. A memory rose, unbidden, of that last word on her lips, so long ago. They'd been touching then, too. Staring into each other's eyes.

He shook his head, shoving the memory aside. Shadow. He had to help Shadow.

He called forth his talent, again and again. Every tremor struck him with a fresh wave of fatigue. By the time they finished healing his bondmate, he felt as if he could sleep for a hundred years. His breath came shallow and quick. His shoulders slumped, the weariness in his body compounding with the pain of his injuries until he was ready to welcome death, if only for a moment of relief.

Ereni pursed her lips, eyeing him closely. "You'd better get some rest before we heal your wounds." She perched atop the forward seat of the little canoe, wrapping her arms around her torso. "I'll keep watch. Sleep."

Conall thought to protest, but it was a fleeting urge that vanished as soon as his head hit the canoe's cold wooden boards. He slept.

Growling woke Conall in the middle of the night. His eyes shot open, pain exploding as he jolted up. *"Shadow, what is it?"*

His eyes quickly adjusted to the moonlight. Shadow had left his side and stood in the center of the canoe, his teeth pulled back, and his golden eyes shining in the dark. But he'd not spotted some far-off danger, like Conall had first suspected. He stared at the bow, his nose twitching, a growl reverberating deep in his throat, his gaze locked on Ereni.

"Brother, calm down." Conall shuffled closer, scooting across the boat bottom using his one good leg and arm. *"She's not here to hurt us. She pulled us from the bog and healed you. She's going to heal me soon, too."*

Shadow snapped his jaw closed, his growl quieting. *"How long have I been asleep?"*

Conall sighed, sinking his fingers into the fur atop Shadow's head. *"I'm not sure. Since before we were pulled from the bog."* He looked up at the sky, scanning the moon's position. *"Half the night, maybe?"*

His gaze drifted back to Ereni. She hadn't said a peep, even with a huge wolf growling at her menacingly. It was soon apparent why. She was fast asleep, curled up in a ball atop the bow seat.

Something wasn't right. Her color was off. He could see her pallor clearly, even in the moonlight. The shudders wracking her thin frame.

He glanced to the side. Not one, but two cloaks rested on the boat bottom where he and Shadow had slept. She'd given them both, and slept alone, with nothing but those ridiculous coveralls.

Conall frowned. *"She's freezing. We need to get her warm."*

He scooted closer, wincing as his broken foot dragged on the canoe's bottom.

"Don't hurt yourself for her, little brother. Not after what she's done."

Conall shook off the words. *"We still need her to heal me. I never learned how to do it on my own."* Of course, that was all. It wasn't like his stomach was turning at the thought of her freezing to death. He reached out with his good arm and slid her off the seat into his lap. *"The cloaks, brother. Bring them over here, please."*

The sweet scent of lavender tickled his nose. He breathed in deeply. There was something else. The metallic tang of blood. Was she injured? Or was it just his and Shadow's blood on her hands?

He scanned her carefully but didn't see any injuries. Just her chattering teeth and blue lips. He grabbed the first cloak from Shadow, doing his best with one arm to wrap it around her before setting her gently on the boat floor beside him. Then he draped the second cloak around them both and stretched out behind her, pulling her back against his chest. Trying to ignore the memories that fought to surface.

How many times had they lain like this? Curled up together, laughing, spent, contentment bubbling up inside, overflowing.

He pushed the thought aside. This was not the same. It would likely never be like that between them again. He just had to keep her alive. Keep her alive so she could return the favor.

"C'mon, you, too. She needs the body heat."

Shadow settled down in front of her, and Conall lifted the cloak again, draping it over all three of them the best he could. Another scent drifted toward him through the fabric. Something familiar, but with the pain in his limbs screaming at him and exhaustion making his eyelids droop, he couldn't place it. Maybe in the morning, it would come to him.

Conall woke with the dawn. Waves lapped against the hull. The croak of some distant reptiles and nearby birds trilled in his ears. Lavender lingered in his nose. The canoe's gentle swaying and the warm weight pressed against his chest sought to lull him back to sleep. But the pain, ever present, decided for him.

He yawned, stretching his sore muscles. His good arm tingled as he rolled it out from underneath his neck.

When he flexed the fingers on his wounded arm, his cheeks heated. At some point in the night, his hand had slipped beneath the cloak wrapped around Ereni's waist, and he found himself holding a handful of warm flesh. He gently removed his hand, careful not to wake her.

Wait—why was his hand wet? His stomach dropped.

The memory of that metallic scent last night made him jerk his hand back, much too sharply for his wounded shoulder. He bit back the cry that rose in his throat and prepared himself for the sight of crimson staining his fingers. But his brows rose instead. His hand glistened with moisture, his fingers slightly pruned, but not a hint of pink painted his skin.

He blew out a shaky exhale. She must be sweating. It wasn't that surprising; she had just spent half the night penned in with a man at her back, a furred wolf on her chest, and two cloaks draped atop her.

He sat up gingerly, flinging the top cloak aside.

"Shadow, wake up. We did our job too well. Ereni's sweating through her coveralls."

Conall paused. That scent he couldn't quite place last night drifted through the air. It was so familiar. He grabbed the cloak and pulled it to his nose, breathing deep.

"Little brother?"

"Hold on a moment." He closed his eyes, bunching the fabric in his hands, sniffing it all over. This was definitely where it was coming from. Herbs of all kinds and hints of flowers, just like when his sister opened up that pack she always carried with her. His eyes widened, his fingers slipping into the pockets. Tiny specks of dirt crumpled beneath his fingers. *"This is Lark's cloak. What is Ereni doing with Lark's cloak?"*

Shadow met his gaze, his nose twitching. *"That's not the only question you should be asking. Human sweat rarely smells this"*—he dipped his snout down, taking another long sniff of Ereni's torso—*"sweet."*

Conall blinked repeatedly, shaking his head. Ereni still slept, oblivious, her back facing him. He gently grabbed her shoulder and rolled her onto her back. Shaking fingers peeled back the cloak wrapped around her chest. The entire front of her coveralls was soaked down to her belly, staining the light gray fabric to a deep charcoal.

"What the blazes?" he said aloud.

Ereni's eyes popped open. Her gaze flicked between him and Shadow, both practically atop her, staring down at her intently. Then she shot up, scrambling away, her legs catching in the cloak and knocking her to her hands and knees before she got far. The boat rocked precariously in the water, and she groaned.

"Calm down." Conall gripped a bench as the water sloshed up along the sides. "You'll knock us into the bog if you're not careful."

"What happened? The last thing I remember I was on watch..." She rolled to face him and shuddered, tugging the cloak higher on her body.

"You fell asleep. Shadow and I woke in the night and found you half frozen. We warmed you with body heat."

Her brows furrowed an instant before her head bowed. "Thank you."

He scoffed. "Sure. Tell me, though." He held the cloak aloft. "What are you doing with my sister's cloak?"

She met his gaze, lips pursed. "It's a long story."

"We've got time." He opened his arms wide to illustrate his point, but the motion set off a shooting pain in his wounded shoulder, and he winced.

"At least let me heal you first," she insisted. She scooted closer on the boat bottom and settled down beside his broken ankle. In the bright morning light, the wound looked even more painful than it felt. His leg throbbed and stuck out at an unnatural angle.

She stared at him, a brow arched. He nodded his assent. She was right. He'd dealt with the pain long enough.

She started digging in a pack. He peered at it curiously, opening his mouth to ask if that was Lark's bag, but he closed it again when he got a close look at it. Lark's bag was plain brown; this one was dyed with bright stripes of rainbow shades.

"I'm afraid this will hurt. I need to set the bones straight before the healing." She thrust something in his direction. "Here, you can bite down on this."

Smooth leather slid across his hands. A knife sheath. The thought of her with a knife set off a momentary jolt of panic before it dissipated. He slipped the sheath between his lips and bit down, closing his eyes.

If Ereni had wanted him dead, she could've simply let the bog carry him away. She certainly wouldn't be going to all this trouble to heal him, just to turn around and stab him in the back. But why? He still hadn't figured her out. Had she only saved him so he could live to see through the battle to come? Or was there another reason—

Snap.

He screamed around the leather, the pain so sharp and strong he fell back, slapping his wounded shoulder against the hard boat bottom. But even that was nothing compared to the agony that tore up his leg, radiating from his ankle all the way up his thigh like a bolt of lightning.

He opened his eyes and spat out the sheath, breathing hard. His leg was straight once again, but now fresh blood gushed out from his boot, the throbbing so intense he could barely keep his eyes open.

Ereni slid her hand beneath his boot, sending another jolt of pain up his leg. "Call on your talent."

Conall sucked in a series of deep breaths, trying to concentrate.

"Now, please."

"I'm trying," he bit out between clenched teeth.

"Sorry, take your time." Ereni's cheeks flushed.

Conall closed his eyes. Lark. He focused on her image in his mind.

Warmth spread along his leg an instant before the boat trembled. The vibration worked its way through his skin, deep in his muscles, rattling his bones. A wave of weariness washed over him just before the pain in his leg vanished.

He forced his eyelids open as Ereni's hand slid out of his boot. He twisted his ankle experimentally. No pain. Normal range of motion. His mouth quirked up in a crooked grin.

Ereni scooted closer. Her breath warmed his cheek as she reached across his chest and lifted his tunic gently, placing her hand on his wounded shoulder. She met his gaze. "Once more."

Again, he closed his eyes. The warmth, the tremor, the weariness, each washed over him again until the pain receded.

He opened his eyes to find Ereni slipping her hand away. He clasped her wrist before she could retreat. Something wasn't right. Her face was pallid, her body trembling. The cloak wrapped around her slipped down, showcasing the darkened stain spread across her front.

"What's wrong? Are you hurt, too?" He stared down at her chest.

She tugged her arm. He loosened his hold, only to watch her wrap her arms around her middle, bowing her head. She shook even harder, saying nothing.

"Ereni," he gripped her shoulders, "tell me. We can heal you, too."

"There's no need." Her voice was a fragile, thready thing, like a single string of silk stretched taut. "Lark already healed me."

Conall frowned at his sister's name. Is that how Ereni came across her cloak? But why did Ereni end up with *it* and not his sister? If it wasn't pain wracking her... He sucked in a breath, his gut clenching. What had she done?

"Then what's wrong? Tell me what happened." He tilted her chin until she met his gaze. Her eyes were flooded with tears, her lips quivering. Conall bit back a gasp, his eyes widening at the guilt and shame writ across her features.

"I-I left her." It was as if she'd erected a dam around her emotions that suddenly collapsed. Tears spilled down her cheeks, her breath heaving in and out in great gasps.

Conall dropped her shoulders, backing away. "What did you do to my sister, Ereni? Where is Lark?"

Ereni shot him a glare, eyes like knives. "Your sister is fine. I'm not talking about *her*." The indignation slipped, replaced with another wave of sorrow engulfing her so strongly it was palpable. "Violet. I-I left her behind."

Conall rubbed his temples, his thoughts spinning. Whoever Violet was, she was obviously important if she was causing this reaction from Ereni. He'd never seen her cry. Just like her mother, she was always so strong. Fierce.

He scooted closer and pulled her into his arms. Ereni tensed for an instant, but then she melted into his embrace, her body wracked with silent shudders.

"It's all right," he said, even though he wasn't sure it was or ever would be.

Lavender drifted up to his nose from her hair. And beneath that, another scent rose. Sweet and subtle but nonetheless distinct. A scent he couldn't remember smelling for many years. Not since his mother held his newborn sister to her breast.

"Ereni." He drew back, holding her at arm's length. "Who is Violet?"

Her answer shattered his heart. "Our daughter."

Chapter 14

"What?" Conall backed away further, until his back rammed into the wooden seat behind him. He must not have heard her right. "How could that be?"

"Do you think I would lie about this?" Ereni hissed. She tugged down the cloak and pulled the soaked coveralls away from her heaving chest. "Is this a lie, too?"

"Forgive me if I don't take every word of yours as gospel," he muttered, crossing his arms.

Ereni stared back at him, the red in her cheeks fading, her eyes turning glassy. She pulled her knees against her chest and curled into a ball on the canoe's floor, her shoulders shuddering.

Conall had to stop himself from pulling her close again. Growing up without a father, with a mother and sister to protect, he couldn't stand the sight of a woman crying. But he needed space. He had to think.

It just didn't add up. It was true they'd lain together. She'd even admitted she wanted his child. But the timing was off. This was months too soon.

Had she been pregnant already when they'd first met?

No, even that timing made no sense. Her belly would've been heavy already, not flat like he remembered.

A strangled sob broke his line of thought. It certainly would explain the way she was acting now. Having a midwife for a mother, he'd heard stories about women reacting strangely after birth, all their emotions worn on their sleeve. Sometimes even making them act irrationally. Harming themselves.

His gaze landed on the empty sheaf sitting on the canoe floor. Then at the sack curled up by her feet.

Whatever he did, he needed to tread carefully.

Conall inched closer. The canoe swayed.

"Don't touch me." She curled up even more, her voice thick with anguish.

He halted. "I won't," he whispered. Then he snatched the bag away from her, smiling triumphantly.

She peeked at him and rolled her bloodshot eyes before her head sank to her knees again. "Have it. It's not even mine."

Conall shoved the bag behind him, not bothering to open it. "Can you just explain it to me?" He winced at his tone. Forced his voice to soften. "Please?"

"Isn't it obvious?" she said. "I summoned without a source."

Conall rocked back, his hand flying to his chest. Of course. How hadn't he seen it? It was the only explanation that made any sense.

"We have a child," he stated flatly. "Are you sure she's mine?"

That was obviously the wrong thing to say. She glared at him, venomous. "Yes."

Conall bristled. "The prince—"

"He never touched me," she bit out, practically seething. She turned away from him again, hiding her face.

Shadow had been so quiet while all this was happening that Conall had almost forgotten he was there. But as silence descended on the canoe again, broken by the occasional sob from Ereni, he spoke. *"What's happening?"*

Conall flinched, his gaze shooting to Shadow. *"I-I—Sh-she."* He drew a deep breath. It was all so bizarre he was stuttering in his thoughts. *"She had a baby. A little girl. My little girl."*

"A cub? That's good news." Shadow's tail wagged. He tilted his head. *"Did you not want a cub?"*

Conall shook his head. *"It's not that simple."* He closed his eyes. Was that even true? Or was he just being stubborn and too quick to believe the worst? First with his father, and now Ereni.

Lark's words on the boat rang in his ears. "People make mistakes," she'd said. From where he was sitting, Ereni's mistakes were myriad. He'd not even had the chance to question her about her betrayal at the Palisade, and here she was admitting to another.

"Why did you leave her?" His voice came out surprisingly even for how much the question weighed on his shoulders.

Ereni sniffed. She was silent for so long he started to believe she wasn't planning to answer. But then she lifted her head and met his gaze. "I didn't want her to grow up without her father."

Her words hit like a punch to the gut. She'd left their daughter to save him?

He opened his mouth.

"Little brother, someone's here."

He snapped his mouth shut, his head swiveling around, searching.

"Wh—" Ereni began.

He thrust out a hand to cut her off as the sound of chattering men rose in the distance.

"Get down," Ereni mouthed, barely audible, catching his eye and slinking down against the boat's bottom.

Conall frowned, following her lead. Shadow lay down, too, without having to be told.

He hadn't given their location much thought, what with everything happening within their canoe, but as he crouched unmoving on the boat's bottom, he took a closer look around.

It appeared that Ereni had chosen the mangrove she'd tied them to carefully. Their canoe sheltered within a pocket of water between two massive trees. They would need to maneuver backward to make their way out to the main waterway, but the spot had one advantage: they were practically hidden. With all three of them crouched down, only a small amount of the hull would be visible to anyone floating by.

His gaze flicked to Ereni. The sadness that had been so evident in her features had been pushed aside. She was on alert; her face pressed to the boat's side, gaze lifted just high enough to peek over the edge.

She'd been expecting this... What else wasn't she telling him?

He slid beside her as the voices came closer. Soon they drew near enough he could make out much of what they were saying, though he still couldn't see anyone between the twisted branches they hid behind.

"Are you sure we're headed the right way?" asked a man with a deep baritone.

"Do I look like an idiot to you?" a different voice answered, this one nasal and edged with steel. "This'll lead us back to the docks."

"I still don't know why we're going back," a third voice piped in. "I'm not gonna let them lock me up again."

Conall's stomach sank. He shot Ereni a sideways glare, but she didn't deign to meet his eye, her gaze still locked on the water beyond their hiding spot.

"We won't let 'em catch us. Besides, you heard the guards before they ditched us. The city is about to be overrun by monsters." Steel Voice chuckled. "Pathetic scared fools, the lot of 'em. We'll have the city to ourselves, I bet."

The waterway rippled, waves spreading down the stream and gently swaying their boat side to side. Out in the waterway, a canoe appeared around a corner, and Conall's throat went dry.

A muscular man stood, shoving a long pole down into the bog, a cudgel strapped to his back. Two more men sat inside, loaded down with more weapons, looking just as menacing. All three sported matching gray coveralls, just like the ones Ereni wore.

What was he to think of that? Had she been locked up, too?

"I wouldn't mind running into Lady Death again," one of the seated men mused, licking his lips. "That was one nice piece of ass."

Another canoe turned the corner, with three more men inside. And then a third and fourth. All of them shared a laugh and murmured agreements while a sick feeling spread in Conall's gut. He clenched his fist so hard his nails dug into his palm, lest he send a wave of water spilling them all into the bog.

But then Steel Voice spoke up again. Conall could put a face to the voice. He was a hulking, balding fellow with a crooked nose and a bevy of scars covering his skin beneath the rolled-up sleeves of his coveralls. "You have fun with that. Won't catch me inviting a mage into my bed. If I see either of those witches again, I'll slit their throats."

Conall held in a breath, his burning lungs a welcome distraction from the images swirling through his mind. From the way Ereni stiffened at the statement, he had no doubt that she was one of the mages they were currently laughing at and plotting to slaughter. Was Lark the other? What had happened? It took everything in him to stay still and silent, his body thrumming with rage.

Conall released the breath as the boats slid away. The echoes of the men's cruel laughter bounced off the water and burned inside his ears.

Once the laughter faded, he grabbed Ereni's shoulder, twisted her to face him, and lifted a brow. "Who are they? What aren't you telling me?"

She only swallowed and lifted a shaky finger to her lips. Then she brushed his hand off her shoulder and stood, making her way to the boat's bow and untying the rope that tied them to the mangrove.

Conall snatched the long pole off the side holder and readied to push as soon as she detached the rope. Ereni met his gaze and frantically pointed in the opposite direction the men had headed.

Soon they were out in the open waterway, gliding away from their hiding spot. It wasn't until they'd turned at least half a dozen times that Ereni finally spoke, her voice barely louder than a whisper.

"They're prisoners. The worst of the worst. The prince left them locked in Southmoat Prison rather than evacuate them with all the other citizens." She sighed. "I guess no one told your sister that. I happened to be walking by the prison and heard something. It's lucky I decided to investigate. The two of us barely made it out of there."

He sucked in a shaky breath. "Did they hurt you?" He exhaled, the lust in the one fiend's voice clear in his mind. "Did they *touch* you? My sister—"

Ereni shook her head quickly. "No. From the looks of it, Lark made them regret trying."

Conall jabbed the pole into the murky water again. Why would Lark try to free criminals? Yet again, it wasn't too surprising. "Lark has always been the type to rush in to save anyone who needs help."

Ereni nodded. "I gathered as much." A tiny smile curved the corners of her lips. "That's why I left Violet with her."

Conall stiffened. "You brought a baby into a prison?"

"No," Ereni replied woodenly. "I didn't have her yet."

"Wait, what?"

"We hid underwater while the prisoners fled through the docks." She shrugged. "We needed to breathe."

Conall almost dropped the pole. "You *just* had a baby. Yesterday?"

Ereni's gaze turned murderous. "Yes."

Conall stopped poling. "If Lark and Violet are back there, then why are we going in the opposite direction?"

"Keep pushing, Conall."

"Not until you answer my question."

"I already tried returning after I pulled you and Shadow out of the bog." Her voice was quiet, filled with a note of defeat. "There's nothing to go back to. Southmoat has fallen. Those men will be heading back this way eventually, and I'd rather not get my throat slit."

Conall's mind raced. What should they do now? "What about the ocean? Shouldn't we be heading for the ocean docks to meet up with the others?"

Ereni shook her head. "The bog doesn't lead to the Eprora Ocean near Flamesmoat. Only the Orddon Ocean to the east and south to Raimire."

If that was true, then his plan to reach the docks last night had never had any chance of success. If Ereni hadn't gone after them...

Conall thrust down on the pole, and the boat picked up speed. "And you know where you're going?"

"Not exactly." She grimaced. "But what other choice do we have? Dracwood is crawling with scourge now."

"No, you're right," he conceded. "Lark and Kayda will head to Joria next, and then north up the coast to the Abandoned Lands. If we can make it to the Orddon, we might have a chance of catching up with them."

"Princess Kayda was with you?" Ereni asked, a single brow arching.

Conall shot her a glare. "Happy to see all your schemes falling into place?"

Ereni frowned. "It's not like that."

"Isn't it?" He scoffed. "Seems to me that all of you mages have been itching for the three of us to fight in the Abandoned Lands for centuries now."

Ereni wrapped her arms around her legs.

"Did you see it, too? Have you met the Winter Witch?"

The startled look in her eyes was enough of an answer. A thought jumped out at him, one that hadn't crossed his mind before, and it settled in his gut like a sunken stone.

"Did you know who I was from the very start? Did you recognize me back in the *Greenvale Inn*?" He drew in a deep breath, his brow wrinkling. "Did your mother send you to seduce me?"

Her gaze burned into his again. "What? Don't be ridiculous, she would never ask that of me."

He didn't miss that she hadn't denied his first accusation. "What do you expect me to believe after what happened? After what you did?"

"I'm sorry for that. Truly, I am. But the wall had to fall. And you couldn't follow me. You *had* to journey north with Mother. Can't you see that now?"

"Why didn't you just tell me that? You lied to me, Ereni. You threatened Shadow. You killed those mages who helped me bring down the Palisade. Am I just supposed to forget about that?"

Ereni shook her head. "I don't expect you to understand." She sighed.

Conall turned another bend and spotted a small, marshy island stretching out between a dense thicket of mangroves to their left. He directed the canoe toward it.

"Where are you going?" Ereni asked.

"I need to stretch my legs." Really, he desperately needed to relieve his bladder, but he was hoping she'd read between the lines.

She seemed to understand, and after scanning behind them, she nodded, gripping her legs tightly. "Me too," she admitted.

He pushed up to the island, and Ereni hopped up to tie the canoe to a mangrove's roots. "I'll be right back," he called over his shoulder, hopping out, Shadow at his heels. Maybe he should've offered to let her go first, but he wasn't feeling particularly generous at the moment.

His stomach churned. Ever since he'd brought up the Palisade falling, he couldn't stop picturing it in his mind. Remembering the agony and betrayal he'd grappled with in that moment, like she'd torn out his heart and stomped on it.

She didn't expect him to understand? That's all she had to say?

He took care of his business quickly and strode back to the water. Shadow stayed behind on the island, digging at a corner of the marshy soil.

"Your turn." He seated himself back inside the canoe.

Ereni stood, meeting his gaze. She looked like she wanted to say something, but after a moment, she dropped her gaze and wordlessly climbed out and onto the island.

Conall kept his stare trained on the water, watching for signs of the men behind them. How had he gotten into this mess? Running from criminals and separated from all of his friends. Stuck on a tiny boat with the woman who'd betrayed him. He sure had the best luck these days.

Shadow returned a few moments later, licking his chops.

"What did you find?" Conall asked, his stomach rumbling at the thought of food.

"Frog. You want me to find another?"

Conall grimaced. *"I'll pass."*

His gaze lit on the rainbow-colored pack he'd stashed beneath the aft seat. He opened it up and dug inside, finding a full waterskin and a pouch stuffed full of jerky. After quickly cramming a mouthful of jerky into his mouth and taking a swig of the water, he continued to dig.

His blood went cold. There was no knife. The sheaf still sat empty on the boat's bottom, but the knife...

Why wasn't Ereni back yet? Conall jumped up, swallowing. Panic made his feet feel like they were encased in rock, every step a struggle.

She wouldn't do something stupid... would she?

He raced behind a pair of mangroves, his boots slipping in the marshy soil. Then he spotted her, an arm's length away, her back turned to him, just lifting the coveralls back over her shoulders.

She spun at the sound of his approach. Her cheeks flushed, and she quickly wrenched the front of the coveralls closed. But not before he glimpsed the dark purple lines snaking across her stomach.

She sputtered, indignation flashing across her face, but before she could say a word, Conall grabbed her and slapped a hand over her mouth. Her eyes widened as he shook his head slowly, staring pointedly behind her.

"Did you hear something?" a hushed voice said an instant later.

Conall stood still, angling him and Ereni behind the mangrove as best he could, praying whoever the voice belonged to would leave them in peace. A moment later, a boat slid by, filled with more rough men dressed in coveralls. None of these he recognized from earlier. How many of them were on the loose?

"I don't hear nothing. Probably just some wild animal," a different man replied. "Keep pushing. If we don't find a way out of this maze soon, I'm gonna go crazy."

Conall held his breath, waiting. Luckily, their boat was heading away from where they'd tied their canoe, so they didn't need to worry about this group catching them—for now. Finally, he judged the boat far enough away to be out of earshot. He released Ereni and backed away, his gaze slipping down the front of her shirt, still gaping open.

She was quick to tug it closed again. "Do you mind?"

"Blazes," he snapped back. "Did you want me to let them find you?"

She finished forcing the buttons back in place and threw up her hands. "Don't do me any more favors. I can take care of myself." Then she stormed off, back to the canoe.

Conall followed behind her, rolling his eyes. This was shaping up to be a fun voyage.

Chapter 15

Lark stared at the blue sea, the tingle of static and moisture in the air surrounding her. Mages at the bow took turns coaxing the water and air currents to their will, leaving a constant grin on Captain Jayan's face, even in the face of shallow waters that few dared sail.

"Incredible, isn't it?" Mika said, stopping beside her. "Here I thought I'd only ever see magic used for healing."

"Yeah, it's pretty amazing." She met his gaze. "How are you doing? We haven't talked since you got back from Northmoat."

It had been two days since they departed the waters off the coast of Dracwood. Mika had been keeping to himself, barely even interacting with the people he'd come with from Raimire.

She'd seen how failing to save the king had affected Kayda. Was it weighing on Mika, too?

He curled a hand through his wild brown hair. A slanted smile crossed his lips. "Have you been looking for me, then?"

"Sure. We were going to train together, weren't we?" Maybe if she could convince him to a join her for a training session, he would open up about what was bothering him.

He chuckled. "Well, if the story of the babe's birth that Dausius has been telling is true, you might have a few things to teach me."

Lark's cheeks warmed. "Oh, you know Daus. He could watch someone washing dirty socks and spin it into a grand adventure."

Mika leaned closer, his golden-brown eyes meeting hers. So close she noticed little flecks of copper in his irises sparkling in the sun. "Is that all it was?" His smile widened. "Somehow, I doubt that."

Mika straightened, breaking eye contact and glancing over her shoulder. "Ah, here's the little one now."

Lark sucked in a breath, strangely jittery all of a sudden. Must be all the magic in the air.

She turned and waved to her approaching friends, Tiora, Meital, and Mazen. Violet cooed in Mazen's arms, her eyes wide open and a tiny line of drool hanging out of her mouth.

"Lark, I've been looking for you." Tiora stopped beside her, brow furrowing. "Actually, it's the princess who's looking for you. She stopped me on the way up from Violet's nap to ask me to send you and Aren her way when we saw you."

Lark sighed. "I guess I better go see what she needs."

"We haven't spotted Aren yet." Meital tilted her head, her gaze flicking to Mika.

"I'll get him. He's with Muse." Lark rubbed Violet's tiny hand. "Do you mind watching Violet a little longer?"

"No, not at all," Mazen chimed in, a mischievous grin on his face. "Meital and I are planning on making her part of our act." He feigned tossing her, earning a set of gasps from Tiora and Meital.

Lark rolled her eyes, spinning on her heel to leave. "I'll be back soon," she called over her shoulder.

Her boots tapped on the deck, a pleasant breeze blowing through her long brown curls. But a thread of tension spooled in Lark's belly as she made her way closer to the aft rail where she knew Aren would be, keeping watch over Whisper and Muse as they soared through the sky, hunting for seabirds.

What could Kayda want? She wasn't surprised she'd asked to speak to her. After all, they had shared history now. And with everything happening in Flamesmoat, there'd been little time to discuss Jett or how they were suddenly related in a very real way.

But Aren... Why would she be asking for him, too?

Soon she caught sight of Aren, leaning against the rail, a wide brimmed hat shading his face, and his gaze on the sky. In the distance, two little specks circled high in the clouds. Lark's breath caught as he turned at the sound of her boots and graced her with a smile.

"Hey." Aren tilted his hat up slightly, his blue eyes meeting hers. "Have you come to watch Muse?"

Lark smiled back, placing a steadying hand on the rail beside him. "No, I came for you."

She cringed inwardly, her cheeks warming. She hadn't meant that to sound so forward.

"Oh?" He grinned. "Did you need my help with something?"

"Yes." She brushed her brown curls out of her face. "Kayda wants to see both of us for some reason. Tiora just told me." She shot a glance at her boots. "I was about to head to her room now..."

"Well, I'll come with you. Let me just signal for the birds." He raised his arm high in the air, and soon, the birds swooped down to land gracefully on the railing.

"Good flying today," Muse said as she landed. *"Not enough seabirds this far off the coast, though."*

"Sorry to cut your session short. I need to borrow Aren for a moment."

"Borrow him? Is that what you're calling it now? Ha."

Lark clicked her tongue. What was that supposed to mean?

But then Aren reached into his pack and pulled out some meat. Muse's gaze zeroed in on the morsel.

Lark shook her head, letting the matter rest. There was no use talking to her when she was eating. Gluttonous little thing.

Aren turned to her. "Ready?"

She nodded and followed him to the closest hatch leading into the inner part of the boat. *Nova's Champion* was a large vessel, originally used for trade before being commandeered by Kayda off the coast of Dracwood. A multitude of rooms spread out below deck, some filled with rows of hammocks, many occupied as the night shift rested. Even more rooms lay empty or were filled with stacked crates and boxes.

It wasn't until they neared the forward hull that they reached the hall that led to Kayda's room. The hallways here were lined with oil lamps instead of the stubby candles affixed in place on the other parts of the ship. Threadbare tapestries were tacked to the wooden walls, showcasing scenes of sea serpents and lush, green islands floating in the sea.

"This is it." Lark stopped beside a closed door. She knocked.

"Come in."

Lark opened the door and stepped inside. The room was small but brightly lit from glass windows along the far wall, the dark blue curtains tied back. A wide wooden desk, scarred with countless gouges, sat front and center. A single hammock hung suspended from the ceiling in the corner.

As they entered, Kayda rose from a wooden chair behind the desk and closed the cover of the book she'd been reading. It was the same ancient book Conall had brought back with him from his adventures in Doln with the Sade Prim.

Lark's curiosity grew. Had Kayda found something in the old tome she wanted to discuss?

But Kayda left the book behind, circling around the desk to greet them. "Lark, Aren, thank you for coming so quickly. I have a problem I'm hoping you can help me with."

Aren clutched his hat in his hands. He shared a glance with Lark before meeting the princess' eyes. "How can we help?"

"We'll be reaching Joria in a few days. I've been planning to send a fast-sailing ship to Doln, to request aid meet us on the Abandoned Land's coast. But Izora told me the tale of how they knew I'd survived the last battle there, and it got me thinking."

Lark nodded, wondering where she was going with this. Did she want the two of them on that ship?

"Apparently there was a pair of cousins passing notes between Flamesmoat and Joria with trained doves. We don't have any doves on board, but I wonder if maybe Muse or Whisper would be up for the task."

Lark's eyes widened. "You want Muse to deliver a message to Doln?" She shook her head, her stomach clenching at the thought of sending her off on her own. "She's never been to Doln."

Aren leaned forward and captured her gaze. "Whisper has. He grew up in the mews in Clan Chief Aundrea's household, in Gransea. The two of them together could make it there, I expect."

Lark frowned. "Are you sure they'll be all right?"

"Sure, why wouldn't they? And they'll arrive there and return back much faster than any sailboat." Aren smiled at Kayda. "It's a clever plan, Princess."

Kayda rubbed her arm and grinned back at Aren before turning to Lark and meeting her gaze with a look of concern. "I know it's a lot to ask, separating you from your bondmate, Lark. I wouldn't ask if it wasn't so important. If the warriors from Doln don't meet us in time..."

Lark bit her lip. "No, you're right. We need all the help we can get."

"Good." Kayda's face lit up. "I'll prepare a parchment for Chief Aundrea and have it ready by morning. Thank you."

Lark forced a smile. "Happy to help." She whirled around to leave. "I better go check on Violet."

"Goodbye, Princess." Aren followed, closing the door behind him.

Lark shuffled a few paces away before Aren caught up to her. He slipped a hand around her elbow, stopping her in the empty hall. "Hey, they'll be all right. Muse and Whisper are a formidable pair."

Lark peeked up at him, blinking quickly. "I know. It's just hard knowing we'll be apart for so long." She sighed.

"But that's not all, is it?"

She grimaced. "No." All the events of the last few days swirled around her mind, pressing down on her shoulders. "Conall's gone again, and I have Violet to care for, and the battle looming. Everything's changing so fast. I just wish I could slow it all down. Get a chance to breathe." She wrinkled her nose, straightening her back. "But I'll be all right."

Aren stared down at her, brow furrowed. Then he let go of her elbow, smiling widely. "Follow me." He beckoned her down the hall.

Lark watched curiously as he stopped in front of a doorway a few feet away, sticking his ear to the door. He listened for a few heartbeats, then shook his head and strode to the next doorway, repeating the action there.

"What are you doing?" Lark quirked a brow and crossed her arms as he stopped beside a third door.

"Shh." He propped his ear on it and must've found what he was searching for. His smile widened, and he fitted his hand on the knob, slowly opening the door and peering within. Then he grabbed her hand and tugged, and they both spilled inside the room, the door banging closed behind them.

Lark giggled, scanning the room. Pots and pans hung on the walls. A hearty stew bubbled nearby, and knives and various half-cut vegetables decorated a nearby countertop.

"What are we doing in here?" She strode to the counter and lifted a carrot. "Did you need a snack?"

"No. I'm just stealing you a moment to think." He grinned, leaning back against the door. "No one ought to come looking for you here."

Lark's heart was like that stew, full and bubbling. She spent all her time taking care of everyone else. It was so nice to have someone worried about her for a change. And not just anyone.

Her mind flashed back to the kiss they'd shared. She could see from the casual way Aren stood, his back pressed to the door, giving her all the space to do whatever she wanted, he'd not brought her in here intending to repeat that kiss. But they were alone. And she found she couldn't think about anything else.

She glanced up at him and glided away from the counter, back toward the door. Back to Aren.

"I've been meaning to ask, how is your sunburn healing?" She reached up tentatively, gently tugging at the collar of his shirt. "Do you want me to take another look at it for you?"

He met her gaze, and his smile brightened. His chest rose as her fingers grazed his skin. But the words he said next had a hard edge. "I didn't bring you here for more work, Lark." He enclosed her hand within his.

"I know you didn't." She blushed, staring down at her feet. "But I don't want to think right now." She peeked up at him, meeting his gaze, her heart thrumming madly.

"No?" His gaze zeroed in on her lips, and her stomach clenched. "What do you want?"

For once, she didn't care a bit about being forward. "You."

That one word was all it took for his lips to descend on hers. She pushed up on her tiptoes, meeting him halfway. The swish of fabric fell to the floor, and then Aren spun her and pressed her against the wall next to the door, his hands tight on her waist.

Lark lost herself in his kiss. Her hands bunched in the silk of his shirt, and she pulled him closer, wedging herself against the hard plane of his chest. Her mind stopped spinning, all the fears and plans for the future slipping out of her mind.

Her world narrowed down to this moment with this man. The blood pounding through her veins. The giddy, wonderful rush of sensation she felt when she was in his arms.

A deafening clang shattered the air. Aren jumped back, breathing heavily. Lark's eyes popped open, and her jaw dropped as she spotted an angry man banging a pot just behind them, the door wide open.

Her face burned. When had he come in? She certainly hadn't noticed the door open or any sound until that awful clamor began.

The chef—she guessed, being as they were in the galley and this man wore a stained apron atop plain cotton clothes—was red faced as well. "Out! Out with you, ya randy buggers," he yelled, shooing them out the door. "Worse than the sailors, you are."

Aren bent down to scoop up his crumpled hat, and they wasted no time hustling out of the room and down the hall.

Lark laughed. "I wasn't expecting that today."

Aren stopped her before they reached the outer hatch. "Lark, I didn't want to..." He trailed off, shaking his head.

Lark frowned, her stomach sinking.

"Not that," he hurried to say. He straightened his hat in his hands. "I wanted to kiss you." He met her gaze, smiling gently. "I just don't want to be another thing that's changing too fast for you. You just finished telling me you needed to slow down, and then I—"

She squeezed his arm. "You're not. I wanted to kiss you, too." Warmth spread in her chest as she beamed back at him. She leaned closer, wetting her lips.

A door somewhere in the hall slammed open, and she flinched. Damn crowded ship. But the noise was another reminder of everything she had to accomplish. As much as she wanted to hide away with Aren, there were things to do. The world didn't stop just because someone wanted to kiss her.

She sighed, pushing open the hatch. "C'mon. We better go break the news to Muse and Whisper."

Chapter 16

Kayda approached Jayan at the helm. A cloud of haze drifted off the ocean in the early morning hours, thickening even more with the mages' constant stream of magic boosting their speed.

"Good morning, Jayan." She handed him a warm cup of tea. "Are we still on track for Port Joria this afternoon?"

"This morning, I expect. Those mages of yours really speed things up. I've never seen anything like it." He swigged from the cup and grimaced, squinting at the horizon. "Once all this mist clears, we should have a clear view of the coast."

Kayda took a deep breath. "I have a favor to ask you."

"Whatever it is, consider it done, Prin— er, Kayda." He grinned.

She raised a brow. "That so? And what if I asked you to throw yourself overboard?"

Jayan pursed his lips and set down his teacup on the deck, then shrugged. "I reckon I could stand a swim." He lifted a foot, untying the laces of his boot.

Kayda nudged his hand aside. "Stop." She laughed. "I'm only joking."

She shook her head. The fool man likely would do anything she asked. But just because his loyalty knew no bounds, she wouldn't take advantage of it.

Jayan straightened, running a hand through his braids. "So, what is it then, if I won't be swimming?"

"On our trip to Sul Hollow, I couldn't convince Lazar to join us. My nurse, Izora, has ties there. She's agreed to travel there to speak with him on my behalf."

"And you want me to tag along?"

Kayda nodded. "I wish I could go with you, but there's too much to do in Joria and not enough time. Do you min—"

"Aye, like I said, consider it done." Jayan grinned again.

Kayda smiled back, then let out a sigh. That's one less task she needed to worry about. Hopefully Izora and Jayan could convince the Sul to fight at their sides.

"Thank you, Jayan. I'll leave you to it, then." She turned to leave, but he caught her arm.

"You take care of yourself while I'm gone." His fingers slid down to her wrist, and he clasped her hand, leaning close. "The Jorians are a strange breed. Half of them would sell their own mother if it would make them a profit." He squeezed once, then dropped her hand and grabbed the helm. "Just be careful who you trust."

She flashed him a half-smile. "I will."

The warning didn't help to ease her anxiety as they sailed closer to port, but she knew she'd be wise to heed his words. Things had changed a great deal since her last visit.

Without Druturion by her side, would the people of Joria still be eager to come to their aid? It was one thing to follow a dragon rider into battle, but now, she was just a displaced princess whose country was under siege.

And she still had the deal with Wyll to solidify. Her father had grudgingly agreed to the terms—her hand in marriage for his family's fleet of ships—but she had a feeling that any wrong move could see the tentative agreement broken.

She wasn't worried about Wyll. Her future husband would likely charm her father easily. But his uncle might be a different story. She had to hope that Wyll's claim about his uncle's desire to have a royal connection at any cost was enough to calm his temper.

Kayda made her way to the forward rail as the mists dissipated, chased away by the bright dawn sun. The noisy hustle on deck was muted with most of the passengers still sleeping.

But not everyone rested. Lark stood at the rail beside a trio of mages at work directing the ocean currents in the sea below.

Lark turned as Kayda approached, no doubt alerted by the gentle tapping of Kayda's boots on the polished deck. She cradled Violet in her arms, bouncing the wide-awake little babe gently.

"I see I'm not the only one who likes to rise early." Kayda aimed a grin at the babe.

"Violet isn't much of a sleeper. Funny thing is, she quiets down every time she's near the summoning at the bow."

"I'm not surprised. Magic is in her blood." Kayda stared into Violet's distinctive reddish-blue eyes. "Huh, in the right light, her eyes almost look violet. I wonder if that's why her mother chose the name?"

Lark smiled crookedly, peering down at Violet. "Yeah, you're right. But I don't know if that's why Ereni picked the name." Her smile faded. "Hopefully one day we can ask her."

Kayda didn't say as much, but she had a sinking feeling that Violet's name might remain a mystery. "We'll be docked in Joria for a few days before we head north. Are you and the show planning to do any entertaining?"

"Not me. I have to hire a new wet nurse for Violet, now that Elmena's leaving. And then Aren and I are planning to accompany Tiora to visit her family." Lark sighed deeply, staring at the sky.

"You're missing your bondmate?" Kayda asked.

"Yes, and no." Lark chuckled. "She certainly hasn't stopped chattering away in my head, no matter how far north she gets. Muse is not a fan of snow, I can tell you that much."

"Really?" Kayda's stomach clenched. "I wish it was like that with me and Dru."

"You can't hear him at all?"

Kayda frowned. "Not since we fled that island mountain top. I don't even know if he's still alive."

Lark squeezed her shoulder. "He is. He'll be back. I just know it."

"I hope you're right."

Without her bondmate by her side, the city appeared so much wilder and foreign. They were one of the few ships to approach the port from the south. Curious children and adults stopped to watch them pass, likely surprised to see a ship so large sailing the southern waters, which usually only the bravest of fisherman dared venture.

The city's southern stretches added to the strangeness. All along the coast, tiny huts and hovels crowded together, more dilapidated than the worst of the brick and wood buildings in Southmoat or the modest tile and clay huts in Joria's northern section.

Kayda's heart broke for the throngs of weary-eyed, malnourished people they passed. With so much wealth and plenty brought in by the silk trade, it was criminal these people were left to suffer.

She clutched the railing, hardening her heart to their plight. This was not her country. She was coming here to beg for help in dealing with the terrible destruction of her own lands. But one day, she would do what she could to set things right here. One day.

As the first glimpse of Port Joria rose in the far distance, Kayda made her way below deck. It was time to shuck off the casual silk shirt and cotton pants she'd grown so accustomed to on board and don something more befitting a princess.

She settled on the lovely golden silk dress Wyll had gifted her. As the smooth fabric slid on, her chest fluttered. Was it from the reminder of the tetrela's silken embrace, or her future husband's kiss?

It still felt so strange, knowing she would soon be wed. In truth, she wasn't ready. Not at all. But it was a sacrifice she was prepared to make. When Izora and Jayan returned with the Sul, they would need ships to bring them all north. She smoothed her sweaty palms down the shimmering silk. This was the only way.

A knock interrupted her musing.

"Come in," she said, pulling a brush through the tangled mess of red heaped atop her right shoulder.

King Gideon entered, smiling as he noted her attire. "You look lovely, Kayda." He twisted his nose, closing the door firmly behind him. "I wish you would let the rest of your hair out of those ridiculous braids, though."

Kayda's stomach flipped. She'd still not explained the story behind her new hairstyle to her father. Could she trust him now?

"You know we're in desperate need of the Sul aid. I thought it wise to adopt some of their customs."

Gideon scoffed. "I don't think the way you wear your hair is liable to matter to those hermits." Then he shook his head, sending her a tentative smile. "But then again, I was never much of a statesman. We'll be pulling into port in just a moment. Shall we head up?" He offered her his elbow.

Kayda set down the brush and grabbed his arm. Soon they were back on deck, watching the city grow large as they docked.

It was just how she remembered it. Sun-drenched and sandy, packed with colorful buildings and people dressed in even more colorful silks, many with their hair dyed to match.

It appeared Wyll had been hard at work while she was gone. The port was much more crowded than their last visit, with rows of ships much like *Nova's Champion* docked. People hustled about the decks, no doubt making ready to set sail.

"Hm, those aren't the type of folk I'd expected to see joining the fight," said a voice at her side. Jett stood beside her at the rail, squinting at the large ships as they passed.

Kayda spun back, her brow furrowing as she spotted all the bright silks the people wore. "They are a bit more finely dressed than I'd expected." She shrugged. "But of course, we are in the silk capital of the world."

Gideon chuckled, patting her arm. "You're right, my dear." He leaned forward and thrust a hand out in front of her toward Jett. "We haven't met. I'm Kayda's father, Gideon."

Jett grasped his hand and shook. "Jett."

Kayda leaned back, her gaze flicking between them as they shook. Time seemed to stand still. Her heart squeezed as she realized she was watching two cousins unwittingly meeting. With their differences in coloring—Jett tanned and dark-haired and Gideon pale and dirty-blond—it was easy to miss the signs of shared heritage. But the more she looked, the more similarities stuck out. They were both tall with strong chins and similar facial features—straight noses and high cheekbones.

Finally, their hands unclamped. Gideon glanced between her and Jett. "How did you two meet?"

Kayda's eyes widened, and she stiffened.

Jett opened his mouth.

"My king." Gawain stepped up beside them, and Kayda's shoulders slumped at the interruption. "You must allow me to accompany you ashore."

Gideon waved off the Guard Captain's concern. "Don't be silly. We're meeting with family. The princess and I will be fine on our own."

Gideon was right—only not about the family part. But they'd risk infuriating Wyll's father by showing up with a contingent of guards surrounding them. And she needed this meeting to go off without a hitch.

Kayda smiled at Gawain. "He's right, Gawain. With Jayan leaving, someone needs to protect the ship. Are you up for the task?"

Gawain's frown deepened, but he nodded. "Yes, I understand. I'll keep watch. Be safe, sire. My lady."

As the gangplank touched down on the wooden wharf, a grin crept across Kayda's lips. There was already one face in the crowd she recognized.

Wyll strode purposefully toward their ship, wearing a green silk suit, his dark curly hair just as perfectly coiffed as always. He captured her gaze and sent her a wide smile. There was that flutter again, spreading through her belly this time.

He met her and her father at the bottom of the gangplank. "Princess, it's a pleasure to see you back so soon."

"Father, this is Wyll," Kayda said. "Wyll, King Gideon of Flamesmoat."

"King..." Wyll's brow furrowed. "That must mean King Quinton..." He shook his head, then gentled his voice. "I'm so sorry for your loss, my dear."

Kayda bowed her head, pushing back the rush of grief that swamped her at the reminder. "Thank you," she murmured.

Wyll turned to her father. "But I suppose congratulations are in order, too. It's not every day we have the pleasure of hosting royalty in our fair city. I would be honored to invite you to breakfast at Oasis Manse."

"That would be lovely," Kayda said.

"Yes," King Gideon agreed. "I would be grateful for the opportunity to get to know you and your family better, son."

Wyll's smile tightened a fraction, then slipped right back into place. "They'll be excited to get to know you better as well, sire. I understand you never traveled to Joria before your betrothal to my late aunt."

"That's right." Gideon rubbed his brow, curling a lank blond strand off his forehead. "I had too many pressing engagements at the time to travel."

Kayda bit back the frown that threatened to spread. She hadn't known that... her father hadn't even bothered to meet the family of the woman he was to wed? No wonder the mages' plot to swap his wives went off without a hitch.

Wyll spread out his arms, gesturing to the waiting city. "Well then, let me be the first to welcome you to Joria. I took the liberty of preparing transportation when I got word *Nova's Champion* was due to dock."

Wyll led the way to a fancy, open wooden carriage at the end of the dock. A pair of short-haired black horses sat at the ready, and a thin, dark-skinned boy of perhaps twelve perched on the driver's bench.

That wasn't the only thing perched on the carriage. Kayda tilted her head, locking eyes with a large black crow balanced on the roof. How strange... She was under the impression crows didn't live this far south.

She opened her mouth to comment on the peculiar sight, but the bird lifted off as they drew close and fled, flying straight out to sea.

"Allow me to give you a hand, Princess." Wyll extended an arm beside the tall carriage steps.

Kayda slipped her hand in his. A gentle tingle spread up her arm and settled in her chest as she rose on the step and met his gaze before stepping into the carriage. His brown eyes twinkled, his smile never slipping as he assisted her up. Then he backed away, making room for the king to hop up, and took a moment to speak with the driver up front.

"He seems a pleasant fellow," Gideon said quietly as the plush silk cushion sank beside her with his weight. "I hope the rest of his family are as accommodating."

Kayda only had time for a smile before Wyll hopped up to join them and seated himself across from them. The carriage rolled off into the city, and Wyll pointed out many points of view along their route. But all the little anecdotes that made her father grin and chuckle slid in one ear and out the other for Kayda.

She clenched the golden fabric of her silk dress in her fingers, her stomach churning far more than it should have from a simple carriage ride over the sandy roads weaving through the city. So much was riding on their families meeting. She tried to bury her misgivings and enjoy the ride, but something inside of her just wouldn't settle.

"You're awfully quiet, my dear." King Gideon patted her knee. "Is anything amiss?"

Kayda forced a smile. "No. Not at all."

"It must be a big shock to lose your grandfather. How did it happen, if you don't mind my asking?" Wyll inquired.

"It was the scourge," Gideon said. "The blazing vermin must be stopped."

Kayda blinked, blowing out a hard sigh.

"I'm so sorry. I heard all about Flamesmoat's fall. I still can't believe the city was overrun." Wyll frowned briefly, but then his smile returned, just as bright as before. "But together, we'll be able to stop the vermin from spreading further." He tilted his head sideways and stared out the window. "Well, enough of that talk for now, yes? Here we are at Oasis Manse."

The beautiful mansion appeared, covered in ivy and bright vibrant blooms. The green grass on the lawn stood out starkly among all the sandy roads they'd traveled across in the dusty city.

"You have a beautiful home, son." Gideon ran an appreciative eye over the grounds.

"Thank you, sire. It's been in our family for many generations." Wyll hopped down after the carriage stopped. He held out a hand to help her down, and then she and the king followed Wyll inside.

Wyll led the way to the left, passing by the bright entranceway with the circular stair she remembered from her last visit, and heading inside a tiled room with massive bay windows. An enormous table sat in the center, heaped with dozens of platters. Fresh fruit, steaming cuts of meat, and fragrant loaves of bread and pastries had Kayda's stomach rumbling.

But the sight of Wyll's uncle, his frown firmly in place at the table's head, was enough to spoil her appetite. He stood as they approached, a hand out to greet King Gideon.

"I hear congratulations are in order for you, sire. It's *King* Gideon, now, I take it?"

"Yes, it is. I'm pleased to meet you finally, Egard." A rare smile spread across her father's face as he clasped Egard's hand and shook. "We spent so long corresponding back when I wed your cousin—it's nice to finally put a face to the letters."

Egard's brow rose, and his jaw clenched.

Kayda's heart sank. She still hadn't told her father that Egard's cousin wasn't her mother. But she should've expected Gideon to bring up his shared history with Wyll's family. Now that Gideon was the only one still in the dark about her true ancestry, she might be in trouble. What would she do if Egard took it upon himself to bring up the truth of the arrangement and revealed how the mages swapped his cousin out for Kayda's real mother ?

But Egard's features smoothed, and he pulled out the chair beside him. "Yes, it's nice to meet you finally as well. Please, have a seat. Let's share a meal and discuss the future of our families, shall we?"

Kayda took a chair across from the older men beside Wyll. The meeting seemed to be progressing smoothly, but she still wasn't sure if the men's big personalities would get in the way. She'd been hoping Wyll's great aunt would be present to guide the conversation if it went off the rails.

She leaned closer to Wyll. "Where is Aurelia this morning?"

Wyll spread a bright white napkin across his lap. "Oh, she had some business to take care of in the city, I believe. I'm sure you'll see her later." He poured her a glass of something pink and fragrant. "Here, you must be parched after that long carriage ride. Have some diquat juice."

Kayda smiled and took a sip. The sweet liquid danced on her tongue. "Thank you. That's delicious."

"I'm glad you like it," he said with a grin.

Kayda glanced across the table and spotted her father draining a cup of juice and holding out his cup for a refill. She swallowed a chuckle. Neither of them were used to the southern heat. She turned back to Wyll and opened her mouth to ask something... but the question slipped out of her mind.

It was like she was swimming in an ocean of cotton, her head heavy and limbs shaky. "I'm feeling strange..." she murmured, lifting a hand to her brow.

Across the table, the king's head smacked on the wooden tabletop with a loud *thunk*.

Kayda's jaw dropped, and her hand fell slack in her lap. The last thing she saw before her eyes became too heavy to hold open was Wyll's face, still smiling.

Chapter 17

Lark waved goodbye to Dausius and stepped out of the *Salty Serpent Inn* into the bright afternoon sun in Port Joria. A bead of sweat rolled down her back. She sucked in the dusty air, happy to be back on solid ground for a change.

"Did you find someone?" Tiora stood from the stoop on the wide wooden front porch.

"Yeah," Lark said. "That was easier than I expected. Violet's new wet nurse will head to the ship directly."

"That's good news." Aren pushed off from where he leaned against the inn wall and crooked both his elbows. "Ready for the next stop?"

Lark smiled, taking Aren's right arm. She peeked around his tall frame and watched Tiora tentatively grasp his left, while releasing a deep sigh.

"Are you all right, Ti?" Lark asked as they strolled southward through the crowded docks.

"Yeah, I'm just nervous, I guess. It's been years since I've seen my family." She threaded a hand through her short brown curls. "Amilya and Cyrie ought to be nearly grown now."

"Don't be nervous." Aren flashed her a grin. "They'll be delighted to see their big sister. I just know it."

But Aren's optimism didn't seem to reach Tiora. She clutched his elbow, her steps carefully measured, sweat dripping down her brow.

Lark couldn't imagine what she was feeling. This would be the first time Tiora had seen her family since she'd sold herself into bondage to save her mother and sisters from sickness and ruin. She'd made that difficult choice all on her own, knowing it was the only way to keep her family safe. Now, she was returning to them, but whether she would be accepted with open arms or pushed out for her decision remained to be seen.

The situation brought back a wash of memories from her own forced separation from her family. Lark might not have the opportunity to reunite with her brother, but she was determined to be there for Tiora while she sought out her kin. And if they even thought to condemn her for the actions that saw her end up a slave, she would be the first to speak up for her friend.

Without Tiora, she would've never survived her own captivity. She would've gone mad locked up with those slavers all on her own and likely never mustered the courage to try using her talent to free them both.

Every step of the journey, Tiora stepped up. Brave beyond measure, always willing to help anyone who needed it. If her family didn't see that instantly, Lark would make them see it before the day was through.

"What's with your face, Lark?" Tiora asked with a giggle. "You look like you're thinking about punching someone."

Lark joined her laughing before quickly schooling her features. "It's nothing, just woolgathering." Time to change the subject. "So, tell me about the city. It's so big and crowded. Way bigger than Flamesmoat."

"It is. We're almost through the dock section. My family lives south of the city proper on the Peat River's eastern banks."

"That's the one you used to swim in practically every afternoon?" Lark fanned herself with her hand, understanding the need for a daily swim in this dry heat.

Tiora sighed. "Yep. We'd swim in the hottest hours and spend the rest of the day scouring the banks for river butterfly cocoons. Anyone who rounded up a basketful could trade them for a coin at the silk factories. Me and my sisters usually gathered a basketful every week."

"A week's worth of work for a single coin?" Aren frowned. "That's all?"

Tiora shrugged. "Yeah."

As they left the dock section behind and tread down the crowded streets to the south, more evidence of squalor appeared. Tiny huts made of mud and clay tiles crowded every block. Not a single person looked overweight. Many even had sunken cheeks and thin, frail limbs.

The beautiful dyed silk clothing worn by the fashionable folk wandering the docks was absent here. The people donned worn, patched rags and dull homespun attire. Everyone she passed was hard at work, stirring vats filled with bright liquid, or hanging dripping cloth to dry.

"Do all the people here work in the silk trade?" Lark asked.

"Most do," Tiora explained. "The dye houses north of the city handle all the fine fabric. They contract out the everyday stuff to workers like my mother, who bulk dye in vats like these."

"And I imagine they aren't paid much better than you were for gathering all those cocoons," Aren said.

Tiora shook her head. "No. No, they aren't."

"You'll never guess what I ate just now." Muse's voice in her mind made Lark flinch. *"It was delicious."*

"You mind filling me in on the details later? I'm a little busy," she replied.

"Fine," Muse grumbled. *"I'm just bored is all, with only the old snoozer for company. Ha, you're gonna owe me big time when I get back."*

"I'll have a big snack waiting. Something tasty, I promise."

"You better."

Despite her bondmate's playful banter, Lark's stomach churned. It was hard to walk past all these people, knowing they'd spent their whole lives toiling just to line some rich trader's pockets. No wonder Tiora had needed to take such desperate measures to save her family.

Tiora stopped suddenly, her golden-brown eyes open wide, staring at a woman stirring a huge vat of dark purple liquid in front of a tiny mud hut, which was identical to all the rest.

It didn't take Lark more than an instant to realize the woman was Tiora's mother. Her dark hair was long and streaked with white, braided into a tight plait resting on her shoulder. Except for the different hairstyle, she was practically identical to Tiora, with the same golden-brown eyes and beautiful features.

Tiora's mother stared down into the vat, absorbed with her task as Tiora blinked back tears, moving closer. It wasn't until they were directly in front of her that her brow furrowed and she glanced up.

She dropped the wooden pole. "Ti-ti? Is that you?"

"Mama." Tiora dropped Aren's arm and rushed around the vat. She thudded into her mother's open arms.

"My baby. I thought I'd never see you again. Oh, Ti-ti."

"Mama, I've missed you so much. I'm so sorry I left."

They clutched each other, laughter and tears bursting free. On the other side of the vat, Lark grasped Aren's arm, her heart so full it was practically overflowing. This was exactly the kind of homecoming her friend deserved.

Two heads popped out of the hut a moment later.

"What's all the noise out he—" the older girl began, only to stop short when she spotted Tiora still clutched tightly within her mother's arms. "Tiora? You're back!"

Then both of the girls jumped in, hugging their sister and mother, squealing and shouting questions so quickly Lark couldn't keep track of what they said. But one thing was immediately clear. There would be no need for her to stick up for her friend during this reunion. The love and relief washing through all the women was immediate. So palpable Lark brushed aside all the worries that any of them would be anything other than grateful for Tiora's return.

After a few moments of hugging, Tiora eased free from her mother's arms, wiping the tears off her face. "Mama, you have to meet my friends." Tiora beckoned them over, a wide smile on her face.

"This is Aren and Lark," she began. "This is my mama, Gisila."

Tiora pointed to the older girl, who looked to be in her late teens, with dark brown eyes and her dark brown hair tied up in a simple bun. "This is Amilya."

Then she turned to the youngest, who appeared to be twelve or thirteen, with her hair wreathed around her head in a mass of short curls much like Tiora wore hers. "And this is Cyrie."

Lark and Aren took turns shaking hands with all of them and exchanging pleasantries. Then they all piled into the little hut at Gisila's insistence.

The inside of the hut wasn't any more impressive than the outside. The single room was barely large enough to fit all of them, with three mats spread out on the dirt floor serving as beds for the women. A fire pit in the corner held a single, worn pot sitting empty atop it.

Lark sat on one of the mats beside Aren and listened quietly while Tiora's sisters and mother grilled her about the last years of her life. Tiora glossed over the details of much of the beginning of her time apart from them, but grew more animated when she shared the last few months of her journey, traveling with the Wandering Bards, and battling the scourge.

"And that's how we ended up back here in Joria. Princess Kayda was promised a fleet of ships from one of the silk traders in the city to help win the fight in the Abandoned Lands," Tiora finished.

"Wow," Amilya exclaimed, her brown eyes wide. "You've been on such an incredible adventure."

Tiora reached into her skirt pocket. "Mama, this is for you." She handed her mother a small coin purse, the metal within clinking noisily.

Gisila's eyes bulged, and she shook her head. "No, Ti-ti. That's yours. We'll get on just fine here on our own."

Tiora frowned. "Take it, Mama. I'll only make more. Performing with the show, it's a good, honest way to make a living." She closed the purse in her mother's hand and smiled at her sisters. "Now Cyrie and Amilya can pay for training in the mills. Or use the coin for a dowry."

Lark's stomach flipped, and she shared a dubious glance with Aren, though she didn't interrupt.

They had to pay to work a decent job, and even pay to marry, here in Joria? It seemed the system was designed to keep the poor from ever gaining ground.

Lark couldn't still the tiny grin that crossed her face. Tiora had found a way. After all her suffering and hard work, she would be the one in a million that broke her family free of the ties keeping them stuck in this trap. It nearly brought tears to her eyes.

Gisila was equally moved. Her cheeks shone with tears, and she clenched the coin purse to her chest, smiling radiantly.

Amilya crouched beside her, leaning forward next to her mother and slipping her hand around the bottom of the coin purse, her big brown eyes going round as she traced the coins inside. "Oh, thank you, Tiora. I can't believe it. I never imagined..." Her voice trailed off, choked with emotion.

Cyrie bit her lip, shaking her head, her legs wrapped tightly around her knees.

Gisila's brow rose. "Aren't you gonna thank your sister, too, Cyrie?"

Cyrie cleared her throat, then reluctantly nodded, glancing at Tiora. "Thank you."

Tiora scooted closer, wrapping an arm around her little sister's shoulders. "What's wrong? I thought you'd be happy?"

"I am, it's just..." A tear slid down her cheek and splattered atop the threadbare silk skirt wrapped around her knees. "There won't be any marriages or mills. Not after they leave."

"What?" Lark's heart thrummed to life.

Cyrie clamped her mouth shut, her eyes widening.

"You can tell us, Cyrie. Maybe we can help," Tiora insisted, rubbing Cyrie's back and staring in her eyes.

Cyrie sucked in a shuddering gasp. "Please, you can't tell anyone how I knew. If anyone finds out, Davit could be killed."

"What does Davit have to do with this?" Gisila demanded. She turned to them. "He's our neighbor's son." Then she glared back at her daughter, still sheltered in Tiora's arms. "What's that boy gone and got you wrapped up in now?"

"It's not like that, Mama." Cyrie scrubbed the tears off her cheeks. "He only told me what's gonna happen. Made me swear I'd keep it a secret. If he's hurt because of me..."

"I don't understand. Why would anyone hurt your neighbor?" Aren asked.

"Davit found a job as a driver at Oasis Manse," Cyrie said. "I guess that rich trader thought a young boy from the slums would be too stupid to piece together what he's been planning, but Davit's smart."

"Oasis Manse?" Lark's jaw dropped. "Isn't that where Kayda was headed?" She stared at Cyrie, her skin prickling with goose flesh.

Cyrie shook her head, sighing deeply. "They haven't been packing those ships in the harbor with fighters and supplies to join your fight. They're planning to run. They're gonna leave us all to die."

"But where will they go?" Aren turned to Lark. "What if it's true? Remember, I told you about how I wanted to sail out beyond the Orddon one day, to search for the island paradise with the clear water that I'd heard about?" He gulped, running a hand down his face. "With all the ships they have, I wouldn't be surprised if they've found it."

Lark frowned. "Are you sure, Cyrie? That trader promised Princess Kayda he'd aid us in our fight. They are to be wed."

Cyrie nodded sadly. "Davit wouldn't lie to me. He's been listening in on them plotting in that carriage for weeks. They aren't planning to help your princess. They're gonna betray her."

Lark's stomach dropped as she stared at her friends. What were they going to do?

Chapter 18

A hazy cloud encased Kayda's mind. Blearily, voices reached her through the fog clogging her ears.

"I think she's coming to," said a familiar voice, one she should be able to place, but couldn't in her current state.

A second voice replied, "Surely not so soon. A single sip of that juice had enough sleeping tonic to knock her out for hours."

She fought to open her eyes as her body jostled, but the task proved impossible. Her eyelids might as well have been glued shut for how much they refused to budge.

"Disgusting," the first voice said. "This pig won't stop throwing up."

"How should I have known he'd drain the whole cup in one swig? Fat bastard," answered the other.

"Leave him. He doesn't matter. All they want is the girl."

A spike of fear shot through her as retreating footsteps echoed in her ears. But even that could not force her eyes to open. Blackness reigned.

She came to sometime later. An hour, a day—how much time had passed was impossible to tell. Light shone in from high windows, revealing a basement room. Dirt walls and floors, bare except for herself and another occupant, sprawled in a heap beside her, his face resting in a pool of vomit.

"Father?" Her voice was hoarse. She reached out to him. Her hand stopped short, encircled by a metal shackle.

Kayda gasped, staring down at her torso for the first time since she awakened. Thick metal chains wrapped around her waist, wrists, and legs. The far end latched around a hook high on the wall. A period of frantic scrambling and tugging proved she was well and truly trapped, unable to move more than a few degrees in any direction.

The morning's events returned to her in a flash. That sweet juice. Wyll's traitorous smile.

Blazes. Why was this happening? What could he hope to gain by capturing her and her father like this? It made no sense.

An echo of the overheard conversation rose, like the hazy memory of a half-forgotten dream.

All they want is the girl.

Terror struck her, and the weight of the chains pressed against her unbearably, squeezing, constricting her limbs. Her breath came, harsh and labored. Who wanted her? Why?

Footsteps pounded just outside the door. Kayda fought to shake off the panic and school her features as the door swung open.

"Ah, finally awake I see." Wyll strode in, his smile still firmly in place, looking for all the world like he'd just happened upon her waking from a peaceful nap.

"What is the meaning of this, Wyll? Set me and my father free. Now."

"I'm afraid that won't be happening, my dear."

Kayda's heart seized. Whatever tiny sliver of hope she'd held that this was all some massive mistake evaporated with those words. That saccharine smile. "But we had a deal."

"Yes, we did. But it wasn't much of a deal now, was it?" He crouched in front of her, meeting her eye to eye. "Our entire fleet, for the hand of a single *bastard* princess?" He scoffed, shaking his head slowly. "Do you really think you're worth an entire fleet of ships?"

Kayda's stomach twinged, his words pummeling her like a gut punch. How could she have believed this snake wanted to marry her?

"Are you mad?" Her voice was surprisingly stable, considering how much her stomach churned with dread. "Don't you see, if I don't bring the fight to the scourge, they'll only spread? What good will your silk trade be with no one left to purchase?"

His smile shifted into a sneer. "You think you know everything, don't you, Princess? That just because you grew up in a castle, sur-rounded by gaggles of fools desperate enough to believe your family had some divine right to rule, that any of that nonsense was true? You couldn't stop the scourge from destroying Flamesmoat. I don't have any faith that you'll keep them from spreading here as well."

She met his stare, her jaw clenched. "Coward."

Wyll rolled his eyes. "Let all the brave fools keep their battles and their graves. I have other plans."

"What plans? There won't be anything left."

He scoffed. "Oh, you truly don't know, do you?" He stood, turning to leave. "I told you once, trade was king here. Someone offered me a better deal. It's nothing personal. I'm sure you understand."

Before he made it to the door, another set of footsteps sounded. Egard appeared in the doorway, carrying a lit candlestick.

Wyll shot him a murderous glare. "Blow that out, now. I thought I told you? No fire near this one."

Egard quickly snuffed out the flame, grumbling, "I didn't know she was awake."

Wyll smirked. "Can't have our little mage burning the place down, now, can we? Don't get any ideas about melting those chains, Princess. I have it on good authority that the talent it would take to manage that task would cost you more years than you have to spare." He laughed, turning to leave again.

"Wait. Please, at least help my father. Look at him, he's not well." The king hadn't moved since she'd awoken, his chest rising and falling in a labored pattern that did not bode well for his state. Surely, they would help him?

Egard set the candlestick down and strode into the room, sneering down at the king on the floor. "Yes, that is unfortunate, isn't it? Don't worry, Princess. I'll help him for you."

"Thank you." Kayda sighed.

Egard leaned over beside the king's head, reaching behind his back. His hand flashed forward, metal gleaming in the dim light. Before Kayda realized what was happening, the knife was at her father's throat, slicing through his neck. Red spurted through the air, the gush of blood pooling on the floor and mixing with the chunks of vomit in the dirt.

"No!" she screamed.

Egard laughed, wiping his blade on the back of the king's tunic as he bled out. "I've been waiting to do that for decades. He thought he could toss Solenne aside and take some dusty Sul for a wife behind my back." He paused, only to spit out a glob of mucus on her father's closed eyelid. "Good riddance."

Kayda's chest burned. "He didn't even know! He never knew. You just killed an innocent man."

Egard frowned for an instant, then shrugged. "Oops." He smiled at Wyll and slid the knife behind his back. "I wonder if we can get a bonus now? They asked for a princess, but we're bringing them a queen."

Wyll shook his head. He stood far back from the blood pooling on the floor, casually leaning against the dirt wall. "No. What is she queen of, after all? Queen of ruin isn't much of a prize."

They left her with her father's corpse. Slammed the door on her, and left her to watch the pool of red creep closer and closer to where she sat, chained and alone.

Long hours passed with nothing happening. Kayda sat, tied in place, watching her father's blood seep into the dirt floor and dry. Her mood shifted, alternatively turning from determination to be freed to despair that she'd never see a way out of this.

Bone-deep regret burned inside her every time she glanced at her father's corpse. If she'd only trusted him, maybe none of this would've happened. She'd been so suspicious of her father's motives. So worried he'd reject her when he learned of her true parentage that she kept him in the dark until this...

He'd taken the first step to repair their relationship when he apologized back in the tower, but she hadn't done the same. Now she'd never have the chance to make things right between them.

Wyll and Egard could not be allowed to get away with this. She needed to find some way out of this prison. She had to make them pay. But no matter how much she wracked her brain, she could see no path out of this basement room.

Was she even still at Oasis Manse, or had the villains moved her while she was unconscious? It was impossible to tell from where she sat. If she managed to escape somehow, could she even find a way back to the docks?

She needed to warn everyone on board *Nova's Champion*. Even now, Wyll and his father might be out there, betraying her friends like they'd betrayed her.

Footsteps clattered outside the door. But instead of the door opening, a harried whisper sounded from outside.

"Kayda? Kayda, are you all right in there?"

It was a new voice that spoke. One she remembered from her last visit. "Aurelia? Is that you?"

"Yes, it's me. I'm sorry, Princess. I didn't know Wyll and Egard were capable of this treachery."

"Aurelia, let me out of here. If you don't agree with what they're doing, then set me free."

"I wish I could. You're locked in, and I don't have the key. Even if I could, they'd never allow it. This is the first chance to get Ignace back."

"Ignace? Who is that?"

"Wyll's brother. He's been missing for over a year. Left on some mission to find a new trade route beyond Saltcliff. Only he's not really missing. He's been captured. By whom, I'm not sure. Wyll's been trying to find some way to trade for his freedom. But no amount of silk could sway these people. There was nothing they wanted. Not until now."

Kayda's stomach roiled. "Me. They want me."

"Yes. I'm so sorry. If I could—" Aurelia's voice abruptly cut off.

"What are you doing down here?" a deep voice boomed. It was that bastard, Egard.

"Nothing, I was only checking on her," Aurelia said.

"Well, come away from there. We need your help to get everything set for sailing in the morning."

"All right, I'm coming." Aurelia's voice faded, and the sound of footsteps trailed off into the distance.

Kayda's mind spun. Who were these mysterious people who wanted her badly enough to arrange all this? What could they possibly offer Wyll that he'd be willing to sell out his entire country? Surely it wouldn't help him to win his brother back, only to have his home destroyed.

Only... what if they offered him a place in this new trade land instead?

There'd long been rumors of islands past the Orddon Ocean. She'd come across plenty of tales in the books in the Royal Library back in Flamesmoat. But she'd always assumed they were tales of fancy. Or the exaggerations of sailors who'd happened upon the tiny string of islands that they knew for a fact did exist in the Orddon Ocean.

Saltcliff was one such island. A tiny isle resting off the coast of Joria in the midst of the Orddon Ocean, only remarkable for its natural salt deposits.

If what Aurelia said was true, then maybe there *was* something out there. But why would they want her?

Chapter 19

C onall pushed the stick into the bog, his shoulders and legs aching. A day and night had passed without another sighting of the armed men sharing the bog with them.

Ereni sat at the canoe's bow, her sharp blue eyes staring ahead. She'd overcome her heightened emotions, returning to the cool, collected woman he remembered so clearly.

"Are you ever going to talk to her?" Shadow asked.

Conall sighed inwardly. *"I don't know."*

They'd spent most of the ride in silence since their last run in with the men. He was beginning to think Ereni would rather ignore him than attempt to right things between them.

There was so much he needed to know. So much he wanted to say.

At first, he hadn't wanted to upset her further, seeing how emotional she was. But now, the silence wrapped around them like a physical thing. A barrier keeping things civil. Part of him wanted to leave it standing until they found a way out of this place.

Did he really want to tear down the wall and peer beyond the cracked foundation at the tormented souls within?

No. They couldn't keep this up forever. He had to think of something to say to break—

"My mother. Is she all right?" Ereni turned, her expression flat, back straight. But her fingers clenched around her coverall's sleeves, betraying the feelings she tried to hide.

Conall shook his head. "I'm sorry. She's gone."

"She told me she wouldn't be coming back. I didn't want to believe it..." Ereni trailed off, her fingers straightening, releasing her death grip on her sleeves. "How did it happen?"

"A fever on our journey to the Northern Depths." Conall frowned. "Wait, what do you mean? She told you she wouldn't be back?"

"It was one of the things she saw in her first vision." Ereni shifted on the bench. "All Sade Prims make the journey to the Northern Depths in their youth."

"You've been there, too," he stated flatly.

"I have."

"Were you meant to be the next Sade Prim, then?"

Ereni nodded. "If things had kept on like they had been, yes."

"But they didn't."

"No, they didn't."

Conall stared at her, so many questions bombarding his mind. He picked the loudest. "Why did it need to be now?"

Ereni shrugged. "The Palisade was weakening. It had been for years. If you hadn't brought it down, it would've fallen eventually."

"Then why didn't you let it?" The faces of Amora and the other mages who'd died at the Palisade's fall flashed in his mind. "You could've saved Amora. You could've spared them all."

"Perhaps. Or maybe more would've died when the wall fell without warning and caught us unawares."

Conall grimaced. He hadn't considered that. She could be right, but there was really no way of knowing that now. "Why them?"

"Mother chose the weakest among us who could still handle the task. And those who would balk when they learned of our plans."

"And me."

"She knew you would survive because of the vision she had of you two traveling to the witch. That you would be aged, but live. I'm sorry."

"How can you put so much stock into these visions? What if they're wrong?"

Ereni scoffed. "They aren't."

Conall glared at her, a single brow raising.

"I told you, all Sade Prims travel there. Sometimes they even bring others with them. Everyone who drinks the dream elixir witnesses things that one day come true; we had a ledger at Mage Keep to record it. Without fail, every vision comes true. It's hard to argue with hundreds of years of results."

"If that's the case, at least we know we'll make it out of this bog and back to the others. I saw myself fighting in the Abandoned Lands with Kayda and Lark."

Ereni flashed a sad half-smile. "That's true. I've seen it, too."

But if that was the case, then was what the Unseen said true as well? Was one of them destined to die fighting the scourge?

Conall's stomach churned, and he stared into the murky water, replaying the vision he'd witnessed beneath the ocean.

He'd seen a glimpse of the battle but not its end. Kayda and Lark were definitely there, and he was as well, but the rest of the battlefield was a blur of chaos in his memory. Except for Shadow and Muse, he couldn't be certain of any other face in the crowd. Not even...

His heart thudded, dropping to his stomach just as the stick dropped to the bog's bottom.

His gaze flicked to the front of the canoe. "Are you there at the battle? What did you see in your vision, Ereni?"

Ereni exhaled and stared at her hands as if gathering her thoughts. Then she met his gaze, her lips parting.

"Brother, I hear something." Shadow sat up straight, head cocked. *"It could be men, talking."*

Conall raised a finger to his lips before Ereni spoke. He pointed to Shadow and tugged his ear, then flicked his gaze to the bog.

Ereni's eyes widened, and she closed her mouth, pressing her lips into a thin line. She pointed at the mangroves looming around them.

Conall squinted, then shook his head.

Last night, just like the first night, they'd found a spot to cram their canoe behind some trees, hiding among the mangrove roots. But the trees here grew tightly together on the waterway's sides. He didn't see any space large enough where they could fit.

Until now, he'd heard nothing strange. Just the normal croaking and buzzing of the reptiles and insects that called this swampy land home. Shadow's ears were far keener than his, after all. But now, the echo of voices carried across the water.

The hair rose on the back of his neck. There was no question now. The sound Shadow heard was definitely men's voices. And if he could hear them, they must be coming closer.

Conall gulped. What were they going to do? If those men found them—which seemed likely, considering they had nowhere to hide—would they be able to fight them off? They were rested now, at least, but they'd be outnumbered. And if they carried ranged weapons with them instead of just cudgels and swords...

Ereni's hand slid out of the canoe and hovered outstretched above the water. Moisture whispered through the air, and a cloud of icicles materialized in front of the bow, sparkling in the late afternoon sunlight.

Conall gritted his teeth and stashed the pole on the canoe's side holder, careful to make as little noise as possible.

The voices grew louder. Someone must've just told a joke; laughter peeled out, rich and hearty, bouncing off the water and filling his ears even as a shiver slid down his spine. His stare locked on the bend ahead of them.

He snaked his hand out of the canoe, joining Ereni's hovering just above the bog. He reached for his talent, pushing the fear of the unknown aside. He had to fight. For Shadow. And Ereni. This would not be the end for them. They *would* join the others. They'd make it to the Abandoned Lands.

The air around their boat thickened so much it was like they slid through a cloud of fog. Ice crystalized, taking shape beside the canoe. He added dozens of ice shards to the ones Ereni summoned. When those prisoners rounded the bend, they'd be in for a wicked surprise.

The first glimpse of wood rounded the bend. Conall held his breath, waiting.

Laughter still rang out, but it was tapering off now. The bow of a second canoe appeared, right next to the first, and then a third, just behind it. Conall exhaled, readying his shards, preparing to send them flying to the unsuspecting men as soon as their faces were revealed.

Then the first man's smiling face appeared, and Ereni's icicles splashed into the water in front of their canoe.

Conall stared ahead, his gaze flicking between the rippling water and the men, all three visible now, each one poling a canoe, their smiles falling and jaws dropping as they spotted them in the water ahead of them.

Why wasn't Ereni attacking? They'd lose the element of surprise if they didn't act now.

But before he sent his ice shards sailing, he stole another look at the men. He didn't recognize any of them. And they weren't wearing the ugly coverall's either. Two of them dressed in dirty overalls and matching wool cloaks. The third sported a cloak as well, but beneath the cloak, sheer green fabric flashed. The same fabric that was so popular in Raimire.

These weren't the prisoners. They'd just stumbled upon a few of the Raimish sailors keeping watch over the bog.

Conall grinned, feeling as lucky as a hare who'd escaped a snare. Just as Ereni spun toward him, he let his ice drop into the bog, splashing the canoe again, tiny waves rippling outward.

"Friends of yours?" he asked.

Ereni shook her head, smiling. "Not exactly, but we've met."

She turned back to the newcomers, raising her voice. "Dal, Fillan, I'm pleased to see you."

The face of the older man wearing overalls screwed up, his gaze flitting up and down Ereni, as if he were not sure where to place her, but the younger man's face lit with recognition.

"Ereni? Is that you?" he asked, thrusting his pole down and gliding closer.

She beamed. "It is. I'm certainly glad to find you out here, Fillan. We could use a guide right about now."

Conall frowned. That must make the older fellow, Dal.

The older man spoke up, shaking his head, pushing his canoe behind Fillan's. "We're not guides. Not anymore. We've been keeping watch over the bog for those foul beasts." He gestured to the Raimish man in the final canoe, who stayed silent, letting the pair do all the talking. "There's more of us, spread out between here and Raimire."

"What are you doing out here?" Fillan slicked back his brown hair. "I thought all the mages fled after the scourge broke loose. Shouldn't you be with the Sade Prim?"

Ereni's smile dropped. "It's a long story. But what matters is my," she paused, glancing at him, "friend Conall and I got separated from the others when Flamesmoat fell. We need to find a way through the bog to meet up with the others on the eastern coast, in the Orddon Ocean."

Fillan exchanged a glance with Dal, and it looked like they held a silent conversation with only their eyes. It was the kind of familiarity that only existed between family or close friends. Conall suspected from the resemblance they shared, it was the former.

Fillan gave a small nod and stared back at Ereni. "You're a long way off track if that's where you're headed. We can guide you there."

Ereni beamed. "Thank you. That would be most kind."

"You haven't come across any other folks in these waters lately, have you?" Conall asked.

Dal shook his head. "Nope. Not a soul."

"About that..." Ereni grimaced. "A handful of prisoners escaped the Southmoat Prison into the bog."

"Prisoners?" Dal's eyes widened. "That changes things. We can't leave the rest of our people without warning."

Another one of those weighted looks passed between the men. Then it was Dal's turn to nod.

"We split up," he announced. "Fillan, you guide Ereni and her friend." Dal thrust his hand backward at his silent companion. "We'll spread the word to the others about this new threat."

With that, they took off. The men spun their canoes around and headed back the way they came, discussing the routes they planned to take and saying their goodbyes, while he caught Shadow up on the new plan. At the first fork in the bog, the Raimish man peeled off, his path leading south. A few moments later, Dal took another turn, headed southwest. That left their two canoes slowly poling eastward.

Moisture flooded the air again. Ereni lifted her hand above the bog, a trio of ice darts hovering before her face.

"What's that for?" Fillan asked, scratching his head.

Conall pointed to a group of small waterfowl floating just ahead of them, atop the murky water. "Watch."

Ereni sent the ice soaring. The darts slammed into three of the birds, striking each of them cleanly in their necks. The remaining birds scattered, squawking and flapping away as quick as their wings would carry them.

Fillan's face lit up, and he shifted his canoe, heading for the carcasses. "Yum, sparling. I've been eating too much fish lately."

Ereni glanced at Conall. "I'll take a turn with the pole if you can handle the plucking?"

Conall passed Shadow, lazing in the middle of the canoe, and handed Ereni the pole, then took a seat at the bow.

Fillan floated up beside them and tossed the birds into their canoe. "I thought watching a falcon and hawk hunt sparlings was impressive, but your method has them beat."

Falcon and hawk... "You must've met my sister Lark and her friends the Wandering Bards."

"You're Lark's brother?" Fillan eyed him up and down. "I see the resemblance now. But she told me her brother was dead."

Conall picked the first sparling off the boat bottom. "Yeah, that's another one of those long stories. She thought I was dead for a while, but we've reconnected." He glanced back at Ereni as she stabbed the long pole down into the bog, then back at Fillan. He seemed a nice enough fellow, and about the same age as Ereni. "How do you two know each other?"

"My father and I hail from Bogsmouth." Fillan clenched his stick so tightly his tanned knuckles turned white. "Well, we used to." He sighed. "Being so close to Mage Keep, we spent a fair amount of time ferrying mages about. I met Ereni a few years back, when we gave her and her mother a lift to Raimire."

Ereni nodded, smiling. "That was one of my first outings as a seer for the keep. I found five talented folks in Slinas on that trip."

Fillan grinned back at her, chuckling. "That's right. The boats were a lot more crowded on the trip back."

Conall's gaze flicked between the two of them, smiling at each other. A sliver of something uncomfortable took up space in his chest.

He tried to shake it off. She could smile at whoever she wanted. It didn't mean anything.

He concentrated on the birds, making quick work of the task with a hunting knife.

Ereni had surrendered the knife that belonged in that empty sheath yesterday. She'd stashed it underneath the forward seat. He'd kept a close eye on it since then, and she made no attempt to retrieve it.

Maybe it was silly—considering her talent, she could harm herself just as easily without it—but having the knife brought him a measure of comfort all the same.

"I suppose we should start hunting for a spot to pull over and cook those," Fillan said.

"No need." Ereni smiled again. "We can cook them on the go."

Fillan leaned back, brow raising. "You can? I've got to see this."

Ereni dug through the rainbow pack and pulled out a tinderbox. She sent a few sparks flying, as she lit a bundle of dried sticks aflame.

"Careful, now," Fillan said. "You don't want your canoe up in smoke."

"Don't worry. We only need it for a short while." She lifted the makeshift torch, holding it above the water, stomping out the few cinders that fell to the boat bottom.

Ereni drew in a deep breath, and Conall's skin prickled all over, like he'd rolled through a pile of evergreen needles. Then the naked birds rose in the air and hovered beside the boat, between their canoes.

She shifted her gaze to him, an expectant look on her face.

That was his cue. Conall closed his eyes briefly. He meant to call on Lark's image in his mind, but all he could picture was a pair of blue eyes instead of hazel. Nevertheless, his talent responded. The birds burst into flames, the fire so bright he flinched back from the heat. He kept the flames flowing until the bundle of sticks in Ereni's hand died out.

Then she sent a wave of air, gliding one of the charred birds into Fillan's canoe, and the others dropped on the boards of their boat, still sizzling.

Shadow popped up from where he'd been napping, licking his chops in anticipation. They settled down to eat, their poles stashed, canoes listing in the gentle current.

"I have to say, that was mighty impressive, too. I've got to travel with mages more often." Fillan chewed, a thoughtful expression replacing his grin. "How come you didn't cook like that the last time I ferried you?"

Ereni glanced his way, swallowing. "We didn't have anyone on board with fire talent then."

Fillan chuckled. "You're stronger together. Makes sense."

Conall glared down at his meat to avoid rolling his eyes.

"It's getting late. We should search for somewhere to tie up for the night, after we're done eating," Ereni said.

"There's a spot close to here that ought to do." Fillan licked his fingers, staring at Ereni. "You can sleep here with me, if you want. I've got extra blankets. Proper wool, even."

Conall chewed slowly. He watched the grin spread across Ereni's face, and his stomach churned.

"And why would I want wool when I have fur over here?" Ereni answered, nodding to Shadow.

"Would be more room is all." Fillan shrugged. "Suit yourself."

"I'm staying here." Ereni tossed the rest of her bird to Shadow. "Besides, you kept me up practically all night on our last trip through the bog."

Her words caught Conall mid-swallow. He coughed, grabbed the waterskin, and met Ereni's gaze. Mischief glinted back at him.

"I did nothing of the sort," Fillan declared.

"Yes, you did. You snore. Loud." She laughed, and Conall's heart squeezed.

He hadn't heard that sound in ages. Now this dirty ferryman had her laughing.

He used to be the one making her laugh. Putting that mischievous glint in her eyes. Now, all they had together was hurt and the shadow of betrayal. Would it ever be easy like that with them again? Did he even want it to be?

Fillan splayed a hand across his dirty overalls, feigning shock. "I never snored a night in my life."

Ereni laughed again and shook her head. "All the same, I'm staying here."

Fillan shrugged then hopped up and grabbed his pole. "Follow me. The spot I was talking about is just ahead."

Ereni manned the pole again, and soon, they were sheltered within a large hole in the bog, hidden by mangrove roots.

Fillan settled down to rest in his canoe without delay by unfolding a stack of wool blankets. "I'll see you guys in the morning."

Conall lounged beside Shadow and stared up at the crooked mangrove branches. Ereni plopped down behind Shadow, snuggling up against his back. Shadow allowed it, stretching and yawning.

Conall's eyelids drooped. The long day of travel and his full belly caused drowsiness to envelop him quickly. Until a loud, grating sound met his ears. His eyes shot open.

"Told you," Ereni said with a giggle.

Conall met her gaze in the dusk light. He cringed as Fillan snored again, the harsh rattle repeating without a discernable pattern. "Yeah, I see what you mean." He sighed, the weariness he'd just been feeling chased away by the obnoxious noise. It was going to be a long night.

"It'll be worth it not to get lost." Ereni tugged one of the cloaks against her back, shivering.

Conall scooted over, lifting the cloak draped atop him. "C'mon, climb in the middle."

"Are you sure?" she asked.

He nodded, and she rose from her spot.

"Roll over, brother. Ereni's cold."

Shadow snorted and cracked open one golden eye, meeting his gaze. Conall sensed he wanted to say something, but he must've decided against it. He simply rolled over and breathed deeply, settling back down to sleep.

Ereni slid in between them. She turned her back to him and draped an arm around Shadow's side.

Conall tucked the cloaks around them. Then he rested on his back and listened to Fillan snore, wide awake.

After a few moments, Ereni stopped shivering. "Do you still want to know what I saw?"

"Hm?" What she saw... Her vision. "Yes."

"It started with the battle. The same one everyone sees. I saw the three of you, all glowing purple." Her voice rose in pitch, sounding hopeful. "Until then, I didn't know it was possible."

Conall blinked. She could see them glowing with her seer sight, even within the vision?

She shifted to face him. Conall kept staring at the branches, but he could feel her stare on his face, her gaze landing on his cheek like a caress.

"Were you there at the battle, too?" he asked.

She shook her head gently. "I don't know. When I think back on it, everything except for you three is all a blur."

Conall inhaled. "Me, too." He exhaled. "What else?"

Ereni tugged the cloak higher on her shoulder. "I almost didn't make the journey to meet the witch. I was planning to leave Mage Keep. Cut ties, live a normal life somewhere."

Conall turned to her, raising a brow. "You were?"

He thought back to when they'd first met. She'd asked him what he planned to do with his life. When he'd told her about the farm, how he'd wanted to settle down and have a few kids, she'd said it sounded lovely. At the time, he'd assumed she'd just been humoring him. Was she envious instead?

"I was toying with the idea. But my mother convinced me to make the journey to the Winter Witch first. And what I saw after the battle changed my mind."

"What was it?"

"A man appeared. One I barely recognized. My father. He died when I was just a child."

Conall's brows pinched together. "I'm sorry."

Ereni smiled. "Actually, it was nice to see him. A relief, in fact."

He could understand that. After all, he'd seen his mother in his vision.

"It was nice until he started speaking. He told me the future depended on me. On my choices. That if I left Mage Keep like I'd planned, the world would be doomed."

Conall frowned, his heart aching for her. "That's awful. Don't the mages have other seers? Couldn't someone else have taken your place?"

"No, you don't understand. This isn't about the Palisade, or the Abandoned Lands. It's about her."

Conall met her gaze. "Who?"

Ereni's eyes were misty. "Violet. Our daughter is going to change the world."

Conall's heart skipped a beat as he realized they shared something much bigger than hurt feelings and betrayal. They had something binding them together, flesh and bone and beyond amazing. Their daughter.

"Tell me everything."

Chapter 20

The night passed slowly for Kayda. After Aurelia's visit, no one came. Not even to remove her father's body from the room. She was left to stare at him while the flies found him. And when night fell, to scream every time a rat slunk out from some hole in the wall to gnaw on his flesh. After the first few times, the wretched things ignored her, and she was forced to listen to them feasting in the darkened basement room.

She couldn't sleep. Not with the awful stench of death clogging her nose and the chains wrapped around her. The thick metal rested heavily on her skin, weighing her down just as surely as grief burdened her heart.

It was all her fault. Her father wouldn't be dead at her feet if she hadn't trusted Wyll and his family. And now he was threatening to steal her away before she could fulfill her plan to save her country. She couldn't let it stand. She wouldn't.

As the first hint of dawn washed over the sky outside, transforming the shadowy black inside her room to a chalky gray, the lock clicked open. The crowd of rats scattered, their claws skittering on rock.

Wyll strode in, nose wrinkling as his gaze flicked to her father's corpse. "My, it is rank in here. Can't believe we forgot to move that body yesterday." He shook his head slowly, meeting her gaze. "Sorry for that, my dear. I really had no idea what my father was planning. You understand he has a bit of a temper. Always one black sheep in the family, isn't there?"

She met his crooked smile with a hard glare. Did he actually think she'd laugh off her father's murder because Egard didn't know how to control his temper?

Wyll strolled closer, straightening his freshly pressed, cobalt-blue silk suit, detouring around the pooled blood that had darkened to a brownish-black stain on the dirt floor. "Let's get you out of here. We have a boat to catch."

A thread of hope unspooled in her chest. If the basement she was currently trapped in *was* in Wyll's house, then they'd need to travel through half of the city to return to the docks. Someone might see her and offer aid. Or better yet, she might sneak close enough to an open flame to burn these chains and free herself.

Wyll led her through the darkened house. The basement did belong to Oasis Manse. He'd made certain not to light any of the candles or lamps, leaving them to shuffle through the dim light filtering in through the drawn curtains.

Soon they made it outside. Kayda breathed deeply the warm dusty air, trying to banish the stench of decay that clung inside her nostrils. Wyll didn't grant her much time for the task. He tugged her behind him to a black carriage tied up in the courtyard. He opened the door, revealing the darkened interior of a closed carriage, much less fine than the one that had driven them here yesterday. And instead of holding out a gentle hand to help her up, he shoved her inside without a word and slammed the door closed.

Kayda's chest burned with rage as she surveyed the empty carriage. Black cloth blanketed the windows, leaving the dreary interior just as dark as her mood. She needed to think of some way out of this. A plan to break free of her chains and put these murdering snakes in their place.

"Kayda."

She was so wrapped up in thoughts of revenge, she almost ignored the voice in her mind.

"Kayda. Please answer me."

"Dru? Druturion, is that you?" Hope exploded, bright and wild, infusing her body with a lightness she'd almost forgotten. *"Where are you? I'm in trouble. I need your help."*

"It's good to hear your voice."

"You too. I've missed you so much. Where are you? Why did you leave me?"

"I'm sorry. There's so much to explain, and I'm afraid there's not much time. Even now, I can feel it trying to take over."

"What? I don't understand." Her eyes widened. *"The Unseen. He's trying to take over you like he has the scourge."*

"Is that what you're calling it? That voice, it's gotten worse. Belstasia and I, we've both been affected. We left the rest of you before it took full control."

Her stomach clenched, his words confirming her worst fears. *"How is that possible?"*

"I'm not certain. It happened already to Bela. She killed the others, but it wasn't her fault. You were right to stop me from harming her in my anger. I see that now. You've given us a chance at a future, Kayda."

"That's good. I'm glad it was the right thing." She sighed. *"But why did you leave?"*

"Distance is the only thing that helps. Bela and I returned home."

"Home? I thought Dracwood was your home?"

"Dracwood was never our home, only our breeding grounds. But much has changed while we've been underground. People swarm the lands that used to belong to only dragonkind."

Kayda gasped. *"There* is *a land out there with other people."*

"Yes. And I'm afraid our presence may have some men here eager to find you, so that they can get to me. I could feel your pain seeping through our bond. I had to warn you."

"You're too late, Dru. I've been betrayed. You have to help me."

"I'm sorry. If I return across the sea, the voice will take over. We might have a way to return, but we need something first. It will take time to procure."

Kayda's heart sank. *"So, I'm still on my own?"*

"For now. Do what you must to free yourself. You must. The Unseen cannot be allowed to flourish. We will be back to join the battle, but you need be there to start it, Kayda."

"Dru! Don't leave. Please. I can't do this all on my own."

"You're not alone. I'm with you, even when you can't hear me. Call on my strength." His voice faded, filled with a note of pain. *"I have to go. I can't hold it off any longer."*

Once again, she was alone. But the conversation with Dru had given her new hope. Even though she was still shackled, just as desperate as before, she had one thing to hold on to. Her bondmate was alive. She would see him again. These bastards keeping her hostage would not win.

Footsteps echoed outside. Kayda drew a calming breath and prepared for the carriage to start. Once it was in motion, she could shuffle sideways and peel back the cloth covering the wind—

The door swung open. Kayda squinted at the sudden light spilling in through the doorway. But it only stayed open long enough for Wyll to slide in and seat himself across from her. The lock outside clicked shut, and the carriage shook, no doubt from someone seating themselves in the front.

Kayda glared across the seat at her former intended. She'd never known a carriage that locked from the *outside*. How long had he been planning to betray her? Not that it mattered. Knowing the details wouldn't change anything. It wouldn't bring her father back.

And now with Wyll in the compartment with her, she'd need to come up with a different plan. There was no chance of him letting her wave for help from the window.

The carriage jolted forward without warning. Kayda's head bobbed against the hard seat back. It was a far cry from the thick cushions she'd traveled on just yesterday.

Wyll grimaced and pulled a small flask from his pocket. He unscrewed the top and took a sip. "Can't say I'm a fan of sailing. A little tipple helps." He offered the flask to her with a raised brow.

Kayda only stared back at him flatly. What was it with men, thinking alcohol could solve all the world's problems? Although...

"Sure, thanks," she leaned forward, opening her mouth slightly.

Wyll leaned forward, too, lifting the flask, only to snatch it back at the last instant. He jerked back in his seat, staring at her with scrunched brows and pursed lips. "No, I think not. I don't like that look in your eye." He twisted the stopper on the flask. "You're liable to spit it back in my face."

Damn. Another plan foiled. Kayda snapped her mouth shut and leaned back, annoyed he could read her so well. She scanned the darkened interior, searching for anything else that might help her break free of this carriage. There was nothing.

The liquor might still work. She'd caught a whiff of it when he held it out toward her. It had practically burned her nostrils. She just had to ensure he took another sip.

"It's funny you don't like sailing, being that you own a shipping company and all." Kayda forced an amused smile across her lips. "I can't get enough of sailing. The waves rolling under you. All that water stretching out as far as the eye can see. The way the water sways you, side to side. It's like being rocked in a mother's embrace."

"And what would you know about that?" A cruel grin lit Wyll's face.

Kayda resisted the urge to scowl, instead gazing to the side thoughtfully. "No, it's more like dancing, I think. Spinning around and around on the floor, the waves heaving merrily. Soft and slow like a ballad until a storm hits, then the water pounds like the drums in a country jig."

"Enough. I get the picture." Wyll grimaced, clutching his stomach. Then his hand slipped into his pocket, and he pulled the flask free.

Kayda set her stare on the carriage floor, feigning disinterest. She wouldn't give him the chance to glimpse anything in her gaze this time. But as he twisted the stopper free, she reached for her talent.

She would have to pay for this with no source. But for what she had planned, it would likely only be a wave of exhaustion and not years of her life.

He lifted the flask. Set it to his lips. And just as the liquid touched his tongue, Kayda struck.

Cold coursed through her body, like she'd been drenched in a vat of ice water. At the same time, she conjured a tiny flicker of flame and sent it right into Wyll's open mouth.

Dizziness washed over her limbs, and she trembled where she sat.

Wyll screamed as the flame whooshed to life using the alcohol as fuel. He dropped the flask, and the flame spread even farther, engulfing his chest and lap as he clutched his throat. Within moments, his screams turned ragged, his voice garbled. He pounded his feet and slapped at the fire coursing across his body.

The noise must've reached the driver. The carriage pulled to a halt, and the door swung open. Egard stared in, his eyes bulging as he spotted Wyll, groaning and slapping out the last of the flames. The scent of charred flesh and burnt silk wafted through the air.

"Healer," Wyll croaked, his voice distorted and raspy. "Now, healer!"

Kayda squinted against the bright daylight and wobbled in her seat. She shivered, fighting to keep her eyelids from closing with the exhaustion weighing her down.

"What did you do, you witch?" Egard spat, fists clenched.

Kayda forced her eyes open fully and met Egard's gaze. "Oops."

Egard's fist flew at her face, and the world went black.

Chapter 21

Lark and Aren arrived back at the *Salty Serpent Inn* just as Dausius wrapped up a long story to thundering applause. They slipped through the crowd, dodging sweaty sailors and silk clad villagers, until they made it to the table where Mazen and Meital sat.

"Hey, you two are back early. I thought you'd be gone for most of the day with Tiora," Mazen said.

"Where's Ti?" Meital tilted her head, scanning the crowd behind them. "How did it go with her family?"

Lark slid into a seat across from the twins. Aren sat down beside her. "It went well. But she left with her sister to find someone. We ran into a problem while we were there."

Dausius strolled up to the table. "Problem? What problem?"

Lark glanced around, well aware of all the eyes and ears present in the crowded inn. "We might want to discuss this in private."

Dausius' brow furrowed. "All right. I'll tell the owner we're taking an extended break. Let's head back to the ship."

Lark nodded. "Good idea. I have to check on Violet, make sure the new wet nurse has everything well in hand."

Soon, they were back outside, the scorching afternoon sun beating down on them. Lark made her way down the wharf, her step hurried.

Poor Kayda. Surely, she would be all right, wouldn't she? With her talent, she could take care of herself. Maybe she'd already figured out some way to turn the betrayal to her advantage.

As they drew closer to *Nova's Champion*, a familiar face hustled toward them.

Lark smiled. "Hello, Jett."

Jett reached her side and clutched her elbow, a wide smile plastered on his face. He spun her around and hurried back the way they'd come. "Hello, dear. I'm so glad you and your friends agreed to meet me for lunch," he bellowed, waving emphatically at the others. "Come, I've secured a private room at the inn, just over here."

Lark quirked a brow but kept step with Jett, allowing him to lead her into a nearby inn. This one was a degree shabbier than the *Salty Serpent*, with only a handful of patrons staring gloomily into their mugs of ale atop worn wooden stools.

Jett led them away from the common room to a side door. They all crowded inside quickly, without a word, until Jett pulled the door shut behind them.

The room was small, housing only a large wooden table and chairs. An untouched pitcher and a pair of glasses rested on the table, and a single man sat behind it. Lark vaguely recognized him as the large man she'd seen following Kayda back from *The Lady Luck* when they left Flamesmoat. Sweat glistened on his brow in the stuffy room, made even stuffier with all the windows shuttered.

"Jett, what is the meaning of this?" Lark asked. "I know I didn't forget any lunch plans with you."

The sweaty man stood. "Something is deeply wrong in this city."

Lark's stomach twisted. She crossed her arms and raised a brow.

Dausius strode forward, sticking out a hand. "We haven't met. I'm Dausius of the Wandering Bards. Who might you be?"

The man turned a glare on Jett. "I asked you to meet me back here with help, and you bring me a traveling show?"

Jett flushed. "At least I found someone, Gawain. I see you've returned alone."

"Gawain, is it?" Dausius withdrew his hand, unshaken. "Aren't you the Guard Captain? What's going on?"

Lark spun on her heel. "I have to check on Violet."

Jett grabbed her arm. "You can't return to the ship. They aren't letting anyone off."

"What?" Aren asked.

"A few hours after we docked, a group of men claiming to be with the Port Master ordered *Nova's Champion* surrounded and quarantined." Jett explained. "They're saying there's an illness on board. But of course, that's a load of horseshit."

"Are you sure?" Lark's heart skipped a beat. "Violet... I can't leave her on board with a sickness spreading."

Gawain shook his head. "It's not true. Jett and I left to take a closer look at the other boats on the wharf just before the quarantine. There wasn't a single word about sickness until the Port Master showed up with his invented claims."

Meital stepped closer, placing a gentle hand on Lark's shoulder. "Even if it were true, Mika's still there with Violet. She'll be all right."

That's right, Mika was there. He wouldn't let anything bad happen to Violet. Lark let out a deep sigh. "I guess this only confirms what we learned while we were with Tiora."

"That's right. You said there was trouble earlier but not what it was," Dausius said.

Lark nodded. "One of Ti's sisters knows someone who works as a driver at Oasis Manse. The boy told her that the trading family Kayda's meeting with is planning to betray her."

"That would explain all the rich layabouts on the ships that we saw," Jett said.

"Rich layabouts?" Mazen asked.

Gawain scoffed. "Princess Kayda was sure that Wyll fellow was prepping those ships to join us in the fight to save Dracwood. Instead, they're practically crawling with finely dressed folk dripping with gems—most looking like they've never worked a day in their lives or know what a sword or bow looked like—much less how to use it. That and a ton of armed men and women hovering over them like it's their job to keep the rich pigs breathing."

"Then it's true. They're not planning to join the fight. They're going to run." Lark's heart thrummed madly. "What are we going to do?"

"Tiora." Aren's eyes widened. "We told her to meet us back at the ship."

Meital stepped toward the door. "I'll find her. C'mon, Maz."

The twins slipped out the door, shutting it firmly behind them.

Dausius paced behind the head of the table, tapping his chin. "We need to find the princess. With everyone stuck on the ship, it's up to us to stop this foul trader's plan from succeeding."

Gawain scratched his sweaty brow. "How is the question? With all the mages stuck on board *Nova's Champion,* we don't stand much of a chance." He gestured to Jett. "The two of us, a few traveling entertainers, and a single mage against the whole of Jorian high society and all of their sell-swords? I'm not a betting man, but I doubt many would chance those odds."

"What choice do we have? Without Kayda, everything falls apart. We can't fight the scourge without her," Lark said.

The door creaked open. Tiora stepped inside.

"You're back." Lark smiled, giving her a quick hug.

"What's going on?" Tiora asked. "Maz and Mei rushed us in here before we could reach the ship."

"I'll tell you everything in a moment," she promised, turning to greet the skinny young boy cowering behind Tiora, next to her sister. "I see you found him. Hello, I'm Lark. It's nice to meet you, Davit."

The boy stared down at his threadbare boots. "Hello."

Lark smiled at him, though he didn't look up to meet her eyes. "Please, we're friends of Cyrie's. And friends of the princess' as well. Can you tell us what you know? We only want to help our friend."

Davit peeled off his dusty hat, wringing it in his hands. "I could lose my job for this."

Dausius dug into his pocket and lifted out a heavy coin purse. Davit's eyes lit up at the jingling.

"I'll pay you handsomely for the information," Dausius offered.

Davit glanced at Cyrie, and after she sent him a gentle nod, he spoke, "It's all true. Everything Cyrie told you. The trading families are planning to flee. I heard them laughing about it. Bits and snatches while they've been in the carriage."

Gawain's neck stiffened, the corded muscle there sticking out. "I knew it."

"Is there anything else?" Lark asked.

Davit nodded. "I drove them there this morning—the king and princess. After I took care of the horses, Sir Wyll ordered me to take the rest of the day off. He *never* gives me the day off."

"She must still be there." Gawain rose to his feet. "We have to save her."

Jett squeezed his shoulder. "Wait. We don't know that for sure. They could've easily moved her in a second carriage." He turned to Davit. "What's their security like at Oasis Manse?"

"They've got a dozen men, at least, keeping watch over the house at all times."

Lark's heart sank. That didn't sound like good odds. They'd have to fight their way inside, without the certainty that she was even there.

"There's more. Sir Wyll and Sir Egard are planning to take the princess with them when they leave on the morrow."

"Are you sure?" Aren asked.

Davit shuffled, his shoulders sagging. "Yes. I heard them say they needed her. What for, I don't know."

"So, they'll need to bring her here tomorrow or at some point in the night," Dausius mused, rubbing his chin. His face lit up. "I have a plan that could work." He spread out his arms, his smile spreading just as widely. "I hope you're all prepared to do what we do best."

Lark stepped down from the tabletop in the *Salty Serpent Inn*, the roar of applause echoing throughout the common room. She displayed what she hoped was a radiant smile, all while exhaustion tugged on her shoulders and apprehension spread through her belly.

The thick crowd parted, allowing her and Aren to make their way to the long table they shared with the rest of the show members. With barely a pause for the clapping to subside, Dausius hopped up on the table and immediately launched into a tale filled with adventure and mystery.

Lark sank into a hard wooden chair, heaving out a sigh. "Any word?"

Meital's gaze flicked to the windows. "No sign of her yet. We might need to keep this up until morning."

Mazen groaned. "Much more of this and my knives are liable to start missing their target."

Tiora squeezed his shoulder, her smile a touch too bright. "Surely not... You're the best there is."

The grin he aimed at her was interrupted by a yawn. "Flattery doesn't work as well in the wee hours as it does when I'm well rested."

The inn door slammed open, and a group of three wobbly sailors stumbled outside into the dark.

"How many is that now?" Lark's stomach churned.

"Don't worry." Meital shook her head. "Did you see the way they were walking? They won't be in any condition for sailing anytime soon."

Lark couldn't stem the unease that swelled inside her chest every time the door opened. They'd arranged an evening of entertainment for the captains and sailors of the ships docked on the wharf. A grand send-off with ale flowing freely and non-stop acts that were supposed to keep all of the crew so enthralled they'd stay the entire night and be in no condition to sail on the morrow.

So far, the plan had been going smoothly, but as the hours passed, more men trickled out, back to their hammocks on their ships. If enough left... She didn't even want to think about what that would mean for the rest of the plan. They had to put on the show of their lives tonight. Kayda's life depended on it.

"What song should we do next, Aren?" Lark scanned the crowd, noting a handful of sleepy-eyed patrons. "I don't think we should chance another ballad. The last one sent that table out the door."

"Shall we do the opener again? We've played all the merry tunes once already," Aren replied.

Lark scrunched the hem of her multi-colored tunic. "Repeating sounds like a recipe for disaster, too." Lark missed her bondmate even more than usual. Without Muse and Whisper, they were down an act, making them rely much more on their songs.

Tiora bit her lip, then leaned over. "What about some new material? When I was at the *Joria Rose*, they hired a singer once a week. I have a feeling the songs she performed would be a big hit with this crowd. They're simple enough to learn. Just a repeating tune and rhyming lyrics."

Lark frowned. "Are you sure, Ti?" Surely remembering her time in that brothel was bound to dredge up some painful memories.

Tiora straightened in her seat and sucked in a deep breath. "I'm sure. I want to help."

Aren shrugged. "It can't hurt to try."

Lark smiled and squeezed Tiora's hand, impressed once again by her friend's incredible strength.

"Does anyone have a parchment? I'll tell you the lyrics, and you can write them down, Lark," Tiora said.

Mazen hopped up. "I'll see if the barkeep has a bit to lend."

"No, don't bother, Maz." Lark pulled her pack from the back of her chair. "I'll add them to the book Daus made me. There are a few blank pages at the end."

As Lark dug out the book and a charcoal, Tiora hummed the tune to Aren.

"Like this?" He thrummed his lute quietly with Tiora listening intently.

"Yes, that's it exactly," Tiora said. "Just keep that up on repeat."

Dausius finished his tale, and the crowd roared again.

Meital stood, clasping Mazen's shoulder. "C'mon, Maz. Ti can sit this one out to help Lark and Aren."

The twins wove through the crowd. The crush of sailors swallowed their multicolored tunics until they replaced Daus on the tabletop and sent their glittering daggers flying to a chorus of oohs and aahs.

Lark wasn't watching. She was too busy trying to keep her cool while her cheeks burned. But she kept writing, copying down the lyrics to some of the dirtiest limericks she'd ever heard. Dausius returned to the table and nearly choked on his water when he discovered what they were up to.

As Tiora finished the last of the verses, she leaned back in her seat and sipped her water. "That's all of them. The ones I can remember, at least."

"These are great, Ti." Lark grinned. "At least your time at that brothel will come in handy for something."

A gasp sounded behind them. Lark and Tiora spun in unison. Cyrie slowly backed away, her hand over her lips and her eyes wide.

"You were in a brothel, Ti-ti?" Cyrie's chin quivered, and her eyes filled with tears.

Lark scrubbed her face as the girl fled the room. "I'm so sorry. I should've never said—"

"I have to find her." Tiora jumped out of her chair and chased after her little sister.

Lark stood, but Daus stepped in front of her. "I'll go after them. Don't worry. It'll be all right. You two are up next."

Lark sighed as she watched him disappear into the crowd. She hoped Daus was right. She'd forgotten Cyrie had volunteered to keep a watch for Kayda's arrival at the docks with her friend Davit. If she'd only thought to peek over her shoulder, or just kept her mouth shut, then Tiora wouldn't be forced to spill all her secrets to her little sister. Lark's stomach knotted from knowing she'd been the cause of it all.

Just then, the applause rose, signaling the end of the twin's act.

Aren slung an arm around her shoulders. "That's us. You ready to try the new songs?"

She bit her lip, wanting nothing more than to tear out the pages from the book and forget these songs ever existed. Not only had they forced a wedge between her friend and her sister, they were definitely not the kind of song she was comfortable singing.

But as she debated internally, another table of sailors rose and headed for the door. Lark pushed aside her misgivings. She had to do this for Kayda. Surely a few moments of discomfort would be worth it to save the sister she'd only just discovered.

"Let's go."

Soon they arrived at the head of the room, and Aren helped her atop the table before hopping up beside her. He strummed the lute, and Lark took a deep breath and sang, choosing one of the milder lyrics to start with.

There once was a young lady of Flamesmoat

Who woke with a tickle in her throat

The healer said sure, I've got the cure

That panicked young lady of Flamesmoat

Lark cringed on the inside while forcing a brazen smile. Silence filled the common room for a heartbeat as all the sailors stared up at them, no doubt shocked at the bawdy innuendo that was much different from the grand ballads and lively dance numbers they'd performed so far.

But then the crowd erupted in laughter. The men who'd been on their way to the door joined in and spun around, heading back to the table they'd just abandoned.

Lark turned to Aren, shaking her head and smiling as she signaled for him to start up the tune again. The things she did for her friends...

The morning sunlight flickered inside the inn windows. Lark stepped down from the tabletop, yet again, and made her way to the table she shared with the Wandering Bards. Exhaustion wasn't just prickling her shoulders anymore. It lay heavy on her limbs like a warm blanket, ready to lull her to sleep. But she couldn't succumb to the urge for slumber. There was still so much left to do.

Dausius hopped up on the table behind her, launching into a humorous story before she and Aren sank into their seats. Lark glanced at Tiora, sending her a wobbly grin.

Tiora smiled back warmly. "Those limericks Dausius thought up are even better than the ones from the brothel."

Lark chuckled and shook her head. "Yeah, who knew our Daus had such a dirty mind?"

Dausius had sat down with the charcoal after Lark's first round of bawdy songs and came up with a dozen of his own, each one filthier than the last. They'd certainly been a big hit with the crowd of sailors. Dozens of men had stayed the whole night. Even now, a few hours after dawn, the room was still full, with more than one group of sailors sleeping on their folded arms atop the tables or leaning back in their chairs, mouths wide open and snoring.

Tiora giggled before turning to gaze out the window.

Lark squeezed Tiora's hand. "I'm sorry again about your sister."

"Stop apologizing. I'm not mad. I'm relieved I got the chance to explain everything to Cyrie." Tiora smiled again, looking hopeful. "I have a feeling that after today, a lot of things around here will end up changing for the better."

Just then, the inn door slammed open, and Cyrie rushed in. She stopped at their table and leaned forward. "They're here. Davit confirmed it." She glanced at her sister and sent her a wide smile, her excitement evident.

Lark sat forward in her seat, the exhaustion that'd just been so heavy lifting with Cyrie's announcement. This was it. She exhaled, her palms moistening and her heart fluttering like a hummingbird's wings.

Meital stood, signaling Dausius at the front of the room.

"That's all for us, my fine friends. You've been a wonderful audience." He bowed hastily and jumped down from the tabletop, quickly joining them.

"We're on." Aren hopped up and strapped his lute to his back.

Dausius blew out a breath, turning to look each of them in the eye. "You all remember your places, yes?"

Tiora bit her lip. "Wait. My mother and sister did as you asked, but Jett and Gawain haven't checked in. Shouldn't we wait?"

Daus shook his head. "No. They were always a long shot. The show must go on without delay."

Lark rose to her feet and walked to Mazen's side. "Ready?"

"Do you need to ask?" He twirled a knife, cocking a brow.

Aren grabbed Lark's arm. "Good luck. Be safe."

"You, too." Lark flashed him a smile and strode to the door, where she waved goodbye to her friends.

Dausius called out to them as they opened the door. "Time to put on the show of a lifetime."

Chapter 22

Kayda woke to her body gently swaying. She groaned, opening her eyes to a world of black, her face swaddled in a layer of dark silk. Her heart pounded as confusion reigned. Images of the tetrela rose unbidden, and she shuddered, twisting where she lay. She flashed back to that dark desert night, her body immobile while being manhandled by the enormous spider. But the clatter of chains against the hard floor she sprawled on brought her back to the present.

What the blazes? What was on her head? And why was her face throbbing?

It all came back to her in a flash. The reek of charred flesh. Wyll's garbled screams. Egard's fist flying at her face. She smiled despite herself, hissing as the action tugged on her swollen jaw. But the pain was worth it to make that bastard pay for what he'd done to her father.

If only it had been Egard in the back seat instead... She clenched her fists, feeling the tug of the shackles attached to her wrists. She might still get the chance to make him regret what he'd done.

Kayda forced the thought aside. There were more important things to worry about now—like where she was and why she couldn't see. The sweat-soaked cloth on her face had to go. She reached up, but with her shackled wrists held close to her body with the metal chain, she couldn't quite make contact with the soft fabric.

She rubbed her head against the floor while taking stock of her body in the dark. She was lying flat on something hard. Maybe with enough wiggling she could... There. After scrunching her body into a ball, she caught a bit of the hem between her middle and ring finger. She pulled.

Kayda squinted, the dim light in the room setting off a cascade of thrashing in her skull. Well, that explained the swaying. She was on a boat. A glass window on a nearby wall provided a view of the waterline. She must be below deck on one of the ships.

Were they still parked at the wharf or already out to sea? With her head still swimming, she couldn't be sure.

One thing was certain—she was alone. The tiny window didn't let in much light, but it did a fair job of illuminating the room. The contents certainly didn't give her much to go by. It was completely bare, with only the darker wood and nail holes on the floor remaining as evidence that anything had once been here.

If she had to guess, she would bet this room was once a cabin. But now it might as well be a prison for all the good it would do her. All she had was bare wooden walls, the black silk shirt clutched in her hands, and what looked like a chamber pot in the far corner. Not much to use to escape.

Kayda sighed, rolling up to a seated position, though the motion made the throbbing in her head intensify so much that she groaned again. Now, to get to the door. It was probably too much to hope her captors had left the door unlocked, but she would be a fool not to che—

Footsteps pounded outside. Her stomach churned as the door swung open.

"Ah, you're awake." Wyll peeked in, an apple-red silk suit covering his tall frame, looking no worse for the wear after the scorching she'd delivered, though his voice was slightly raspy. He sent her a wide smile from the doorway. "You were hoping to see me burnt to a crisp, I expect. Sorry to disappoint."

Kayda glared at him. Guess he'd found a healer in time to avoid any permanent damage. Damn.

Wyll tossed a sack inside the room. "Now that I've seen my investment is intact, I'll be on my way." He chuckled. "We'll hand you over to your new *friends* in a few days."

"Wait," she said before he shut the door. "You don't have to do this. There's still time for you to free me. I can ensure that your father pays the price for his crimes and you're let off easy."

Wyll sneered at her. "It's adorable you think you still have anything left to bargain. Can't you see you've been outmaneuvered? Don't fret, my dear. Happens to the best of us, from time to time."

"That's where you're wrong. I *will* be at the battle in the Abandoned Lands. It's fated. Your plans will be foiled, and when they are, I won't go easy on you. This is your last chance, Wyll. Set me free. Now."

Riotous laughter met her statement. But after a moment, Wyll's laughter cut off, and he clutched his throat. Kayda bit back the smirk that fought to spread at the evidence of the damage her fire had wrought.

Wyll cleared his throat and narrowed his eyes. "You actually believe that dreck? Puh-lease. Let me break it down for you. You've lost your dragon. Every member of the royal family is dead. No one knows where you are, and even if they did, there's nothing they can do about it on your *stolen* ship, since it is currently under quarantine with all souls stuck on board for the foreseeable future. No one is coming for you, and your magic won't be any help without a source. You've been outplayed, Princess. The sooner you get used to the idea, the easier it will be for you. Now, if you'll excuse me, I have more important things to see to than delusional *former* royalty."

With that, he slammed the door, and the click of the lock reverberated in Kayda's ears.

Quarantine? *Nova's Champion* was quarantined? Kayda's heart sank. She couldn't expect any help from there.

What was she going to do?

She had to find some way to escape. There was no way she would let herself be carted across the sea to become some stranger's slave or used as leverage against Dru.

With that thought in mind, she slid across the floor toward the sack Wyll had tossed to her and grasped it with her shaking fingers. Was it too much to ask that he'd slipped up and gifted her something she could use to escape?

Apparently so. All the sack contained was a stale loaf of bread and a full waterskin, neither of which would be helpful. As unappealing as the loaf looked, it still made her stomach rumble. She tore off a corner and stuffed the hard bread into her mouth, considering while she chewed.

Jayan and Izora were still out there with the Sul. Surely, they would come to her aid. But how would they know she was in trouble? And could they make it to Joria from Sul Hollow before the ship set sail?

From what she'd overheard in the basement, it had sounded like they'd been planning to set sail straight away. But the longer she sat still on the floor, the more she suspected they were still at port. The boat was certainly not swaying the same way *Nova's Champion* did while they were at sea, and all the boats she'd seen on arrival appeared so similar; surely it would feel the same, too…

Perhaps her little trick in the carriage had slowed their timeline, but whether it would be enough, she had no idea. She needed to slow them further. If they set sail, all hope was lost.

Kayda swallowed the chalky lump in her mouth and cast her gaze about the room again. There was nothing. Absolutely nothing.

Wait—maybe the silk could be useful. She scrambled to her knees and across the room. She crammed the fabric beneath the door. All she needed was another small spark. If she was lucky, the door would catch.

Let's see how they deal with a fire on board.

But before she could call on her source, something clattered in the hall. Kayda stilled, listening intently. Were those footsteps? These were much softer than Wyll's had been, but after a moment, she was certain it was footsteps—and they were coming closer.

She snatched the silk from under the door and scrambled back. A few moments later, the sound halted, and something strange took its place. The gentle clinking and scraping of metal on metal.

She barely had time to wonder what the sound meant before the door popped open, and a wave of relief crashed into her so strongly she nearly squealed with glee. "Lark, thank the Lord Dragon! How did you find me? Wyll said the ship was quarantined."

Lark slipped into the room with one of the twins she performed with, both of them wearing multicolored tunics and wide smiles. "Kayda, it's good to see you. I'll explain everything in a moment. Let's get you out of those first." After eyeing the chains, Lark turned to her companion. "Maz, can you unlock these chains, too?"

That's right—Kayda remembered their names now. Mazen and Meital, the knife jugglers.

Mazen closed the door gently behind him, then crouched beside her and grabbed the lock on her chains. "Yeah, this one looks easy. I'm glad my years as a pickpocket and thief are coming in handy." He sent Lark a mischievous grin. "Never thought I'd be stealing a princess."

Kayda didn't have long to ponder over that. Lark knelt on her other side and gripped her jaw gently. Kayda winced as Lark's fingers prodded at the flesh on her chin.

Lark's brow furrowed. "Looks like someone clobbered you pretty hard. Don't worry, I can fix it." Lark released her chin, pulled the pack from her back, and dug inside. "Do you have any other injuries?"

"No. I'm all right." The lock on her chains clicked open, and Kayda sighed. "Forget about healing me. It can wait. Let's get out of here."

Lark nodded, replacing the bag on her back. With the three of them working, they removed the chains quickly, and Kayda breathed out her first deep breath since she woke with the heavy weight dragging her down. All the while, Lark kept up a steady stream of chatter, filling her in on everything that had happened while she'd been trapped by Wyll.

"So, you got all the crew too drunk to sail?" Kayda chuckled. "That was smart thinking."

Lark smiled. "Not quite all, but enough of them they won't be sailing anywhere for a few hours. We have a few surprises in store if we catch any trouble on the way out, too."

"Where is the king?" Mazen asked. "Do you know where they're keeping him? We can get him ou—"

"No, we can't." Kayda's voice shook. "He's dead."

Lark squeezed her shoulder. "I'm so sorry."

Kayda heaved out a deep breath and nodded once. "C'mon. Let's go."

They made their way through the barren room's door. The hall looked identical to the ones found on *Nova's Champion*, except all the candles and oil lamps that decorated the wall had been removed. Wyll clearly wasn't taking any chances that she'd get close to an open flame.

"Blazes. Where's a torch when you need one?" Kayda mused.

"I almost forgot. I brought you something." Lark pulled the pack from her back again and removed a metal tin and a long stick wrapped in cloth.

"Here, I'll light it while we walk." Kayda grabbed the supplies. She quickly opened the tinderbox and worked the flint and steel, thankful for Izora's instruction with the same materials back in the tunnels beneath Kings Keep. Within moments, she lit the torch, just before they opened the door to the outer deck.

The bright torchlight and near blinding sunlight made Kayda squint as they strode out on the deck. Then the door they'd just exited slammed, and a pair of women popped out from behind it. They tossed buckets of water on her, extinguishing her torch and drenching her golden silk dress. They moved so quickly Kayda only had time to gasp before she stood there soaking and stuttering.

"My, my. I hope you weren't planning on leaving already?" Wyll's deep voice greeted her as a circle of armed men and women surrounded them. Kayda spotted at least a dozen and knew there were likely more that she couldn't see, all with weapons trained in their direction, their faces locked in hard stares.

Wyll elbowed between a scowling, dark-skinned bald fellow with a bow pointed at Kayda's face and a pale long-haired man wearing a bored expression behind the longsword he aimed at Mazen's throat. Behind them, a crowd of finely dressed folks lounged on the deck, smirking and snickering at each other quietly.

"Did you think you'd escape so easily? Your little group of tricksters won't be enough to free you, my dear," Wyll said.

Lark stepped forward, ignoring the blade a grizzled, bearded man held at her throat, raising her voice far louder than was necessary. "Who said we were alone?"

A whistle rang out, and Kayda's eyes widened. A series of sharp whistles followed, each one fading in succession in such a way that she was certain each whistler was further away than the last. Then chaos erupted.

Several multicolored tunics flashed in the streets as the rest of Lark's performer friends emerged. With them, hundreds of people flooded the docks, pouring into the streets like a swarm of bees whose hive had been kicked. The buzz of all that angry humanity rose in the air and reached the armed men on the deck. Most stood strong, but some turned in astonishment, shifting on their feet.

"A few laborers with sticks won't stop us," Wyll announced with a scoff. "Will they, men?"

With that, even more armed people revealed themselves, stepping out from doorways and rounding the nooks and crannies they'd been hidden in.

Kayda gulped as her gaze flitted between the mercenaries on board and the crowd. Wyll was right about one thing—the caliber of fighters the performers brought definitely didn't match the men Wyll hired to protect the ships. The men and women on the docks carried rusty old knives and homemade weapons—some indeed held what looked like nothing more than sharpened sticks.

Kayda's heart thundered to life. She'd seen what could happen when a few trained men stood against the common folk. Would this be a repeat of the battle in Kings Keep on the night she found Dru?

She shook off the worry. No matter her misgivings, these people were here for her. To save her and stand up to the rich cowards who'd built a fortune with their labor, only to abandon them when their lives were on the line. They deserved a chance to stand up for what was right. And the gutless traders deserved to pay for their cowardice.

Kayda dropped the useless soaked torch and flicked her wet braids out of her eyes, stepping beside Lark. She projected her voice loudly, booming above the buzz of the commoners. "Your time as leaders of this city is over. The people have spoken."

The mob responded with hoots and cheers. Wyll backed away a step, scanning the crowd warily as it continued to increase in size. The other rich traders watching on deck edged away from the rails or hurried to the hatches leading inside the ship.

Kayda smiled brazenly. "These people might not be slaves in name, but what has their freedom earned them? Just a life lived in squalor and a ruling class that would abandon them at the first sign of trouble. Trade is *not* king here anymore. It stops today."

Wyll's eyes blazed with barely contained fury as he signaled for the fighters to spread out. "This mob doesn't stand a chance against these fine fighters. Let's see how long they stand when they start dying in droves. Men, it's time to do what you've been hired for."

Kayda's stomach clenched as the fighters stepped forward to the rails. Beyond them, she saw similar action happening on each ship on the dock. This would not be an easy win for the common people. She held her breath, waiting for the first arrow to fly and the blood to flow.

But then a new voice roared above the mayhem. "Interlopers! Remove yourselves from our ships."

Kayda's heart stalled. She knew that voice. Her jaw dropped for a heartbeat, and then a smile slowly spread across her face.

Lazar pushed through the crowd with Izora and Jayan at his side—and surprisingly—Jett and Guard Captain Gawain. Dozens of Sul, armed with pole knives and bows, followed at their backs.

"Your ships?" Wyll scoffed, his voice sounding equal parts incredulous and drenched with hate. "These ships are *mine*."

Lazar didn't balk at the enmity aimed at him. He strode forward, the silver streaks in his braided hair gleaming as the crowd parted in his wake, allowing even more Sul to filter into the streets. "No. These ships have been promised to the sandborn. They *will* ferry us to the great battle to come. Remove yourselves or prepare to return to dust."

The fighters who'd appeared only mildly wary of the commoners were clearly shaken now. They shot each other wide-eyed glances, hands shuddering on the hilts of their swords and quivering against their bowstrings. When a group of mages appeared from the direction of *Nova's Champion*, elements swirling in their outstretched hands, Kayda knew they would fold.

One by one, the fighters backed away from the rail and marched to the gangplank, sheathing their swords and shouldering their bows.

"What are you doing?" Wyll grabbed closest mercenary's arm, trying to tug him back to his spot at the rail. "I hired you to defend the ships. Do your jobs or you can forget your pay."

The man shook off his hold and pressed forward. "You can't pay the dead. I'm out of here."

Kayda strolled forward. "I'm afraid you've been outplayed, *my dear*. The sooner you accept it, the easier it will be for you."

Behind her, the door to the inner hull cracked open, and the traders inside filed out. They crowded around on the deck, gathering their things and scrambling to leave. Chaos flooded the streets and the boats. The common people, who'd been happy to let the sell-swords pass unmolested, were not so kind to the traders. Screams broke out on all sides.

Wyll backed away, blinking wildly. At that moment, Egard burst from the nearest porthole, rubbing the sleep from his eyes.

"What is the meaning of this?" Egard bellowed. Then he took stock of the scene, and his fat face blanched.

Wyll grabbed his father's arm, tugging him backward toward the gangplank.

"I hope you're not planning to leave already?" Kayda grinned, taking extreme pleasure in echoing Wyll's words back at him, yet again.

Wyll and Egard flinched in unison. They scanned the crowd as another trader screamed out in pain, trying unsuccessfully to escape the bloodthirsty mob. Egard's gaze locked on a trader just beyond the gangplank as a trio of youths with sticks wailed on him, the dull *thwack* of their hits beating in time with the surf against the hull.

The man spotted him looking, and he reached out, desperation shining in his eyes. Then one of the boys struck him hard across the jaw. His head jerked sideways, and blood sprayed in a fine mist. His golden chains swung as he crumpled, and the mob swallowed him.

"Please, Princess. M-my queen. Have mercy." Wyll fell to his knees in front of her, and in less than a heartbeat, Egard followed suit.

"Help us," Egard chimed in, his head bowed.

"And what price will you pay for my help?" Kayda smiled. She strode up to Mazen and grabbed one of the thin daggers strapped to his back, flicking the blade up and hiding it behind her wrist.

"Anything you want," Wyll rushed to offer. "Take all the ships. They're yours."

Kayda smirked, striding closer to the kneeling pair. "Perfect. Then of course I'll help."

Egard's shoulders sank, and his head bowed even further. "Thank you. Oh, thank the gods."

Kayda knelt beside him and sliced the blade across his throat. "Have all the help you gave my father."

Wyll scrambled back from Egard as blood spurted from his neck, painting the deck red. Wyll trembled, a stain quickly darkening the crimson trousers of his finely pressed silk suit. Then, like the coward he'd proven himself to be time and again, he ran. He made it to the aft rail and jumped, splashing into the bay's deep water.

Kayda rose to her feet, shook Egard's warm blood from her fingers, and strolled to the aft rail. She leaned over the side and spotted Wyll surface in the ocean. He spun back and stared up at the boat, a smirk on his face, before he lifted an arm to swim away.

The glint of silver flashed in the air just before a pole-knife lodged in Wyll's throat. Kayda smirked back at Wyll one last time before he slipped beneath the waves. Then she turned to the wharf, in the direction the pole-knife flew from. Jayan stared back at her and winked.

Kayda met his eyes and winked back.

Chapter 23

The days in the bog passed in a predictable routine. Each morning, Conall woke, bleary after a night spent tossing and turning, to spend countless hours slowly poling eastward through the maze.

But despite Fillan's snoring, Ereni proved all too right to trust him. It was soon apparent they'd had little hope of ever finding their way to the Orddon Ocean with how much the tangled waters weaved. Luckily, the young ferryman knew every twist and turn of the bog. Eventually, they grew close enough to the coast that a seabird's cawing joined the familiar croaking and buzzing of the Boglands' critters.

"How much longer until we reach a sea pass?" Ereni asked from her seat at the bow. Shadow's ears twitched at the sound of her voice, but he didn't glance up from where he napped in their canoe's center.

"Not long now." Fillan pushed on his pole, easing his canoe forward. "An hour or so, I expect."

Conall's heart lifted. It couldn't come too soon for him. Day after day spent penned up in a tiny boat with only a few short breaks to stretch his legs on solid ground wasn't exactly his idea of a good time.

Not to mention, they hadn't exactly been prepared for the journey to begin with. Fillan lent each of them a set of stained overalls so they hadn't been forced to spend the entire time in the same set of clothes, but rinsing out his shirt and trousers in the murky bog water hadn't exactly cleaned them properly. He was dying for a change of clothes and a chance to wash up with soap and clean water.

There would be all that and more on *Nova's Champion* once they met them on the coast. He smiled, picturing Lark's face when she spotted him and Shadow returning. He couldn't wait to reunite with her once again. And it wasn't just his sister waiting for him on board. There was someone else he was eager to meet.

He flicked a quick glance at Ereni, and his stomach fluttered. The time spent in her company had reminded him how much he once cared for her. It wasn't quite the same, yet, but he was beginning to think that in time, they might regain some of that ease. Perhaps even more. Especially now that they had Violet.

What would their daughter be like? Despite himself, a tiny spike of fear prickled his chest. Would Violet like him? She was only an infant—he knew it was silly to worry, but he couldn't help it. It was so strange knowing there was a piece of him out there, completely unaware that he even existed.

Would she cry when he held her? He tried to mentally prepare for the very real possibility that the babe would wail and treat him like a stranger for long after they first met.

He'd still not fully wrapped his mind around everything Ereni told him about their daughter's future. It was strange to think she would one day grow up and hold the fate of the world in her hands. But then again, there was no shortage of prophecies latched to the members of his family.

Conall sighed, thrusting the stick down from the back of the canoe. He may not have met her yet, but he was already determined to be a part of his daughter's life. If she was destined to change the world, then someone had better do a damn good job of raising her right.

He might not be the perfect man for the task, but he knew from experience there was plenty of evil out there. The least he could do was ensure that Violet grew up happy and healthy, with parents who'd love her and teach her everything she'd need to navigate a harsh world when the time came for her to fulfill whatever task fate demanded.

His stomach clenched as the Unseen's words returned to haunt him—*Three will come, but only two will see the next day.* He'd not forgotten that he might not have the chance to be a part of Violet's life. But if he was one of the two that survived, would that be any better? That meant either Kayda or Lark would be the one to fall. Could he live with that, if one of his sisters died instead of him?

Shadow's ears twitched again, and his head lifted. *"I hear voices."*

Not again. Conall had hoped they'd traveled far out of the escaped prisoners' path. "Fillan." He waved his arms, speaking barely above a whisper. "Shadow hears voices. Could it be your men?"

Fillan frowned. "It's possible, but we better take cover in case it isn't. Quick, follow me."

Fillan led them to a spot where the mangroves thinned and craned his neck behind the branches. He used his stick to brush a few wispy tendrils aside and beckoned them forward.

Ereni's brow furrowed as they slid inside. "Wait, there's not enough room."

Conall peered around the small hole behind the tree. She was right. Although the shrubbery hid them well enough that he couldn't see much of the waterway beyond the leaves, the space was far too narrow to fit more than one canoe inside.

"Don't worry. There's another spot just ahead." With that, Fillan dropped the branch and slipped away in the water just as the voices rose enough to become audible, although they were still far enough away that he couldn't make out what was said.

Conall squinted, bobbing his head to keep an eye on Fillan's canoe as it slid through the waterway. His heart raced as the voices grew louder and louder. Fillan still hadn't stopped, his head flitting frantically around the tree bank on the waterway's opposite side.

Conall gritted his teeth as he heard the first words clearly.

A loud smack rang out before a voice grumbled, "Blazing bugs are gonna be the death of me. At least back at the prison, we weren't getting eaten alive."

Oh no. Fillan had to hide now.

Conall crouched down in the canoe, making himself as small as possible, all the while keeping a watch as Fillan struggled to locate a spot on the other side of the bog.

Suddenly, a second voice rang out, clearly coming from a different direction. "Hey, is that you, Garnell? Where are you blokes?"

A chorus of voices answered, all of them louder than the last.

"Hey, over here!"

"Where've ya been?"

"We're over here."

There were so many. Fillan scrambled faster. He shoved his pole into the bog and brushed aside branch after branch, peering behind them. Conall sighed as the ferryman's canoe finally slipped behind a large mangrove close to the nearest bend in the bog.

He'd hidden not a moment too soon. Just as Fillan's boat disappeared completely, the water rippled around the bend. One boat appeared, then a second. Soon, five boats perched in the waterway outside of their hiding space, all the men hollering hello to a single canoe that approached from the opposite direction.

Conall's heart skipped a beat. Had that man been trailing them? They'd been lucky to happen upon the larger group when they had, or the single man might've snuck up behind them without notice. Unless he was in the habit of talking to himself, it would've been unlikely for them to hear him speaking in enough time to hide.

"So, did you find anything?" a bald man from the larger group asked.

The single fellow puffed out his chest, smirking. Conall recognized him as the same hulking man he and Ereni crossed paths with the first day, with the crooked nose and scarred arms. The same man who'd threatened to slit the girl's throats. "Wouldn't you all like to know?"

"C'mon, Reg. Don't be like that. We want a way out of this maze as much as you do," pleaded a short man with a cudgel strapped to his back. He slapped his wrist loudly and grumbled under his breath.

"Bah, he's just as full of shit as always," a new voice declared.

"He must've found something. Where else are the rest of the blokes he brought with him?" said the bald man.

"I found it all right—the answer to all our problems. If you joker's wise up, you'll come with me and see for yourselves." Reg sent them a wide grin full of confidence.

Conall watched the larger group as they circled together and argued among themselves in hushed tones, flicking occasional scowls in Reg's direction. Finally, they broke apart.

The bald man pushed his canoe to the front of the group. He lifted a worn bow from the bottom of his boat and slung it over his shoulder. "All right. We'll go see. But if shit goes sideways, you're gonna get an arrow in your back."

"C'mon, Garnell, would I do that to you?" Even from their hiding spot, Conall glimpsed the cruel glint in Reg's eyes that contrasted his affronted tone.

It seemed Garnell wasn't buying it either. His hand tightened on his bow, and he rolled his eyes. "Enough chatter. Lead the way to our *salvation*."

"Don't worry. You won't be disappointed." Reg chuckled. "You're gonna love him."

"What was that all about? Who could they be meeting?" Ereni whispered after the men's canoes disappeared down the waterway and around a bend.

Conall shrugged. "No idea. But at least they're heading in the opposite direction."

He backed out of their hiding spot, returning to the waterway's center. Fillan joined them and silently motioned them to follow. They slid further away from the prisoners until even the echo of their voices receded. When Shadow's ears finally fell and he rested on the canoe bottom, the last of the tension in Conall's limbs lifted.

Ereni leaned forward, pitching her voice softly and meeting Fillan's gaze. "Are you sure you'll be all right heading back into the bog? Why don't you come with us?"

Fillan shook his head. "Nah, I'll be fine. If I sail south when we split up, there's no way those men will catch me before I make it back to Raimire."

Conall frowned. "I'm sure you're right about the route, but how can you be sure there's no one else out there? Or what if those men turn back? Ereni's right. You should come with us."

"I can't leave my dad that long. He's the only family I've got left."

Conall sighed. He could certainly understand the need to be with family in these trying times.

"Don't worry. If there's anyone else, I'll hide like we did back there." Fillan flashed a lopsided smile. "And I'm not worried about the last group. They ought to have their hands full where they're headed."

"What do you mean?" Ereni asked.

"That bend they turned down leads to Bogsmouth. Nothing there these days except for the scourge."

Conall's brow furrowed. Strange. Why would Reg lead them there? Could he be leading those men into a trap?

He tamped down the questions. There was no way to find out without following them, and despite his curiosity, that wasn't a path he would be taking. All that mattered was finding the ocean and meeting the ships before the battle started.

They continued eastward as the sun sank slowly in the sky behind them. Little clues emerged that the ocean was close at hand. The few patches of dirt planted among the mangroves shifted from deep brown to a sandy tan, littered with chipped shell fragments. The cawing of seabirds intensified and was eventually joined by the gentle roar of the surf.

Fillan stopped in front of a fork in the bog and pointed down the path behind him. "Here's where we part ways. This will lead you to the ocean. Here. You're gonna need these." He scooped something out of his canoe and tossed it to Ereni.

Conall leaned forward, but before he got a look at the object, Fillan sent another one sailing at his face. He scrambled to catch the small oar.

"I noticed your canoe didn't have any. Be careful out there. The swells close to shore can be crushing. Even with the oars, you might struggle until you sail beyond them."

Ereni grinned. "We mages have our ways of handling the current. Thank you, Fillan. For everything."

"Yeah, thanks, Fillan." Conall lifted the oar and waved.

"It was no trouble. Tell Lark I said hello when you see her." With that, he pushed on his pole and slid away, heading south.

The mouth of the waterway widened as they sailed closer to the ocean. When Conall stuck the pole down and it didn't connect with the ground, he realized the water was growing deeper as well.

"Do you want to row, or handle the waves?" he asked as he stashed the pole on the side holder.

Ereni handed him her oar. "I'll summon."

She settled down in the front of the canoe and stuck her hand out the side, sucking in a deep breath.

Conall shivered as the air simultaneously clouded with moisture and crackled with electricity. He dipped the oars into the water, rowing them forward even as the wind and water sought to force them forward far quicker than he could accomplish with the oars alone.

Soon, they passed the last mangroves and burst out into the open sea. The waves jostled them fiercely, even with Ereni smoothing them with her talent. Beyond the mangroves, huge rocks littered the surf, sticking out high in the air like forgotten monuments to the earth. From far away, the surfaces appeared glossy and smooth, no doubt chipped away by the surf over countless days. But if the rocking waves smacked them into one of the monoliths, their boat would not survive the experience. Worse, there might be even more sharp peaks hidden below the surf's surface, ready to impale the bottom of their boat.

"Ereni." His voice wobbled as they approached a large rock formation. A tremor crawled up his spine as the waves crashed around them, splattering them with a fine mist of salt water. He pulled furiously at the oars, seeking to turn them sideways and around the behemoth.

"No, head straight."

Conall gulped, catching a glimpse of her blue eyes—normally so bright, clouded over—as she flicked a glance back at him, only to spin back and stare ahead blankly.

"What? We'll crash," he insisted.

"There are rocks below," she said simply. "I'll guide us through. Trust me."

Was she using her talent to sense the rocks below the surface?

"What's happening, little brother?" Shadow cowered on the boat bottom. The wet fur on his face matted against his skin, and when he aimed his wide golden eyes backward, Conall had to shake off the desire to pet him—Shadow looked miserable and adorable all at once.

Instead, Conall rowed, steering straight as directed. *"Don't worry, brother. We'll get out of this. Ereni knows what she's doing."*

He hoped the statement was not proven a lie as they sailed straight toward the colossal rock.

When they were only a boat length away, Ereni screamed, "Break right, now!"

Conall dug in with the oars, pounding the water. The left one bounced off the surface of something hard below the waves.

Ereni's hands flew through the air, directing the wind and sea, buoying their little canoe. They slipped past the huge boulder not a moment too soon, and Conall sighed.

But they weren't out of the woods yet. More rocks littered the water, and the surf still pounded, seeking to shove them back to shore. Each stroke of the oars was hard fought, and Conall's shoulders ached from the constant motion.

"Conall..." Shadow's panicked voice made him pause. He flicked a glance at the boat bottom and spotted his bondmate slinking backward from a puddle slowly growing larger. He gulped, realizing it was

filling too quickly to be from water splashing over the sides, though he couldn't see a hole.

"We've sprung a leak," he yelled over the crashing waves.

Ereni shifted, her eyes still glazed over, before turning back to stare forward. "Call on your water talent, push the sea out. I can't spare the concentration now."

He flashed Shadow a crooked grin. *"Don't worry. I'll fix it."* He hoped.

Conall pulled at the ocean all around him, using it as his source. He closed his eyes briefly, picturing the puddle flowing back down the crack to join the sea. When he lifted his lashes, he smiled, watching the puddle slowly decrease in size until he could finally see the source of the problem. A small crack marred the wooden floor, almost directly in the center.

Great. But at least it was dealt with, for the moment. He kept the magic flowing, using a constant stream to keep the water from seeping back in. Now it wasn't just his shoulders aching, but his whole body, the exhaustion of summoning quickly compounding with the physical ache until he was ready for a nap.

At last, they wrestled free of the huge rocks and into the deeper water beyond the coastline. The hum of vibration in the air faded, and Ereni peered at them, her eyes back to their normal bright-blue. "You two all right, back there?"

Conall nodded. "That was intense."

"Which way should we head?"

"You're asking me?"

She craned her head sideways, gazing up and down the coast. "I was hoping when we made it to the ocean, the ships would be here to greet us, but it looks like we'll need to find them. Do you think they made it off the coast of the Abandoned Lands yet, or should we head south toward Joria? The way I see it, we have a fifty-fifty chance either way."

The ocean spread out before them, empty of ships in every direction. Worse still, the coastline was littered with more rocks. To the south, the mangled mangroves stretched far into the distance, and to the north lay high cliffs that even the strongest of climbers would likely struggle to scale.

Conall's stomach sank. The leak in their boat would require constant supervision from here on out. That, coupled with the summoning they'd need to navigate and avoid being driven back into shore, spelled exhaustion for them both. If he chose wrong here, it could be a death sentence.

Ereni spoke up, breaking the silence. "I trust you, Conall. You'll lead us the right way."

His heart stuttered. He met her gaze and saw the certainty there. After everything, all the harsh things he'd said, she still trusted him?

Conall closed his eyes. If it really was fate that he found them, he couldn't choose wrong now, could he?

Lark, where are you?

His eyes flicked open. "South. Let's go south."

Ereni turned forward, moisture and static flooding the air instantly.

Conall dipped the oars into the sea and prayed he hadn't just killed them.

Chapter 24

"**L**ark." Muse's voice woke Lark from a dead sleep.

"Ugh, what is it?"

"Ha, cranky much?"

"I was sleeping."

"In the afternoon? You've grown lazy while I've been gone, I see."

"You try being woken by a babe half a dozen times a night," Lark grumbled.

She rolled out of her hammock in the single room Kayda had arranged for her to share with little Violet and the wet nurse on board *Nova's Champion*. She crept over soundlessly and peered into the tiny bassinet in the corner. Lucky for her, their silent communication didn't bother the babe.

"Hm, remind me to spend the night with Aren when I get back. I don't need any noisy critters waking me all night long."

The reminder of her bondmate's return made Lark smile after she rolled her eyes. *"How far away are you?"*

"We're close to the Boglands' northern edge."

"*Good. We've been passing the bog all day. You can't be far off now.*"
Lark snuck over to the window and peeled back a corner of the curtain. Streaks of pink and purple painted the clouds. How long had she slept? "*Jayan will likely drop anchor soon. Maybe you and Whisper ought to stop for the night and meet us in the morning?*"

"*We'll fly for a little while longer. If we don't spot sails on the horizon before dusk, we'll stop.*"

Violet stirred. Lark quickly let the curtain fall back into place, but it was too late. She was met with a hearty wail.

"*Violet's awake. I'll talk to you later. Be safe.*"

"*You, too.*"

"Hey, little one. I'm here." Lark cradled Violet in her arms, rocking and shushing until she quieted. "I bet you're hungry after that big nap, hm? Let's find Indra."

She found the new wetnurse in the mess hall, chatting up a table full of sailors. Her brown eyes twinkled, and the sailor's brash laughter filled the air.

"Hello, Miss Lark. Is our beauty ready for her dinner?" Indra called out as Lark entered the room. She flicked her long, black curls off her chest, unbuttoning her top.

Most of the men turned aside as Indra settled Violet on her breast, but one bold man stared unabashedly. Lark glared and stopped in front of him, blocking his view.

Indra only chuckled. "Go on, Miss Lark. Me and Violet will be just fine on our own. I'm sure you have plenty to tend to."

"You sure?"

"Of course. I've got this. Go."

Lark sent Indra a smile and the forward man a parting glare, then made her way to the top deck.

Lark passed Kayda, who chatted with a group of Sul warriors. Her golden dress was long gone, replaced with a simple shirt and trousers and a wool cloak, much like her own.

The Sul huddled in groups, clutching blankets around their shoulders or shrouded in thick furs. Lark pulled her own cloak closed as the chill air hit her. It was easy to forget it was early winter in Joria. She might be more used to these northern climes than the desert dwelling Sul, but the closer they sailed to Dracwood, the more the sea breeze bit.

"Hello." Aren greeted her with a grin, tipping back his wide-brimmed hat.

Lark smiled back. "Aren, hi."

"I'm glad I found you. I have a surprise."

"You do?"

"C'mon." He beckoned her to follow.

Lark's boots tapped on the wooden deck as Aren led her to the center mast. She stopped beside him, her gaze flitting all around but spotting nothing different.

"What did you want to show me?"

"Oh, it's not here." He tipped his hat up further, nodding to the crow's nest perched above them. "It's up there."

Lark's stomach dipped. "You left me a surprise in the crow's nest?"

"Yep. It's no different from climbing the diquats in Raimire." His brow furrowed. "If you don't want to climb, I can fetch it down."

She spared the rope ladder a dubious glance before turning to Aren. "Are you coming up with me?"

"Mm-hm. I'll be right behind you."

"All right." Lark grabbed the rough rope and scaled the shaky ladder. Then she clambered onto the circular wooden balcony, high above the midship deck. Aren arrived just behind her.

The boat's swaying intensified, but luckily the chest-high railing left little chance of her falling. Lark clutched the rail and peeked over the edge. Her stomach wobbled when she realized how far up they'd climbed, and she tore her gaze from the deck to look back at Aren.

He smiled at her before leaning down to grab a small covered basket off the nest's floor. He lifted the lid, revealing a loaf of bread and some cheese. "I saw you missed lunch, so I thought we might have a bite to eat and watch for the birds at the same time."

"What a great idea. Thank you." Lark grinned.

She reached inside the basket and broke off a small piece of cheese and a hunk of bread. Then she shifted to stare out at the northern horizon. The pinks and purples painting the clouds had only intensified since she'd first woken, making for a gorgeous sunset. A small flock of birds flew in a 'V' ahead of them, but they didn't come close to matching the grace of Muse and Whisper.

"Muse just told me they were closing in on the Boglands' northern edge. Do you think they'll reach us before dusk?"

Aren set the basket down again and joined her at the rail. "With how fast they fly? Yeah, I think they might." He popped a bite of cheese into his mouth and chewed thoughtfully. "I bet you're excited to see Muse again."

"It will be good to have her back. She certainly hasn't been quiet in my head while she's been gone, but it feels strange being apart from her all the same." She took a bite of the bread and cheese, savoring the sharp flavor.

They ate in companionable silence for a time. It was certainly lovely up here. And quiet. But the wind—she shivered and adjusted the collar of her brown wool cloak as the breeze picked up, whipping her curls against her face.

"Here." Aren grabbed a folded bundle off the nest floor, quickly shaking out the plaid wool blanket and wrapping it around her shoulders. "I thought the wind might kick up while we were waiting."

"Thank you. You thought of everything, didn't you?"

Aren shrugged. "When you grow up where it snows more than half the year, you learn to prepare for the cold."

Aren blew on his cupped hands, then stuffed them into his black cloak pockets.

Lark opened one side of the blanket and held it toward him. "There's plenty of room under here. We can share."

Aren grinned and wrapped the blanket around them both, tugging her tight against his side. Lark snuggled against his chest and sighed.

"I've been wondering something..." Aren started, pausing to gaze down at her face.

"What?"

"Have you decided what you'll do after the battle is over?"

Lark bit her lip. "I'm not sure. Honestly, I haven't given it much thought. I mean, I haven't had much time with a new problem popping up every other day."

"Yeah, I get that. I know it's hard to picture the future with this battle hanging over our heads." He stroked her shoulder gently.

"Why do you ask?"

Aren's hand stilled. "I haven't gone home to visit my family since I left. I want to travel back to Gransea. Maybe not right away, but in the spring or summer, for sure."

Lark blinked. "That's right. You told me the whole show was planning to travel to Doln in the spring, didn't you?"

"Yeah. They might still be planning to, but after that last show in Joria, the inn offered Daus a permanent spot. I'm still not sure if he'll take it, but either way, I want to go home—at least for a week or two.

With everything that's happened, I feel like I need to see my mother and father again."

Lark nodded. She could understand that. It was only natural to want to spend time with family, especially now. If she were in his shoes, she'd likely be dying to know how her parents were holding up, and she'd want to make sure for herself, in person.

"I was hoping you'd come with me."

Lark's heart skipped a beat. She stared up into Aren's blue eyes.

He watched her intently, and his hand tightened slightly on her shoulder. "If you need time to think about it, I—"

"Yes." A grin stretched her face so wide her cheeks ached. "I'd love to."

Aren's answering smile was blindingly bright. "Really? Great—that's great." He pulled her closer, wrapping her in a tight hug. Then he pulled back to peer down at her face, his smile falling. "There's one more thing I've been wanting to tell you."

Lark met his gaze. Why had he turned so serious? "What?"

Before he could answer, the wind whipped to life, and a huge bird zipped behind Lark's head, making her jump.

"Blazes." She spun around, spying Whisper landing on the rail just behind her. She beamed at Aren. "They're back." She swiveled around, searching for Muse.

Aren let go of her shoulder and slipped out of the blanket to greet Whisper. "Hey, buddy. I missed you."

Whisper shifted on the railing, his head tilting and pupils dilating the same way Muse always did when she was excited about something. Lark might not be able to speak to Whisper, but she had a feeling he was happy to see his handler again.

She turned again to watch the sky for Muse's return. What was taking her so long?

"Whisper just showed up. Where are you?"

When she didn't answer immediately, Lark's stomach churned. Aren joined her, staring at the sky.

"I don't see Muse yet, do you?"

"I just called to her, and she didn't resp—"

"Hey, I'm here."

Lark gripped the railing, and her shoulders slumped. She sent Aren a half-smile. "She's there. Let me find out why she's so far behind."

"What's taking you so long? Whisper beat you here. I didn't realize you'd grown lazy in our time apart."

"Ha. Lazy, am I? I'm not lazy at all. Just for that, I don't think I'll tell you what I spotted."

"C'mon, don't be like that. I was only joking."

Aren squeezed her arm. "What is it?"

"She spotted something, but she's got her feathers all ruffled and won't tell me what."

Aren chuckled and shook his head. He carefully examined Whisper and began untying the folded parchment strapped to his leg.

"Oh, you're gonna love this," Muse exclaimed.

"You sure about that?"

"Hey, didn't you say Jayan was liable to drop anchor soon?"

"Yes, he always does at dusk."

"Yeah, you don't wanna do that. Make sure he keeps sailing."

"Muse—what is it already?"

"It's your brother. He's not far from you, on a tiny boat close to the shoreline."

Lark gasped. "Conall. Muse found Conall." She headed for the ladder. "I need to ask Jayan to keep sailing until we reach him."

"All right. I better bring this parchment to Kayda." Aren waited for her to mount the rope ladder, then followed just behind her.

Kayda was there to meet Lark as her boots thumped down on the deck.

"I saw one of the birds made it back. Did they bring news?" Kayda asked.

"Yes." Lark's words spilled out breathlessly. "Aren has a parchment for you. And Muse just spotted Conall ahead of us, near the coast. Where's Jayan? I have to make sure he doesn't drop anchor."

"He should be at the helm."

"Thanks." Lark sped off, her heart racing. Conall and Muse were both coming back. The news had her grinning like a fool as she spotted Jayan.

"Captain Jayan." She waved frantically and jogged up to the helm. "There's a boat just ahead we need to locate. My brother is on it."

Jayan glanced at the darkening sky, then turned to frown at her. For a heartbeat, Lark thought he might say no, but when Kayda ran up just behind her with Aren in tow, the parchment clasped in her hands, he said, "Aye. I reckon we can handle that."

"Thank you." Lark left the helm and raced to the bow railing. Where were they?

I got the boat to keep sailing. Are you with Conall still? How is he? she asked Muse as she reached the rail and stared out at the slowly darkening sea. She still didn't see any sign of either of them.

I'm keeping an eye on them from above. He seems all right, if a little wet.

Who's with him? Shadow?

Yep. Ha. He looks miserable. The humor in Muse's tone made Lark want to roll her eyes but reassured her they were safe. She knew her bondmate well enough to understand Muse wouldn't joke if they were injured or in serious distress.

"Good." Lark grimaced. *"Not that he's miserable. You know what I mean."*

"Guess what else?"

"What?"

"Remember when I said it would be weird if that wind mage found your brother?"

"Ereni, Violet's mother? Yes, I remember."

"Ha. I was right. She's here, too."

Lark sighed, and another weight lifted off her chest. Not only was she getting her brother and her bondmate back, she could finally reunite the child she'd cared for with her mother. Today was shaping up to be an amazing day.

Aren caught up to her, carrying a coiled rope in his hands. Kayda walked just behind him, the parchment unfurled and her gaze dancing across the page as she read.

"Have you spotted them yet?" Aren asked.

"No. Not yet." Lark bounced on her toes, her gaze flitting around ahead of them.

A crowd gathered, no doubt alerted by her shouting at Jayan. Soon the rail was crowded with dozens of people staring out at the sea, everyone murmuring excitedly and smiling.

Lark turned to Aren, her brow furrowing as a thought struck her. "I'm sorry. You were in the middle of telling me something earlier when Whisper landed. What was it?"

Aren opened his mouth, then glanced at the crowd around them and shook his head. "It's all right. It can wait." He squeezed her arm gently.

Lark flashed him a smile then stared off the bow. The sun was nearly fully set now. The clouds darkened to a deep blue-violet, the sky an ever darkening blue-black. A crescent moon rose in the sky, hovering over the eastern horizon further out to sea.

Lark's smile widened. "I can see them." A tiny dot appeared far off ahead in the sky, a slightly larger shape beneath it on the shifting waves.

A few of the folk gathered at the rail sent her dubious glances, then squinted into the shadowy dusk ahead. Of course, no one else could see them yet.

Lark had grown used to spotting far-off things much quicker than others. After meeting Kayda and learning a little more about the boons that bondmates brought to their pairing, she could only assume that was the reason for her advanced eyesight.

After a few moments of sailing, the little canoe grew nearer. The people sending her doubtful looks stopped, and everyone began pointing and waving. An air of excitement broke out, even more so when the few mages gathered at the bow spotted Ereni in the front of the canoe. Magic hummed to life on deck as wind and water mages sent gusts into the sky and surf to advance the ship forward more quickly.

Muse landed on the railing beside her. *"Told ya, you'd be excited. Now that I found your lost brother, I think you owe me a treat."*

Lark chuckled and grinned at her bondmate. *"Name it, and it's yours, my fine feathered friend."*

"Ha. I like the sound of that." Muse puffed up her chest, then turned to stare back at the ocean. *"Don't worry, I'll think of something."*

Finally, the canoe pulled up alongside them, and Aren tossed the rope down. Ereni was the first to climb on board. All of the mages crowded around her as soon as she touched down on the deck, still wearing the ugly gray coveralls they'd been forced to don back in Flamesmoat, her brown hair tied back in a ponytail, damp and askew.

Ereni only spared the mages a small smile before craning her neck around, as if searching intently for something—or someone. When Ereni's gaze locked on Lark, she pushed through the circle of mages and strode up to her.

"Violet. Where is she?" Ereni's eyes were wide, her jaw clenched tight.

"I left her below deck in the mess hall, with Indra, the wet nurse I hired," Lark replied.

Ereni pressed a hand to her chest, then sighed deeply. "Thank you, Lark. I can't thank you enough." Ereni strode off, heading for the closest hatch.

Lark smiled at her retreating back, then leaned over the bow railing. Aren had thrown the rope back down to Conall while she'd been talking with Ereni. Shadow was already wrapped in it and being hoisted into the air by Aren with the help of a trio of sailors, who gripped the rope behind him. They strained and groaned under the large wolf's weight, but soon, he thudded down on the deck.

Lark rushed forward to untie him after seeing no one else was brave enough for the task. Shadow met her gaze with his golden eyes, his sopping wet tail wagging, though he dutifully stood still to allow her to unknot the rope.

Sunny appeared out of nowhere, her tail spinning and her whole body thrumming with excitement. Once Shadow was released from the rope, he padded up beside her and they rubbed flanks. Lark watched on her knees, her chest tingling with warmth and her eyes filling with moisture.

Then it was Conall's turn to climb aboard. Lark rose to her feet as his boots hit the deck. "Brother. You're late." She only gave him enough time to grip the railing and right his balance before thudding into his chest and wrapping her arms around him.

"Lark. I told you I'd meet you on board." He squeezed her tightly, his voice filled with joy. But he only hugged her for a few heartbeats before pulling back and staring down at her.

His clothes and hair were soggy, but his smile was exactly the same as she remembered. The sight of it filled her heart with glee. But the next thing he said wiped the grin from her face and made her knees buckle.

"I hear I have to thank you for more than just waiting for my return. How's my daughter?"

Chapter 25

Kayda stuffed the crumpled parchment in her pocket and strode forward to greet Conall as he released Lark from a tight hug.

"...How's my daughter?" Conall said.

Kayda halted beside them. Lark's mouth dropped open, her eyes just as wide.

Kayda raised a brow. "I didn't know you had a daughter."

Conall flashed a crooked grin and rubbed the back of his neck. "Yeah, me either. Hey, Kayda, it's good to see you."

Kayda sent him a tentative smile in response. Should she hug him, too? Or maybe a handshake?

She was saved from deciding by Lark's gasp. "Don't tell me I've been taking care of my own niece all this time."

Kayda stifled a gasp of her own. "Violet's yours?"

Conall nodded. "Ereni and I traveled to Mage Keep together last summer."

For half an instant, Kayda's heart sank. That meant Tarquin... No. This was much better. Violet would grow up with her father by her side.

Lark squeezed Conall's arm. "Ereni already went below deck to find Violet. She's with the wet nurse. I'll show you."

"If you don't mind, I'll walk with you," Kayda said. "I have some news to share."

"All right, let me just tell Shadow." Conall flicked a glance at his wolf, who sat on his haunches while Sunny circled him whimpering, her tail whipping nonstop. Conall chuckled, then turned to them with a smile. "Let's go."

"What news do you have?" Lark led the way to the nearest hatch. "Are the Doln on their way to meet us?"

Kayda stepped into the candlelit hallway. "Yes. It seems they're not far. We should both arrive off the coast of the Abandoned Lands tomorrow afternoon."

Conall frowned. "So soon? I knew we were close, but I'd hoped we'd have more time..."

Kayda stopped outside the door to her room. "It appears so. I don't want to keep you from your family, but if you could both meet me back here. There's something we need to discuss. It won't take long."

Conall glanced at Lark and then back at Kayda. His brow furrowed, and he shifted his weight, then motioned Lark to follow. "If it won't take long, we can discuss it now. I have something I need to tell you both as well."

Kayda's brow rose. "Are you sure?"

"Yes. Ereni will be happy for a few more moments alone with Violet, anyway."

Kayda nodded once, then unlocked the door and slipped inside. She held the door wide for Conall and Lark to file in behind her.

The room was dim, lit with only a single oil lamp strapped down on the dinged desk. Kayda closed the door and strode to it, where she quickly worked the wick to brighten the room. She inhaled, gathering the courage to spill all the secrets she'd learned from Izora. Now that Conall and Lark were here together, and before the battle began, she had to tell them the whole of it. They deserved the truth.

She turned around, but before she spoke, Conall broke the silence.

"One of us is going to die."

"What?" Lark practically gasped out the single word.

Conall paced, his clunking boots echoing the thudding beat of Kayda's heart. "I'm sorry I didn't tell you sooner. I assumed the Unseen was just screwing with me. That he'd say anything to stop the battle from happening. But then Ereni told me it all comes true. Every single vision for hundreds of years."

"The Unseen predicted one of us would die in your vision?" Kayda rubbed her forehead.

"Yes. I didn't believe him, or I would've told you when we sailed to Stoneshore."

Lark stepped into her brother's path, halting his pacing. "It's all right, you're telling us now. The Unseen didn't say who?"

Conall shook his head, his face grave. Lark blanched and splayed a hand over her chest.

"It doesn't matter," Kayda said. "This changes nothing. There's always the chance of death when you engage in battle. At least now we know two of us will survive."

"You're right. There is that," Lark agreed.

Kayda drew in a deep breath. "In fact, this news makes me even more sure about the favor I have to ask of you both."

"Whatever you need, we'll help you, Princess," Conall insisted.

"Actually, it's *Queen* now," Lark said.

Conall's eyes widened. "What did I miss?"

Kayda sighed. "A lot, I'm afraid. Lark's right. Technically, I'm Queen of Dracwood. My father and grandfather are gone."

"I'm so sorry." Conall moved closer, his hand outstretched, but Kayda waved him off.

"Thank you. But I didn't ask you here for your condolences, as much as I appreciate them. The fact is, I'm alone now. Should I die, the kingdom would have no heir."

Lark bit her lip. "There isn't any other family to step in? A cousin, or uncle?"

"No. I'm afraid not." Kayda looked them both in the eyes. "Just a half-brother and half-sister."

Conall's jaw dropped.

Lark shook her head and backed up until her shoulders struck the wood-paneled wall. "No. You can't mean us? We aren't royal. And if you tell anyone we're related, they'll know you aren't royal either."

"I thought the same until after Flamesmoat," Kayda admitted. "Then Izora told me the truth about what happened with Jett and my mother all those years ago. All three of us have royal blood in our veins."

Lark's brow furrowed, and she stared down at her feet. "I don't get it. How could that be?"

Conall appeared just as confused, his lips pursed and brows sunken. But then he stiffened and inhaled sharply. "Jett didn't know who his father was."

"His father was King Quinton," Kayda explained. "My grandfather. *Our* grandfather. I'm sorry he never got the chance to meet you both. I know he would've loved you dearly if he had the chance."

"That must be why the mages made Jett leave. They didn't want him around to put two and two together." Conall bit his lip and stared at his feet.

Lark shook her head even more forcefully. "But Kayda, you can't possibly want us to rule. We don't know a thing about rul—"

"And you think I do?" Kayda waved a hand. "There will be plenty of people around to help with the minutia. What the country really needs is a figurehead. Someone they can rally around. Whoever survives this battle will certainly qualify. If I end up being one of them, then you two don't need to worry. But if I don't... Someone has to step up. After everything that's happened, we'll need to rebuild."

"What about Jett?" Lark asked. "If what you said is true, then he's just as royal as we are."

Kayda smiled gently. "I talked to him yesterday. He doesn't want any part of ruling—not that I planned to ask him. He agreed with me that both of you have proven your worth. Even before learning the Unseen's words, I was planning to ask you to be my heirs, should I fall. Before we met, you both fought to overcome the evil plaguing our lands. You stood by my side when I lost my bondmate. And we will stand together to put a stop to the Unseen. You deserve to reap the rewards, and I have every faith that you can handle the responsibilities that come with it."

Conall straightened. "All right. I agree. But on one condition."

Kayda met his gaze. "Name it."

"If it's me who falls, then I want Violet taken care of. Who knows what will happen tomorrow. Ereni could be hurt, too." He rubbed a hand across his chest. "Violet deserves a decent life, with family that loves her. If I'm not there, then I need—"

"Done." Kayda agreed. "She can live at Kings Keep."

Conall shook his head. "No." He grimaced. "No offense, Kayda, but she doesn't need a life of luxury. Violet—she just needs a normal life."

Kayda blinked, shifting on her feet. "I understand. I'll keep an eye on her from a distance, if that's what you'd prefer."

Conall nodded.

Lark wrapped her arms around her middle. "I don't like this. I don't want to think about either of you dying. It's not fair."

Conall pulled her into a hug. "What about you, Lark? Would you watch over Violet for me?"

Tears spilled down her cheeks. "Do you even have to ask? Of course I will." She sniffled. "And you, Kayda. I'll do whatever I can to help, if it comes to it."

Kayda blinked back tears of her own. "Good. So, that's settled." She turned to her desk and lifted the ancient book off the top. "Lark and I have already read this cover to cover. We have a few ideas that might come in handy for the battle. We should discuss it together before we arrive tomorrow, but that can wait. Go. Spend some time with your daughter, Conall." She handed the book to him. "You can have this back. Thank you for letting me borrow it."

Conall grabbed the book. "You're welcome—sister."

For a moment, she thought he would leave it at that, but the next instant, he pulled her into a tight hug. Lark thudded against them both a heartbeat later.

Kayda couldn't stop the smile that split her cheeks.

Just a few weeks ago, she'd been so certain this kind of love would never be hers. Tarquin had certainly never treated her like this. Like a treasured friend. Now she had a brother and sister who would stand with her and stare down the end of the world. It was more than she'd ever dreamed of.

She only hoped it would be enough.

Conall and Lark left with a parting goodbye. Kayda strolled to the window and stared out at the dark sea.

"Dru, are you there?"

No answer.

"We'll reach the Abandoned Lands soon. I really need you."

Still nothing. She sighed.

"Conall says one of us will die tomorrow. If you don't make it back, then this might be goodbye."

A tear slid down Kayda's cheek, and she brushed it away with the back of her fist. *"I'm sorry for what happened to your kind. I wouldn't blame you if you wanted to stay away. To stay in your home and build a new future with Bela."*

She exhaled, closing her eyes. *"I love you, Druturion. I only wish you could hear me."*

Chapter 26

Conall followed Lark down the dimly lit hall, clutching the ancient book in his hands. This was it. He was finally about to meet his daughter. They'd stopped in the mess hall, only to learn that Ereni had taken Violet back to her room.

"Almost there." Lark looked up at him with a grin. "Oh, I almost forgot. I don't want you to be alarmed when you first see Violet. She looks a bit different from other babes, but it's nothing to worry over."

Conall halted, grabbing Lark's elbow. "What do you mean, different?"

"I'm not sure if it's because of the nature of her birth, being fast tracked and all, but Violet was born albino."

"Albino." Conall's brow furrowed. "Like that goat we had the one year on the farm?"

"Exactly. Just like Snowy."

Conall chuckled and resumed walking. "You had me worried for a moment there."

Snowy had been a favorite of Lark's the year she'd been born. The nanny looked a bit peculiar compared to the other goats but was normal in every other way. Surely, it would be the same with Violet. And who knew, the pale hair and skin might even suit her.

"Yes, like I said, nothing to worry about. She is on the smaller side as well, but she's catching up quickly. She's thriving." Lark beamed up at him and turned a corner, then stopped. "Here we are." She pointed to a door in the middle of the hall. "I'll leave you to it then." She moved to leave.

"Lark, wait. Are you all right, after my news earlier?"

Lark's smile shifted, suddenly looking a touch too bright. "Yeah. I—yeah, I'm fine."

He grabbed her arm. "Really? Why don't you come with me? We'll talk some more."

She shook her head. "No. I just have someone I need to talk to, is all. And you need time alone with your little girl." She squeezed his hand. "I'm all right, I swear. I'll see you in the morning."

Conall frowned but let her go. Sometimes, it was still hard for him to not see the little girl that begged him to play dolls in her room. But Lark wasn't a little girl anymore. She'd grown so much in the time they'd been apart. He had to keep reminding himself she could take care of herself.

Conall turned and strode to the door. He stopped just outside, his palms moistening with sweat.

Footsteps thumped down the hall, and he spun toward them.

"Jett?"

The older man rushed forward and pulled him into a hug. "Son. I'm so glad you're back."

At first, Conall stiffened, but after a moment, he wrapped his arms around Jett and returned the embrace. Memories flooded back, unbidden, of so many other hugs. It wasn't the same—back then he'd barely reached his father's chest after all—but the feeling, the love, washed over him just like it had when he was a child.

"When you didn't come back to the docks, I didn't know if I'd ever see you again. I know we didn't have time to talk, but—"

Conall pulled back and met Jett's gaze. "Wait. I have something to say."

Jett's mouth snapped closed.

"I'm sorry for the way I reacted to your story. I—It was hard for me to wrap my head around it all, but I understand now."

"You do?"

"Have you met your granddaughter yet?" Conall inclined his head to the door beside them.

Jett's eyes widened. "Violet—she's yours?"

Conall nodded. "I still haven't met her, but as soon as I learned about her, I understood the choice you made. If I could guarantee Violet would have the kind of life she deserves, even if I would never get to be part of her life, I would take that deal in a heartbeat."

Conall flashed back to the conversation in Kayda's chambers. In a way, he'd already made that deal.

Jett's gaze darted between him and the closed door. "You haven't met her yet..." A wide grin split his face. "Go on then, son. I won't keep you." Jett squeezed his arm and stepped away.

"Thanks, Father." A rush of rightness spread through his chest as the words left his lips. He still wasn't happy about all the years they lost, but he could admit now that Lark was right. He refused to hold on to the anger and hurt when forgiving his father meant they'd have a chance at a future spent together.

Jett sent him a parting smile and disappeared down the hall.

Conall turned to the door. He knocked gently, then tried the knob. It twisted open, and he peeked inside.

Ereni perched on the edge of a hammock, her dirty coveralls replaced with a plain brown dress. She gently rocked a blanket-wrapped bundle in her arms. She glanced up, her eyes shining, as he slid inside and smiled.

Conall set the old book on an empty side table and strode over to the hammock.

Ereni stood as he approached and glided toward him. "Do you want to hold her?" she whispered.

Conall stretched out his arms. Then the slight weight of his daughter landed on his chest. He stared down at her face, her eyes closed in slumber, and his heart melted.

"Hello, Violet," he whispered. He hadn't meant to wake her, but either the low rumble of his words or the motion of being transferred made her eyelids pop open.

A pair of eyes the most beautiful blend of blue, red, and violet greeted him. As he gazed down at her, he was overwhelmed with love unlike anything he'd ever felt. This little girl had taken his heart and wrapped it around her finger so thoroughly with that one simple look. He would never be the same. He was a father now.

She opened her mouth and wailed.

Conall laughed. "Well, she has a good set of lungs. That's for sure." He rocked her gently. "Shush, little one. It's all right." After a moment, she quieted.

He flicked a glance at Ereni. Tears slid down her cheeks.

"Hey, what's—"

The door creaked open, halting his words. A voluptuous, dark-haired woman slipped in, heading straight for Violet. "I see I'm right on time for Little Miss' next meal. She's up like clockwork, this one." She stopped before him and lifted the hem of her dress, performing a shallow curtsy. "I'm Indra, Violet's wet nurse. You must be her father. It's nice to meet you, sir."

His heart squeezed at her simple statement. Her father—he was a father. "Please, call me Conall. It's nice to meet you as well."

Indra held out her arms. "I'll bring her back as soon as she's fed."

Conall's brow furrowed. So soon? He'd only just got her. But, of course, she needed to eat. He passed her over. "All right. Thank you."

Indra slipped back into the hall and pulled the door closed behind her.

Conall exhaled, then walked to Ereni's side. She'd stationed herself beside the window, staring out at the dark sea. Moonlight filtered in, making the tears on her cheeks shimmer.

"Hey, what's wrong?" he asked.

Ereni shook her head and forced a smile. "Nothing. It's nothing." She scrubbed her cheeks with the sleeve of her dress.

"You can tell me." He tilted his head to meet her gaze. "Aren't you happy to have Violet back?"

"I am. Of course, I am." Her chin wobbled. "She's so big already. When I saw her last, she was such a tiny thing. Now..." She waved a hand, then crossed her arms. "It's silly, I know. It's only been a few weeks, but I feel like I missed so much."

"I'm sorry for that. If you hadn't come after Shadow and I—"

Ereni squeezed his forearm. "No, I didn't mean that." She dropped her gaze and pulled back her hand. "I'm not sorry I saved you. I would do it again. And not because of the battle or even for Violet."

Ereni sighed and turned back to the window.

There was still one question he'd been wanting to ask her since she found him. For whatever reason, he'd kept it buried, but he found he couldn't bear having it unanswered any longer.

Conall took a deep breath. "Ereni?"

"Hm?"

"What was I to you, back then?"

She spun to face him, her brows sinking. "What are you asking?"

Conall stared down at his boots, gathering his thoughts. Why was this so hard? His heart raced, and his stomach knotted.

"You knew who I was when we first met. And you knew you were destined to have a talented daughter like me—to have Violet. When we were together, was it just because of fate? Did you ever care for me at all?"

Ereni didn't balk at the question or at the hint of accusation in his tone that he couldn't hide. She met his gaze and smiled gently. "Yes, I cared for you. I still do."

Conall bowed his head and closed his eyes. When her arms wrapped around him, he leaned into the embrace, the scent of lavender tickling his nose.

"Do you want to know what I was thinking when we first met?" she whispered.

He nodded wordlessly against the top of her head.

"I thought you were handsome and far too trusting. And a bit naïve."

He grunted. "Naïve?"

"Yes. Like when you tried to convince me and everyone else that Shadow was only a simple hound." She chuckled. "But the more I got to know you, the more I saw what a wonderful man you are. Walking across the country to find your sister. Treating a stranger you'd only just met like a true friend."

He pulled back and stared into her blue eyes. "So, you weren't thinking the whole time about the vision you had?" He cocked a brow. "I find that a bit hard to believe."

Ereni sighed. "There was that as well."

He tried to pull away fully, but she tightened her grasp on his waist.

"I won't lie to you. I knew from the start." She pursed her lips. "If I could go back in time, I would do things differently."

"What?" Conall shook free of her hold and backed away.

"No—you don't understand." She stepped toward him, but when he backed away further, she furrowed her brow and turned to the window. "I wouldn't change what happened. Not in a million years. Those days we spent traveling together—they were amazing. You were amazing."

Her words calmed his racing pulse, if only a little. "Then what do you mean? What do you wish you'd done differently?"

"I would tell you all of it from the start. The truth about the Palisade. The vision I had about Violet. I should've never lied to you. I'll regret that for the rest of my life, Conall. I'm sorry."

Conall stilled, watching Ereni closely. She didn't make another move to draw nearer, just remained staring forlornly out the window.

"You can't imagine the debate I held in my mind when we first met. I've never been one to accept my fate easily. I think we're alike in that." She glanced at him and smiled half-heartedly before gazing at the window. "I didn't want to be a mage. You would think growing up surrounded by them, I would want nothing more, but I didn't. I wanted a simple life. But fate had other plans for me, just like it did for you.

"After I visited the Winter Witch, it all changed. I stopped trying to fight becoming a mage. Especially when we were set upon by thieves and my talent was awakened. But then, when I first met you, it started up all over again. I didn't want to surrender to fate and bind myself to someone I barely knew, no matter that I felt something for you instantly. I spent so long fighting against it. Trying to convince myself that I wouldn't let fate control me."

Conall recalled those early days they'd spent together. All the mixed signals she'd sent him, flirting in one breath and then giving him the cold shoulder the next... Was this why? She'd been fighting to stop herself from caring about him? To avoid the fate that was meant to be her destiny.

He could certainly understand the feeling. All that time he'd followed Delyth, the weight of his fate had burdened him exactly the same. Like he'd been locked into a future he had no say in. Was that what he'd been like to Ereni?

"Do you know what I realized?" Ereni turned from the window. "When I stopped fighting, for just one instant, and really thought about it, there was no question. That first night under the stars, *I chose you*—not fate. I chose you then, and I would choose you again if you'd let me."

He stared back at her. He saw the question in her eyes that she left unspoken. Would he choose her, too?

Ereni held his gaze, her chin lifted, chest heaving. She made no move closer—she just stood still, waiting.

The moment stretched out. He stayed there, glued to the spot, his mind reeling and his tongue tied just like it had been the night the Palisade fell. Back then, he'd cursed himself for a fool. But as he stared back at her tonight, he felt far from foolish.

Finally, he moved.

Ereni's head dipped, and she silently shuddered as he left her side and strode across the room to the door.

Conall slid the lock closed with a *click*.

The sound was deafening in his ears, but Ereni didn't seem to register it. She wrapped her arms around herself and sank to the floor.

It wasn't until he stopped directly in front of her that she lifted her tearstained face to look at him, her eyes widening.

Conall knelt beside her and pulled her into his arms. She climbed atop his lap and buried her face in his neck, her body trembling.

"I'm sorry," he said.

Ereni stilled in his arms and pulled back to peer at his face, shaking her head. "You don't have anythin—"

"No, listen. Please."

She nodded gravely.

"All my life, I've been so certain about what was right and wrong. But I've come to realize things aren't always so simple. Sometimes people do the wrong thing for the right reasons." He grimaced, recalling how he'd lied to make sure Brenna received the punishment she deserved. "I've even done the same. I can't keep blaming you, Ereni. I won't."

Her lashes lowered, and she nodded again.

"Just promise me one thing. We can't keep each other in the dark anymore. Never again. We have Violet now. We have to be on the same page if we're going to raise her together."

Her blue eyes collided with his. "Never again. I promise."

Conall lifted his hand and caught the teardrop that slid down her cheek. Ereni tilted her head, leaning into his touch. But then she exhaled and sat up straight, wrapping her legs around his back.

"Is Violet the only reason you want to be together?" She traced her fingers across his chest, the shadow of a seductive smile on her lips.

But when he looked into her eyes, he saw the vulnerability she tried to hide. The wounded heart that craved the answer to the question she'd been too scared to voice.

"No, she's not." He caught her hand in his and stilled its exploration, making sure her gaze stayed glued to his. "I choose you, too."

He watched the last flicker of doubt fade from her eyes, and a smile slowly spread across her lips. Then he kissed her like it was the last thing he'd ever do. Like this was the last time he'd ever get the chance.

Who knew, maybe it was? In the back of his mind, he realized he had to tell her. They'd just promised not to keep each other in the dark. He needed to tell her he might die tomorrow.

But then her fingers tangled in his hair, and she did that thing with her hips that drove him crazy.

Later. He'd tell her later.

Chapter 27

L ark strode away, leaving her brother to meet his daughter. She grinned alone in the dimly lit hall.

Conall was a father. And to the sweet little girl she'd just spent so long taking care of. It was all so strange—but in the absolute best way.

If only all of his news had been so pleasant. She shuddered, pushing the thought from her mind before tears filled her eyes again.

Not now. She had other plans for tonight.

"Have you seen Aren?"

Muse's scoff reverberated through Lark's mind. *"I've been gone for ages, and all you want to ask me about on my return is lover boy?"*

Lark shook her head. *"You're right. How are you? What's happened that you haven't reported back to me in excruciating detail? How about your lunch? Did it make a reappearance like you thought it would, or did you manage to keep it down?"*

"Ha. You've got jokes now. Nice. Aren's out here with me and the old snoozer, up top."

"Thanks." Lark opened the nearest hatch.

The cold night air rushed forward to greet her. She shivered and pulled her cloak closed, then strolled toward the ship's center. It didn't take her long to find Aren. He stood next to Whisper and Muse, tossing them little tidbits from a pouch he wore around his waist.

"There you are. Let me guess. You want to borrow *him again? Ha."*

Lark rolled her eyes. *"So what if I do?"*

Muse cocked her head. *"Fine, just let him finish feeding me first."*

Aren turned, following Muse's gaze. He smiled when he spotted her approaching. "Lark. Everything go all right with Conall?"

She stopped in front of him. "Yes, and no. I need to talk to you about something."

Aren's brow furrowed, and he cinched his waist pouch closed. "Sure, what is it?"

"Hey," Muse squeaked.

Lark giggled. "Do you mind doing me a favor first and leaving my gluttonous bondmate a pile of whatever it is you've got in there?"

Aren chuckled. "Sure." He opened the pouch again and dumped a handful of dried meat on the deck in front of each bird.

"That's better." Muse hopped down and gobbled at the meat greedily.

"So, what do you want to talk about?"

Lark grabbed his elbow. "Not here. Come with me." She pulled him back through the hatchway to the inner deck.

She grabbed a candle holder off the closest wall, then set her ear to the nearest door. When the muted sound of chatter reached her ears, she lifted her head and moved on.

"Don't try the galley this time. I don't think the cook will be too happy to see us again," Aren whispered, his eyes twinkling.

At the next door, she found what she was hunting for—silence. She cracked open the door and peeked in. Perfect.

She turned to Aren. "In here." She grabbed his hand and tugged him inside.

They entered a wooden chamber filled with piled cloth. What at first glance looked like the perfect spot for a little privacy lost a bit of the appeal upon closer inspection. The musky scent of sweat lingered in the air. Lark wrinkled her nose. This must be the crew's laundry room.

Aren coughed as she shut the door behind her and set the candleholder on a wall hook.

"So what—"

Lark silenced his question with a kiss. Aren stiffened for half a heartbeat, but then his lips parted, and his arms wrapped around her waist.

Lark closed her eyes and leaned into him, sliding her hands up his back. This was what she needed. If tomorrow might be her last day, then she would make every moment count until then. She trailed her hands around to Aren's chest, her shaking fingers working the buttons at the neck of his tunic.

Aren pulled back, his chest heaving as her hands slid off his neck. "Lark, wait. What's wrong? You're trembling."

She met his gaze in the dim candlelight and shook her head. "Nothing." Her voice cracked, and his eyes narrowed. She reached for him again, tipping her face up. "Please, I don't want to talk."

Aren didn't take the bait. He traced his thumb over her bottom lip and pressed their foreheads together. "What aren't you telling me?" he whispered.

Lark shuddered and sank into his arms. "What if we die tomorrow? I just wanted to..." Lark's cheeks heated, and she started to pull away, but Aren squeezed her tighter.

"You're not going to die."

"There's a good chance I will."

Aren stepped back, raising a brow. "What are you talking about?"

"Conall told me and Kayda one of us would die during the battle. That out of the three of us, only two would survive."

"How could he know that?"

"The Unseen told him, during his vision. The same visions that always come true."

Aren bit his lip and stared at the ground. But then his face lit up, and he smiled. "It won't be you."

Lark barely resisted rolling her eyes. "You can't know that for sure."

"I do. Don't you remember what Daus said?"

"Daus says a lot of things. You're going to have to be more specific."

Aren snorted. "Yeah, he does." Then all the humor faded from his face, and he stared at her intently. "I'm talking about in the boat outside of Bogsmouth. The girl who saw his future. She said we would save the world—together. Together means you're there, Lark. You're *not* going to die."

He said the words with such confidence, such unwavering belief, she almost believed it, too.

"But—what if you're wrong? I don't want to have any regrets."

"Neither do I."

Her heart fluttered, and she stepped closer. "Good."

"That's why this is a bad idea."

Lark halted, her stomach sinking. "Oh." She turned to the door.

"W-wait, I don't mean it like that." Aren grabbed her wrist and spun her around. "It's just this room. The smell. The door that doesn't lock." He flashed a lopsided smile. "I have a feeling if we do what you're thinking here, we'll have a whole heap of regrets. It's not a bad idea—just bad timing."

Blazing timing. Lark sighed.

Aren tipped up her chin, and she met his eyes. "I want you, Lark."

Her heart thundered, and she gulped.

"I don't think I've ever wanted anything more. But I can wait until we have a proper bed and the specter of death isn't forcing our hand."

"It's not force—"

"Are you sure about that?" He reached past her and lifted a dirty pair of trousers by the bottom hem, wrinkling his nose.

Lark laughed. "Put those down."

Aren dropped the pants and grinned down at her.

Lark smiled back, but she must've let something slip on her face.

"Something's still bothering you, isn't it?" he asked.

Lark frowned and stared down at her boots. How could he read her so well?

Aren grabbed her hand. "Tell me."

"Conall has Violet now. And Kayda's the queen. They both have people depending on them." Her voice wobbled. "I can't help feeling like it should be me."

"It should be—no. No." Aren shook his head. "That's just not true."

Lark glanced into his eyes. She saw the certainty there but couldn't find it in herself to agree.

Aren squeezed her hand—hard. "You're a healer, Lark. Think of all the people you've saved. All the people you'll save in the future. The world needs you."

"I suppose that's true."

"And it's not just that. I need you, too."

Her heart beat frantically. "You do?"

He nodded, loosening his grip and stroking the back of her hand. "Remember, I wanted to tell you something earlier?"

She met his gaze, her lips parting. "Yes."

"I love you, Lark. I fell in love with you the first moment we locked eyes back in that clearing in the middle of nowhere."

"Really?"

Aren stepped closer. So close she could see the flicker of the candlelight reflected in his irises. He swallowed. "You don't have—"

"I love you, too."

He chuckled and pulled her close, grinning like a fool. "Good."

She rose on her tiptoes, meeting his lips. The kiss they shared was different from all the rest. It still sent a jolt through her body, weakening her knees, but the desperation from before was gone, replaced with a warmth in her chest that resonated deep within her soul.

Lark hummed with contentment. This kiss was everything. This kiss felt like home.

Then the door popped open, and a shadow darkened the entrance. Lark and Aren pulled apart, turning wide eyes toward the new arrival.

"You again," the chef blubbered as he hustled in, his arms loaded with a stack of dirty white aprons. "Get out, you randy buggers. Out, I tell ya!"

They spilled into the hall, laughing and rushing away from the cook's continued verbal assault.

"What is it with that guy?" Aren leaned in conspiratorially, lifting his brows. "Do you think he's following us?"

Lark chuckled and linked their hands. "I think he might be."

They rounded a corner and bumped right into Tiora. "There you two are. I've been looking all over for you."

"You have?" Lark asked.

Tiora flicked a glance between the two of them, lingering on their linked hands before smiling widely. "Mm-hm. I see you've been busy."

Lark's cheeks warmed, but she couldn't wipe the grin off her face. "I guess you could say that. What's going on?"

"Daus offered to put on a bit of a show for the sailors before everyone turned in for the night. Are you two coming?"

Aren quirked a brow. "Duty calls."

Lark squeezed his hand. "Let's go."

Lark opened the hatch and shivered. Her breath clouded in the afternoon air like a fine white mist.

She walked to the bow railing, a smile on her lips as the swaying boat sparked a memory of last night. Singing and dancing. Laughing with her friends. The night might not have turned out as she'd first envisioned, but they certainly made every moment count.

"Good morning," she said around a yawn.

Conall whirled around, his wide-eyed daughter resting in his arms. "Don't you mean good afternoon?" He chuckled. "I would ask if you'd slept well, but it looks like you did."

Lark grinned. "It was quite nice to have my slumber uninterrupted for a change." She leaned closer, cooing at Violet until she met her gaze and gurgled happily in response.

Lark straightened and stared off the bow. "Did I miss anything?"

"Not yet." Conall pointed ahead of them. "You're just in time."

Lark's eyes widened as she spotted a fleet of ships approaching from the north. "Yeah, it looks like I am."

At least a dozen sets of sails approached their position. When added to the handful they'd brought with them from Joria, they'd make an impressive force. Still, Lark's stomach churned as her gaze drifted to the west, and she spotted the coastline. They'd left the bog behind and sailed beside a charred wasteland she'd been told was once a gorgeous coastal plain.

The Abandoned Lands. They'd arrived.

A whisper of the creeping shiver she'd grown to associate with the scourge crept up her spine.

They hadn't even landed, and already she could sense it. This place felt off. Wrong on a visceral level that made her stomach roil more than the motion of a ship ever had.

Kayda strolled up beside them, frowning. "That place gives me the creeps. Every time I get close to the scourge, I have the strangest feeling. Like someone's watching me."

Lark shuddered. "I do, too."

Conall nodded. "Me, too."

The three of them exchanged a look, their faces grave and unsmiling.

"Are you ready to talk strategy yet?" Lark asked.

Kayda shook her head and gestured to the ships fast approaching. "We might as well wait on the Doln. I'm sure they'll wish to be included in our discussions."

Ereni appeared from a nearby hatch with Indra in tow. Conall turned, a wide smile lighting his face.

Lark's gaze darted between her brother and Ereni as they drew closer. She could practically feel the air thicken with the force of their undisguised attraction.

So, her brother was in love. That much was plain to see. And from the way Ereni's eyes lit up as she stared back at him, she could only assume the feeling was mutual.

Conall had a fling or two with girls back in Greenvale, but she'd never seen him look at anyone like this. It warmed her heart to know that he'd found someone he cared about so deeply.

"Ereni. It's good to see you again," Lark piped up with a smile.

Ereni glanced at her and nodded. "You too, Lark." Then her gaze swung back to Conall in a flash. He'd still not taken his eyes off her.

"Hello." Conall's grin widened as Ereni stopped in front of him.

Ereni's cheeks flushed a deep red. Lark had a suspicion it wasn't just from the chill air. "I brought Indra to collect Violet for her next feeding."

Conall's smile slipped, and his fingers tightened around his daughter. Then he sighed and planted a gentle kiss on Violet's forehead and handed her over to Indra.

The wet nurse disappeared without a word, just as the lead Doln ship pulled alongside them. Within moments, the crew on both ships tied the boats in place, and boards slammed down, forming a makeshift walkway between the two vessels. Lark followed Kayda toward the ship's center, watching silently as the sailors gave the all-clear that the bridge was ready.

A flurry of motion began. Lark expected a bevy of pale-skinned blondes to come rushing over—and granted, there were plenty of them included—but just as many white-robed elders pounded across the wood, clasping hands and hugging the young mages that crowded around on deck.

Two beefy men in thick fur coats brought up the rear. The leader was a head shorter than the second man, but he swaggered forward with an air of confidence, his shoulders thrust back and a wide smile on his lined face. He halted midway across the planks and peered around until his gaze lit on where Conall stood between Lark and Ereni.

In a few short steps, the Dolnman stopped in front of her brother and thrust out his hand. "Conall of Greenvale. Why am I not surprised to find you here?"

Conall clasped his hand, wincing slightly as they shook. "Clan Chief Aundrea. I'm glad to see you're well." He peered behind him at a younger, red-bearded man. "Taul. How are you?"

Taul stepped forward, clasping Conall in a quick hug. "Mighty fine, now that we've a battle to begin."

Conall held out his hand and quickly made introductions. Lark smiled politely when he introduced her but kept quiet. The men nodded in response but seemed to dismiss her in favor of staring at Kayda once Conall introduced her as queen.

"Perhaps we should adjourn below deck to talk strategy?" Kayda offered.

They all followed her inside the cramped halls and down to her room.

Kayda closed the door and turned to the clan chief with a grateful smile. "I must thank you again for coming to our aid, Clan Chief Aundrea. I know I said as much in my letter, but—"

"Think nothing of it, my lady. The scourge—and this Unseen that's controlling them—are a problem for us all, not just you Dracians. And we Doln have never been ones to back down from a fight."

"I'm glad to hear it," Kayda replied. "Should we talk timing? I expect everyone is itching to begin the battle, but I wonder if it would not be more prudent to wait until morning to sail ashore." She strolled across the room to the window, gesturing outside. "It's fairly late in the day already."

"I'm afraid that may not be wise, my lady." Taul frowned. "We brought a weather seer with us. He predicts a storm is not far off. A big one."

A weather seer? Lark lifted a brow. She'd never heard of any such thing. But perhaps she could help.

"I could ask Muse to take a look," she offered.

Kayda nodded. "That would be helpful."

Lark reached out to Muse in her mind. *"Hey, are you busy?"*

"Nope, unless you count napping as being busy."

"Would you mind taking a quick flight and checking the weather headed our way? The Doln seem to think we're due a storm soon."

"All right. Give me a moment."

Lark turned her attention back to the conversation that had kept up while she chatted with Muse. Ereni, Kayda and the Clan Chief crowded around a map, debating where to send which forces.

"If the battle is anything like the last time we fought in the Abandoned Lands, then we'll need to keep an eye out for the scourge swarming up from the ground," Ereni said.

"Speaking of underground." Conall stepped forward and exhaled a deep breath. "That's where I have to go. That's where the Unseen will be."

Lark's brow furrowed. "Underground. Are you certain?"

Conall nodded. "Yes. In my vision, I was shown a tunnel. I saw it all so clearly. That's where he'll be."

"We'll form a party to go with you. Will you need soldiers? Mages? How will you get there?" Kayda asked.

Conall shook his head. "I took another look at that book Delyth gave me last night. I found something that should work, but it's not without risk. It's best if I go alone. In case I fail, the rest of you will need to find a way below ground."

"Lark, they're right. Snow and ice is on the way. A few hours, tops. It's a big one."

"Thanks, Muse," Lark replied, even as her stomach sank.

"Muse confirms it. There's a storm coming. A big one," she said.

Kayda stood straight, speaking with an air of command. "Then we better hurry. We can't wait until after the storm, or the bog might ice over and allow the scourge to spread south. We need to stop them now."

"That's what I like to hear. To battle." Taul hefted his axe with a wide grin.

The young man's smile was infectious, but Lark's stomach churned. This was it. The day she or one of her siblings would die.

She couldn't help worrying it would be her.

Chapter 28

Conall stared at the coast. It was even more devoid of activity than the last time he'd been here. But where last time it looked like a paradise of untouched fields and trickling streams, today, the surface echoed the ugliness that dwelled below.

The ground was charred and littered with bones. The cold wind blew across the landscape, flicking motes of dust and the first glittering sprinkles of snow.

There was no time to waste. Even now, a handful of small boats filled with fighters were on track to land ashore. The ships' captains pulled as close to shore as they could, but without a proper port, they were forced to drop anchor in the bay. But they couldn't rely on the dinghies for everyone. With all the fighters they had, it would take a full day to transfer them all.

Luckily, they had other plans.

Everyone remaining on board gathered on deck, shouldering weapons and stretching. They hugged their friends and family, whispering harried goodbyes before the chaos began.

Beside him, Ereni slid her hand into his and squeezed. He met her gaze.

They'd spent long hours last night curled in each other's arms, alternately making love and scouring the ancient spell book, searching for answers. Just before dawn, he'd happened upon a page that made his lips quirk with a grin. But when he'd shown the passage to Ereni, she'd been less than enthusiastic about his plans.

Now he could see the echo of that conversation shadowed in the blue depths of her eyes. But before she left to rally the mages, Conall tugged her hand and pulled her into an embrace. Their lips met, and a spark hummed through his veins.

After only a moment, he ended the kiss and stared down into her face. "Stay safe," he whispered. His stomach churned as she nodded and silently walked away.

She had to live. Violet would remain on board with the wet nurse, but Ereni was determined to stand and fight. And though a part of him wanted to plead for Ereni to stand aside for Violet's sake, he knew his pleas would fall on deaf ears.

This battle was as much Ereni's as anyone's. More so, since she could trace her ancestry back to the first mages who'd built the Palisade. She'd admitted to him last night that the ancient book Delyth had gifted him was a family heirloom. Generation upon generation of her family had stood guard over the Abandoned Lands, waiting for this day. Waiting for their chance to destroy the evil that plagued them.

"Time to link," Ereni's voice rang out behind him.

The mages hustled to comply. Conall watched from his spot at the rail. The forces in each boat pulled alongside mirrored the movements on theirs. Young mages stood shoulder to shoulder with white-robed elders, linking hands.

On each ship, one mage strode to the front of the pack. Onboard their ship, the task fell to his sister, Lark.

Lark lifted her hand. A bucket full of dirt sat on the deck next to her. She closed her eyes, and a vibration hummed through the ship, tickling the soles of his feet.

The next instant, soil flew into the air, forming a wide plank-like shape hovering beside the ship. The rattling vibration intensified as the other boats lined up in the water beside them followed suit.

"Hurry, now. Everyone on," Ereni ordered.

Conall was one of the first to hop on the dirt platform. Shadow bounded on beside him.

"You all right?" Conall asked as Shadow wobbled precariously atop the floating dirt.

"Yes. It's strange, is all."

It seemed Shadow was not the only one who held reservations about traveling in this fashion. Though some warriors hopped off the boat readily, others had to be coaxed. The linked mages were the worst of all, requiring a helping hand, their step wobbly and faces flushed. The exhaustion of linking appeared to be already taking its toll.

Kayda hopped onto the platform beside him, a glowing oil lamp strung around her neck. In her hands, she carried another, already lit. "I've been looking for you." She thrust the lamp toward him. "Here, you're gonna need this, I wager." She pulled a stack of handkerchiefs from the pocket of her black cloak. "Stuff it down your tunic, and the heat won't be a problem."

"Thanks." He took the supplies and arranged them as she'd suggested. He had a full waterskin on his belt, dirt stuffed in every pocket, and now this.

But although he had all the elements at his disposal, he still couldn't fully banish the tiny voice in his mind that screamed it wouldn't be enough. That this battle was doomed before it even began.

No. Conall shoved the doubt aside. He crushed it with the staggering weight of his determination. He would make sure they won this fight. Even if he wasn't around to see the battle's end, he would ensure they succeeded, one way or the other. He had to. For Violet.

Before long, the deck emptied. Conall wobbled as the dirt beneath him began to move. The icy breeze rushed past, stinging his cheeks. Lark kept their platform moving, swiftly dragging dozens of people with it, closer to the shoreline and lower in the air until they floated just above the rolling surf.

Somewhere beside them, a massive splash sounded. Conall gulped. Another group had failed, the linked mages unable to keep their boatload of fighters afloat. He swiveled his head and watched as they surfaced, their heads bobbing in the dark water.

From across the platform, Ereni met his eye and shook her head. Conall's stomach clenched, but he nodded once. They'd known this might happen. It was why they'd chosen to split the mages into groups on each ship rather than risk everyone falling together. The few sailors left on the boats would fish the unlucky folks out of the sea.

Conall sighed, setting his sights back on the coast. Perhaps they were the lucky ones, after all.

Ahead, the first of the dinghies ferrying fighters arrived on the sandy shore. They'd barely stepped foot on dry land before the scourge emerged, bursting out of the ground in the thousands. Steel flew and shrieks of the dying vermin rose in the air, joined in time by grunts and screams of wounded fighters.

Before long, the fighters were massively outnumbered. Sul pole knives sliced into the crowd of vermin, and the Doln axes and swords cracked and whistled, painting the surf red with blood. But even so, many among them faltered, falling to the ground with ravenous beasts gnawing and slashing at their throats.

There were too many for the few men who'd arrived to handle. They had to do something.

Lark seemed to have the same thought. They soared above the surf, picking up pace. Within moments, their earthen raft reached the shore and disintegrated, dropping them all into the sand behind the first wave. The linked mages collapsed, panting, their energy spent.

"Form up," Ereni shouted, blasting a wave of air ahead and displacing a manic group of beasts that leaped for them immediately. "We need a shield, now."

Conall rushed to comply, joining Lark at the head of their group. He called on his talent, the image of his daughter fresh in his mind. The vibration thrummed in his blood as a massive semi-circle of dirt coalesced in the air before them.

The formerly linked mages were protected, for now, along with a large number of the struggling fighters who'd been close by. With the shield in place, they would have enough time to recover from the weariness washing over them.

"Archers," Ereni shouted, even as the first of the bowmen burst forward.

Lark's friend Aren was among them. His bowstring twanged as his first arrow flew over the shield into the ever-growing crowd of scourge.

With every passing moment, the scourge came, throwing themselves upon the shield relentlessly. By now, the shield was half the size it had been when it started. The weakened mages staggered to their feet behind him, slowly catching their breath.

They just needed a few more moments. Conall dug deep, throwing more magic at the shield, desperately seeking to shore up the holes. But with every hole he patched, two more appeared, until he was certain the thing would fall at any instant.

Lark staggered beside him, her hands flying furiously. They held on for one heartbeat, two. Then the shield crumbled to dust, and chaos ensued.

Snarling filled the air. Conall strode forward with static coursing across his skin, flinging blasts of air in all directions, shoving the beasts back. All around him, steel rang out. Shadow leaped forward, snatching a scourge mid-jump and crunching down on its neck.

Kayda appeared at his side, the oil lamp bouncing against her chest. Fire blasted from her hands, and the stench of roasting flesh and singed hair enveloped him, making him want to gag.

"C'mon," she yelled, as she carved a clear path ahead of them.

Conall followed, grateful for her help. He had to trek further inland for his plan to work. Lark and Ereni closed in on either side of him, and they all moved together through the chaos, sending blasts of magic in every direction.

The further inland they fought, the more that strange, lingering sensation grew, until he felt certain someone was watching him. When the prickle of eyes on his back became unbearable, he halted. "Here," he shouted over the roar of battle.

Lark knelt in the dirt, her arms spread wide. A smaller shield coalesced around them in a tight circle. Ereni and Kayda stood watch, tossing balls of fire and air over the shoulder-high dirt wall to push back the scourge that sought to intrude inside their bubble of protection.

Despite that, many rammed into the shield, displacing earth at a sickening pace. He didn't have much time.

Lark met his gaze, her hands still in motion, flinging dirt all around. "Good luck."

Conall nodded and knelt beside Shadow, wrapping an arm around his back. *"You ready for this, brother?"* he asked as he tugged the waterskin from his belt.

"Always, little brother."

Conall dumped the water into his palm and closed his eyes. Then he did something he'd only done once before. He called on all the elements in sync.

Warring sensations buffeted him. A cold chill crept up his spine. The air around him moistened and crackled with static. The ground below trembled and rattled his teeth.

The book told the story of a young mage who could transport below the earth. Her earth talent was so strong she could pass through layers of rock and dirt into the tunnels deep down below.

But the story had been a cautionary tale. The mage only managed the feat a handful of times before disappearing. A few days later, her waterlogged corpse was discovered floating in a deep well.

Would he be able to do what that mage had failed to accomplish? It was time to find out.

Conall clutched Shadow tightly. His eyes shot open. He met Ereni's blue stare one last time before the ground below opened up and the earth swallowed them.

Chapter 29

Kayda gulped. The ground opened up like an angry mouth, splitting apart beneath Conall and Shadow and sucking them down. An instant later it snapped back, reforming in their wake and leaving only a mound of loose soil as evidence of their disappearance.

It all happened so fast, if she'd blinked, she'd have surely missed it.

Please let them be all right.

Kayda shook off the thought and focused on the battle. She had to trust Conall to take care of his part of the plan on his own.

Lark's earthen shield was close to crumbling. Once it fell, there would be nothing holding back the vicious beasts. They'd been the first to reach this far inland, but while they'd been shielded, many warriors and mages had caught up. The scourge flowed around them all in a massive wave of fur and destruction.

Kayda gritted her teeth and called on her talent. The chill spread through her veins, cooling her even as flames licked her skin. When the shield fell, she was ready.

Fire flew furiously. She would make them pay for what they'd done.

Destroying her country. Sacking her city. Killing her king.

In the back of her mind, she knew if what Conall saw proved true, they were not the true villain. But it didn't stop her from unleashing her fury upon the beasts. It was as if every shred of rage she'd shoved down burst loose and flowed through her hands.

Kayda smiled, reveling in the destruction. Burnt hair and flesh stung her nostrils and the coppery tang of blood flooded the air as she watched the sea of beady eyes turn into a molten river of ash and flame.

The warriors from the boats spread around her. To her left, a small group of Sul fought in a ring, pole knives flashing furiously. Two archers remained protected in the center, shooting arrows above the warrior's shoulders wherever the scourge sought to pounce on the fighters unawares.

To her right, Clan Chief Aundrea and his son bowled through the crowd. Taul's axe and Aundrea's great two-handed sword hammered into the mass and sprayed blood in all directions, carving through the mound of beasts like they were shoveling snow.

Beside her, Lark and Ereni fought. Blasts of air and earth pummeled the scourge, unleashing death on all sides. Together, they pushed forward, gaining ground slowly until they mounted a small hill.

At this slight elevation, Kayda gasped and spun in a slow circle. The devastation spread out on all sides. From within the crowd, it was easy to lose track of just how many beasts swarmed the land. They carpeted the earth, so much that it was hard to glimpse any dirt beneath all the fur and teeth. It was truly mind-boggling.

Yet, still more came. They spilled out of tiny holes, popping up and jumping upon unsuspecting warriors. Even more poured out of a few larger holes, set within small hills like the one she stood on.

"Hey," Kayda yelled to Lark, sending a blast of fire ahead. "Can you block a few of those?"

Lark glanced at one of the hillside holes just as her falcon swooped down and snatched a scourge out of the air mid-leap. The crack of its neck snapping echoed in Kayda's ears.

Lark grinned. "Yeah, good plan."

Kayda led the way down the far side of the hill they'd mounted. Sure enough, there was a hole just like others she'd seen, cut into the very bottom of the mound. It was small enough a human would need to crouch down and shimmy through, but big enough to let a half dozen scourge out at a time.

"Go for it," Ereni shouted to Lark as she thumped to the ground beside her, hurling a blast of air that sent dozens of scourge scrambling backward. "We'll cover you."

Lark knelt down, filling her hands with charred soil. A heartbeat later, the thrumming in the ground intensified so much Kayda's feet buzzed in her boots. Then the mouth of the hole collapsed, crushing dozens of *ichneumons* and sealing the hole.

Kayda whooped. "That ought to slow them down."

With the multitude of tiny holes in the ground, caving in the large holes wouldn't stop the scourge completely, but maybe if they filled enough of them, it would turn the tide. It might give the fighters a chance to cull the massive herd while Conall sought the Unseen.

"C'mon," Kayda yelled, "Over here." She blasted fire in a wide arc, heading for the closest hillside.

They burst through the scourge, felling them mercilessly. Twice more, they stopped and collapsed a hole, each time heading further inland until they were so far from the main mass of fighters the sound of battle faded from an overwhelming din to a mere clatter in the distance.

The third hole they approached was set in a hillside much larger than the rest. The entrance rested on the hill's far side, and when they thumped down to the ground before it, the hill blocked their view of the ocean and most of the fighting.

It sent a shiver up Kayda's spine the moment she set her gaze inside the yawning hole. This one was large enough she would only need to duck her head to enter, instead of crawl.

A massive crowd of scourge lay in wait at the tunnel mouth. Unlike the rest, these weren't racing away, heading for them or to the larger battle beyond. These sat still, teeth bared, almost as if they'd been stationed there, guarding something within.

The eerie feeling that had first struck her only intensified as she set fire to the beasts and they squealed where they stood, unmoving even as they roasted to death.

Lark sank her hands into the earth, and the ground rumbled in response. But though the earth shook harder than ever, and flecks of dirt flew, joining the ever-increasing misting of white flurries, the hole refused to collapse.

Lark frowned, staring into the dark cave mouth. "I don't know why it's not working."

Kayda whipped around, pausing the fire flowing from her hands long enough to quirk a brow at the tunnel entrance, still standing stubbornly. "Try ag—"

"Funny finding you here, sister," called a voice from within.

Kayda gasped, her hand flying to her chest. It couldn't be. Surely not.

She shook her head, squinting into the dark. That voice. She would know it anywhere. Her heart skipped a beat.

"Tarquin?"

No, he was dead. She'd watched him die months ago, in the first battle here in the Abandoned Lands. He and his entire contingent of guards had been overwhelmed, swarmed by hundreds of the scourge. Eaten alive.

But even as she convinced herself otherwise, he strode out of the cave mouth, ducking his head until he halted before her and straightened to his full height.

Kayda's jaw dropped.

"No." She shook her head again, flicking it so strongly her braids whipped against her cheek.

How was this possible? She'd watched him die.

One of his blond brows arched, his voice dripping with malice. "Aren't you happy to see me, sister? Why am I not surprised?"

Beside her, Ereni stiffened at the sight of him. She turned from the crowd of scourge at their backs and blasted a wave of wind directly at him. The wind flew around him so strongly that just being in its periphery, Kayda nearly stumbled. But Tarquin only strolled on, his dark blond hair flickering, but his body unmoved.

Kayda's stomach plummeted.

Tarquin spared Ereni a glance and sneered. "Deal with them, will you?" He called back over his shoulder. "I've need of a private word with my little sister." His smile curved up as he lifted his hands.

Kayda caught a single glimpse of shadowy forms emerging behind him before the remaining scourge suddenly became unglued and burst into motion. They crowded around them and stacked atop each other, forming a wall of bodies much like the circular shield Lark had crafted out of earth.

Kayda stared, stunned.

Tarquin smirked.

"What? How?" Kayda backed up, coming close to ramming into the wall of scourge.

"What's the matter, Kayda? You look a little surprised."

That was an understatement if there ever was one. Kayda stared wide-eyed at the wall of scourge caging her. Her stomach churned uneasily. "Why are these vermin listening to you, Tarquin?"

From somewhere outside, male voices rang out, filled with violence, but their words slid through her ears, unheard. She could only stare at her half-brother. He looked exactly the same. Tall and strong. Still wearing that haughty smirk.

"I only took what I deserve."

"What you deserve?"

He sneered at her. "I will be the new king of these lands. Not just our country—all of them. A king for a new age."

"What are you talking about? The scourge will destroy us all." Despite herself, she couldn't stop a pleading tone from infecting her voice.

"Oh, but that is only the first step. After Father's had his fill, it will all be mine."

"Father is dead. And he never wanted—"

Tarquin's lips curled back. "Not that drunken fool. My true father."

Kayda gasped. No. Even Tarquin couldn't be that stupid. Could he?

"You allied yourself with the Unseen?" But even as the question spilled out of her lips, she knew it was true. That's why the scourge listened to him. And why he'd survived the attack that destroyed his men. "No." She shook her head vehemently. "How could you?"

Tarquin glared at her. "How could I? Easily." He stabbed a finger at his chest. "It should've been me. I should've been the special one. Not you. I was only righting a wrong."

Kayda drew back at the cruel glint in his eye. "But what the Unseen is doing is wrong. After he's finished, there'll be nothing left. You'll rule over a land of ghosts and bones. Can't you see that?"

Tarquin scoffed, waving a hand dismissively. "We're merely wiping the slate. Washing away the filth that inhabits this realm and starting anew. We're the cleansing fire that will render this world to ash and allow something stronger and better to rise from the ashes."

Kayda wobbled on her feet. "That's insane. All those people..."

Tarquin rolled his eyes. "There will be others. New rules. A society built in whatever way I see fit. No savages to the north and south to defy me. It will be a paradise."

How could he be so cruel? Willing to dispose of people like they were refuse tossed in a slop bucket.

Kayda planted her feet and squared her shoulders. "I won't let you."

Tarquin turned to stare at her full on, and he laughed. "You think you can stop me? Go ahead and try," he forced out between maddened chuckles.

Kayda raised her hand, her fingers twitching. "Please, Tarquin. I don't want to kill you. It's not too late to put an end to this. You can join us and defeat the Unseen."

He stopped laughing. "No." He stared pointedly at her hand.

Kayda gulped. Tarquin had seen her blast fire from her hands before. He knew what she could do.

"Go ahead, sister. Destroy me like you've always wanted to." He took a step closer. "Or are you too stupid and weak? I'll never stop. And do you know why? Because I don't want to live in a world where fate would choose an ugly, conniving little bitch like yo—"

Fire flew from her hands, cutting off his cruel words. Tarquin's clothes caught first, and his golden hair. Then his skin sizzled.

Kayda gagged but kept the flames flowing until he fell to a knee in front of her, his entire face blackened, and his clothing reduced to crumbling ash.

Then she backed away, a hand at her mouth, struggling not to vomit.

She expected him to fall fully after that. To slump face-first in the dirt and remain unmoving. But after only an instant, he started pushing up off the ground.

Kayda gasped again, her gaze glued to him as he rose. The damage her fire wrought stood out starkly. His flesh was black and red, covered in massive blisters.

But right before her eyes, Tarquin's skin began to heal itself. The blisters faded and disappeared. The redness receded, his skin returning to a pale, creamy white. His hair grew back, covering his head so quickly it was hard to remember it had just been burned to a crisp a moment ago.

When he rose to his full height and brushed the blackened remains of his charred clothing off his body, he was almost good as new, only a few tiny red marks and blisters remaining.

Tarquin strode to the piled scourge, seemingly unconcerned with his nakedness even though his breath clouded in the cold air and snowflakes landed on his shoulders. He grabbed one of the beasts by the throat and strangled it. The scourge made no move to defend itself, just whimpered pitifully until Tarquin snapped its neck.

Kayda's eyes bulged as the last of the redness and blisters faded away on Tarquin's skin.

"Blazes," she said. "What have you become?"

Chapter 30

Conall fought not to panic as darkness closed around him. The lamp dangling from his chest ensured it wasn't as complete as it could be. Even still, it was hard to remain calm as the earth dragged him down.

"Are you all right?" he asked Shadow, the comforting feel of his fur clutched tightly under his arm.

"Yes, I'm fine, little brother."

Conall sighed. That was good. Besides being uncertain this would even work, he'd also been unsure whether he could bring anyone with him. He'd convinced the others to stay above ground, but Shadow had insisted on coming. With the earth surrounding him like a grave, he was grateful for his bondmate's insistence.

They sank slowly through the earth. Conall's heart thrummed faster than a scared hare in flight. He'd expected to flash under, transported from one spot to the other in an eye blink like he'd done in the strange waking dream he'd experienced while the Palisade fell. But this was a whole different story. He fought through the descent, pushing aside the earth below while keeping a much smaller version of the shield Lark had constructed above intact around him and Shadow. It was slow going and exhausting, but it was working.

Long moments passed with nothing happening except for that slow sink. The air in their little shielded bubble grew stale, the same way it had when he'd been trapped below the snow with Quent. Conall forced himself to remain calm, praying they'd find a tunnel or cave, something to refresh their air supply before they passed out.

The surrounding ground, which had started out almost as chilled as the winter air on the surface, slowly warmed. He remembered the dream. The heat that had seeped off that red-lit tunnel where he'd first spoken to the Unseen. They must be getting closer.

Shadow stiffened at the same moment Conall gasped. The slow but steady movement changed to a sudden plummet and a shocking splash. Water flooded up from below, soaking the bottom of their shield of dirt and seeping into Conall's trousers.

"Don't worry, brother." Conall took a deep breath and pulled gratefully at the fresh air, ensuring their protective sphere didn't become waterlogged. But as the water trickled out to rejoin whatever underwater stream or lake it came from, Conall spotted a new problem. They'd stopped sinking. The ball of dirt and air was floating.

He banished a small section of dirt above his head and peered out, pulling at the fire in the lamp and sending four fireballs flying out the hole and across the ceiling. His eyes widened. It was definitely a lake. A huge one from the looks of it. He spun sideways and spotted water stretched out in every direction. The cave's roof hovered over his head, just out of reach, making it even harder to make out how big the chamber was or where it ended.

Shadow peered over his shoulder. *"What now?"*

Conall gulped. *"I'm not sure. Give me a moment to think."*

He wasn't having much trouble keeping them afloat. Granted, it required constant concentration and a steady stream of magic, but he could see them floating long enough to reach shore. The question was, how long would it take? How much energy would he be forced to spend in the process? How many people would be killed by the scourge while he and Shadow sailed?

Would it even be enough? He closed his eyes, concentrating on that vile wrongness. The further down they traveled, the feeling had steadily increased, but still couldn't match level he remembered from his dream. His instincts howled, demanding he listen.

The second option, then.

"We're going down."

Shadow cocked his head. *"Is that wise? What will we do for air? Ereni—"*

"I know. Let's just hope it's not deep." Conall petted him reassuringly. Shadow nodded. *"I trust you."*

Conall took another deep breath, gripping Shadow even tighter. Then he banished the earth surrounding them, and let the water take them.

He kept a bubble of air locked around their heads, lifting the lamp close to his face. Wouldn't do to lose the light now that they sank into the black water below. Conall shivered as the water soaked his clothing. But though their legs and torsos quickly submerged, the bubble of air kept them close to the surface.

Conall kicked his legs. All the hope he'd held that the water would be shallow evaporated as his toes met no resistance. There was no way to tell how deep this water went. But that changed nothing. They had to keep going.

Using his talent, he forced the water to part below them, letting them sink further even with the air bubble around their heads seeking to buoy them. But as they dropped away from the surface—away from the air—a wave of exhaustion slammed into him.

Somehow he'd been able to maintain the bubble of air with the dirt wrapped around them, but underwater, it was a different story. The bubble slowly shrank with each breath they drew, forcing him to summon more out of thin air—or more like thin water. The exhaustion quickly compounded, making him dizzy.

How much longer until he passed out, and they drowned? Or how much of his life would this cost him? Ereni had lost months when she'd summoned a handful of bubbles to save herself and Lark. If this water was much deeper, he might start losing years.

Before the thought could make his stomach plummet as surely as he and Shadow sank through the water, Conall's feet touched bottom. He immediately pulled at the dirt and formed a shield, sinking back down into the earth. Slowly he forced the water out, watching in the lamplight as it trickled into the dirt and rock. The bubble of air stabilized, and the worst of his exhaustion lifted.

"Do I look older, brother?" Conall's voice wobbled in his mind and his shoulders stiffened as Shadow's golden eyes shifted across his face.

"No, you look the same."

Conall relaxed slightly, some of the tension lifting. *"Good, I'm glad that water wasn't deep—"*

His thought ended in a gasp as their shield of earth plummeted again. This time, the bottom wasn't met with a wet splash, but with a jarring thud. The earthen shield absorbed the worst of the blow, but Conall's legs still smarted from the collision.

He banished a section of the shield, lifting the lamp. They were in a tunnel. One with a red glow seeping through the air, along with a moist heat.

"I think we're here." Conall let the shield fall completely and stood on wobbly legs. The ceiling was too low for him to rise to his full height, but at least there was air and no water. He tugged his soaked clothes and set the lamp down so he could quickly shuck off his boots and spill out the water filling them.

Shadow shook out his fur, then shifted to stare down the long tube of dirt where the red light emanated. *"You sure this is it?"*

Conall shoved his feet back into his wet boots as that slithering wrongness crept across his skin, stronger than ever. *"Yeah, I'm sure. Let's kill this bastard."*

He took a step toward the light.

Chapter 31

Lark's stomach dropped as a wall of scourge formed around Kayda, blocking her and the smirking blond man from view. She and Ereni fought on, desperately flinging magic at an unending stream of vicious beasts throwing themselves at them from all sides.

Was that really the prince—back from the dead?

Whatever the answer, it didn't matter. She couldn't just let the bastard cut Kayda off from the rest of the battle. He could be doing anything to her in there.

She pulled at the earth, readying an enormous blast that would hopefully destroy the wall of vermin shielding the pair.

"Lark, look out!" Muse chirped, full of alarm.

The same instant, a deep voice spilled out into the night, and a bevy of shadowed forms appeared in the cave mouth, slinking out behind the wall of scourge. "Lady Death, we meet again."

A man with scarred arms was the first to emerge, an evil sneer twisting his lips. At least a dozen men joined him, all faces she recognized. The same men that stared at her with overt lust while she'd been trapped in that prison cell were here to greet her, clutching weapons in their fists, their faces full of amusement and rage.

Lark's stomach dropped. Blazes. She blasted the earth meant for the scourge in his direction. The man ducked, his reflexes somehow lightning fast, and the dirt pounded into the cave wall behind him.

"Bet you're wondering how we got here. Bet you thought we'd die in the bog or be eaten alive by the scourge."

Lark scrambled for a reply, tongue-tied in her shock, even as her hands went right back to moving, flinging a dart at a beast that leaped for her chest. He was right. She'd been sure she'd never see those men again.

"No one cares, Reg," Ereni shouted. She jumped up beside Lark while hurling a blast of air toward the men and a second behind her at the scourge. "Lay down your weapons or prepare to die."

The man's brows shot up as Ereni named him. "You witches are full of surprises, aren't you?" But he shook off his surprise and strode forward, a lecherous glint in his eyes as he scanned them. They both wore close-fitted cloaks and trousers, much more suited for battle than the normal skirts and dresses Lark was used to, but Reg's gaze lit on their simple attire like a starving man at a feast.

Lark spared a glance behind him and spotted a similar hunger on all the men's faces. It made her stomach knot like crazy, especially since none of them had moved to fight them. At least not yet.

A second man spoke up. "Bet if we drag them inside, we can have a little fun before the rest of the fighting reaches us."

"Not going to slit our throats?" Ereni shot back.

Lark's stomach dropped. Why was she goading them? Not that she could blame her. The thought of being dragged back into the caves with those men was worse than death.

Reg stilled in his tracks, staring at Ereni strangely. "She's right. These witches need to die." He growled, raising his spear and stabbing right for Ereni's chest.

Ereni dodged, blasting a wall of air at Reg and sending him sprawling backward on his ass.

But though Reg fell, a trio jumped at her next. Ereni spun sideways, barely staying out of reach of their blades and staves before pushing them back with another blast of air.

Lark's heart hammered as she fought by her side, sending darts of dirt in every direction. Muse swooped down and snatched a scourge who came close to landing on her back in the chaos. She snapped its neck.

Lark's breath came hard and fast. It was too much. The three of them against more than a dozen armed men and hundreds of ravenous beasts. They wouldn't be able to hold them off forever. But if they could just hold out until the rest of the fighting reached them, then maybe it would be enough.

She'd left her friends with explicit instructions to remain in the back of the lines. She'd even made Tiora and Dausius promise to stay close to Mika. Mika, Vespen, and a handful of other healers volunteered to care for the many injuries their force would be sure to receive. Lark knew Aren and the twins could handle themselves in a fight, but Ti and Daus—not so much. She'd pleaded with them all to stay back. To stay safe. She hoped they'd listened.

But her friends weren't the only ones out there. The Doln warriors and Sul had been close on their tails not long ago. If she and Ereni could hold out a little longer, maybe they would catch up, and they might actually have a chance.

Even as hope spooled around her heart, she tripped, slamming hard to the rocky ground. A snarl filled her ears, and she jerked her wide-eyed gaze sideways, spotting a black and silver flash speeding straight for her throat.

The beast was impaled before it could reach her, the blade of a stave catching it in the ribs. A squeal of pain replaced the snarl an instant before the blade twisted viciously and retracted, flicking a cascade of hot blood across her face.

Lark turned, meeting the cruel stare of the prisoner who'd just saved her. But it was clear he hadn't done it for her benefit when he flipped his weapon around, aiming the blunt end for her forehead.

She could see it in his eyes. He would knock her unconscious and drag her off into the cave. Into the dark.

Lark dug her fingers into the rocky soil beneath her. The man drew his arms back, readying to thump the stave into her skull. Then a golden flash of feathers and fury shot into his face, wicked talons carving up his skin and tearing at his eyes.

The man shrieked, blood pouring down his neck. He dropped his stave and screamed, his hands flying toward his face, desperate to knock Muse loose.

Lark scrambled to her feet while they grappled. *"I'm up, fly,"* she screamed in her mind.

Muse unlatched her claws from the man's face, but not before he shot out his fist and slammed her into the cave wall.

"Muse, no!" Lark barreled between them and flung dirt at the man's bleeding face, using her talent to make sure it caught him in the eyes. He staggered back, scrubbing his face and yowling.

But one man down didn't mean she was safe. A pair of muscled brutes jumped up to take his place, one with a cudgel and the other a short sword. Lark dodged a blow from the sword but was too slow to avoid the cudgel. It slammed into her stomach in an explosion of pain, forcing the air from her lungs.

"I'm up." Muse screeched as she lifted off the ground. She flew right for the man holding the cudgel, momentarily blinding him and giving Lark the chance to catch her breath and scurry backward.

The sword came flying at her face again, but she speared a dart of dirt into the man's stomach before his swing landed, making his aim go wild. She sprinted away from the pair, scattering dirt behind her in a cloud, praying it would blind the men so she could regroup.

She almost ran into Ereni, who held a man immobile with her air talent, her fist outstretched. She calmly walked to his side and slashed his throat with her hunting knife. Blood spattered the ground and spurted into the air. Then Ereni dropped her fist and let the man's dead weight crumple to the ground.

Blazes, she was fierce. Lark made a mental note never to get on her bad side.

"C'mon." Ereni mounted the hillside, flinging a blast of air ahead of her. "Climb to the high ground."

Though Lark sent a wary glance back at the cave mouth—back to Kayda—still hidden behind the shield of scourge, she followed. Soon they made it to the top of the small hill, and Lark gasped as she caught a glimpse of the larger battle beyond their small clash.

Though the rest of their forces had only scourge to contend with, they weren't faring any better. If anything, they were worse. Blood soaked the ground, and far too many bodies lay in a tangle of limbs on the battlefield. Many more than their few healers could save.

The number of scourge had not lessened in the slightest, even after they'd plugged the few cave entrances. They swarmed across the land, overwhelming the tiny pockets of fighters with their immense numbers.

As she watched, a circle of Sul warriors fell, and the scourge piled on them so quickly they were lost to her view in the blink of an eye.

Lark's stomach churned as she swiveled around, forcing her gaze away from the melee behind them. From the cave mouth, a blast of fire roared, the heat so strong, a warm gust of air blew across Lark's face.

But then a handful of men emerged, scrubbing dirt from their faces and mounting the hillside.

The same villain who'd tried to slam her head with a stave clambered up the hillside. Lark locked stares with him, and her jaw dropped. His face, which just moments ago had been torn to shreds from Muse's talons, appeared to have partially healed already.

That shouldn't be possible. Did the men have a healer of their own?

The man sent her an evil grin, then stomped viciously on a scourge, grinding his boot into its back. The instant the vermin's squeals died, the rest of the gouges on the prisoner's face disappeared.

Lark bit back a gasp. What the blazes?

Ereni blew the men backward, and the air crackled from the force of her talent. But her brow was wet and her breathing erratic. Lark's own body slumped with exhaustion, her sore stomach heaving as she sent a hail of dirt pummeling into the scourge that sprang up at them.

How long could they last out here? How could they hope to defeat these men who had some mysterious way of healing themselves? She had no idea, but she wasn't about to stop trying.

Conall. Brother, you need to hurry.

Chapter 32

Kayda stared bewildered at Tarquin's healing body. How was it possible? She'd never seen anything like it.

Tarquin flicked a hand at the scourge, a sly smirk on his lips. The beasts moved in unison, the circle around them morphing into a wide wall that blocked the cave mouth.

Kayda gaped, watching them reform without him even speaking a word. How did he get them to listen? Did his pact with the Unseen grant him the power to control the beasts, too? It was all so strange. She was trapped, cut off from the battle, stuck with her brother, who'd become indestructible somehow.

Tarquin strolled over to a fallen man whose throat had been slit. Blood pooled around his neck and chest, soaking his dirty tunic.

"What's happening, Tarquin? I don't understand."

He knelt beside the man and tugged off his boots and his trousers, then quickly dressed in the fallen man's clothes, covering his nakedness. "Well, sister, I know you've always had a sick little thing for me, but I'd rather not fight like this."

Kayda shot him a disgusted look. "Don't even... That's revolting and not at all what I mean. How are you still standing?"

"That's all you have to say after trying to scorch me to death?" He straightened, adopting a mocking tone. "How are you still standing?" He bent at the waist and picked up the fallen man's discarded weapon—a short sword. "Isn't it obvious? I beat you at your own game. I was cheated out of the magic I deserved, so I found my own. And now, I'm going to enjoy watching you die."

Kayda backed away warily, forming a fireball on her outstretched hand. "Stay back, or I'll—"

"You'll what? Burn my clothes off again? Haven't you seen the futility in that? You spent your whole life with your nose in those books, yet you're still dumb as a rock."

Kayda trembled. He was right. He should be dead now, burnt to a crisp like anyone else would be after being struck by so much fire. But he wasn't.

How could she hope to defeat him when he would just heal himself?

Tarquin advanced, an evil grin on his face. He lifted the sword over his shoulder, pacing slowly toward her.

"Kayda, I'm almost there. Hold on."

Kayda stifled a gasp as Dru's voice reverberated in her mind. Yes! Dru would help her out of this mess.

"I'm stuck behind a wall of scourge in a cave mouth. Hurry."

She dodged a swing from Tarquin's sword, ducking under the blow and scurrying to the opposite cave wall.

"Where? I don't see you?" Dru replied.

Kayda blasted the fire on her hands at the wall of scourge. *"Look for the flames."*

Tarquin dove for her again. Kayda cut off the stream of fire and leaped away, but not before the blade caught the string holding the oil lamp around her neck. The lamp shattered on the floor. The oil ignited so quickly she barely jumped away before the flames engulfed her trousers.

Blazes. She didn't have much time before her source disappeared. She blasted another wave of flames at the scourge blocking the cave entrance. The reek of charred hair and flesh wafted through the air. Though many of them died, the beasts remained stacked, only squealing as the flames roasted them.

Tarquin didn't give her long to focus. He charged at her, his blade swinging straight at her neck.

Kayda dodged again, blasting a fireball at his face.

Tarquin grimaced as it connected, but paid his burning flesh no mind. Kayda's jaw dropped as his skin immediately began reforming before her eyes.

Then he flicked his hand, and the scourge shuffled around them, encircling them in a tight ring.

Kayda gulped. There was barely any room to dodge now.

Tarquin sneered down at her, his blackened, blistered skin already partially healed. He snatched another scourge off the pile and snapped its neck casually. Then he stomped out the flames lingering on the cave floor.

"Goodbye, Kayda." He lifted his blade, the metal glinting dangerously.

Fire blasted from the sky. A black shadow hovered just beyond the scourge. Druturion!

Kayda called forth her talent again, using Dru's flames as her source. Her blood ignited with liquid ice, chilling her body even as flames surrounded her. The scourge burst into flame from Dru, but Kayda aimed all her fire at Tarquin. She screamed, pelting him so intensely he staggered backward and dropped his blade.

After a moment, she relented and shoved her way through the scourges' burned carcasses, leaving her brother in a heap of ash and bloody blisters.

"Dru, you're back." She raced forward as he landed, a huge smile on her face, and clutched his neck.

"I am. Quick, hop on. We've got more vermin to kill."

Kayda vaulted atop his back. *"I hate to break it to you, but he's not dead, Dru."*

Even as the words filled her mind, Tarquin staggered to his feet behind them. The scourge he'd used as his puppets lay in waste, but somehow, he was healing himself yet again.

"Is that your brother? I thought he died months ago."

"Me, too. He's made some vile pact with the Unseen. No matter what I do, he won't die."

"We'll see about that."

Dru whipped around to face him and spewed fire in a molten stream. Tarquin dropped to his knees, his skin peeling and bubbling from the heat.

Kayda watched his smoldering body until more scourge diverted her attention, leaping at them from the outside of the cave. She blasted them back, but more kept coming, attracted to Dru like insects to a flame.

"C'mon, Dru. We have to fly. There's too many."

Dru cut off the stream of flame and burst into the sky. They left Tarquin in a pile of blackened flesh. But Kayda didn't hold out much hope that would be the end of it.

Dru flew low to the ground, and Kayda concentrated on destroying the scourge. Now that she was free from the cave, she could see the battle was not going as well as she'd hoped. Thousands of scourge swarmed up from the ground, and the fighters and mages struggled against the massive numbers.

Kayda's heart lifted as she spotted a white dragon barreling toward the coast. *"Bela's back."*

Belstasia dove, shooting blasts of ice at the scourge attacking the fighters near the coast. Their forces cheered, and it seemed like everyone fought with renewed strength. Surely now, with two dragons on their side, the tide would turn. Maybe they could actually win this fight.

Atop the hill, she spotted Lark and Ereni fighting back-to-back, sending wave upon wave of dirt and wind at armed men and countless scourge.

"Let's help those women on the hill."

Dru banked toward them, opening his mouth and spilling fire down at the ground. Kayda threw out her hand, adding her flames. Soon, they rendered the scourge to ash and set the men on fire.

Lark and Ereni whooped with delight. But Kayda gulped as one man brushed the flames off his body and rose off the ground. Then another.

"They're getting up, too?" Dru circled back, sending more flames at the men.

Blazes. Those men were just like Tarquin—somehow able to heal from her magic. How would they ever defeat them?

A thought struck her, and her stomach fluttered. *"Wait, there was a corpse on the ground in the cave that had his throat slit... If a mortal wound to the neck worked, then maybe one to the heart or brain would as well."* Kayda scanned the ground, spotting a few more corpses nearby that weren't moving. It must be true. They just needed to kill them quickly and get up close. *"Drop me back on the ground. You scorch the bastards from above, and I'll stab them."*

"All right. I'll stay close so you can use my flames as your source."

Dru dropped her next to one of the corpses, and Kayda snatched his discarded stave off the ground. She headed straight for the closest man as he skewered a scourge on the end of his blade, and the burnt skin on his face and arms healed.

He faced her with a smirk, but Dru wiped it off his lips the next instant, catching him in a blast of flame. Kayda strode up to the man as he dropped to the ground and shoved the stave into his heart.

She tugged the stave free and held her breath, half-expecting the man to climb back to his feet. But he stayed down. *"It works."* Kayda grinned. *"C'mon. Let's kill them all."*

Chapter 33

C rouching, Conall shuffled further down the narrow tunnel.

"How much farther, do you think?" Shadow's fur bristled. *"That awful feeling keeps getting worse. I'm not sure if I can bear it much longer."*

Conall shuddered. *"I don't know. I can feel it, too, but I still can't hear him."* That repulsive, crawling itch had returned with a vengeance.

"I wonder why the Unseen's only spoken to you, little brother? Even when it infected your mind at the fire moat, I still could not hear it, though our thoughts are connected."

Conall shook his head, ducking beneath a dripping stalactite. *"I don't know. But maybe we can use that to our advantage. If he can't sense you the way he can me, maybe he'll assume I've come alone if we don't speak."*

"Good plan, little brother. We must think of a signal. When you give it, I will stay silent."

Conall pondered that for a moment and settled for a double tap on his thigh. *"How's that?"*

Shadow inclined his head. *"I will watch for that movement."*

Conall sent him a half smile and crept forward. The eerie red glow increased with every step, as did the heat. Sweat slid down his back beneath his tunic, and his trousers stuck to his skin, the humidity making them slow to dry even with the heat baking him. He'd long ago shucked off his sodden cloak after stuffing all his supplies in his belt pouches.

In a few spots, holes in the walls and floor revealed a molten river of glowing, bubbling lava somewhere below.

Conall's eyes widened as he skirted the edge of a wide hole. The heat rose, crackling against his cheeks. *"Careful."*

Shadow sidestepped the hole deftly, though his tail hung low between his legs.

The tunnel ahead split, and Conall's stomach roiled as he stopped before the fork.

"Which way?" Shadow tilted his head, his golden eyes flicking between the two tunnels, each practically identical.

Conall rubbed his chin, then shifted his touch to his aching neck and shoulders. He couldn't just stand here forever, crouched and indecisive. But the wrong choice would cost them time and energy. Force them to backtrack and possibly lead to hundreds more killed on the surface.

Then the distant snarl of the scourge echoed down one of the paths, and he shuffled toward it. *"Keep a wary eye out, brother. Sounds like we're heading for a fight."*

He hoped he'd chosen right, and the presence of the scourge meant their leader was nearby, but only time would tell.

He pulled at the flame in the lamp dangling against his neck and readied a fireball as the beast's skittering claws and screeching grew louder. The chill of fire magic spread through his veins, and he shivered, though he welcomed the icy bite if only for a brief reprieve from the stifling heat all around.

He didn't have long to revel in the sensation. They rounded a bend and entered a wide, rocky chamber. But though the ceiling here was finally tall enough for him to straighten to his full height, there was a big problem.

Dozens of scourge blocked the path. Conall sent out wave after wave of flame. The answering shrieks of the vermin rent the air.

A few dodged the flames, leaping sideways and bouncing across the walls. A pair came at him, snarling, hate spewing from their beady black eyes. He gasped, certain they would leap for his neck and tear him to shreds before he could react, but both of the beasts ignored him and leaped straight for Shadow behind him.

Blazes. That was worse than if they'd come for him. Conall roared, turning from the huge crowd of scourge he'd already scorched.

Shadow caught the first beast mid leap, snapping its neck with his powerful jaws. But the second beast landed atop his back, and its claws sank deep into his hide, drawing blood.

Conall blasted fire balls at two more who leaped for his bondmate. His brow raised as they both ignored him once again, even though he was closer than Shadow.

Why were they not attacking him? It made no sense.

He shoved the thought aside and swung back to Shadow, where he grappled with the last scourge. The vile beast's jaw clamped down between Shadow's shoulder blades, holding tight even while he bucked and rolled, attempting to dislodge the beast.

"Stay still, brother," Conall shouted in his mind.

Shadow complied instantly, and Conall dumped a handful of water from his waterskin into his palm. Then he sent a globe of water to Shadow's back, fully submerging the scourge.

As the water surrounded the creature, it finally opened its wicked jaws and unlatched from Shadow's back. As soon as his bondmate ducked away, Conall sent the water and the scourge sailing into a hole.

The beast descended into the heated glow, the water sizzling as it evaporated.

Conall sucked in a deep breath and took a step toward Shadow. *"Are you all right, bro—"*

Conall staggered. His foot slipped in a puddle of blood, and he fell, smacking hard into the rocky cave floor. Pain, sudden and sharp, exploded behind his eyes, and the world twirled. Blearily, he lifted a hand to the back of his head and warm wetness coated his fingers.

Blazes. *This can't be good.*

Darkness reigned.

Chapter 34

The spearhead shoved into the charred man's chest. Kayda grunted as she twisted, then pulled out the spear with a wet *thunk*. She raced up the hillside to Lark and Ereni's side.

"Magic alone doesn't work," she yelled, slamming a scourge out of her path, which Druturion kindly roasted from his spot in the sky. "They need a mortal wound."

Lark's eyes widened, and Ereni nodded. Behind them, Kayda spotted more of their fighters closing in on their position. Belstasia's bolts of ice were turning the tide. But it wasn't time to celebrate. Not even close.

"Sister," a voice bellowed below. "Where are you?"

Even dragon fire had not been enough to kill him. A jolt of panic lanced her chest until she remembered the spear in her hands. It was time to end this.

Kayda spared a glance for Ereni and Lark. Lark sent darts of dirt shooting into a crowd of scourge. Four fell with spikes sticking out of their necks and chests. Even more flew off course, only to jolt back up to their feet and leap toward the pair again.

Ereni let one man get uncomfortably close. He raised a cudgel over his head, a menacing cry tearing out of his throat. Before he connected, Ereni's hand shot out. She held him immobile with what looked like nothing, but Kayda suspected from the crackle of static on her skin, it was a cage of air. Then Ereni strolled up to his side, lifted a blade off her waist, and stabbed the side of his neck. Blood gushed out, spurting like a red geyser.

"Sister!" Tarquin shouted again.

Well, it appeared that Lark and Ereni had things handled here. Especially now that several of their fighters closed in on the hillside. She smiled, spotting Jayan hovering close to a white-haired woman spewing out flames—Izora.

Kayda raced down the hillside, heading for the cave mouth. *"C'mon, Dru."*

Druturion followed, spreading flame around her path in all directions to keep the scourge at bay. Kayda lifted her hand, banishing the burning grass before her to clear a path through the fire. Her boots kicked up ash, and specks floated to her face, joining the cold snowflakes stinging her cheeks.

The snow fell in earnest, sizzling as it struck the fire and sticking to the grass everywhere else. The scourge's pelts were dusted with white, but the weather didn't slow their ferocity in the least.

Soon, their forces would begin to struggle, if they weren't already. The snow made everything slicker, and poor footing during battle could easily become a death sentence. The Sul, in particular, had never battled in these conditions. Kayda's heart ached, picturing Jayan and Lazar—all the sandborn who'd answered her call. Had she led them to their ends?

Tarquin's still healing face appeared before her, and she forced her worries aside. She could protect the Sul after she put her brother down—for good this time.

Tarquin smirked at her, then opened his mouth.

"Now, Dru."

The awful words he'd no doubt been about to spew were swallowed by a scream of pain. Fire cascaded around Tarquin once again. He shielded his face with his arms, and the skin peeled back, giving Kayda a glimpse of the bloody bone beneath.

Kayda marched up to him as Dru cut off the river of flame. She gritted her teeth and thrust the spear into his chest. She waited for the wave of remorse to wash over her, but nothing came. Even as she pulled the spear free, and his charred body crumbled to the ground.

Tarquin was no more. He'd never talk down to her again. Never plot against her and their kingdom. It was over.

Dru stiffened above her. The flames he'd been spraying at the scourge disappeared, and he roared as if in great pain.

"What's wrong?"

"Kayda. It's the Unseen. I feel him trying to take over." He shook his head and groaned.

"Fight it, Dru. You're stronger than he is. I believe in you."

The great black dragon wobbled in the sky. For a moment, she was certain he would come crashing to the ground, crushing her beneath him. But he suddenly stabilized, hovering easily once more.

"He's gone. I don't know how he reached me after our wish." He pivoted, sending another blast of fire into the scourge surrounding them.

Kayda pulled at the flame in his chest and added her own fire to the fray. *"Your wish?"*

"Yes, we—"

His explanation was cut off by manic screaming echoing across the snowy plain. Kayda raced sideways, rounding the hillside.

The sight that met her sent a chill down her spine. Belstasia had turned on them. Instead of blasting ice into the scourge, she sent great blasts of ice spiraling into the fighters on the beach. People fled in every direction, jumping aside and screaming.

"Bela!" Dru bellowed.

"Go," Kayda insisted. *"Stop her, Dru."*

Druturion took off like a shot across the sky. Kayda whirled around, her gaze on the scourge surrounding her. She couldn't afford to watch them grapple, not while she was surrounded by a sea of beasts.

She grimaced, realizing she'd just sent her source away. Kayda ripped the pile of handkerchiefs out of her tunic. She didn't need them to shield her breast from the lamp's heat any longer, but they could still come in handy.

She skewered them atop the spear and quickly shoved it inside a flame that'd already begun to sputter out on the ground. Luckily, the fire caught. It wouldn't burn for long, but maybe it would buy her enough time to reach Izora so she could share her source.

Kayda strode away from the hill and stopped as a strangled murmur reached her ears.

"Sister, don't leave. This isn't over."

Horror struck her, and she spun around. Behind her, a great clash exploded, no doubt from the dragons fighting, but she didn't turn to look. Her attention was entirely wrapped up in the nightmare before her.

Tarquin rose off the ground, the huge gaping hole in his chest where her spear had skewered his heart slowly closing. His skin reformed, his eyes burning with hatred and his smirk as haughty as ever.

"Did you think that little trick would work on me? Me!" He scoffed, staggering closer. "You can't defeat me. Not now. Not ever. As long as there is a single bone left in my body, I'll return to plague you." His smirk grew larger. "Not that you'll be around much longer to bother."

"What are you?" Kayda's brows sank, her jaw dropping with revulsion and disgust. "Why won't you die?"

She lifted her hand and sent more flames at him. But even as he writhed beneath the onslaught, his skin reformed. He flicked his wrist, and a line of scourge appeared in front of him, stretching out at his feet on cue so he could stomp on one with every lumbering step he took.

And like a curse from above, the snow shifted to sleet and fell in a great sheet upon them. Within a few instants, the fire atop Kayda's spear snuffed out, leaving her with nothing to draw from.

She cut off her stream of fire, shuddering as Tarquin stalked closer until he stopped directly in front of her. He smacked the spear from her shaking fingers. His hand shot out and seized her neck.

Kayda tore at his wrist, desperately seeking to dislodge his crushing grip. She couldn't breathe. The edges of her sight darkened. This was it. She was about to die.

Jayan leaped at Tarquin with his pole knife raised. He stabbed Tarquin's back. Blood spattered Kayda's face as the tip of the blade poked out from the spot in his chest that'd just healed.

Tarquin tossed her to the ground and rounded on Jayan with malice in his eyes. His hand shot out, and with a single strike to the chest, he blasted the huge, muscled Sul aside like he was a doll made of paper. Jayan slammed into the ground and rolled, landing on the hill's far side.

When he didn't jump back up, Kayda screamed, her throat hoarse and painful. She rolled up to her knees, ready to race toward him, but

Tarquin snatched her hair, gripping a handful of her braids with an evil smile. "Get back here, you bitch."

Kayda grimaced, still on her knees, as her head snapped backward in his grasp.

Then a fireball slammed into his face.

Tarquin roared and shoved her to the ground. Kayda's head bounced on the hard dirt, her head swimming as Izora burst into view. She sent wave after wave of fire at Tarquin, her face filled with grim determination.

Tarquin, his skin sizzling, knelt down and lifted something off the ground. Her discarded spear.

Kayda fought to push through the pain. To rise and fight. But before she could recover enough to do more than lift up on her elbows, Tarquin sent the spear flying through Izora's chest.

"No!" Kayda screamed, watching with dawning horror as her grandmother tilted forward, falling upon the spear and driving it further within her chest. The fire on Izora's hands died, and her eyelids fluttered shut as blood poured out her open mouth.

Tears spilled down Kayda's cheeks. She reached out, wanting to run to Izora. To hold her in her arms and clutch her tight one last time.

But Tarquin had other plans. He grabbed her outstretched hand and slammed her to the ground again. His strength, even while his skin still smoldered from Izora's flames, was inhuman. He flung her to the ground like she was a bug he intended to stomp on.

Then he rounded on her as her head swam with dizziness and pain, the icy sleet smattering her face and mixing with the hot tears running down her cheeks.

Tarquin crouched by her side and stared down into her eyes. "I told you we would wipe the slate. I am the destroyer of worlds—the cleansing fire. I've become so much more than you could ever be, even with your little flames and your dragon. I am a god!"

How had it come to this? Tarquin had spent his whole life cutting her down with sly remarks and constant casual cruelty. Always acting like he was better than her. Like she was nothing. She could handle it when it was only directed at her. But this—he'd taken it to a whole new level of insanity.

Kayda stared up at her half-brother's crazed face. He truly meant it. There was no question he believed he'd become a god. He would destroy this world without a second thought, just like he had Izora.

Kayda's gaze flicked to the side. Izora lay next to her, the spear deep within her chest and the end of it caught on the ground, leaving her top half dangling in the air as her body slowly slid down the wood. The oil lamp on her chest swung in the wind, still burning brightly.

Tarquin's voice boomed again. "Any last words, sister?"

Kayda met his gaze. She stared back at the man who would happily hold a flame to the world and watch it burn. She couldn't let him get away with it. She wouldn't.

"You're wrong about one thing."

"What's that?" A sly smile crossed his lips as his fingers closed around her neck.

"You're *not* the fire. I am."

Kayda pulled at the flame in the lamp and sent it at him. Then she dug deep down inside. She grasped the pain welling within her for Izora and Jayan and let it flow through her, and the flame burned brighter and hotter than ever before. Just like back at the guard tower, it spilled out of her in a bright blast.

Tarquin staggered back, his eyes widening with horror before they popped and sizzled within his skull.

Kayda shook her head. It still wasn't enough. He'd said as long as he had a bone left, he would return. She had to make the flame burn long and hot enough that there would be nothing but ash.

Her talent screamed through her veins. She shivered uncontrollably; the icy sensation so strong her skin froze like she'd been dunked in the Northern Depths.

The flesh bubbled on Tarquin's skin, but he was still moving. Still trying to reach for her, to choke the life from her.

She wouldn't allow it.

Kayda flicked a glance at the coast where Dru and Bela hovered, battling each other with bolts of fire and ice. Her bondmate's words returned to her, replaying in her mind. "Even if I'm not with you, I'm there. Call on my strength." He'd never told her in so many words, but in that moment she instinctively knew. This was the boon dragons brought to humans they bonded. This power she had access to, the power to decimate her enemies, it came from Druturion.

She dug deep down and pulled at her talent with everything she had. A scream spilled out of her lips as the fire brightened, burning white hot. It seared her, bursting out from deep within her soul, drawing strength not just from her, but from her bond as well.

Tarquin's jaw opened on a silent scream even as his body burst into pieces, disintegrating.

That was the last thing Kayda saw before something within her exploded, and she crumpled to the icy ground.

Chapter 35

Conall's eyes flicked open. He rubbed a hand over his face, blinking repeatedly. "Not this again."

Conall floated on an undulating metallic sea. How had he returned here? This was supposed to be destroyed...

Whatever the answer, at least he knew what to do. He sighed, scanning the surface for a floating figure. There.

He jumped and landed next to a sleeping woman. One he recognized instantly.

"Delyth." He shook her shoulder gently. "Wake up."

Her eyelids fluttered open, and steely blue eyes speared him. "Conall?" Her head swung around, making her gray braid bob across the shoulder of her white mage robes. "Where are we?"

Conall stifled a groan. If she didn't even know that, then what were the chances she'd have any other answers?

"The Palisade. This was exactly how it looked when we brought it down."

Delyth's mouth opened on a silent oh.

"I have no idea how I ended up back here, though," Conall continued. "Or how you're here with me. Last I checked, I was searching for the Unseen, and you were—"

A thought struck him, and the word caught in his throat. Delyth was dead. Did that mean... Was he dead, too?

Would he ever see his friends again? Had he survived a magical trip through the earth, only to have a blow to the head end him?

"I'm dead, aren't I?" Delyth's voice was surprisingly steady for someone grappling with such news.

"I'm afraid so."

She gasped and splayed a wrinkled hand across her chest.

"I'm sorry, Delyth. I wish I could've saved you, but we were stuck on that barren island and—"

The look of surprise on Delyth's face vanished, and she waved a hand. "No, not that." She stared off into the distance, rubbing her temple and muttering under her breath so quietly Conall had to strain to hear her words. "That damn feather. I thought it was a dud. But it worked." A smile slowly spread across her face, the expression so reminiscent of her daughter it made his heart ache.

Conall leaned in, a single brow raising. "What feather?"

Delyth's gaze met his. "Hm?" Her smile fell. "Tell me, what's happened since I died? Quickly now."

Conall frowned, but then he filled her in on the events of the last few weeks. She listened quietly, and the urgency in her expression had him rushing through the tale, leaving out the finer details.

"And then I struck my head and passed out. I guess now that I'm here with you, it means I was the one who was destined to fall." Conall shuddered, picturing poor Shadow slumped distraught beside his cold body. Hopefully, the others would find him when they descended to finish what he'd started—defeating the Unseen.

Delyth squeezed his forearm. "Dear boy, you're not dead."

He met her gaze. "I'm not?"

"No. I've been given this one last chance to guide you. It was my greatest wish."

Conall's brow pinched. "I don't understand..."

"It's all right. You don't have to. Just know this; the Unseen, he will offer you things—wonderful, amazing things. But you must be strong and resist. He must be destroyed."

Conall drew back, trying not to let the offense bubbling within him color his tone. "I would never accept anything from him."

"That's easy to say now, but when he tries to hand you all your wildest dreams on a platter, you might think otherwise."

No. She was wrong. He'd never align himself with that sickening presence, no matter what he offered.

"Please, Conall. Listen. You have to know. The Unseen wants you and you alone. It has to be you who defeats him."

"Me?" His eyes widened. "Why does he want me?"

Delyth opened her mouth, but before she could speak, her body was rocked with a violent convulsion. Conall's heart sped up as he gripped her shoulders, trying to still her quaking.

Finally, her body quieted. She lifted her face to stare at him, and Conall swallowed a gasp.

She was changed. Aged just like the poor souls who'd held tight to the Palisade beside him so long ago. Her hair fell out in clumps atop her shoulders, and her face was so heavily lined and gaunt she looked only moments from death.

She cleared her throat and leaned closer, the voice escaping barely a whisper. "Some lines, once crossed, can never be redrawn. Don't—"

Her words were cut off by another round of convulsions. "Delyth." He clutched her tightly, until a tremor of his own ripped across his spine.

Blazes, that hurt. His arms detached from Delyth and wrapped around his middle instinctively. He clamped his eyes shut, praying for it to stop.

Please, make it stop.

The pain faded as suddenly as it had started, replaced with a new, strange sensation. A wet rasp grazing the back of his head.

Conall groaned. His eyes jolted open, and his hand rose to prod the sore, wet spot on his skull. He whipped his hand away when it encountered something rough and wet against his scalp.

"Little brother, you're awake."

"Shadow, were you just licking me?" he asked, incredulous, turning to stare at his bondmate's yellow eyes.

Shadow's tail flicked happily. *"I see you still have much to learn. It is helpful to lick a wound. The bleeding stopped, thanks to my help."*

"Thanks, I guess." He scanned Shadow, paying special attention to his back where the scourge bit him. *"What about you? Are you all right?"*

"Yes, it was just a scratch. I'm not bleeding anymore."

Conall sat up, staring into the cave's red-lit recesses as Delyth's words reverberated in his mind. *"I just had the strangest dream,"* he said, though a part of him was certain it had been no normal dream. He gasped, remembering the convulsions. *"Do I look different, brother?"*

Shadow tilted his head. *"No, a little banged up and wet, but the same as always. Why do you ask?"*

"It's a long story." He sighed, wobbling to his feet. *"I'll tell you once we get out here. C'mon. We've wasted enough time as is."*

They hiked deeper into the cave, stomping through the burned scourge's ashes. At the back wall of the large chamber, another tunnel stood. Conall ducked down, forced to crouch once again in the narrow dirt tube.

They walked long enough that his back and shoulders ached, but finally, they approached the entrance to another large chamber. This one was almost blindingly bright red, and so hot the sweat that had only trickled down his skin so far poured in rivulets.

He had a sudden urge to drain his waterskin, but his hand stilled before he removed it from his waist. He might need water magic more than he needed a drink. Best to conserve his source.

They crept inside the chamber. Here the roof rose again, allowing him to straighten, but the relief he felt was short lived. He fought down the urge to gasp aloud.

The chamber was enormous. Far larger than the last, perhaps as big as Flamesmoat, or at the very least, as big as all of Southmoat with some of Northmoat thrown in for good measure.

Bubbling pools of molten rock dotted the landscape, surrounded by great swaths of humongous circular rocks. And in the center, one rock stood out, larger than all the rest, made of a shining metallic substance that was unlike anything he'd ever seen.

"Ah, you've finally come. Just like I knew you would."

Conall flinched, and he tapped his leg twice, flicking a glance at Shadow. Shadow inclined his head in response, then tilted his jaw toward the center rock. Conall nodded, setting off on a straight course toward it.

No doubt Shadow could feel it as well. That revolting feeling emanated from that shimmering boulder. That was where he needed to go. He was certain of it.

Shadow darted sideways, leaping behind one of the huge round rocks. Conall's heart thudded harder being separated from his bond-mate, but it was a wise plan. Maybe if they were lucky, they could catch the Unseen unawares.

Time to be the distraction. *"Yes, I've come. But not to join you, like you claim. I've come to destroy you."*

Laughter reverberated in his mind. That same sickening chortle he remembered so clearly. *"Why would you want to do that?"*

"Why shouldn't I?" Conall edged forward, only turning when he needed to dodge one of the huge boulders. *"You've set the scourge loose to destroy my home. You want everyone to die."*

"Not everyone. Some—yes. But they are nothing in the grand scheme. A trifling price to pay to get what I need."

"That's sick." He scanned all around, searching for signs of anyone in the vast chamber. So far, nothing. The place was quiet as a tomb, except for the bubbling lava. *"I'm here to make sure you don't succeed."*

"Even if what I need is you?"

Conall paused, fighting to tamp down his revulsion. Delyth was right, yet again. *"Why? Why me?"*

"I've waited eons for one such as you. Can't you see? Together, we will be unstoppable."

"I'll never join you." He took another step forward, craning his neck for any sign of movement. Where was he?

"Don't be so quick to refuse. Not after everything I've given you. It can all be taken away just as easily."

"You haven't given me anything."

The Unseen chortled again, and his laughter set Conall's nerves on edge.

"Where do you think you humans got that magic you waste, building walls that should've never existed?"

Conall's stomach dropped. *"That's not true."*

"Oh, but you don't believe that, do you? I told you I was the giver of gifts. The taker of lost dreams. The evidence is right there before your eyes, if you'd only look closer."

Conall's step slowed. He swiveled his head, scanning the chamber. What did he mean? His knees wobbled, and he rested a hand on the huge rock beside him. He only shifted a portion of his weight before his hand smashed through the side of the rock, shattering the fragile surface that wasn't solid at all. His eyes widened so much his vision blurred.

They weren't rocks. They were eggs.

Conall gazed inside the massive cracked egg. He spotted a body, at least as big as he was, but far different. The beast was winged and had a skinny tail wrapped around its shrunken, stunted form.

Suddenly, Delyth's cryptic last words began to make sense.

"What did you do to them?" But even as the question left his mind, something inside him revolted. He remembered the words in that ancient book. *"Dragons used to be the only ones who summoned elemental magic..."*

"Vile, disgusting creatures. I only spread the gifts they'd been so greedily hoarding."

Conall's stomach roiled, and his mouth watered so badly he almost heaved. The Unseen had killed all these young dragons, only to somehow siphon their elemental magic to mankind. How? Why? His head spun as he tried to get a handle on this insanity.

"All those years I spent searching for the perfect vessel. Someone worthy of all of my gifts. Finally, you've come to me."

Conall reared back, a hand splaying on his chest. *"Me?"*

"Of course. You can summon all elements. You have the gift of bonding. I knew if I spread enough magic through the humans, one such as yourself would arise. Join me and take what you deserve."

A vessel... What did that mean? It wasn't making any sense.

"Show yourself. Talk to me in the flesh," he cried out in his mind.

The Unseen scoffed. *"Not until we come to an arrangement."*

The coward. The Unseen wouldn't show himself until he agreed to his disgusting scheme.

Conall could play that game. But he couldn't sound too eager, not after he waltzed in threatening to kill him. The Unseen would never fall for it. Delyth said he'd make promises. Maybe he could pretend to be swayed by them.

"Why should I? I already have all the magic I need. You've admitted it yourself."

"Haven't you ever wanted more? Oh, the things I could give you."

"I'm listening." Conall left the egg behind and strolled toward the large rock in the room's center.

"How about your youth? Wouldn't you like the years back those witches stole from you?"

He was playing dirty. All those years he wasted tearing down the Palisade—he thought they were lost to him forever. *"You can do that?"*

"Mm-hm. Better than that—by my side, you will live forever."

Conall swallowed a gasp. Surely not. No one had that kind of power. *"That's not possible."*

"Don't you know how long-lived dragons were? I didn't just take their magic. It's all right here, waiting for me to gift it. How about your family and friends, hm? Wouldn't you like to give them the gift of perfect health and long life? I can arrange it."

"Y-you can?"

"Yes. All that and more." The Unseen's voice was a gentle purr, coiling around his spine, full of forbidden promises.

Even though it was impossible, he allowed himself to picture it for a fleeting moment. Lark. Ereni, and Violet. Shadow. All of them, living with him forever. They could travel the world, rebuild the farm. Anything they wanted for all of time—together.

He shook off the thought. No. He wouldn't allow himself to be swayed. Not truly. But for the Unseen's behalf, he had to act like he was considering it. In another life, he might've even wanted to take him up on his offer. It was certainly tempting.

"And what do I have to do for this gift?"

"You must swear to be my holy vessel. I cannot venture above without one. But together, we will rule the world. I've waited so long to find one worthy of my greatness. Out of billions of humans, it is you I've chosen. You should be honored."

"I-I need to think..." He let his voice trail off as if he were actually considering it.

"Don't wait too long. Even now, the last of the dragons battle above. After I turn them to our side, the silly war the humans have waged will be lost. I would hate to see your loved ones fall while you are considering my generous offer."

He was turning the dragons against them? Could he do that? But really, it wasn't too much of a stretch to imagine after everything else he'd claimed.

Conall rolled his shoulders back and strode forward confidently. *"All right, I've decided. I want to save them. Give me the gifts you've promised."*

"So, you swear it then? I have to hear it."

"Yes, I swear."

"Come to me."

Conall's feet dragged him forward as if they had a mind of their own, leading him straight to the metallic boulder in the chamber's center. He halted before it and stared up at the craggy surface as a hole opened in the rock's top.

Out of the hole, a creature slid, eerily reminiscent of a snake. It slithered across the jagged rock, its sinuous body a black so dark it seemed to suck all the light in the room toward it. It slinked closer, leaving a trail of gray sludge everywhere it touched.

His feet locked on the ground, Conall attempted to raise his arm. His stomach hurtled into his throat as his limbs refused to budge.

The creature slid closer, and the waves of revulsion emanating from it made him certain this strange beast was indeed the Unseen.

"Open your mouth," a gleeful voice commanded in his mind.

And though he wanted to do nothing less in his entire life, Conall's jaw dropped on cue. His heart hammered, his eyes bulging. Why couldn't he move? Was this disgusting thing controlling him already?

The vow—he'd made an awful mistake. He should've never let those words leave his lips.

The disgusting creature snuck closer, weaving across the rock's surface and dropping to the ground. Then it coiled up, no doubt preparing to leap atop his legs and slink all the way up to his mouth until it worked its way down his throat.

Conall gagged at the thought, but his traitorous body still refused to move. This was it. He was about to die.

A blur of gray fur leaped into sight, snatching the Unseen out of the air just as it jumped for him. Shadow bit down with a wet crunch and shook, only to toss the beast aside an instant later, yelping and rubbing his jaw with his paws.

But thankfully, Shadow's actions unlocked his frozen limbs. Conall jolted forward and raced to his side. *"Brother, are you all right?"*

"Yes. That thing's blood burns. But I'm fine." Shadow shook his head and coughed. *"Find him. Finish this, little brother."*

Conall nodded and rose. He scanned the ground, searching. There. He followed that nasty trail of sludge and found the Unseen cowering on the ground behind one of the petrified dragon eggs. Trying to find safety among the creatures he'd betrayed and slaughtered.

"Wait. It's not too late." The Unseen's voice had lost its cruel edge; it warbled, pained and full of panic. *"If you destroy me, all that I've given will die with me. Would you curse the world to live without elemental magic? Will you give up eternal life? The safety of your family?"*

Conall stopped before him and called forth his talent, using the flame dangling around his neck as his source. A cold chill seeped across his skin, but the sensation was barely discernible with the disgusting filth roiling around him being in the Unseen's presence.

As a fireball coalesced on his hand, he took another look at all the boulders surrounding him. There were so many. Hundreds.

"You really thought we'd do anything to keep your gifts, didn't you? But some lines should never be crossed. We don't want anything you've stolen. Here—have it back."

Conall sent the fireball at the Unseen and smiled as he watched him burn.

Ice cooled Conall's veins as the Unseen writhed beneath the flames. He wriggled and squirmed, letting out an unearthly screech as his oily black scales shriveled and cooked. The smell was horrendous, worse than garbage set out to rot in the summer sun. But Conall bore it silently, holding his breath through the worst of it. Once the Unseen stopped moving, Conall stuttered out a breath and killed the flames.

"Shadow." He raced back to his bondmate's side, sensing his discomfort through their bond even before he spotted him trotting toward him. Shadow met him halfway, pausing every few paces to rub

his paws against his mouth. *"Here. Let me help you."* Conall grabbed the waterskin off his belt and poured the liquid in Shadows mouth, washing off the last of the foul black blood.

"Thank you, little brother. I think I'll be tasting that for days."

"I hope not." Conall peered inside Shadow's mouth as the water spilled out. *"Your tongue looks a bit swollen, but I think you'll live."*

"Conall!"

Shadow's warning was the only thing that saved him.

The Unseen, charred and still smoking from the scorching, leaped at Conall's chest.

Quicker than ever before, Conall called forth his talent. The very air sizzled, bursting with so much current every hair on Shadows body fluffed up instantly. Conall slapped the Unseen with a wave of air, knocking him off course.

The vile serpent shrieked, coiling back to strike. *"This isn't over. It will never be over!"* he hissed.

But Conall saw his chance. He didn't even bother to respond. He just sent another blast of air at him, knocking him back.

The Unseen's ruined skin sheared off in layers as he clung to the dirt, refusing to give up. *"You might kill me, but you won't win."* More of that black ooze poured out, hitting the ground and sizzling. The smell was so wretched Conall nearly backed away. *"You've already lost."*

"No. You have." With those words, Conall dug down deep. He pictured the faces of everyone he loved in his mind's eye. A rumble reverberated up his spine as he dug his fingers into the cool soil in his pocket and used it to loosen the earth beneath the Unseen. Then he sent a final blast of air at the villain, gritting his teeth and screaming.

The Unseen tumbled up, dislodging from the dirt and whipping into a hole soaked in red. An inhuman screech cut through the air, before choking off into a pained gurgle.

Conall crept closer to the hole's edge and stared down at the boiling molten rock.

"You did it, little brother. Nothing could survive that. Not even him."

Conall smiled weakly at Shadows assurance and decided to trust the evidence in front of his own eyes, no matter how much that vile creature insisted this wasn't the end.

He was wrong.

The Unseen was dead.

"Let's get out of here." Conall turned his back on the hole and walked away.

Chapter 36

Hundreds of voices screamed out in terror. Lark spun slowly, her eyes widening with horror as she spotted the cause. The white dragon, the one Kayda called Belstasia, sent great bolts of ice into the crowd.

But she wasn't attacking the scourge any longer. She was targeting the people crowded around the beach.

"My friends." Lark turned back to Ereni, who fought by her side atop the little hill. Together, they'd put down—for good this time—about a dozen prisoners. There were only two left she could see still fighting their way toward them.

"Go," Ereni shouted over the melee, her voice barely loud enough to be heard over the pained screams from the shore. "I've got this."

A spike of indecision warred within her. It was her fault these men were here. If she'd never freed them, they'd have died when Flames-moat fell.

Then another bolt of ice pounded into the beach, spraying great gouts of sand into the air. The faces of her friends rose in her mind. She wanted them safe, but trouble had found them anyway.

"Muse, back to the beach. We need to help the others."

A blur of gold and brown darted through the sky above her. *"On it."*

Lark ran. She hustled through the crowd of scourge, felling beasts in every direction with blasts of earth.

Why had she insisted they stay so far away? She should've kept them with her, where she could protect them. Now they were being pummeled with ice and there was nothing she could do.

She pushed her legs like she'd never pushed them before. Snow and dirt kicked up in her wake, but she only ran faster. The snow battered her face and slicked the ground, but somehow, she kept her balance, even when countless warriors slipped and slid.

"She's heading for Aren," Muse cried.

Lark gulped, flicking her gaze to the sky as Muse flew directly toward the white dragon. Fear clawed up her spine. Muse would get herself killed, tangling with that huge beast.

"What are you—are you mad?" her own voice warbled in her mind, full of panic.

"Just a distraction. Hurry."

Even though she was already running faster than she'd ever run, Lark forced herself to race faster. The fighter's features blurred as she passed them. The muscles in her legs burned like she'd been doused in lava, but still she pushed. At this speed, she didn't trust herself not to hit the wrong target while she weaved between the fighters and scourge. She summoned the shape of a dart and clutched it tight in her fist, the vibration thrumming through her blood a welcome sensation as she barreled forward.

Finally, she glimpsed Aren's blond head peeking out from behind an overturned canoe, bow drawn, sending arrow after arrow into the scourge's ranks. His eyes widened as he spotted her racing toward him.

Belstasia was right behind him now, hovering in the sky, mouth open to spew more ice at the beach. A few of the fighters panicked, running and screaming, heedless of the scourge in their haste to escape the fearsome dragon. Aren stayed calm, using his bow to pick off beasts that leaped for the escaping fighters.

Muse darted in front of Belstasia, clawing and pecking at her eyes. But the dragon only shook her off, sending Muse flying aside and screeching in anger.

Lark's heart stalled as Bela opened her wicked jaw and a bolt of ice coalesced. She aimed down at the beach below. Right where Aren stood.

No!

With a final burst of speed, Lark jumped, simultaneously spinning the dart in her fist into a dirt shield. She landed in the sand next to Aren just as the ice slammed down, hammering the shield and shattering into thousands of tiny shards that pummeled into the sand harmlessly.

The blow made her shield collapse. Tiny flecks of dirt rained down on them as Aren turned to face her. "Lark, you're—"

His gaze flicked to the sky, and he stopped speaking just as a second dragon, this one black as night, slammed into the white dragon above them.

"Muse, are you—"

"I'm fine. Run before those beasts hit you."

She saw the sense in her bondmate's warning as the dragons started battling each other, throwing blasts of ice and fire. Most of the magic landed on its target, but whenever the dragons dodged, the ice and fire blasted to the ground instead, hitting whoever happened to be below, scourge and human alike.

Lark grabbed Aren's elbow, towing him aside. "The others, where are they?" She threw up a shield as they shuffled down the beach, away from the behemoth's battle.

Great sheets of sleet fell, sneaking between cracks in her dirt shield. Lark's teeth chattered as her sweat-soaked skin cooled beneath her cloak.

Aren frowned at the sound, wrapping his arm around her shoulder and shifting slightly, aiming for a circle of overturned boats further up the beach. "I left them here, helping Mika."

Lark breathed out a sigh as she spotted the circle of canoes, a dirt shield covering the top in a wide dome. Suddenly, a light flared further inland, white hot and blindingly bright. So bright, she was forced to shield her eyes and turn her head aside as she staggered across the sand.

"What's that?" Aren asked, squinting beside her.

"I don't know."

"Muse, can you see that from above?"

"Too bright. I can't focus on it." Her voice turned grave. *"But it's back where we just were."*

"Kayda." The word came out as a strangled whisper.

Aren's brow wrinkled. "What is it?"

The light cut off, and the black dragon roared so loud she thought her eardrums might burst.

Oh no. Kayda. What happened?

"I have to go back," Lark said.

They'd just arrived at the circle of canoes. She peeked over, spotting Dausius and Tiora, safe beneath the shield of swirling sand and dirt. Mika crouched over a man sprawled out on the ground, and the old, white-robed mage Kayda had brought back from Northmoat, Vespen, stretched out his hands, his face the picture of deep concentration.

Mazen and Meital were nowhere to be seen, and Lark's heart sped up for an instant until she forced it to slow. With their knife skills, she could count on them to take care of themselves.

Dausius spotted them approaching and dropped the bandages in his hand to sprint over. "Make a hole," he yelled over his shoulder.

Aren met her gaze and nodded as Vespen obliged, banishing a small section of the swirling dirt in front of them. "Be safe," he yelled, and then he released her shoulder and ducked beneath Vespen's shield.

Lark ran again, heading back to the hill where she'd left Kayda and Ereni. The sleet pelted her, raining down on her shoulders and face like tiny arrows. Her cloak was soaked, but she ignored the shivers and rushed toward Kayda, her stomach clenching.

As she approached, she spotted a brown ponytail bobbing, and a small smile tugged at her cheeks. Ereni was surrounded by a group of Sul and a handful of Doln warriors now, the front lines having managed to push through to their position.

Behind her, a great crashing *boom* rocked the earth. Lark halted as the ground shook beneath her, nearly throwing her to the ground. She swiveled backward, her eyes bulging.

Belstasia had fallen. She sprawled on the beach, laid out on her back. Dru hovered above her, watching as every scourge battling nearby stopped what they were doing and made a beeline for the fallen dragon.

Bela opened her jaw and aimed up at Dru. But before she could let loose, a scourge jumped atop her and dove straight down into her gaping maw. Two more leaped in right after, before she could snap her mouth closed.

Lark's jaw dropped. But she couldn't just stand there and stare. She whipped around and jerked back into motion as another one of those deafening bellows tore out of Druturion's throat.

Lark slowed down as she reached Ereni's side. She'd stationed herself above a crumpled man on the hillside.

She swallowed a gasp when she recognized him. Jayan, the captain. Was he...?

"He's still alive. Can you heal him? I'll cover you both," Ereni shouted.

Lark knelt at his side and reached into her pack. There was no time to examine him thoroughly, but if the huge lump on his forehead was any indication, he had a head wound, at the very least.

She slicked a handful of her mother's ointment—the one with countless ingredients—over his forehead. Then she wished. The tremor pulsed through her and shot into Jayan's skull. An instant later, he gasped and jolted up, his gaze jerking wildly while he sucked in huge gulps of air.

"You're going to be all right," Lark said.

He pointed, one long finger shooting toward the cave entrance as he struggled to his feet. "Kayda," he croaked.

Lark straightened and raced ahead of him, quickly overtaking Jayan's staggering steps. When she circled the hillside, her heart dropped.

Izora and Kayda were both down. The old nurse's blood spilled down her lips and onto her chest, a spear skewed through her heart, the only thing holding her up off the ground.

Bile rose in Lark's throat. The mage was clearly dead, so she sidestepped around her and raced to Kayda's side.

Kayda sprawled in a heap on the dirt, her head pressed into the snow, hiding half of her face. Lark's stomach roiled as she dropped to her knees beside her.

She reached out a trembling hand and shook her shoulder. Nothing. She slid her hand over her neck. No pulse. She slipped her hand in front of her nose and mouth, praying for a miracle.

She dug in her pack, slapping a handful of cream on Kayda's cold, lifeless cheek. She wished and wished—harder than she'd ever wished in her entire life for her sister to rise and live again. The magic pooled through her, rattling the earth beneath them both as it slammed into Kayda.

Still nothing.

A hand landed on her shoulder. She lifted her swollen eyes to meet Ereni's, steely blue and full of remorse.

"You can't heal the dead, Lark. I'm sorry."

Jayan screamed behind them, falling to his knees.

Grief tore at her heart, threatening to overwhelm Lark. But she couldn't give in. Not while they still fought.

Even though it killed her to leave Kayda behind, she rose to her feet and scanned the battle. The front lines had fought ahead of their position, affording them a bit of protection. But still the scourge came, an endless wave of gnashing teeth and razor-sharp claws.

Lark rolled her shoulders back, readying to run again so she could take out her righteous anger at her sister's demise on the enemy.

But then another crash shook the earth just beside her. Druturion landed next to Kayda and let out an anguished roar as he stared down at her lifeless body.

Suddenly, he clawed at his chest, his talons tearing at the scales on his front. Blood spattered the ground.

What was he doing?

Something golden flashed, fluttering to the ground among all the blood. Then Dru spread his wings and hunkered down, covering Kayda protectively beneath his outspread wings.

"Lark, the scourge, look!" Muse's voice rang out in her mind, full of—delight?

She swung around and gasped, her hands covering her wide-open mouth.

Everywhere she looked, the beasts fell, writhing and squirming on the ground. All around, fighters paused, catching their breath and staring, dumbfounded, at their enemies as they fought a losing battle with an unseen foe.

The Unseen.

Lark laughed. "He did it! Conall did it. He killed the Unseen." It was the only explanation that made sense.

Her laughter spilled out, boisterous and more than a touch manic, as she watched the vile creatures' shudder and eventually go still.

It was over. Blazes, it was over. They'd won.

But then her gaze swung back to Jayan, and her laughter died, choked off in a throat gone dry.

They may have won, but countless lives had been lost. Kayda and Izora were far from the only ones. Bodies littered the ground, and blood splattered everywhere, painting the snowy landscape a lurid red. What a steep price to pay.

Lark shivered, the sleet raining down on her like frozen knives.

A petite mage approached their group, and she shuddered, too, then she reverently tugged the lit oil lamp off Izora's chest and wrapped it around her own.

"Here." She lifted a hand, and the cold momentarily worsened before a blast of fire appeared on the ground before them, and the flame's warmth washed over them.

Ereni gasped. "Karina, stop. Stop. Now!"

The mage lifted a brow, but obeyed, cutting off the stream of fire. "I know it won't last long in this weather, but we can't all freeze."

Ereni scrubbed her face, blinking repeatedly. "No, that's not it. Your glow. While you summoned, you lost your blue glow. It's half-faded away already." She spun her head around and shouted across the battlefield. "No one summon! Something's wrong."

Just then, the ground rumbled off to the right. The dirt opened up in a small circle, and out of it, something rose.

"Conall!" Lark raced forward, arriving at her brother's side just as he and his wolf emerged from the ground. It reformed beneath him, the dirt covered by a thick layer of lush grass. She thudded into his chest before he could stand from his cross-legged position and caught him in a tight embrace. His arms wrapped around her instantly as he squeezed her back tightly.

Ereni arrived a moment later, her eyes wide. "Your glow. It's so red. It's barely purple anymore."

Conall cleared his throat. "When I defeated the Unseen, we lost our elemental magic with him. It was never ours to begin with. He stole it from the dragons and gave it to us as some twisted gift."

Gasps spilled out from the crowd gathered around them. Voices echoed, everyone no doubt relaying Conall's words far and wide.

Ereni glanced around at all the mages, and then down at her own hands. "That must mean after we use what magic we have left, it's gone for good."

Lark released Conall and rocked back on her heels. All that work she'd put in to become a healer was about to vanish. But what was the alternative? Letting the Unseen live and wreak havoc just to be a mage? With *stolen* magic, no less? The choice was obvious—Conall had made the right call.

Ereni helped Conall up to his feet and hugged him tightly. Then she drew back and nodded. "All right, everyone, save your talent. We'll use it to link to the healers and save all the injured we can."

The mages scrambled, preparing to follow orders.

But something about the words felt wrong. They twisted in Lark's gut as she stared at the fresh green grass she knelt on. She glanced up as a tinkling noise whispered on the breeze and caught a glimpse of Dausius approaching, his lanky arms swinging and a wide smile stretching his face. The rest of her friends followed in his wake, all of them covered in blood and mud and soaked from the sleet, but each of them wearing matching grins. All of them, still standing strong—together.

"Wait," Lark shouted. "Don't use your talent. I need it. We all have to link."

Ereni turned to her, brow raising. "What?"

Lark bounced to her feet, pointing at the patch of grass that was already quickly being covered by the icy sleet. "We need to save Dracwood. Heal it. Trust me."

Ereni glanced over at Conall. He met her eyes and nodded.

"Change of plans, all mages, come together and link with Lark," Ereni bellowed.

As the mages surrounded her, everyone linking hands, putting their trust in her, a rush of elation spread through her. This was right. Something deep down in her soul demanded it.

Conall had defeated the Unseen. Kayda destroyed the Unseen's greatest champion before succumbing to the prophecy and falling. This—this was her purpose here.

She met Dausius' gaze across the crowd as his tale from so long ago rang in her ears. They'd been stuck on a boat in the bog, watching the town of Bogsmouth burn after the scourge first ascended from the earth to plague their land. He'd told them all the tale of his lost love and her prophetic vision on her deathbed about the songbird who he was destined to save. She'd said—*together* they would save the world.

Conall and Ereni both grabbed one of her shoulders, completing the linked chain of mages. Lark sank her fingers into the earth, and she wished. She wished for the world to be as it was, before all this death and destruction. For all the charred earth and ash to disappear and green grass and trees to return to their rightful place.

Warmth flooded her and colliding sensations surrounded her. Tingles, chills, moisture and tremors, like nothing she'd ever felt, struck her body and sank into the ground. Power—blissful, healing power—drained from all the mages and spread through her hands and shot down into the ground like a shockwave.

Then it was over.

Lark rose from her spot on the icy ground, frowning.

Ereni's jaw dropped as she stared at the crowd of mages. "So much blue, gone," she whispered in a choked voice, tucking her head into Conall's shoulder.

Lark's heart thudded madly as she looked around. She despaired. Nothing had changed. The landscape appeared just as barren and destroyed as it had before they'd sunk the last of their magic into it.

"Lark, you won't believe this!" Muse called out, just as the ground rumbled beneath their feet.

Something shot out from the tiny finger holes she'd left in the small patch of grass. Jaw dropping, Lark backed away just as a massive willow tree burst free from the ground. She slipped in her haste and landed on her backside on the hard ground, her head craning up to stare at the gorgeous green tree in front of her.

Movement and gasps demanded her attention beside her. All around, wounded men and women staggered to their feet, shaking out limbs that had just been broken and staring down at wounds that had miraculously closed. She splayed a hand on her stomach, surprised to discover the dull ache from the cudgel blow had completely vanished.

Lark beamed, warm tears spilling into her eyes. *"What is it?"*

"That tree isn't the only one that just rose from the ground. The forest—Dracwood is regrowing. You did it!"

Lark stumbled up to her feet and raced across the field toward the ridge that hid the rest of Dracwood from the Abandoned Lands. After a long trek through the sleet, she finally mounted the hillside, and a huge smile broke out on her face.

All the trees the mages had been forced to burn to slow the scourges' advance stood once again. Dracwood was back. They'd healed it.

Chapter 37

Blackness surrounded her, and warmth pooled deep in her belly, buzzing through her veins. She could sense she was not alone. A familiar presence called to her, silently demanding her attention.

"Dru? Are you here? Where am I?"

"Kayda? Oh, it worked. I'm so glad it worked." His voice was strained, a quiet murmur in her mind, but nonetheless, her bondmate's words washed over her, calming the panic that fought to overwhelm her in the dark.

She rolled over, the pleasant warmth slowly receding as if it had seeped away into the cold hard ground beneath her. *"Why is it so dark?"*

"You are sheltered beneath my wing. I'm sorry. I'm afraid I don't have the strength to lift it presently."

Kayda lifted a hand and sighed as the leathery texture of Druturion's wing met her fingers. Following the curve of his wing, she scooched across the ground and laid a hand on a smooth scale on his side, then curled up beside him.

"I can't remember... Where are we now?" She leaned against his hide, taking comfort in his presence as something outside shocked her memory.

Excited chatter and whoops of delight echoed around her. She stiffened. That's right! They were in the Abandoned Lands fighting the Unseen. But why was it cheers she heard and not screams of pain and snarls?

"The battle. Do you remember now? We've won," Dru said.

Joy blossomed at his words, but then she quirked a brow, rubbing her aching skull. *"We have? I don't recall the end for some reason..."*

"That's because you were dead."

"I was—"

Dru convulsed beside her, his big body shuddering so forcefully he rocked the ground beneath her.

"Dru! What's wrong? Please, tell me how to help," she cried out beside him.

After a long moment, his body stilled. His voice returned to her mind, quieter than before. *"Nothing can help me now, I'm afraid. But it's all right. You're safe."*

"I'm safe? What about you?" Kayda's chest tightened, and she rubbed her hands across Dru's flank, desperate to soothe him.

"I've lived a long life, Kayda. So long, you can't even imagine. There's not much time. Please, you must listen."

Kayda nodded, then realizing he likely couldn't see her in the dark, she spoke, *"Yes, I'm listening."*

"Know that I don't have any regrets. But the magic I used to save you—it requires sacrifice."

What magic was he talking about? She knew of no magic that could heal the dead. Her throat constricted, and she clutched it as she asked, *"What sacrifice? Did you forfeit your life to save mine?"*

"No. My death was already sealed the moment the Unseen fell. The scourge, Bela, everyone who still shared a bond with the Unseen in some way, was destined to fall when he did. I will too—very soon."

"No. Dru. I can't lose you."

"You must go on, Kayda. You must live without me, as you did before we met."

"But you'll still be with me, won't you? That's how bonding magic works. The voices of your dead bondmate's live on, if only within your own mind. We'll be together always."

Dru shuddered again, and Kayda tensed. But this time, the convulsions only lasted an instant before he shook them off. *"No, Kayda. Not this time. The sacrifice demanded it. When I die, I'll be gone for good."*

She splayed a hand on her throbbing chest, her mind reeling. Ever since she'd learned about the strange quirks of bonding magic, she'd been afraid. She was terrified that the madness that infected her grandfather would one day be passed on to her. But now that Dru was dying, and leaving her for good, it didn't seem fair.

"It's all right, Kayda. I'm ready to rest. It's been so long. So, so long." Druturion sighed, his chest sinking and rising as the deep breath whooshed out of his body. *"I have one favor to ask, my friend. A final wish, if you will."*

"Anything."

Another convulsion rocked through him. This one went on for so long Kayda bit back a scream, certain he was about to die before revealing his last request. But then his shaking ended, and Dru sucked in a wobbly breath.

"I—need you—to—find them." His voice quieted even more, every word forced and clipped.

"Find who?"

"Our—eggs."

Eggs? Kayda gulped. He couldn't mean... Did he have young out in the world somewhere?

A flash of their conversation while she'd been imprisoned in Joria replayed in her memory. *You've given us a chance at a future.* Did that mean... had he and Bela procreated while they were in hiding from the Unseen?

"Where are they, Dru? I'll find them. I promise. I'll find your eggs."
Druturion didn't answer.

"Dru?"

When only silence greeted her, she knew he would never answer her again. He was gone.

Kayda sat in stunned silence, her heart shattering and stabbing outward, agony piercing through her core and deep down into her soul. Druturion—she would never speak to him again. It hurt. Blazes, it hurt far more than she could bear.

Eventually, the darkness beneath Dru's wing wore on her. The weight of it settled on her shoulders, stifling and ominous.

She had to get out. She had to escape.

Kayda crawled on the cold hard ground, her fingers reaching, scrambling for purchase. She couldn't breathe. She had to get out. Had to—

The leathery tip of Dru's wing slid over her scalp, and she pushed forward into the freezing air outside. Sleet rained down on her face and hands, but Kayda's panic only grew.

The darkness had not receded. Her eyes. Why couldn't she see?

Chapter 38

Conall stared out the porthole at the black night. The sea swelled, waves crashing against the hull in the storm's aftermath.

It had taken long hours to ferry everyone back to the ships. Even now, a few straggling canoes dotted the ocean with the last of the fighters on board.

He turned back to survey the room, and a wave of gratitude washed over him so strongly he almost collapsed from the force of it. All the people he loved most were still alive, crowded around him. Ereni sat in the single chair, cradling their sleeping daughter in her arms. Lark perched beside Kayda on the worn desk, holding her hand and humming softly.

When Kayda crawled out from beneath Druturion's wing, that had been the ultimate shock. But as soon as he saw her crouched there, her eyes wide open and changed from their familiar brown to an unfocused, startling crimson, the Unseen's word struck him anew. "Only two will *see* the next day." Kayda certainly wasn't seeing anything now, but at least she lived.

What he still didn't understand was *how*. Lark swore up and down that Kayda had been dead when she checked on her. That though she tried to heal her, her magic had no effect. The last of the elemental magic they'd sunk into the earth somehow miraculously healed all of their injured fighters, but Kayda was the only one who rose from the dead.

They'd tried asking her, but so far, Kayda had not said a word. Losing her bondmate and her grandmother had surely taken its toll. Not to mention everyone she'd lost already. Had she been struck not just blind but mute as well? Or was she in shock over the battle's end?

None of them knew for sure, so they'd decided to simply stay with her, patiently awaiting her words. Whether they came today, tomorrow, or never again, they would wait with her. They were family now. Not just by blood but forged in action. No matter what happened next, they would stick together. Conall was determined to keep both his sisters safe from now on.

"You still haven't told us about the Unseen. What was it like down there?" Ereni asked.

Conall shuddered. "It was awful. Just being near him—" He shuddered again. "He wanted to use me. Called me the perfect vessel. If Shadow hadn't stopped it, he would've slid down my throat and wedged himself inside me and used me like some kind of twisted marionette to take over the world."

"I'm glad that didn't happen," Ereni said. "I've never read about any creatures with that kind of power before. What was he, I wonder? Where did he come from?"

Conall shrugged. "I don't know. I don't know if we'll ever know, now that he's gone."

Ereni pursed her lips, letting the matter drop.

Maybe he should've grilled the Unseen for more answers. At the time, he'd only been worried about defeating him, but in hindsight, he couldn't help worrying that decision would come back to haunt him. Especially when he recalled the end of the cryptic message the Unseen had delivered to him. *Three will come, but only two will see the next day. Even then, it won't be enough...* The Unseen had been right about the first part of his message. The evidence was plain to see whenever he stared into Kayda's blind eyes. Would the second part of his message prove true as well?

"I wish I could heal you, sister," Lark said.

Conall shook his head gently. A mage who'd spilled into the bay had tried healing Kayda when they made it back on board. But even with the last of her magic, she'd not been able to return Kayda's eyesight.

Ereni tilted her head. "We'll figure something out."

Conall stole another glance out the window. "Maybe we should let her rest. It's getting late."

Lark patted Kayda's hand gently and peered at her closely. "What do you think, Kayda? I bet some rest would do you good. I can stay with you tonight, if that's all right with you?"

Kayda just stared blankly, her startling red eyes looking so strange.

Lark rose from the desk and tugged Kayda's hand. "C'mon, sister. I'll help you climb into the hammock. There's enough room for us both."

Ereni yawned, rising from the chair with Violet cradled in her arms. "I'm wiped, too. I might sleep all night and half the day as well."

Conall rubbed the small of his back, following Ereni to the door as Kayda took careful, mincing steps across the room at Lark's instruction. "That sounds like a plan. And then a huge meal when we wake. I wonder if the chef has any eggs?"

Kayda stilled. "Wait," she croaked.

Conall turned from the door, meeting Lark's gaze as a bright smile lit her face. "Kayda." She clutched her chest and let out a deep breath. "It's so good to hear your voice."

"Eggs. I need to find them."

Conall quirked a brow. "Do you want me to see if the chef is awake?"

Kayda shook her head vehemently. "No. No, not those kinds of eggs. Dragon eggs."

Ereni stepped away from the door. "Maybe we should sit back down."

They all filed back to their spots, Lark guiding Kayda as she spoke, "Druturion told me when he saved me I had to find them. Bela must've laid a clutch in the weeks we were separated."

Conall perched on the windowsill, the chilled glass pressed against his back, echoing the chill spreading through his veins at Kayda's news. "There are more dragons out there, somewhere? Did he tell you where to look?"

Kayda shook her head again. "I'm afraid not."

Ereni sank down into the wooden chair. "There was a book in the library at Mage Keep about dragons. If I'm remembering correctly, then we have time. Dragon eggs need many years to mature before hatching and a great deal of heat as well. I believe the book said the average was twenty."

"Well, that explains why the egg remnants I found with the Unseen were in a chamber surrounded with lava." Conall rubbed his chin. "We'll have to search for somewhere else like that. Maybe they buried them out in the Suland Waste?"

"Or maybe they're somewhere else entirely," Lark said.

"I think you're right," Kayda agreed. "The rumors of a land somewhere beyond the Orddon Ocean are true. Druturion confirmed as much to me. We'll need to scour the seas for his lost eggs." She sighed. "But at least now we know we have time. With all the chaos the battle created, we'll have a host of problems to deal with at home. Most of the crops we've stored will have undoubtedly been destroyed. So many people have been displaced from their homes. Not to mention the minor revolution in Joria we had a hand in starting will need to be dealt with in order to reestablish trade routes."

"We'll all help, of course," Conall insisted.

"You can count on us, Kayda," Lark agreed, squeezing her hand.

Kayda closed her eyes and rubbed her fingers across her eyelids.

"Are you all right?" Lark asked.

After a long moment of silence, Kayda nodded, a tentative smile spreading across her face. "Yes. I'm not giving up. Even if I never get my vision back, I won't stop until I find Dru's eggs. I owe him that much after he saved me."

"How did he save you?" Ereni asked. "I didn't think it was possible to heal the dead."

"I'm not sure. Whatever magic he used, he told me it required sacrifice. He's gone for good now, even from my thoughts."

Lark leaned closer, rubbing a hand gently across Kayda's back. "I'm so sorry."

Conall's brow scrunched, and he shot a glance at Ereni. She wore a pensive stare, her nose wrinkled, and her lower lip caught between her teeth. It seemed even with all the books on magic she once had access to in Mage Keep's library, she was just as stumped as the rest of them when it came to this new magic.

There was so much to do. Dragon eggs to save. A new portion of the world to explore. Political unrest to squash and scores of towns and homes to rebuild.

He wasn't sure how they would accomplish all of it, but he was sure of one thing—they could handle it. Together, they'd just defeated an evil force set on destroying the world.

The Unseen was wrong. He'd told Conall if they'd joined together, the two of them would be unstoppable. But Conall already had people in his life who could help him tackle anything. As long as his sisters stood by his side, nothing was impossible.

He glanced at all the strong, incredible women he was lucky enough to call his family and smiled. "So, what's first?"

Epilogue

L ark curled back the curtain on the carriage and peered through the glass. Sunshine filtered in between the new green buds bursting from the trees. Excitement welled in her belly. They were almost there.

She turned back to the interior of the carriage and smiled. "Are you excited to be going home?"

Conall spun toward her, peeling his gaze from the opposite window where Shadow and Sunny happily trotted beside the slow-moving carriage. "Yeah. I can't believe it's been so long since we left."

Kayda frowned from her spot beside Lark on the plush cushions. "I'm sorry for that. I should've arranged this trip sooner." Kayda's red eyes stared unseeing across the cabin, her head no doubt aimed at the sound of Conall's voice, but her gaze landing slightly askew.

"You don't need to apologize," Conall said. "It's just an empty plot of land. I've been happy to stay and help get everything sorted in Flamesmoat."

"We both have," Lark agreed, squeezing her sister's hand.

It had been a long, cold winter. Even with the land magically restored, there'd been so much to do. And without magic to rely on, everything had to be rebuilt the old-fashioned way. But now, spring was here and the hard work of the last few months was finally slowing into something approaching normal.

Her friends in the Wandering Bards were long gone. They'd agreed to be part of the peace forces Kayda sent to Joria to help set things right in the bustling port city, given the absence of the exploitive trade families who'd been ousted.

Well, most of them had. Lark's cheeks warmed. Aren stayed behind, determined to fulfill his promise to take her on a trip to Doln. They were planning to leave on the morrow, in fact, then they would travel to Joria to meet up with the rest of the Wandering Bards after.

But Lark had insisted on making this trip first. It wasn't so long ago that she'd left her home behind, determined to never step foot on the land again. Funny how that worked out in the end. She was on her way back, only to leave again.

Lark snuck another glance at her brother's face as he returned to staring out the window. A tingle of anticipation slid up her spine, and she had to tamp down the smile that fought to spread. She couldn't wait to see his face when they emerged from the woods.

"I see it. You weren't kidding," Muse chirped.

Lark's gaze shot out the window, but she couldn't spot Muse flying overhead with all the tree cover. *"How's it look?"*

"Just like you described it. He's gonna love it."

Lark couldn't still the grin then.

Conall didn't miss it. "What's got you so chipper?"

"Nothing. Just excited about my trip tomorrow," she lied.

"Hm." Conall cocked a brow. "You sure you want to travel all the way up north? It just started getting warm here."

"She'll have Aren with her to keep her warm," Kayda teased.

Conall shot Kayda a glare, not that she noticed. She probably wouldn't let his sour look bother her even if she could see it. Lark only giggled, squeezing Kayda's hand again. "You're right. I'm quite looking forward to that."

A gruff noise across the cabin made Lark's eyes widen. "Did you just growl at me, brother?" She chuckled. "I think you've been spending too much time with your hounds."

Conall rolled his eyes then met her gaze. His expression turned serious. "I want you to be happy, Lark. But you're still my baby sister."

Lark leaned over and patted his knee. "Hey, we just defeated an army of scourge. I can handle a trip with Aren to meet his family." She smiled warmly. "You don't have to worry about me. I am happy."

Conall grinned back. "Good."

The carriage jolted to a stop. Conall peered out the window. "Why are we stopping here?"

Lark reached for the door. "I asked the driver to stop just before we exited the woods. Let's walk the rest of the way." She opened the door and slid out before he could question her further.

Conall hopped out next, then lent a hand to Kayda. They hiked the final distance through the trees, and Lark's smile spread even wider at her brother's gasp.

"The house." He spun to face her, his eyes glossy and his mouth hanging wide open. "What? How?"

Lark giggled, staring behind her brother at the brand-new farmhouse perched in place of the burned-out shell she'd left behind last summer. Muse was right—it looked exactly the way she'd described it, an almost perfect replica of the home she'd destroyed. "We called in a few favors. Do you like it?"

"Do I like it? I love it." The longer he stared, the more his smile spread, until it practically burst across his cheeks. He squeezed Kayda's hand. "You had a hand in this, too?"

Kayda nodded, her own grin just as luminous. "It's the least I could do after—everything. I would give you more, but I had a feeling this was all you'd accept."

"You're right. It's everything I want and more." He breathed out a deep sigh, and his expression turned contented. "It's practically perfect."

Shadow and Sunny loped ahead as they started across the grazing field, barking and chasing each other merrily. Then the kitchen door popped open, and Ereni emerged, beaming, little Violet wrapped in her arms.

Conall stilled, his eyes gleaming. "I take it back. It *is* perfect." He smiled at Lark and squeezed Kayda's hand. "Thank you, both."

Conall rushed ahead, leaving Lark to follow more slowly, holding Kayda's arm. "He's so happy. And the house looks amazing. I wish you could see it."

Kayda sighed. "Me, too."

Lark's stomach clenched. "Kayda, are you sure you're all right with both of us leaving? I can always postpone..."

Kayda shook her head. "No. I want you to go. I appreciate everything you've both done for me these past months, but if I want to be taken seriously as queen, I have to learn to stand on my own." She tilted her head and aimed a grin at her. "I need this, too. I need to prove to myself that this"—she waved a hand in front of her red eyes—"won't hold me back."

"It won't," Lark said fiercely, squeezing her hand. "You were made for this, Kayda. My sister, the queen. Never forget, your family is so proud of you."

Kayda teared up, and she clutched Lark's arm, then pulled her into a hug. "Thank you, sister. I'm so glad I found you."

"Me, too," Lark said, squeezing her back just as tightly. "Now, how about we go see what our big brother thinks of his new house?"

Kayda pulled back and rubbed her cheeks with her sleeve. "After you."

Lark grabbed her sister's hand, took a step forward, and smiled.

The End

Also By

Shadows That Bind Us — Palisade Trilogy 1
Muses That Align Us — Palisade Trilogy 2

Would you like to read more about Dracwood? Sign up for my newsletter for a free standalone prequel novella that tells the story of how the Palisade was built centuries ago.

You'll find the link on my website amberlwerner.com

Look for the next installment in the world of Dracwood — Fall 2023
Book One of the Blood Song Trilogy
Bloodfeather Lullaby

About Author

Amber L. Werner loves to write about magic, monsters and mythical creatures. She lives in Norristown, PA with her husband and two children. The Palisade Trilogy is her debut series.

Follow her Facebook page Amber L. Werner
Or Instagram amberlwerner

Sign up for her newsletter and receive a free novella.
Find it here amberlwerner.com

9 781960 073020